HER Knotty List

an

MVP: MOST VALUABLE PACK

novel by

Ari Wright

Published and formatted by Blue-Eyed Books

Knot Her Goal, MVP: Most Valuable Pack Book 4

ebook ISBN: 9798991446419

ISBN: 9798991446426

cover design: Quirky Bird Covers by Staci Hart

For everyone who's ever felt stupid for having hope during the darkest of times:
People like you are the reason there's still beauty in the world.

Thank you for believing in the good... and inspiring more of it in the process.

WHAT IS *an omegaverse?*

An **Omegaverse** is an alternate universe wherein humans have evolved a biological hierarchy based on three individual designations: **alphas, betas, and omegas**. In an Omegaverse, every person falls into one of those three categories (or "designations") by the time they reach adulthood. Their **designation** then determines certain elements of their physiology, psychology, and physical appearance. The humans in this Omegaverse are not shifters.

Alphas are large, strong, dominant, possessive, and territorial. While civilized, they often struggle with the urge to use force or exert their dominance over others; particularly fellow alphas. Optimized anatomy makes them physically superior in many ways, including reproduction.

Male alphas have a "knot" at the base of their penises. This **knot**, much like the penis itself, becomes engorged when they are aroused and expands to its full size upon completion, "locking" an alpha into his partner. Female alphas have a "lock" inside their vaginas that perform a similar locking maneuver on their partners.

Alphas are biologically compelled to find compatible partners based on individual scents. They also tend to form **packs** with others. Omegas often become the center of packs because they are the only designation capable of creating **bonds** between others. There is rarely more than one omega in a pack. Once a pack bonds with an omega, all of their scents alter subtly. This shift helps protect bonded omegas from unwanted advances.

Betas remain the most similar to everyday humans. They do not have intense scents or the same biological compulsions that alphas and omegas share. Many beta-beta relationships resemble traditional monogamous partnerships. Because they cannot bond among themselves, they often choose to marry instead.

Omegas are smaller and softer in stature, naturally submissive, wary of violence, fearful, emotional, empathetic, and magnetically attractive. Omegas' bodies are built to endure the demands of an entire pack of partners, emotionally and physically.

Omega biology draws alphas in. When omegas are aroused, their bodies send nearby alphas a signal by **perfuming**. Omega perfume is a concentrated hit of their specific scent, intended to lure an alpha to their aid.

Alphas and omegas each have distinctive scents. Their bodies produce these scents at all times, but they are particularly strong when the individual is sexually aroused or emotionally distressed. Alphas and omegas can have very intense, all-consuming physical and emotional reactions to each other's scents. While uncommon, the phenomenon is called **scent-sensitivity**.

Scent-sensitive alphas and omegas are referred to as **mates**. By some twist of fate or biology, they are near-irresistible to one another. Separating from their scent-sensitive mates would cause an omega extreme pain and distress.

Omegas experience **heat cycles**. These "heats" are spurred by the biological imperative to mate/bond with an alpha (or group of alphas) who will provide for and protect them. When an omega goes into heat, he/she will experience intense physical pain unless they are knotted by their alphas regularly. Heats send omegas into a state of limited lucidity that is known as a **heat haze**. This haze makes them extremely vulnerable and unstable.

Omegas can take **suppressants** to lower their hormone levels.

Suppressants help make the pain of heats tolerable for omegas who do not have alphas. Unfortunately, over time, suppressants become less effective.

Unbonded alphas who encounter an unbonded omega can experience **rut**. Rut is a condition wherein an alpha loses his/her mental faculties and gives in to the biological imperative to knot/lock an omega. Rut is often dangerous for omegas.

Omegas **nest** in order to feel secure. An omega's nest should be a soft, round place that feels low to the ground and dark. Omegas take great pride in building their nests to their individual tastes and their alphas' approval. It is their alphas' duty to provide this space and the resources to outfit it.

Courting is the process by which alphas can press their suits with an omega of their choosing. It is generally a task undertaken by the entire pack in pursuit of their one chosen omega.

A note about bonds: Omegas may form individual bonds with various alphas without creating a "pack bond" to connect them all. This is done by individually bonding each separate alpha without bonding a designated pack leader first.

If an combination of alphas, betas, or omegas wish to have a pack bond (where they can all be connected to the omega *and* to one another *through* the omega) the pack leader and omega must bond first. The other members of the pack (including any betas) join after the initial pack bond is established (via the omega and designated leader).

To form a true pack bond, the alpha of the pack must bond the omega first. Otherwise, the omega may make individual connections to separate alphas but they will never be bonded as a pack.

ari's knotty list

triggers & content

Welcome to the **MVP** omegaverse

I'm so glad you're here!

Her Knotty List is the fourth installment in the *MVP: Most Valuable Pack* series. If you haven't read Books 1-3, please don't worry, this is intended to be read as a *complete standalone*!

This is a why-choose Omegaverse romance. It includes lots of knots, tons of spice, and absolutely no choosing!

If you don't like grumpy alphas, swoony mates, and group sex scenes (including packmates lending each other a hand and catching feelings, too), this may not be the HEA for you <3

Trigger Warnings: rejection/abandonment, car accident, sibling rivalry, grieving/loss of a parent.

Content includes: Christmas/holiday content, age gap, breeding k*nk, "Daddy" soft-dominant, exhibitionism, spit-roasting, c*ckwarming, primal/CNC, voyeurism, double penetration/DVP, dubious consent, MM content.

her knotty list playlist

'tis the damn season — Taylor Swift
White Winter Hymnal — Fleet Foxes
July — Noah Cyrus
Blue Ridge Mountains — Fleet Foxes
Evergreen — Richy Mitch & The Coal Miners
Lorelai — Fleet Foxes
Warm December — Sabrina Claudio
Silver Bells — Josiah and the Bonnevilles
Jingle Bell Rock — Bobby Helms
Santa Baby (feat. Steve Davit) — Marian Hill, Steve Davit
Changes — Langhorne Slim
misses — Dominic Fike
Sweet Creature — Harry Styles
Slow It Down — Benson Boone
Little Saint Nick — The Beach Boys
December — Kira Kosarin
Carry You Home — Alex Warren
What A Wonderful World — Sofi Tukker
New Year's Day — Taylor Swift
The Christmas Song (Merry Christmas To You) — Nat
King Cole

Run Rudolph Run — Chuck Berry
My Favorite Things — Elliot Lee
Silent Night — The Lumineers
Belong Together — Mark Ambor
Lover - First Dance Remix — Taylor Swift

remember the packs?

Don't worry: Her Knotty List is a stand-alone! But here are the names of the packs from the first three MVP books to help with the character's cameos in this book.

🏈 ASH PACK 🏈

OMEGA: Meg

PACK LEADER: Ronan Ash

PACK ALPHAS: Declan

Archer

Theo

🏒 PIERSON PACK 🏒

OMEGA: Remi

PACK LEADER: Smith Pierson

PACK ALPHAS: Damon

Cassian

🥊 THORNE PACK 🏈

OMEGA: Serena

PACK LEADER: Tristan Thorne

PACK ALPHAS: Avery

Spencer

Jonah

prologue

one year ago

YOU KNOW THAT PHRASE, *too stupid to live*?

Well, I knew it applied to me, but I didn't realize it was *literal*. "Ope!"

My heel slips as I skirt around the edge of my big brother's swimming pool. The lanai isn't even slippery—and these heels aren't even that high. I'm just... a *little* spin-y and *a lot* clumsy.

There was plenty of champagne in the house. There were also three of the happiest packs I've ever seen. And plenty of "Poor Single Emma" looks.

It would probably be more annoying and less gut-wrenching if my beloved big brother wasn't one of them.

Theo has always been a romantic. But ever since his pack

found their mate, Meg, a couple of years ago, he's turned into an absolute pile of mush. I swear his pupils turn into little hearts the second she walks into the room.

Which just makes all the pity in his eyes when he looks at *me* even worse.

Like, *I get it.* I'm twenty-five and single, and I've had a dozen heats in clinics. I'm not sexy or graceful the way omegas are supposed to be. I'm not super smart like my best friend, Bridget. Or talented with home-making like Meg's best friend Remi. I don't even look as pretty as my own dang sister.

When Remi's twin Serena joined our group, I thought maybe she'd be more "normal"; but, no, of course, she's every bit as stunning as Remi—and so sharp, I usually get the sense her mind works several frames ahead of any of ours.

Maybe I need some less impressive friends.

No! That's a terrible thought. *C'mon, Emma! You're better than this!*

Am I? I think so...?

Good Lord, how much champagne have I *had*?

I'm definitely going to end up sleeping on Theo's couch, aren't I?

I cringe as I narrowly avoid the raised corner of the swimming pool. *Passed out drunk on my big brother's sofa. Not the most auspicious way to ring in the New Year. But you know what? That's okay. That's* good, *actually, because... um...*

Before I can come up with an explanation to comfort myself, my gold heel catches on the edge of another shiny black paver. This time I flail back, squawking, "Oh holy night!"

Until two muscled arms hook around my waist, and a solid, warm body appears behind mine.

Chuckling.

A deep, darkly amused voice asks, "Did you just say, 'oh holy night'?"

I gulp in some of the cool, humid air hanging around us and

whip my head around, sending bouncy blonde curls over my bare shoulder.

Huh. This dress has no sleeves. Shouldn't I be cold? Maybe I am cold, but I can't feel it because of the champagne and the—

Man.

The manly alpha man behind me. Being manly. And warm.

And *gorgeous*.

Oh holy n—nnnevermind.

I blink, trying to absorb the perfect symmetry of his slashing features. Two thick brows, darker than the sandy brown of his shaggy, artfully mussed hair. A straight nose, a jaw sharp enough to cut glass. Thundercloud-gray eyes. Not to mention his sculpted mouth and perfect teeth.

The corded muscles of his arms flex under the rolled-up sleeves of his blue button-down. I watch them shift beneath his tanned skin, and then, like magic, I'm upright.

His brawny hands linger on my middle, pivoting me toward him—and the famous smirk on his beautiful face. Recognition finally pings through my laggy brain.

Oh. My. God.

"Y-you're Gunnar Sinclair," I squeak.

And, guys, I swear, it feels like a movie meet-cute. The two of us, alone on the dark lanai with the sounds of revelry ringing inside the house. A chilly breeze that has me hovering closer to his broad, hot body. Those strong hands spanning my waist to hold me steady while we stare right at each other.

Flecks of gold shimmer in his irises—little bursts of lightning streaked through the storm. His chest—so muscular and so close to my face—expands a deep breath, his own scent swelling under whatever neutralizers he has on.

They work too well, masking the core of his essence completely. I only get the salty-sweet edge of something toasted, but I lean closer anyway, sniffing him.

Visibly.

Because I'm *too stupid to live*.

But, for a moment, even that feels like part of our fairy tale. Instead of looking at me like I'm a lunatic, Gunnar's lips twitch wider as his eyes trace my chagrinned expression.

And it's all *perfect*.

Until he replies, "Yeah, squirt. You're Theo's little sister, right? Lucy?"

He thinks I'm my sister.

And he just called me *squirt*.

A totally unnecessary whine sticks in my throat. I swallow it down, not wanting him to feel bad.

It isn't *his* fault everyone always mistakes me for my little sister. She *is* the prettier, more extroverted, more interesting of the two of us, anyway.

I should probably start taking people mixing us up as a *compliment*, really, because—

"Lucy?"

Oh, right. He asked me a question.

Or, really, he asked *my sister* a question.

Too bad for him; she's with her sorority sisters in Cabo for winter break.

A sudden wave of dizziness flurries over me. I try to step back and give him his space, but my body doesn't want to cooperate. It tilts to the side and he rights me again, frowning.

"Or are you Theo's other sister?"

Ugh.

I wish that was a new moniker, but I've been Theo Matthews' "other sister" for as long as I can remember. Theo was always wildly popular, even before becoming a pro football player. Everyone knew him... And then, when Lucy finally got to high school, two years after me, she practically ran the place.

So Theo was *Theo Matthews*. Lucy was his even-more-popular, even-better-looking little sister.

And I was "the other one."

Or, I guess, I *am* "the other one." Still.

Sheesh. A minor humiliation has no business being *this* painful. I'm going to have to unpack this in therapy later.

Would anyone calling me "Theo's other sister" trigger me? Or am I feeling especially nauseous because it's *Gunnar Sinclair*?

He's almost as famous as Theo. The "hot-shot" forward for the Orlando Timberwolves hockey team has his gorgeous face all over social media and sports networks. They all boast his scoring record and ability to avoid penalties. After just two seasons with the team, he's become their star player.

"With a smile as wicked as his slap-shot," the tabloids say.

Can confirm, my brain pings uselessly as I stare at his face, trying to come up with a not-pathetic way to correct him.

Turns out, there really isn't a not-pathetic way to tell someone they mixed up your name with your all-around-better little sister's.

Maybe I just... won't?

Cheese and crackers. This is going to be so humiliating when I have to explain it to Meg—and, worse, Remi.

Two of Remi's alphas play with Gunnar on the Timberwolves. According to her, Gunnar needs to settle down and quit "hopping around with puck bunnies."

Not really sure I want to know what that means.

But pretty sure I'm about to find out.

Gunnar's gray eyes suddenly spark as he looks me over. Almost as if he's just now realized that I'm *a woman*. Who is wearing the ridiculous black body-con dress Meg shoved at me.

My sister-in-law and I are *mostly* the same size, except for my stomach. And thighs. And my butt. Which may or may not be hanging out the back of this thing.

Thank God Gunnar is so tall, he'll never be able to tell. My forehead only comes up to the base of his throat. Which suddenly smells...

So good.

Whatever he's seeing must be enough to push his alpha

pheromones up several notches. Scent spills over the chemical edge of the neutralizers covering his neck.

It's sweet and salty and rich, too. I lean a bit closer, inhaling deeper. Delicious nuttiness rolls down my throat and shimmers in my lungs. I tremble as my back snaps straight and a thick gush of wetness seeps into the tiny black panties wedged between my thighs.

When I gasp, he rears back, eyes flying down to the sliver of space between our bodies. His nostrils flare, storm-tossed irises flashing as he—

Lets go of me.

Gunnar lets go of my waist and wipes his palms against his slacks as mortification curdles my middle.

I guess I didn't realize how much of my weight he was holding. Because when he steps back like he can't get away from me fast enough, the whole lanai lilts sharply to the left.

Oh. Nope.

The pool deck isn't tilting. That's just me.

Falling into the pool.

chapter
one

"EM," the enormous blonde sitting across from me muffles around a cream-filled bon bon. "I swear, you could not get any prettier."

It's hard not to smirk at her for numerous reasons. First, Meg's just patently wrong. Second, she only has one leg of her panty hose on.

And third, lying on the bridal suite's chaise lounge, with her fleshy preggo-Spanx pulled up to her under-boob region... my sister-in-law sort of resembles a beached seal.

But, like, in an ethereal grower-of-life sorta way.

Meg drops another crème puff into her mouth the exact way a

SeaWorld handler might drop a herring into the mouth of a walrus. This time, I can't swallow my laugh.

She shoots me a pissy glare, narrowing bright blue eyes. "Just wait," she grumbles, swallowing.

"You're short like me, and I thought"—she drops her voice into an irritating whine, highlighting how annoyingly naive past Meg sounded—"oh, I'm petite, I'll be a cute pregnant lady. NOPE. Just means we get *double* the stretch marks other women get and look even *more* ridiculous when our mammoth alpha babies start crushing our internal organs. Give it one year and you'll be just as huge and uncomfortable and *hideous* as I am now!"

Her voice cracks as fat tears roll down both sides of her face. It would be concerning, if she hadn't already cried over her pantyhose being too tight, her hair being too frizzy, a cloud that looked like a ducky, and the fact that she wanted more bon bons but was mortified to order a fourth plate.

Yes. *Fourth.*

In retrospect, it was probably a bad call to ask my nine-months-pregnant sister-in-law to be my only bridesmaid.

I'd never admit it, but she wasn't my very first choice. I would have asked Lucy, if anyone could nail her down for longer than a few days at a time. And Bridget, who has been acting truly bizarre for the last six months...

The door clicks open and my big brother sticks his head into the bridal suite with his palms clasped over his eyes. "Safe to look?"

I giggle, "Come in, come in. We better order your poor wife some more crème puffs before she dehydrates."

Theo ambles into the room, looking every inch the oversized pro football player despite his tailored blue suit. It might be the height of fashion on another man, but he just looks like a blond yeti playing dress-up. Probably because his hair is as unruly as mine, only his is tied up in a man bun and comes with a matching beard.

We also share the same lighter complexion and green eyes, but the similarities stop there. He's 100 percent alpha—huge and bulked, with broad features and more body hair than I like to think about.

Conversely, I'm about as omega as I could get. Basically the human equivalent of a sloopy bowl of vanilla ice cream. I even melt down with alarming ease.

In that way, it's actually sort of nice having Preggo Meg around. At least I know I am not currently the craziest omega in this hotel.

"Peaches," my brother croons to his mate.

I turn and notice she's glaring at him. He holds up his hands. "I know you said not to come in here. And I know you've been pushing us reassurance in the bond. But, precious, this is your third time crying in twenty minutes. You know the rule."

Meg huffs, crossing her arms and wiggling higher in the chair. Well, trying to wiggle. Theo crosses the room in five steps and gently helps prop her up while her eyes burn laser holes into the side of his face.

"What's the rule?" I ask, dabbing fresh powder onto my nose, hiding the big freckle dotted there.

Theo sighs, sinking into a crouch beside Meg's chair. "We all agreed not to hover or overreact when Meg is feeling *big feelings*. And she agreed not to get mad at us for interfering if she's truly upset or if she's cried more than three times in twenty minutes."

Oh wow. Those rules sound... *specific*. And likely honed from a lot of unpleasantness.

Theo notices my eyes go wide and shoots me a panicked get-it-together look. It's too late, though. Meg sees me and wails into his shoulder, leaving puddles on his lapel.

"Now she's going to think I'm crazy!" she cries. "And I'm ruining her wedding!"

My big brother easily lifts his omega into his arms and sits with her tucked into his chest. His purr rattles while I rush to reassure Meg.

"You aren't ruining anything! This is just the rehearsal!"

Tomorrow will be a whole different beast. Because tomorrow, I'll be bonded to the Dunlap Pack. And I have to be *perfect*.

Well.

As close as I can get.

My soon-to-be alpha, William, loves to tease me over what a hot mess I am. Clumsy and prone to saying the most inappropriate things when I get nervous.

I'm also more emotional than anyone in the Dunlap Pack would prefer, but try as I might, I can't seem to fight how my feelings swell to fill my entire body. It's taken months of practice to keep the sensations to myself, even if the way they singe my scent can't be helped.

Science doesn't lie, though. And the Dunlaps were matched with me through the most elite, successful match service in the country. We have a super-high compatibility rating of ninety-five percent. Just over the threshold that makes us scent-sensitive.

Mates, my mind corrects. *They're your mates!*

A queasy roll of nervous excitement flips my stomach every time I think the word, my Omega desperately whining at me. *Mates, mates, mates.*

Geez.

I hear you, I tell her, exhaling shakily. *They'll be ours tomorrow.*

Thinking about it sends another swoop of anxiety through me. My mind races, leaping through all the things I have to get done. *Still have to build the nest for the ceremony, but I can't start that until after the dinner because they can't see it until tomorrow. And I need to wash my hair and shave my legs again and make sure I don't trip in my heels and—*

I've never been particularly organized or elegant, but for my new pack, I will try my hardest.

I can do this!

Totally.

Theo strokes his ham-hand over Meg's head but turns his eyes to me. They crease with fresh concern. "You good, baby sis?"

Oh. My scent. My alpha big brother has always been able to tell when I'm upset.

But I'm not *upset*.

This is just nerves. I'm *great*.

I blink at Meg and Theo, noting the way she turns her face into his chest, burrowing closer to his purrs. The weak, melty part of me wants to whine.

Gosh, that looks so nice. I wonder if I could get William to purr for me before dinner. Or Rob, if he'd agree this time... He probably will..? Of course he will. I just need a little bit.

Two minutes, tops.

It can't hurt to ask, right? These guys will be my alphas tomorrow. And their beta—*our* beta—Renee, is always demanding I tell them what I want.

"Y-yeah," I swallow, sliding toward the door. "I'll just... be right back."

Theo's eyebrows fold down, but he nods. "Mom is looking for you, anyway. Better run while you can."

Oh geez. Mom. She's been an absolute watering pot this whole weekend. Crying happy tears every time she sees Meg's belly, every time we take a big family photo, every time she sees me with my soon-to-be pack.

This is all of her dreams come true. Me, marrying a scent-matched pack the way she did back in the day. Her alpha son doting on his expecting omega.

"By the way," Theo adds, "My buddy Gunnar is here. I hope that's cool with you. Mom said we had enough food for a last-minute invite."

I trip over my own feet and lurch into the doorframe. "*What?!*"

When I whip my head around, I find Theo and Meg staring, their faces crumpled into matching masks of confused concern.

Their bemusement is justified, I suppose. After Gunnar all but shoved me away from him at their New Year's party last year, I didn't have the nerve to admit the real reason I'd ended up in the swimming pool. He was gone by the time I doggy-paddled my way out, and I was too embarrassed by his reaction to my scent to tell anyone we'd even *met*.

I *definitely* didn't tell them that the humiliation of meeting Gunnar Sinclair, being confused for Lucy, perfuming, and getting pushed into the pool because he couldn't get away from me fast enough was the *real* reason I finally gave in and agreed to a scent-matching service.

I'd been resisting for years, even while Lucy and all her friends dabbled with the concept. I knew some of them had even found scent-sensitive mates—the way Remi and her alphas did—but I had all these silly, romantic fantasies of meeting my mates *organically*.

Dreams that drowned in the deep end of my brother's swimming pool.

For weeks, I couldn't get the horrified look on Gunnar's face out of my mind. I spent the remainder of winter break whining in my nest, my Omega and I equally devastated by the memory.

I never wanted to endure a rejection like that again. I needed to know, beyond a shadow of a doubt, that the next alphas I touched were attracted to me.

For a while, even that seemed hopeless. Theo was all-too happy to foot the bill for my sign-up. But after I sent in my samples, I didn't hear back for *months*.

It may have taken Forever Matched longer than average to find alphas who wanted me, but at least I knew I'd never have to see Gunnar Sinclair's shocked revulsion ever again.

Or so I thought.

"My buddy Gunnar?" Theo repeats. "He plays on the Timberwolves? He didn't have anywhere to go for the holidays, and he's been having some issues with the team, so I invited him. You don't care, right?"

...

Crap on a catfish.

Before I can react, Meg wails. "Oh *no*! I told them you

wouldn't care, and *you do*! I'm ruining *everything*! I'm the worst maid of honor *ever*! You should have Lucy take over when she gets here—you shouldn't even let me come to the w-wedding!"

A bolt of panic shoots through me as she collapses into sobs. *Meg can't step down as my maid of honor! My sister isn't even going to get here until tomorrow morning, and someone is supposed to give a toast tonight!*

My new alphas had very specific plans for all of this. If I ruin them by scaring off the only bridal party I have, they'll be so disappointed in me.

A whine scales my throat, but Theo tugs his mate into his roaring purr, casting me a wide-eyed *fix-it Emma* look.

Meg babbles on, snot running from her red nose as she turns her anguished aqua eyes on mine. "You've been the chillest bride *ever*!" she cries. "I *really* didn't think you'd care about an extra guest, but we should have *asked*! I'm so s-*sorry*!"

... Am I a bridezilla if I agree with her?

This does seem like the sort of thing someone should have run by me... then again, I *have* been really hands-off with the planning. And no one knows that Gunnar and I met last year.

If this was some other friend of my brother's, would I still care?

I don't really get a chance to contemplate it, because the door next to me flies open and smacks me in the face.

Um

Ow.

No one notices me recoil with a pained whine, because three suited-up, furious alphas suddenly storm into the room.

My brother's pack bursts past me, erupting in growls and purrs as they scent Meg's distress and fly to her side. Their pack alpha drops to his knees, cupping his tattooed hand around Meg's face.

"Baby girl," he grits. "What's wrong? Tell Daddy."

Meg stammers, trying to explain. As soon as she says my name, Archer and Declan whip their heads in my direction. The doctor's kind, dark eyes are the very picture of disappointment.

And Declan looks *enraged*. A growl builds in his broad chest as he pierces me with neon-blue spears of accusation.

Archer notices the way I tremble under the quarterback's glare and places a hand on his packmate's chest. He casts me a tired look. "Emma, would you excuse us for a few moments so we can work this out?"

I should nod and walk away without issue, right? I *love* Meg— I know she didn't mean to upset me. Plus, she's so pregnant, she's practically *insane*. I should have compassion for that.

I definitely shouldn't feel sorry for *myself*.

Yet, a tender lump fills my throat, wetting my eyes. My nose smarts, tingling with tears and whatever mark the estate house's heavy antique door just left.

My alphas, my Omega whines, shoving at me.

She's right. I just need to find my alphas, and I'll be okay. They'll... make it okay?

Totally. Yes.

I bob my head at Archer and slip out of the room, praying no more trouble finds me before I find my pack.

chapter
two

IT'S hard to say what should have been my first clue.

Was it the strained silence at the end of our first date? The way I sometimes got the feeling I was walking into a room where everyone had just been talking about me? Renee's slightly abrasive lectures on how to be more appealing to *her* alphas? Or their absolute insistence on me getting rid of my apartment and job before they agreed to bond with me?

None of that was great, admittedly; but none of it ever felt like a reason to *run*. There were some... not-quite red flags. Some *maroon* flags. Or coral, if you will. Blush.

But never *red*.

At least, I wouldn't have said so.

Ironically, William and Rob probably would've told you that was exactly the problem—*I* wouldn't have said so.

As in, *I* am the problem because *I* can't seem to keep my chirpy, stupid heart and my own dang optimism in check.

Just like *I*, apparently, cannot suss out who is trustworthy and who is a raging asshole.

It's never really bothered me before. Sure, I can be gullible. But, even if it makes me naive, I like to believe in good things and good people.

So, *of course* I believed that my perfectly scent-matched pack would be good, too.

That just felt obvious. Like, yes, hello, water is wet, and fated mates are good.

Except not mine.

Apparently.

Stupidly oblivious, I round the corner of the stately mansion's third floor. The bedrooms here have all been converted into dressing rooms for brides, grooms, and family members. I count the doors in the hallway, remembering my pack was supposed to be getting ready in their own suite.

When I find the right one, I nearly bust in the way the Ash Pack did, but Renee's shrill whine stops me.

"*Willyyyy*," the beta groans. "Do we really *have to* bond with *her*?"

I hear the slap of a palm against Renee's butt, which is probably Rob.

No, *definitely* Rob. I'd recognize that possessive little growl anywhere. For months, I've been longing for him to use it when he looks at me, but he usually seems more interested in Renee sexually.

I figured that was natural. They've all been together for ten years. It would make sense for him to feel more possessive of her than he did with me.

Remember how I said I was too stupid to live?

"You know we have to bond with her," Rob grumbles. "It's the only way for us to be bonded to *you*, Renny."

My body starts to shake as I take a step back from the door. My thoughts race, blurring and blotting into a big, inky mess.

My Omega is weirdly silent. Almost like she's... letting me to listen? Wanting me to *hear*?

But my brain trills, *William! William wants us. Remember how he gave us his knot? And made sure our bonding was right before our heat? He definitely loves us and wants us and*—

"Renee, sexy," William croons, "I know you hate her, but if Rob and I have to tend to an omega during their heats, we need it to be someone who at least smells decent. You know we don't actually *like* her, right?"

The words are a hot lash, slicing my stomach. My hands drop to clutch at the beaded fabric of my white dress, fingers trembling as my Omega tunnels into her hole, covering her eyes and hiding like she can't bear to watch me finally piece together something *she's been trying to tell me, damn it*—

They don't... *like* me?

It's one of those moments I experience often. Where I know —I *know*—that somewhere, deep down, this shouldn't be shocking.

Sure, they courted me and asked to bond with me. But they've also made it very clear that there are many ways they felt I could improve. On *everything*.

I try really hard not to pull up my mental list of personal improvements to make for their sake, but it's a little challenging, with Rob basically enumerating things out loud.

"She's the neediest, naivest klutz that's ever lived," he crows, laughing. "And *dumb*. Even stupider than her rocks-for-brains big brother. I still can't believe he signed her trust fund over to us."

Panic jabs into my diaphragm as I gasp silently. The truth is, Theo *didn't* want to give any of my alphas access to the savings he set up for me. His pack leader, Ronan, was even more pissed about it. They both begged me to let them set it aside, as a safety net of sorts.

I was the one who insisted they sign it over to Rob and William.

My future alphas asked me if I could contribute to the household/pack fund, and it was the only way I could think to help. My job as an elementary school guidance counselor didn't exactly pay dividends to start with, and with their insistence that I quit and stay home... I didn't know what else to do.

Besides, I never expected *this*.

I thought—I believed they—

"You don't *really* want her, right?" Renee asks, her normally-confident voice wavering. "I know she can take your knots and I can't."

"No," Rob snarls. "Of course we don't want her. We want *you*, sexy. Only you."

My Omega doesn't make a peep. I would feel abandoned right about now, but that wouldn't be fair. Because I'm not even sure I'm *breathing* at this point; how can I expect any different from her?

What little oxygen I have left in my body punches out of me when William sighs and agrees, "God, all that cellulite on her ass. Not to mention the mess she makes of any bed we use. Disgusting."

Rob snorts. "Yeah, even if we were into her, the squirting ruins everything," he gripes. "We would have asked for another match if that had been in her file."

I can practically hear Renee roll her eyes. "No, you wouldn't have," she harrumphs. "You knew as soon as you realized she was Theo Matthews' sister that you wanted her."

"Wanted her *money*, Renny," William corrects. "Although having Ronan Ash in our back pocket definitely won't hurt our start-up. You know we're doing all of this for you. Because our sexy girl likes nice things."

Is Renee... crying?

I'm so shocked by all of it; that one appalling detail is the only thing to sink in. Along with a heavy dose of my Omega's *outrage* —because every time we've ever teared up in front of her, Renee has been nothing short of...

Well.

A bitch.

Now, she sniffles openly. "I hate that we *need* her just to be bonded. I wish I could do it."

I hear shifting and shuffling. Enough to make me peek into the dressing room... just in time to witness both alphas hugging Renee and each other, purring as they comfort her.

"We know, Renny," William whispers. "We know you would do this for us if you could. But we're going to take care of it. And once we're all bonded through the omega, the three of us can shut her out whenever we want. Then it will just be us, okay?"

I start to back away from the door again, feeling so nauseous that I think I may actually upchuck in the hallway of the state's most prestigious antique estate.

Where my parents and *all* their friends are waiting downstairs.

To watch me practice walking down the aisle.

To marry and bond with a pack that doesn't even *like* me.

And wants to use me to make their own separate bond *right through me.*

Oh my God—I'm going to have to tell everyone this was a mistake. That, once again, silly, forgettable Emma has been taken for a ride.

They won't even be surprised.

This is what I do, remember?

Making messes, tripping over myself, trusting blindly.

The neediest, naivest klutz who ever lived. And dumb.

I know I said I need to stop believing everything I hear, but honestly? That seems like a pretty astute assessment at the moment.

What do I do? Who do I tell?

How will I ever face anyone after this?

The gold-foiled wallpaper rasps against my beaded dress as I back into the opposite wall, attempting to stay upright. My legs quiver, knees knocking while I swallow an endless whine.

Shh, I hiss at my Omega. *If they hear us, they'll come out here. And then—*

Oh God. I'll die.

I'll *die* if I have to face them after what I just witnessed.

It's inevitable, though, isn't it? Even if I run to my parents... or Theo... eventually, I'll have to confront *them*.

I need help.

Stumbling, sobbing, I scurry back to my suite as quietly as I can. Every second I spend in the halls is another chance someone will see me falling apart—and word will spread all the faster. I duck into the room without pausing, fear tunneling a pit into my stomach.

All four Ask Pack alphas snap their attention to me as I dash in. Ronan is under Meg, her side pressed along his front; Declan crowds behind her, his hands spread possessively over her baby belly.

She sobs into her hands, inconsolable, while Theo stands like a statue at the end of the chaise, staring at his mate and pumping sour lemon stress into the air.

Archer is the only one not glaring. He glances up from his place on the floor, kneeling as he checks his omega's heart rate with his fingers.

"Emma," he sighs. "Could you get ready in another room, perhaps? Meg isn't ready to apologize yet and—"

Declan's growl rends the air, sending my Omega scrambling back to her bunker. "She has *nothing* to apologize for," he defends, vehement.

Ronan's heavy silver eyes land on mine, sifting like smoke, full of the sort of disapproval that sticks in my soul like a splinter. He doesn't speak, but a flex of dominance draws a whimper up my throat.

I have to tell them what just happened. They need to know so they can try to fix the bank accounts or undo the honeymoon they paid for or—

"Theo."

My big brother has always been my hero. He'll take pity on me and listen.

I squeak his name, barely able to eke it out between gasping sobs. But my brother doesn't look up.

I say it louder, "Theo!" and he finally snaps to. Pivoting to face me.

And *glaring*.

"Jesus, Emma!" he snarls. "*Get out.*"

The bark scrapes my insides, grinding everything to a halt. My body moves, carrying me from the room and flinging me flat against the wallpaper again. I blink through my tears, bewildered and betrayed.

Theo's never barked at me. Ever.

His command loops through my mind. *Get out. Get out. GET OUT.*

Honestly, it sounds like a good idea. *Get out* of here and never come back. Run and hide from all the people I've let down by being so dumb and naive and needy. Escape before anyone can find out that I blew up my whole life and lost millions of dollars over a *sham*.

Not to mention—somewhere, in this very building, Gunnar Sinclair is waiting to watch me walk down the aisle. And he'll be here to witness every mortifying second to come.

For some reason, that lone fact finally sends me over the edge. My Omega snatches the reins, desperate to steer us off any course that would lead to ruining Gunnar's opinion of us.

Too late, babe.

But it's also too late to reason with her.

Or me.

Get out. Get out. Get out.

And the next thing I know, I'm running.

chapter
three

I CAME to escape the soul-crushing dread and familial obligation.

I'm staying for the cinnamon rolls.

Or whatever the caterer is cooking up for this bonding ceremony because, *damn*. It smells *great*.

I probably don't deserve so much as a piece of cake for what a shitty wedding guest I've been. I didn't bring a gift; I didn't RSVP. Hell, I'm technically not even *invited*.

It's weird, being somewhere I wasn't asked to be, against my will.

But leave it to my boss and his pack to utilize any means necessary to get my sorry ass in line.

Or attempt to, at least.

They've been trying to kick me into gear all season. Our hockey team, the Orlando Timberwolves, went to the playoffs for the last two years running. Now, with our other star forward and our goalie happily bonded with our team owner and their omega, this was supposed to be *the* season.

Since Smith Pierson took over, the team has run smoother than ever. We all make more money; our facilities are flawless. Their omega, Remi, bakes great muffins.

And they have me.

I'm supposed to be the game-changer. The one who turns the tides in our favor.

Instead, I'm the one fucking everything up.

The leaden weight of dread rolls through my middle again, along with a cringe-inducing jag of guilt. I hate that *I'm* the one ruining everyone's season.

I hate the reason for it even more.

When it first happened, I thought there had to be a right way to tell people. I mean, surely, when they asked how my summer off had been, I wasn't supposed to say, "It was bullshit; my mom died."

I spent weeks mumbling my way through half-assed explanations and weird, stilted apologies. *"Yeah, sorry—I can't make it to that camping weekend after all. Turns out, I'll be burying my mom."*

See?

Fucking *dark*, right?

But what the hell else do you say?

No, seriously. If anyone figures it out, let me know. Because I still haven't.

Which is why I stopped telling people altogether.

Now, I'm less and less sure that complete honesty isn't the best policy. Just rip the Band-Aid off and let the ugly wound show.

I tried that last week, though, and it didn't exactly work in my favor. When Smith pulled me into his office to have a "talk" about "my future" and asked what the hell was wrong with me this season, I wound up blurting: "My mom died six months ago, my dad already has a new wife, and I'm supposed to show up for *Christmas* like all of this is *normal.*"

Without setting the tree on fire.

Or the house.

My mom's house.

Jesus. Maybe I shouldn't even be at this wedding. I'm pretty sure I have a permanent storm cloud hovering over my head. A stray bolt of lightning might hit the bride or something.

Emma.

That's a cute-ass name. I've never met the woman, but I met her sister Lucy at a party last New Year's. Where she perfumed and then got pushed into the pool.

Okay, okay.

I pushed her into the pool.

Not on purpose, of course. Lucy perfumed, and my body *reacted*. Saliva welled, my dick filled. I had to rear back and lock myself down before I could inhale, lunge forward, and sink my teeth into her.

But then... *splash.*

It was an honest-to-god accident, but I didn't handle it particularly well. Partly because I'd been drinking all night, and partially due to the fact that my entire body felt like it'd been flipped inside out and dipped in a vat of squirming, life-altering *urgency.*

I didn't even get a whiff of the girl's scent. Just watching a shiver of arousal move through her, knowing she was about to perfume, was enough to turn me into a maniac.

So I kind of panicked. I just knew I had to do something—get out of there before I scented her and wound up truly losing my shit. I left the party before anyone could confront me, unable to shake the image of what Theo's face would look like if he walked out of his house and caught me mauling his baby sister.

At first, I was in denial. Because, well, nothing happened, right? I didn't scent her. Our skin didn't touch.

I figured my Alpha just had a weird moment. Too many nights with puck bunnies drenched in fake-omega perfume had finally gone to his head, maybe.

But as weeks lapsed into a month, then two... I barely made it through the season without hunting Lucy down. I had to remind myself—over and over—that she was *Theo's little sister.*

Off. Limits.

Because I couldn't just *tell* one of my *best friends* that I wanted to court his *sister...*

Right?

Right. I don't even have a pack. And then there's, you know, my—admittedly—questionable history with dating.

By the time summer came, I hadn't been able to enjoy a hook-up since New Year's, and I was almost ready to admit defeat. I figured I'd go crawling to Theo, begging him to give me a shot at courting the little blonde I couldn't get out of my head.

But then my mom got sick. And died.

And suddenly, everything seemed pointless.

Hence me sucking ass this season and Smith trying to get me in gear with a mandatory one-month suspension.

So, yeah, I have time to kill. But when Theo suggested this last-minute wedding invitation, I'd be lying if I said that Lucy wasn't the real reason I agreed.

She must be here, right? This is her big sister's wedding.

Which... I'm crashing.

I don't have much of a choice, though. The other options were actually participating in my father's farce of a family holiday or sitting in my apartment alone for the entire break.

I get what Smith and the Ash Pack are trying to do. They want to help me get my head on straight before the seasons starts to heat up, and they think time off, around friends, will help.

It makes *sense,* but it isn't *true.*

Because I'm starting to realize: Nothing will ever fix this grief. And I just have to *feel* it.

Forever.

See what I mean? I'm *bleak*. I don't think I can bring this energy into a wedding ceremony—or even this rehearsal dinner.

For a moment, I wish I had my vape in my pocket. Eying the distance to my Jeep, I consider grabbing it. *Maybe... but Smith would have a shit fit.*

He's around here, somewhere, with his pack. They offered to let me fly on the private jet with them and Theo's pack, but I decided to drive. Between the Piersons' twin babies and another pregnant omega, it was just way too happy-family flight-from-hell for my bachelor ass.

Also, I may or may not have been too chickenshit to sit on a plane with Lucy. You know, just in case she's still pissed about being pushed into the pool.

Unfortunately, ten hours alone in my car didn't do much for my mental state, aside from making me bitter as hell. By the time I got to the grand mansion hosting the event, I had questions.

Who, exactly, planned a wedding this close to the holidays?

And also, why?

And *how the fuck* did I get suckered into this?

Which then reminded me that I had no other options. And triggered *more* bitterness, which—

The side door of the stately manor house suddenly flies open.

Fuck. I automatically step behind the nearest column, scrambling to avoid being seen. The scent of the caterer's delicious dessert wafts out of the kitchen, into the freezing air.

Because, yeah, in addition to all the other reasons I'm miserable—it's like ten goddamn degrees out here. Frigid wind whips over the side of the mountain, rustling through all the bare, anemic trees.

That doesn't stop whoever has stomped out of the house. A woman, I think. The quick clack of heels rings across the cold, quiet parking lot, along with the scraping sound of a suitcase dragging across the gravel.

I deflate, snapping back to bitterness. Not wanting to talk to *anyone*, let alone whoever got in a fight with their boyfriend or girlfriend and is now dramatically rushing out of someone else's rehearsal dinner.

C'mon, lady. I may not be a model guest, but I'm not *that* bad.

Snow starts to flurry, the clean coolness of it smothering my scent before the person fleeing can catch wind of it.

Good. God knows it's probably a burned-up mess.

Omegas have been *running* from me when I bump into them lately.

I can barely see through the white fluff swirling around, but when I squint hard enough, the tiny figure hauling an overstuffed suitcase into the trunk of a rental car has the distinct shape of a female omega.

For a second, I feel like a dick. I could have carried that bag in one hand—what the hell is *wrong* with me? My mom would have swatted the back of my head if she'd seen me hide from a fellow wedding guest and *then* watch her struggle with her bag.

Guilt presses me into motion. I step out from my hiding place and onto the threshold of the side door. Something crumples under my foot, so I stoop to grab it, thinking she must have dropped her packing list or a goodbye letter.

Pretty, girly handwriting stares back at me, only slightly smudged from the snow.

Um. Whoa.

I blink at the paper, all sorts of words I've never seen in print blurring in front of me.

Holy shit. It's a list of... sex stuff?

Correction: a list of *incredible* sex stuff.

I'm ashamed to admit it distracts me long enough for the omega chick to get into her car and slam the door. My head snaps up at the sound. I squint through heavier snowfall just in time to watch the little silver sedan whip out of its spot and take off.

She sure is driving fast for a random person leaving a random wedding.

The name at the top of the personalized purple stationery clamped in my freezing fingers finally registers: *Emma Matthews*.

Emma. As in, Theo's other sister? The *bride*?!

Oh, *fuck me*. Did I just witness *the bride running away*?

Two hazy red lights swerve through the snow, already halfway down the winding road up to the house. For a second, I'm completely still. Frozen between wanting to run after her myself and racing inside to tell someone.

But if she's really running, will there be time? What if I'm the only one who saw her leave? What if she didn't bring her phone or has it turned off and no one can find her?

Lucy might be able to forgive me for dunking her in Theo's pool; but she probably won't get over me losing track of her runaway sister the night before her wedding.

"Goddamn it," I growl, shoving the paper into my pocket and grabbing my keys.

Guess I'm going after the bride.

chapter
four

IT'S SORT OF hard to see with fake eyelashes falling off your eyelids.

Every time I swipe at the massacre of mascara and tears, I come away with more lashes stuck to the back of my hand.

The snow isn't helping, either. Driving in the rain is normal back home in Florida. But this? I can barely see anything, even with my brights on.

The heater's at full blast, but my fingers still ache from the cold as my teeth chatter around sobs. It just keeps getting darker, too. And creepier.

A while ago, I sped up to get away from some headlights I thought might be tailing me and did the smartest thing I could think of—driving a little way up the road before pulling off into a rest stop and waiting for the shiny black SUV to pass. Since then, I haven't seen anyone else.

I guess most people wouldn't drive in this weather unless they had to.

Which, *I do.*

I *had* to get away from everyone who only pretended to like me. And Gunnar-freakin-Sinclair. And my brother, who will be even *more* furious with me once he finds out my trust fund is gone, and it's all my fault.

At least, that's what I'll tell my parents whenever I finally get up the courage to check my phone.

I packed in a blind panic, throwing my iPhone into my suitcase without texting anyone or turning on the ringer. Then, I left a note so no one would think I'd been taken or murdered.

It's fine. I'll be home soon anyway. I've been driving for an hour. It shouldn't be long before I'm far enough south for the weather to break up a bit. And by morning, I'll be back in Florida.

Of course, once I get there, I won't have anywhere to *go.* The Dunlap Pack made me give up my lease last month. All of my stuff is sitting in a storage unit, waiting for me to get back from my honeymoon.

Dang it. I totally should have stolen the tickets to Bora Bora. I could have taken Meg and Remi and Serena. Well, maybe not Meg, with the baby coming so soon. Or Remi, since her pack is in the middle of hockey season right now, and she has the twins. Plus, Serena's baby is only like a month old...

A fresh ache squeezes my lungs.

I was *ready*—to be a wife, a pack omega. To be bonded and have babies. I wanted it *so badly.*

How did I screw all of this up?

We were *scientifically matched.* And they didn't even *like* me.

What will I do now? I gave up my job because Rob hated me "bringing home germs from the kids." I let my apartment go when William asked me to. I even dropped out of my church choir because Renee liked to sleep in on Sundays and I didn't want to trouble anyone.

Stupid. I was so *stupid.*

And naive. And annoying. And covered in *cellulite,* apparently...

But mostly just *too stupid to live*—because a second later, I realize I've been driving *uphill* this whole time.

My rental car may not have fancy GPS or a touch screen, but it does have a meter to tell you how far above sea level you are. And I'm about a mile in the air right now.

I never say this.

But...

Shit.

My ridiculous brain instantly chimes in with its usual optimism. *It's okay. We're okay. We'll just call for help or figure out where we are and find a hotel for the night.*

It's probably safe. People around here are supposed to be nice, right? Southern hospitality? Is that a thing? It's totally a thing. I'll just grab my phone and—

Slowly lifting my foot off the gas, I contort myself into a pretzel, trying to get the cell out of my bag without taking my eyes off the flurry of white flouncing in front of my windshield. When I finally grasp it and plop back down into the driver's seat, a wash of relief rolls through me.

Just in time for my car to careen into a snow bank.

chapter
five

KNOX

MY DOG HAS LOST his mind.

I honestly can't blame him. Though, I will say—of the two of us, all alone up here? I definitely thought I'd crack first.

Instead, my Bernese Mountain Dog has decided today's the day he's going to choke himself to death on his lead.

"McKinley," I grunt, tugging him back and putting some bark into my command. "*Heel*."

He whines but slinks back to my side, giving up on his crusade to asphyxiate himself. For all of two minutes. Then he's right back to dragging me frantically.

I bark again, shooting him a glare. We hike this path three mornings a week, and he never tries to pull me off it. He's a smart dog. I've raised McKinley in this wilderness since he was a puppy. He knows there's a highway on the other side of the pine thicket he's gunning for.

Normally, I don't even have to keep him close. The fresh powder on the ground is the only reason I opted for the leash; I didn't want him to wander into a soft spot and break a leg.

The fifth time I have to yank him back, I start getting uneasy. It isn't even light out yet, although it's possible he's seen or heard something.

If living in the middle of Bumfuck Nowhere for the last seven years has taught me anything, it's not to ignore animal instincts. They usually know important things way before logic does.

"Fine," I growl, easing up on my grip and letting him pull. "We'll take a five-minute detour."

McKinley's tail wags, but it's brief. He has his nose up, his ears back. The farther we wade into the copse of trees, the more the hairs at the ruff of his neck stand on end.

Fucking hell.

"I swear," I mutter low, "if you're leading me into a bear den, I'm going to throw your leash and let them eat you."

McKinley stops so suddenly I wonder if he's understood me. Then, the bastard takes advantage of my surprise and *bolts*, tearing the lead right out of my hand.

Goddamn it. I haven't even had coffee yet.

I take off after him, running like a jackass in my hiking boots and thermal pants. Fresh, fluffy snow and pine needles fly behind us while we cut a path right to the side of the fucking highway.

I told you this dog had a death wish.

"McKinley!"

He doesn't stop. Instead, he veers to the right and launches himself directly at... a snowball? A boulder?

No. It's a car. A car that seems to have run off the road and tumbled into one of the mountain's rock formations.

While McKinley frantically digs at the back door of the sedan, I freeze, assessing. There's smoke rising off the engine. I don't see footprints or markings to indicate that anyone got out and walked away—

Shit.

I fumble for my vest pocket, ripping out the satellite phone I carry in case of emergencies. There's only one number programmed into it. I go to dial, but a breathless voice interrupts.

"I—already—called—"

Snarling instinctually, I whirl to find another man emerging from the path on the opposite side of the road. He's as tall as me, an obvious alpha, reeking strongly of chai spice—

And dressed in a fur Speedo? With... a matching robe?

What the—am I awake right now? Is this some weird dream hinting at latent sexual desires?

That would be news to me. But I *have* been alone in the woods for quite a while.

The other alpha catches his breath fairly quickly, tossing an unstyled pompadour of black hair off of his forehead. He narrows his eyes at the scene in front of us and vibrates with tension.

"Fuck, man, I don't know what to do. I'm not from around here. I was sleeping in my tent, woke up to take a piss, and saw smoke when I looked out my window. But it took me like twenty minutes to get down the motherfucking mountain and—"

I'm not a great alpha in a lot of ways, but I do have a quick mind. It snaps the pieces together in seconds. "You're from that goddamned glamping site up the way, aren't you?"

He has to be. What other "tent" would have windows? And he's dressed like a tool. If he doesn't put some pants on, he's going to freeze his dick off.

Although, that pimp coat and the fur-trimmed boots he has on look about right for these temperatures.

Another thing he said registers. "It took you twenty minutes to get here?" I shout. "That site is five minutes away! It's right off the highway! All you have to do is cut through the trees!"

He scowls at me. "I took the trail, dude. Like I said—I'm not from here. I don't know where the fuck I even am."

We're wasting precious time, I realize, jolting into action. While I charge forward, I grit my teeth to temper the command I toss behind me. "Follow my footsteps. If you step in the wrong place, you could fall into a ditch and break your ankle."

The guy starts mumbling insults at my back, but follows all the same.

chapter
six

THIS GUY IS A FUCKING ASSHOLE.

But—with the flannel shirt and the worn canvas baseball cap pulled low over his brow—he has the grizzled look of a mountain man, so I decide I'll follow him to the car buried under a snow drift.

Fuck, it is cold out here. When my followers voted on this location for glamping, I thought I'd gotten off easy. It wasn't the Himalayas or the Rockies. Or some glacier in Alaska.

The Blue Ridge seemed like a good spot for a bit of holiday content. Lots of snow, pine trees, mountains. Just... you know, no death.

Or, so I thought.

But, right now, there is totally a dead chick in the front seat of this car.

Oh God. Oh hell. Shit. Motherfucker.

Mountain Man knocks at the frosted window, trying to rouse her. But she doesn't even twitch, as far as I can tell. The glass is fogged from the extreme cold, but it looks like she isn't moving.

I start to pant, the cold, thin air doing little to fill my lungs. The guy next to me—possibly the alpha-iest alpha I've ever met in passing, *goddamn*—reaches over and pounds his thick fist into my bare chest.

"Breathe right," he orders. "And close that stupid coat. We already have one person in need of medical care. If you pass out, too, I'm leaving you in the snow."

See? He's a dickhead.

Cute dog, though.

The sleek tri-color pup digs at the car's door, paws flying at the snow built up against it. His owner scans his eyes over the scene, analyzing. "You said you called the fire department?"

I nod, feeling dumb. "Called 9-1-1 and got the fire department." Now that I think about it, that's weird. "You guys don't have, like, emergency dispatch or whatever?"

He snorts, wading closer to the car. "No. Just the local fire station. The closest hospital is almost forty minutes outside of Knotty Hollow."

I try to do the math. The Hollow is the nearest "town."

You have to use air quotes when you call it a *town*, because it's literally, like, one street. Maybe four, if you count crossroads.

My inbox had a few suggestions for the little hamlet while I'm here, but they all made me scoff. When I looked them up, I found that the recommended coffee shop is, in fact, the *only* coffee shop. Ditto the barbecue place and the local gym.

What is it they call it? A one-horse town?

Yeah, this place doesn't even have a horse.

Maybe some goats.

The closest city is Asheville, but I don't know jack about how to get someone there if they need emergency medical care. Guess that's why I need the Brawny Paper Towel Guy next to me.

His blue eyes are intense, running over every part of the car and the blurry shape of the woman inside. When he notices me staring, he grunts. "I don't want to move her in case her neck is broken. And if I open the door and she's already hypothermic, she'll only get colder. I don't have a heating blanket on me."

He flicks a look at my content-filming ensemble. "You clearly don't either."

Well, he's got me there. I don't think anything else would fit into these furry briefs. I can already feel one of my ass cheeks trying to escape. Fortunately, all this snow has my junk shrunk up, so there's some extra room if I shift around a bit.

The things I do for the 'Gram.

Honestly? This? Standing in a snowbank with my package wrapped in faux fur? This doesn't even rank.

While my unfortunate companion continues to analyze the situation, his dog goes fucking ballistic. I feel bad for him.

Taking pity on the poor creature, I crouch a bit and reach to pet his head. "I know, dude. Shit's rough. Bet you wish you could get in there to help."

The dog bounces a bit, whining and licking my chin like I'll let him assist if he can convince me he's a good boy.

"No convincing needed," I tell him, blowing out a breath. "You're obviously a good doggo. I just can't let you in, man. I don't even know how to unlock the door. But good on you for trying."

He chuffs at me, sending a puff of fresh snow into his own face.

Damn, he's cute. Maybe I should get a dog. I could film a shit-load of content with one.

Jesus, Zane. Not the time.

Mountain Man watches the way his pup winds between my legs for more pets and begrudgingly offers his leather-covered hand. "Knox."

I shake it, standing back up. "Zane."

He narrows his eyes. "Your name is as stupid as your outfit."

I shrug. He isn't wrong. "And you have no social skills."

He nods, like he agrees that this exchange accurately sums up the situation. Before I can ask him what the fuck we're going to do, headlights appear on the horizon. They approach from the opposite direction this girl was traveling in—down the mountain instead of up. Judging by the huge flash and the rumble under my feet, it's a big-ass truck.

Knox mutters, "Thank God."

So I assume he recognizes the blue Ram rolling right up to us.

Another guy jumps out, covered head-to-toe in padded fireman-red cold-weather gear. His black rubber boots crunch through the snow surrounding the car as he approaches.

With a hood over his head and snow flurrying, it's hard to see what he looks like, but I glimpse dark-brown skin and lighter eyes as he notices me and shoots a curious look at Knox.

I raise my hand. "Zane. I called in the crash when I saw smoke from my campsite."

The fireman nods, his expression grave. "Smart. Most people would have waited until they got here, and that wastes a ton of response time. It's good you called when you did."

Without another word, the guy pulls out a hatchet—an actual fucking *mini-axe*, people—and shatters the car window. His gloved fingers fumble with the lock. Then he's in, bending over the woman on the seat. As an afterthought, he reaches up and unlocks the door on our side, too.

Knox immediately dives for the handle. Trying to be useful—since the extent of my medical training is, like, *Grey's Anatomy*—I drop into a crouch and wind my hand around the dog's collar, holding him back from jumping on the woman.

"It's okay," I murmur while he wiggles. "They're going to help her, dude. We just have to be patient."

The fireman shucks his gloves and starts a careful examination. "Unconscious," he reports, solemn. "She has a pulse, but it's thready. Mild head contusion. No external bleeding—oh, wait. Here."

He feels around the blonde curls cascading over her shoulders, up to her hairline. "I feel a lump," he says, bending closer. "No blood..."

He turns to look at the dashboard, where I notice a crack in the windshield and a set of spent airbags. "She probably hit her head when the airbags deployed."

He sighs, leaning back to take in her exposed, pale limbs. "She might have passed out on impact. If not, I bet she was disoriented and scared to get out of the car alone. She may not have a cell phone signal up here."

"So, you don't recognize her?" Knox asks.

Fire Guy shakes his head. "She definitely isn't local. Just look at her clothes."

He has a point. The girl—I can see now that she's young and *seriously* fucking pretty—has on a beaded white flapper dress. It's paper-thin. I go to shuck my coat automatically, wanting to cover her, but Knox stops me.

"You'll be just as cold as her in five minutes," he grumbles, removing his own vest and coat. Under the blue corduroy and puffy down, he has on a red flannel shirt.

Because, of course he does.

Fire Guy looks me over, notes my outfit, but doesn't comment. I decide I like him better.

Turning his focus back to the girl, he sighs. "I don't see any reason not to move her. We need to get her vitals and warm her up. She's between the second and third stages of hypothermia. If it gets any worse, I won't be able to help her, and we'll have to call for a med-evac."

Knox tosses me a look, translating with a grunt, "Helicopter."

Okay, fuck. That sounds serious. The fire guy nods at me, his expression mirroring my concern. He turns back to Knox. "Your place is just up the road?"

Knox seems to hesitate—like he isn't sure he wants this shit-show at his house.

And, *seriously,* bro? Man *up.*

I slap his shoulder. He growls, then grits, "Yes. Two miles down the highway and one more up the switchback."

The other guy nods at him. "Help me get her in the truck." He tosses me a look that isn't completely devoid of amusement. "You can grab her purse."

chapter
seven

I'D BET ALL seventeen of the dollars in my wallet that this beautiful, half-frozen woman is an omega.

Normally, I wouldn't presume based on appearance. I could ordinarily just scent her subtly. But she's too cold to even have a scent. Her pores are completely sealed, trying to retain what little body heat she has left.

There are a few other clues, though. For one, it's cold out here, but not cold enough to send a beta or an alpha into hypothermia this quickly. Granted, she's completely exposed in this outfit. Still, anyone with alpha or beta biology would generally be a bit hardier.

Her instinct to stay put and essentially hide is another tip-off.

My little brother is an omega; I recall many times during our childhood when he opted to hide in his closet instead of rough-housing with the rest of us. And I know from volunteering at the tri-county's only heat clinic that it's normal for omegas to cower when overwhelmed.

Poor little thing, I think, gently pulling her slumped body out of the backseat.

Solid and covered in soft curves, the way she fits against my chest makes my heart leap, but I ignore the impulse. It's just my physiology reacting to hers.

Knox doesn't seem to be faring much better. He comes to my side, his hands hovering like he's ready to catch any part of her I might drop.

That won't happen, though. I have a firm hold and she's the perfect size for my arms.

Knox helps me load her into my truck. "Sit with her," he suggests, climbing into my driver's seat.

The other guy comes to the passenger side, still holding McKinley's leash and our patient's purse. It's tiny and covered in pearls. He tucks it under his fur-coat-covered arm and climbs into the truck, sprawling like he walks around in furry briefs every day and doesn't mind displaying his entire naked body in the process.

I mean, whatever. To each their own, I guess.

He obviously isn't local. Even if I didn't know every single person in the tiny town I grew up in, I would know he doesn't fit in here.

For one, his clothes. Then there's the haircut. His bare-ass chest doesn't have a single hair on it. And—dear God—does he *trim* his *underarm* hair? It's all the same length—only a bit longer than the stubble on his face.

I remember we're right near the new "glamping" site on Highway 64 and resist the urge to snort a laugh. Paying eight hundred dollars a night to *camp*? City people. I swear.

Knox cranks the engine and blasts the heat. I move carefully, pulling the omega halfway into my lap. My right arm locks around the nip of her waist, holding her steady as her head lolls slightly in my lap.

The sunrise is just starting to turn the sky from pitch black to muted gray. I squint through the gloom, taking my first good look at her face.

She's *beautiful*.

Most omegas are, but she's especially striking. Something about the turn of her nose, I think. The freckle dotted there. And all of her other dainty features. Even her mouth is little more than a shrunken rosebud.

I look over her fancy outfit, wondering where she was heading and why she was alone on these treacherous roads at night.

Was she going to a party? Leaving one?

Leaving... *some*one?

Another wave of sympathy crests inside of me. I settle my hand on top of her head, petting her hair back while I gaze down at her shut eyes, wondering.

"What's her name?" I murmur.

The stranger in the passenger seat rifles in her purse, wincing like he hates to go through her things. It's a point in his favor. As is the way Knox's dog has his whole body draped over the dude's lap.

"Her ID says Emma Matthews," he replies. "Twenty-five. Her home address is somewhere in Florida."

So that explains why she had no idea what to do with the snow or the mountain roads, then.

My arm flexes around her protectively. *She must have been so scared.*

"I'm Zane, by the way," he adds, reaching over to shake my hand. "Zane Madani."

"Micah Patterson," I tell him. "We're lucky you heard the crash. I'm not sure how much longer she would have lasted."

I don't tell either of them that I'm still not sure. It isn't good that she's unconscious. I'm hoping her deep sleep is just the result of mild hypothermia and that lump on her head. But if it's more serious, at least I know Knox's place is well-equipped for getting her help.

I catch the billionaire's frosty glare in the rearview mirror. "You still have that helipad on the roof?"

He grunts and nods. Zane's eyes fly wide. "A *helipad*? What the fuck, Grizzly Adams?!"

I smile. "Knox is loaded. His house has everything."

Knox's silent glower intensifies. Zane gives a strained laugh. "No shit? Damn. So I guess you guys are friends?"

Now I have to chuckle. "God, no. Knox Beckett doesn't have *friends*. He hates us all. I only know him because he volunteers at the firehouse sometimes."

It's half-true. I know I'm about as close to an acquaintance as the guy has, which is sad because the last time I saw him was the Fourth of July.

He's a recluse, always holed up in his insane mountainside compound or trudging through the wilds with his dog. The only time any of us sees him is when he comes into town once a month to restock on coffee beans from the local shop. Rumor has it he gets all his other shit airlifted in.

Because, you know—helipad.

"Volunteer firefighters are real?" Zane asks, grimacing. "I thought that was only true on, like, *Yellowstone*."

Knox rubs his eyes. "Jesus Christ."

"Our town only has four firefighters," I explain. "We keep a rotation of volunteers in case there's a forest fire or something big like that. They're unskilled labor."

Knox grumbles, "Even a monkey can hold a hose."

I keep smiling, but it feels a bit frozen with this omega lying so perfectly still on my lap. "My point exactly."

With an even deeper scowl, Knox navigates my truck up the winding snow-covered road to his place. Honestly, unless you knew exactly what to look for, you'd never know the whole damn property was back there. From the road, it all just looks like trees, trees, and more trees.

Until Knox pulls a small remote out of his thermal hiking pants and hits a button; then, the nearest group of trees *moves*. It takes a moment to realize they're fake—attached to a concealed gate that falls away, revealing a winding driveway.

"Holy fuck," Zane spits. He turns to our host. "Who *are* you?"

Knox scowls. "I'm the guy who's going to kick your ass out of my house if you don't put pants on."

chapter
eight

I WAKE to the toe-curling scent of cedar and pine.

The smell is like a treasure chest full of family heirlooms. Or a quiet forest after the rain.

It's so comforting; it takes me a minute to realize I'm awake. And that's fortunate since I wasn't able to keep my eyes open the last time I tried.

"Hey."

I gasp, bolting upright.

In the foggy, pain-filled moments after my car hit the snow drift, I remember feeling panicked that I couldn't seem to stay alert long enough to find my phone or get out of the car. I had freaky visions of *Deliverance*-style cannibals coming for me. Which seemed a little silly at the time, but—

Turns out, I had good reason to worry.

Because I'm now in an unfamiliar bedroom with a strange man looming over me.

I yelp. I can't help it. The shrill sound slips out while I rush to gather the many blankets draped over me and bundle them around my chest. I note with relief that, while my dress is gone, my tights and bra are still firmly in place.

The man's expression falls. Then his long, square features and black brows crease into a pained wince. He holds up two hands in a supplicant gesture.

"Sorry, sorry," he says, voice low and steady. "I didn't mean to startle you. Someone saw smoke from your crash and called it in. I'm an EMT."

My eyes fly over him nervously, noting the fire department symbol etched into the puffy red jacket zipped around his big body. Very deliberately, keeping his hands up, he takes a step back.

"W-wh—" I try to ask where I am, but my anxiety rises too fast for me to contain it. A whine slips out of my throat, and the fireman cringes with his whole body.

Alpha, then, my unhelpful brain supplies. *Even more dangerous.*

"I'm sorry, I'm sorry," he repeats, desperate to calm me down. "I was coming off a shift when your accident got called in, so I came straight away. I don't have any colleagues that aren't alphas, but I can call my brother to come if you want another omega with you."

The whines tumbling out of me won't stop. I try to speak around them, but words tangle with the fear vibrating in my gullet, choking me. Tears stream out of my eyes and trail down my cheeks.

I'm so scared. My head is pounding, and my feet feel numb. I just want my big brother. Or my dads. Meg would know what to do. Or Serena—she's the toughest omega. Hell, my mom would be just as freaked out as me, but I'd even take her hysterics at the moment.

The poor man facing my breakdown runs both his hands over his buzz cut...

Then he crouches right to the floor.

...*what?!*

Another whine jags out of me. His expression looks a lot like heartbreak. "Aw, sweet girl. You're killing me. I promise I'm not here to hurt you. What can I get for you? Is there someone I can call?"

I try to say Theo's name, but I can't get it out. I'm shaking so hard my teeth chatter. Right as another loud whine rips out of me, a second man appears in the doorway of the palatial bedroom.

"What's going on?"

His voice *booms*. I shrink back, my fingers digging into the bed. The alpha kneeling on the floor casts the new alpha a glare. "Knox, *lower your voice*. Emma is scared."

The brunet alpha in flannel only peers out from under the brim of his canvas hat long enough to confirm this. He then turns on the heel of his hiking boot and leaves. A second later, a *third* guy shows up.

Seriously?

Three of them?

When I cower again, the guy on the floor sighs, exasperated. "Perfect. Yeah, just come on in, Zane. Pay no mind to the panicking omega."

The third guy—what kind of name is *Zane*?—looks nothing like the other two.

Because he's basically a God.

Seriously. Rich tan skin, perfect musculature. The sort of thick black hair and slashing features that grace the covers of magazines.

And he's also naked.

Aside from... furry panties?

Oh my God, *where am I*?

The third difference between this guy and the other two becomes apparent immediately: he has absolutely no chill. Doesn't even pause as he sweeps into the room and comes right at me.

I scrabble back and whine again. But he's fast. One second, he's in motion—and the next, he's sitting beside me on the bed, his furry hip touching mine through the layers of blankets between us.

The mostly-naked guy reaches both his hands over and cups them around my head, staring deep into my eyes with his endlessly dark gaze. "*Shhhh*," he barks softly.

It's like hypnosis. The bottomless depth of his eyes; the steady, sensual rasp of his voice. "*Settle*, baby," he murmurs, shifting a bit closer. "*Settle.*"

I gasp in a deep breath, and he nods, smiling just enough to incapacitate my brain. *Holy*—

"That's a good girl, Emma," he says, his voice almost a purr. "Relax for me, okay? One more breath."

I listen, unable to break from the swirling brown irises. This time, as air fills my lungs, the scent wafting off his bare chest hits me.

It's *chai*—as rich as it is complex. Citrus, clove, cardamom, and a delicious thread of sweetness.

Inhaling him is like taking a hit of ecstasy; I feel my pupils bloom while my whole body trembles. He grins, and I suddenly can't breathe again.

"Mmm," he comments, noting my expression. "Nice to meet you, too, gorgeous. I'm Zane. That guy on the floor is Micah."

He turns and smirks at the other alpha. "Dude, get up here. I don't know what the fuck I'm doing."

Soft morning light grazes Micah's flawless brown skin as he quietly gets to his feet and ambles over. His long fingers start to reach for my neck but stop. "I won't touch you unless you want me to, sweet girl, but I should check your vitals."

Sweet girl?

My brain feels like it's rebooting. I can't *think* about *anything*. My entire existence has narrowed to the chai spices wafting in the air.

Every time I dare to inhale, a new shiver races through my blood. I feel like I should be perfuming, but trembles quiver through my body without landing between my hips.

Seriously, *what is happening?*

I feel dizzier by the second. So I finally nod, wanting the fireman—Micah, I guess—to tell me if I'm having some sort of seizure.

At this point, a seizure might actually be a relief. Seizures make you smell stuff, right? I think I remember seeing that on *Grey's Anatomy.*

Pretty sure you're supposed to sense burnt toast and not whatever this panty-creaming, decadent, delicious *spice* is... but still.

Micah kneels again, trying to cram his broad shoulders into the space between my body, Zane's knees, and the bedside table. He pauses, quickly assessing the available area, and decides to shuck his puffy jacket.

It doesn't really help.

He's still wide and rounded with muscle, all straining under a thin red thermal. With a grunt, he shifts closer, knocking Zane's legs out of his way.

The chai alpha doesn't seem bothered. He leans further over my lap, his hands sliding off my cheeks to brace beside my hips, holding himself up.

Micah looms closer. Lovely, concerned hazel eyes scan my expression before settling on my gaze. He frowns, all sincerity.

"I'm so sorry this happened to you, Emma. Can I check your pulse and your temperature? I just want to make sure we don't need to call a helicopter."

I can't even get caught up on the idea of calling a frickin' helicopter—*what?!*—because I'm barely letting myself breathe. I don't want to perfume accidentally and turn these seemingly nice alphas feral, but Zane's scent makes that blunder increasingly likely.

What I wouldn't give for someone familiar. Theo, or my parents, or one of the Ash Pack alphas. Hell, at this point, I'd even take Gunnar Sinclair.

With a pitiful whine, I manage a half nod. Micah immediately gets to work, his touch professional but warm as he skims the pulse in my unmarked throat.

"You're unbonded," he notes quietly, flashing a disarmingly genuine smile. "That's surprising."

It's a harmless compliment, but I shiver all over again. His lips quirk in another concerned frown. "Steady pulse," he reports, moving to touch my forehead. "You still don't feel quite warm enough, but you have no fever."

He stretches his torso to maintain a respectable distance as he reaches up to my hairline and feels for the place where I hit the windshield. As soon as his fingers brush the bump, I gasp in pain.

Bad move.

Such a bad move.

The lungful I suck in comes directly off his exposed throat.

And it. Is. Impossible.

The scent of... winter? Sharp peppermint and cool frost and a friendly flurry of flakes. It's an enchanted forest with a thermos of mint tea. It's the first breath of air on the first snowfall of the season.

Magic. Rejuvenation and possibility and *magic*.

And *now* I'm perfuming.

Thank God there are about eighteen thick blankets trapping the smell of my shame.

Good Lord. I've been thinking of this whole thing as one of the Shakespearean tragedies Bridget loves so much, but I think we're firmly in sad-clown comedy territory. I feel more like a jester by the second. If someone gave me a hat with bells on it, I wouldn't even be offended.

Micah misinterprets the way my spine snaps straight and

backs off instantly. "I think the contusion is mild," he mutters. "But does it hurt? Do you have a headache? Dizziness? A stiff neck?"

The bump hurts, but only when he touches it. And I'm sure the dull ache in my skull will subside soon... I shake my head, holding my breath again.

He smiles that same kind, pure-hearted grin. "That's great. I'm going to go make you some hot broth, okay? That will get your temp up a few more degrees. Come on, Zane. You need pants."

Zane makes a face. "Do I, though?"

Micah shoves his shoulder on his way past. "If you don't want Knox to kick you out, then yes."

With a flirtatious wink, Zane vaults off the bed in one easy move and follows his friend out of the room.

Okay...

What?!

Panting, I scramble to get a good look around. The room is huge. A big square with rustic wood floors and matching blank timber on three sides. Across from me, though, the wall is made entirely of windows. From the walnut underfoot all the way up to the A-frame of the room.

There are beams supporting the ceiling. Thick black, metal ones that go with all the plain black furniture. It's all metal, too. Masculine. No throw pillows or pops of color.

A man's bedroom, for sure. One of theirs? Or the other guy they mentioned?

It's... tidy? Too clean, really. Almost sterile, somehow, despite the breathtaking view of the sunrise over the smoky Blue Ridge Mountains. Instead of adding charm, the surreal vista only under-scores the empty—almost *lonely*—vibe in here.

Lonely but not *scary*. There aren't dead animal heads on the walls or knives laid out on the dresser. I see no evidence that a deranged mountain-dwelling psychopath lives here.

I see no evidence that *anyone* lives here.

Part of me wants to get up and go through the bathroom cabinets. That's where everyone keeps their dirty secrets, after all. The minute I move these blankets, though, my perfume will fill the whole room.

But I'm desperate for more information. I don't see my phone anywhere. Or my purse. So unless something in this room can tell me whose house I'm in, I'm sort of at the mercy of these strange alphas.

On impulse, I tug open the bedside table's drawer, fully expecting a loaded gun or some equally terrifying weapon. Instead, there's—well, I don't even know what.

A tube?

It's a flesh-colored tube.

At first, I think it's a dildo. Because it's a long, rubber object in a drawer. In my omega world, that translates to a dildo. Only, it has no penis-like features.

Curiosity is the first non-terrifying emotion I've had since I opened my eyes. My dumb, positive brain latches on to it with a vengeance. I find myself reaching for the tube, wanting to inspect it closer.

I only have to turn it in my hands to discover that I'm holding a masturbation sleeve designed to look like a woman's—

"*What* are you *doing*?"

It's the flannel-wearing, booming-voiced alpha. Aghast, he stands in the doorway and gapes across the room.

A squeak flies out of me. I jump, tossing the pussy replica away like it's burned me. The masturbator goes sailing through the air...

...where a big black dog leaps up to catch it.

While I watch in horror, the pet clamps its teeth around the silicone tube and snatches it. Then he happily trots back to the alpha in the doorway, wagging his tail as he drops the fake vagina in front of its owner.

Is it too late to have the other guys come back in here and murder me?

Because I want to *die*.

Furious, the man snatches the sex toy off the floor and throws it at the leather chair shoved into the corner beside the window. Which would be fine, except the dog goes for it again. And when the alpha shouts, "*McKinley, down!*" the pup spins, changing course mid-air to obey—

But his whipping tail knocks the flesh tube into the huge window.

Which *cracks*.

Oh holy night.

chapter
nine

FOR A MOMENT, the alpha gapes at his cracked window. Then, ever-so-slowly, turns to glare at me.

His expression is terrifying. I duck on instinct, immediately burrowing into the blankets the way I would normally hide in my nest back home.

The home I no longer have.

Because I gave it up to bond to a pack who only wanted me for my money.

A pack who is probably looking for me right about now. Or... maybe not, since they didn't like me to begin with.

In fact, this is sort of perfect for them, isn't it? I disappear and they get all the money. They can find some other omega to build a bond through—perhaps even one they'll all have real feelings for.

I burst into a fresh round of tears, cowering under the comforter. Beside me, I hear heavy footsteps and the harsh *snap* of the bedside drawer slamming shut.

Something pokes the blankets covering my shoulder. I crouch lower, whining. Hoping this is all some bad dream I'll wake up from.

Another poke. "Omega," the hard voice says. "Answer me."

It isn't a bark, though, so I ignore him. There's a heavy sigh and that leather chair scrapes toward the bed. It creaks when he lowers himself into it.

The hand that previously poked me lands on my arm, stroking gently through the blankets. "Listen," he says, still gruff. "I didn't mean to scare you. You just shocked me. I'm—"

He grits his teeth audibly. "Just come out." He pauses, grunting like he's in pain as he adds, "Please."

I gasp around a sob. "I b-broke your window."

Another sigh. "My dog broke my damn window. And right now, you're breaking his heart with those whines of yours, little omega. Could you come out here before he bites my balls off for barking at you?"

I almost come out. The idea of the sweet puppy feeling upset nearly forces me. But I'm way too mortified and freaked out to do anything aside from sniffle.

I feel a soft pat on the bed beside me. "McKinley, up."

The mattress jostles. One moment later, the unmistakable warmth of a canine companion settles along my side.

McKinley snuffles at the top of the blankets piled over me, burrowing his snout far enough in to sniff my hair. When his cold nose bumps my forehead, I peer up at his face.

Dang, he's cute. A Bernese Mountain Dog. Fitting. And *adorable*. My trembling hand slips over the silky hair on top of his head.

"S-sorry, baby boy," I whisper. "It's n-not your f-fault."

McKinley chuffs his agreement, gradually sticking more and more of his body into my cocoon, destroying it. Until the gap over my head slips down to expose my face. And I find a pair of intense, icy eyes staring at me.

His hat is in his lap, curled into his white-knuckled fist. Without it shielding some of his potency, I can't hold his gaze for long. The dominance burning in the blue makes me skittish.

Instead, I fling my eyes over the rest of him, cataloging details. No guns. No knives. Just a pair of navy hiking pants, some major boots, and a flannel shirt. I peek back at his chiseled face to see if he's still looking.

Yep.

The grooves around his mouth pull tight as his jaw flexes. He looks older than me—maybe early forties—with some sun damage on his skin and a short beard that matches the dark-brown hair swept back from his forehead.

If he didn't look so utterly intimidating, I might think he looked sort of like the guy on the paper towel box.

When I finally work up my nerve, we stare at each other, neither of us speaking. My brain replays the sight of his fake pussy flying through the air. A completely inappropriate snort hitches out of me.

His thick brows lower. "Something funny?"

My terror has melted into hysteria, apparently, because I suddenly can't stop giggling. I bite my lip, trying to stop the sound from bubbling out of my mouth.

This serious alpha isn't laughing, though. "What, exactly, is so hilarious?"

Sniffling loudly, I use the heel of my shaking hand to wipe tears off my cheeks. "I just... I've never seen a fake vagina before," I gasp. "I learned something new today."

His ice-blue eyes trace my expression, narrowing like he's calculating something. "I live alone," he finally says, as if that explains everything.

Which, I guess it does.

It certainly explained all twelve sex toys in my nightstand at my former apartment, right?

I nod, doing my very best to compose myself. "I'm not laughing at you," I assure him, swallowing another fit of giggles. "I think I'm"—*chortle*—"in shock."

"Guess that makes sense. Car accident and whatnot."

Car accident. Fleeing the scene of my wedding. Being homeless.

One of those things, for sure.

He gives me that heavy sigh again. As though no one has ever been as troubled as him. "What do you need, omega?"

chapter
ten

THEO

EMMA

WHERE ARE YOU

Please come back.

I'm so sorry.

LUCY

Theo! What did you do?!

Mom is blowing up my phone!

...

YOU LOST EMMY?????

THEO

Meg was melting down and I freaked out and barked.

LUCY

THEODORE MATTHEWS

EXCUSE ME

> **THEO**
> Lucy, I've been out driving all night and so have the rest of the guys.

> This is really bad.

> When will you be here?

> **LUCY**
> I'm in an Uber now!

> **THEO**
> Do you think she might be with my buddy Gunnar?

> He's not here either. Meg just told me.

> **LUCY**
> GUNNAR SINCLAIR?!

> **THEO**
> Yes! Does Emma know him?

I'VE BEEN DRIVING all night by the time Theo calls me.

I pull off the highway I've been driving up and down for hours, searching for any trace of the silver sedan I lost. Sighing, I rest my forehead on the steering wheel and smash the button to answer the call.

"Yeah?"

My friend's voice is a frantic croak. "Gunnar! Is Emma with

you? We've been looking for her all night, and then Smith noticed you were gone, too. Do you have her?"

I look around at all the bleak white-and-gray winter. "No. I saw her leave the venue and tried to go after her, but I lost her in the storm. Did you see my texts?"

I've written and called a few times, making sure they all knew what had happened. Theo must not have noticed, though, because he curses, and I hear him fumble with his phone. "No. Fuck. Sorry. We're all freaking the fuck out. My phone's been going off like crazy since we realized she left back around midnight."

Midnight? The hell? "She left way before that," I growl. "How did no one notice? Not even her pack?"

Theo pauses. "There was... an incident. We thought she would be hiding somewhere in the house or on the property. We didn't find her note until midnight."

I'm relieved she left an explanation. "What does it say?"

He's unnaturally quiet for a long beat. "It's an apology. For leaving."

Damn. Something really bad must have happened.

"I know," he rasps, reading my silence. "Now these assholes are saying they don't want an unstable omega. They're asking us to pay them back for their 'expenses' for the wedding. Not sure what the hell they mean since I paid for all this shit, but... It's fucked. Wait. Did you say you've been driving around looking for her?"

He sounds so incredulous; I'm insulted. "Of course I am!" I snap. "What—was I just supposed to let her run off *alone*? In a *storm*? In the *mountains*?"

"Good point," he mumbles. "You should come back and get some sleep, though, Gunn. There's no point in you getting into an accident because you fell asleep at the wheel."

I blow out another breath, knowing he has a point. "Okay. I'll circle back and be there soon." A feeling I remember but haven't felt in a while seethes in my stomach. *Pity.* "We'll find her, man."

He doesn't sound convinced, even as he agrees, "Yeah. Of course. Lucy is almost here. I'm sure she'll have some idea where Em went."

Lucy.

My blood hums at the thought of her big jade eyes and angelic curls. *Am I really going to give up on finding her sister for her?*

Then again, I'm not sure I can stay away now that I know she'll be at the estate house.

"Okay. I'm on my way."

The call clicks off and I roll my shoulders, glancing out my frosted window at the looming shadow of the mountain beside me. *Emma wouldn't have gone up there, right? Unless she got turned around...*

Theo said she was really upset. I suppose it's possible.

With Lucy's face in my mind, I blink exhaustion from my eyes and turn my Jeep around. I'll go up the mountain, make sure Emma isn't there, then I'll go back and do everything I can to comfort the sweet omega I made a horrible first impression with.

Who knows—maybe she won't mind that I'm not in a pack. Maybe she'll have others in mind, and we can make our own pack.

Holy shit. Was that a hopeful *thought?*

I'm so tired, I'm losing my mind.

I follow an off-branch of the main highway, winding my car up the side of the steep mountain. It takes me twenty minutes to clear the first third of the behemoth, where the road suddenly veers into a sharp incline.

And there, buried in a snowbank, is a little silver sedan.

FUCK.

I leap out of the car and wade through snow up to my knees, fighting my way to the car. Noting that it's empty, aside from a familiar purple suitcase in the backseat.

Fuck, fuck, FUCK.

This was her car. And she's gone.

I wrestle her bag out. My mind reels and I go for my phone, only to realize it's sitting in my cup holder. My eyes leap around the snow surrounding the car, trying to make sense of the tracks. They're pretty fresh—the fine powder falling from the sky hasn't obscured them yet.

It looks like three sets of men's shoes. Two on the passenger's side and one here, where the driver's window has been smashed in.

Shit. Did someone find her here and *take* her?

I note the other tracks, then. A set of thick truck tires that seem to have taken off with our runaway bride.

I don't even think. The next thing I know, I'm back in my car, following the swerving tracks further up the mountain.

chapter
eleven

KNOX

I SEE the way the omega holds back whatever she's about to say
—and it isn't a good sign.

Bad enough that I have a strange woman in my bed. Worse
that she helped herself to what is, arguably, the most private
drawer in any residence. Now she's withholding information?

Leaning forward, I set my elbows on my knees and lock eyes
with her, not allowing myself to be swayed by the pretty jade
irises.

"What are you doing up here?"

The girl—*Emma*—swallows visibly. Her tiny hand comes up
to touch her blank neck, fingertips stroking that smooth, milky
throat.

Goddamn it. I grind my molars as my cock ticks in my snow pants, roused by the way she touches her own creamy skin as much as the sight of her flawless flesh.

She's a beautiful woman. And an omega. I remind myself that this is just our biology, playing tricks on us. But as her light-green eyes slide back to mine and tears gather on her smeared lashes, I can't deny the tug deep in my abdomen.

That desire to lean closer beats at me, pounding under my ribs.

Closer. Closer.

Protect. Problem-solve. Provide.

Hell. This is why I avoid people.

Emma opens her mouth to speak, "I was... at a wedding." She ducks her head as if she's ashamed and corrects herself. "I was at *my* wedding. But then... I had to leave. So I took a rental car, and I thought I was going down south, toward my home, but I guess I went the wrong way. It was dark, and I'm not used to driving in the mountains..."

Right, she's from Florida. It's flat as a pancake down there.

Her eyes suddenly go wide and fill up again. "I didn't hurt anyone, did I? Or hit a deer?"

McKinley seems to hate her crying as much as I do. He burrows into her lap and licks her arm. It looks like she has bruises there. Maybe from the crash?

...they better *be from the crash.*

"No," I tell her, finding her green gaze. "Your car has to be towed into town, though. I've already left a message for the local mechanic. I can have them return it for you after they fix it if you find another way home."

Emma swipes at her eyes, offering a tremulous smile that tightens my chest. "Thank you—um, what's your name? I'm Emma."

She lifts her hand, letting the blankets piled on top of her slide down below her strapless white bra. I carefully focus on her fingers, reaching out and taking them in mine. "Knox."

When I seal my palm against hers and feel her trembling, my hand clenches, holding on. I cup the other one around hers to steady it. "You're shaking."

She gives a quivering nod. "I probably will for a while. Normally, I'd go in my nest or call—" She cuts herself off, angrily swiping at another tear as it escapes. "Never mind."

Her ex, I surmise. *Or exes*. Most omegas seek a pack. It's just one of many reasons why I'm out here all alone.

I hum, scowling at my bedroom as though a nest will magically appear for her. I know damn well there isn't one here. *By design*.

It pisses me off that I even care. But I'm a slave to my instincts. And right now? They're more dominant than ever, suffocating all notions of self-preservation.

There's also an edge of desperation I don't understand. Something about *this* omega, specifically. I've been fighting it off from the moment I saw her face through her frosted car window, but it finally overwhelms me. I clutch her hand tighter in both of mine.

"What else calms you?" I inquire, scanning her face. "Anything."

A full-body shiver moves through her when I say the word. My cock notices and twitches to attention. I smother a growl and wait for her reply.

She blinks up at me. "Um... hot showers? Baths, sometimes. Once my hands stop shaking, I guess I could read."

I don't have a bathtub in the master since I designed it with only myself in mind. But I do have a shower. And there's a library down the hall. It's full of business books, though.

Wait. What am I thinking?

She isn't *staying*. She needs to go back to wherever she came from, and I need to get my head examined.

"A hot shower is a good idea."

Micah's voice interrupts my internal tirade. He comes shuffling into the room with a mug clasped between his hands. Behind him, the tool in the fur underpants leans his bare body along the doorjamb.

His shiny eyebrows wag at me. "Got any spare pants, Grizzly Adams?"

I get up to make space for Micah. He hands the mug of broth to Emma and immediately backs a polite distance away. His eyes jump to mine.

"Can she use your bathroom? Or should I show her the guest one down the hall?"

I don't like the idea of him going anywhere alone with her. Especially since I know she doesn't have any clothes on. Suddenly, I'm the only person in the world I trust with this lost, vulnerable woman.

"Mine is fine," I grunt, walking over to flick on the ensuite's lights and pull a stack of fresh towels off the built-in rack.

Emma carefully tucks three full-length blankets around her cold, pale body before she slides out of bed. McKinley follows her into the bathroom. I'm about to correct him, but she coos her praise and promptly closes the door behind them.

Well, damn.

Even my dog likes her.

We all wait, frozen, until we hear the water running. I stalk to my dresser, dig out a loose pair of black joggers, and throw them at Zane. "Take them and get out of my house."

Zane just grins. "Aw, man, don't be like that! I'm going to the airport today, anyway. If I stay, I can give her a ride."

And leave this madman alone with the omega? For the entire two-hour ride into Asheville? I practically snarl. "Fuck, no. She's staying here until someone she trusts can come get her."

The waxed, muscular alpha yanks my joggers on and shrugs loosely. "What makes you think she feels any safer all alone here with you?" he drawls, smirking. "Maybe she likes me better. She certainly liked my scent well enough."

I turn to Micah, looking for backup, but his expression is grim. He nods. "She did. I saw it."

I hold up my hands, halting the conversation. "It doesn't matter whose scent she likes." *Or how insanely, irrationally jealous it makes me feel.* "The woman was half-dead an hour ago. She isn't in any position to be choosing sexual partners."

Micah shrugs his agreement, but Zane's dark eyes light up. "Sometimes a little sexual healing is just what a person needs. How do you know she wouldn't be into it?"

I think about the shame on Emma's face when she told me about her night. My voice drops low. "She just ran out on her own goddamn wedding. That's why she was all dressed up, over-wrought, and lost, okay?"

Zane's eyes fly wide. "*Fuck.*"

Micah hisses an inhale, wincing sympathetically. "Poor thing. Did she say why?"

I think of the tears in her eyes, my mood darkening by the second. "No. She didn't."

Zane surprises me by looking contemplative. "Must have been bad," he mutters, scuffing his bare foot against my floor. "If she ran away."

We all listen to the water running. There's a soft voice woven into it, singing a song. When I look over at the other two, Micah is staring at my closed bathroom door like he's seen a ghost, and Zane grins widely.

"I like her," he decides. "Let's make her breakfast and figure out how we can help."

I frown at him. Secretly, some part of me is still hellbent on having them all leave. Immediately. "I don't cook. Besides, I'm sure Micah is tired. He worked all night."

Micah looks like he's in a trance. He speaks without blinking, staring at the door while he mutters, "I slept at the station. And I could eat."

"Great." Zane claps. "I'll cook."

I eye him dubiously. "You?"

"Yeah, Ebenezer," he chuckles. "Me. I'm a food and travel

influencer. I have twenty-four-million followers. Got a recipe for just about everything."

God help me. I don't even know where to start with that statement. So I grit back, "Ebenezer?"

He shrugs his bare shoulder, already striding off. "Yeah. You're old and rich. You live alone and have no Christmas tree. Sounds like a Scrooge to me."

I'm really regretting letting him keep his coat on earlier. Should have let the bastard freeze his balls off.

Grumbling under my breath, I stomp back to the dresser and pluck out enough clothing to keep Emma covered from the tips of her toes to her chin. When my pile contains a long-sleeved thermal, a fuzzy gray hoodie, fleece-lined joggers, and warm socks, I drop the bundle at the bathroom door and turn to Micah.

Who is *still* staring.

"What?" I demand.

"Nothing," he denies, blinking at the door. "Nothing at all."

chapter
twelve

KNOX HAS to grab my arm to physically shove me out of his room.

I let him because I know he's right. Obviously, the omega deserves her privacy. And obviously, I'm acting weird as hell right now.

It's just... her voice. I've never heard anyone else sing so beautifully. And that *song*...

The further I get from Knox's bedroom, the sicker I feel. My stomach is in knots, dread riding me hard.

At first, the heavenly smell of cinnamon buns makes my gut tweak harder. But after just a few seconds, my mouth waters. Damn, that smells delicious.

How the hell did Zane get something so good in the oven so fast?
I wonder while Knox leads me down the black iron staircase that
drops us into his family room.

The house is palatial.

I remember when he built it. The whole town practically
rioted. Some hoity-toity billionaire asshole buying up three whole
properties? The guy practically owns half the mountain.

They all hate that. When he submitted his plans to construct
this monstrous house, people legitimately lost their shit.

I, for one, didn't see the problem. It's all his land. No one can
see any of it through the forest... unless they're on a neighboring
mountain looking over at this one.

Even then, the enormous A-frame cleaving to the side of the
peak doesn't seem out of place. Whoever designed it went out of
their way to make the structure as organic as any five-thousand-
square-foot mansion could possibly be out here.

The person who did the outside obviously didn't do the
inside, though. This place is *stark*. There aren't even pillows on
the rounded leather sectional in his sunken living room. Nice
enough flat screen hanging over the enormous slate fireplace,
though.

The view really can't be beat, either. Just like the picture
window in his bedroom, Knox has an equally large, unobstructed
vista of the horizon here. The sun crests over it as we cross
through his foyer and into the kitchen.

Zane is at the stove, whistling while he adjusts the heat on the
gas range like he owns the place. I notice his shoulders are tight.
They hitch up higher and higher as the mouth-watering aroma of
fresh cinnamon rolls gets stronger.

While I take a barstool at the massive white-marble island,
Knox slinks out to his garage, and Zane soldiers on, adding bacon
and sausage to a cast-iron skillet before whipping a big bowl of
eggs and chopping an onion.

I have to say, he does move like a guy who knows what he's
doing in the kitchen. The extent of my culinary knowledge is fire-

house chili and cornbread from a box, but he dices and slices like a pro.

A door opens somewhere upstairs, and McKinley trots into the room a moment later, looking pleased with himself. "Yeah, yeah," I grouse, patting his head, "You got the girl. We know."

Zane flinches and shoots me a suspicious look. "Do you smell that?"

I don't smell anything apart from whatever miracle he has in the oven. I glance over at it, but the thing doesn't even look like it's on.

Knox storms back into the room, carrying... a glass repair kit? *Weird*.

Even weirder is the look on his face as he stops short, nostrils flaring. I chuckle, trying to play peacekeeper. "I know, right? Whatever cinnamon rolls Zane whipped up smell like heaven."

Zane turns his dark eyes on me. "What are you talking about? I'm making omelets."

We all blink at each other.

The real reason for the delectable scent dawns.

Holy fuck.

My pheromones spike, along with both of theirs. The room is suddenly an absolute maelstrom of scents. Pine, peppermint, spice. But nothing as strong as the sticky, sugared cinnamon wafting off the tiny omega who appears in the doorway.

chapter
thirteen

OH.

Oh.

OH.

Is this—is *this* what this is supposed to feel like? Because I have been around omegas all my life, but *this*? This is different.

This is *everything*.

It's only muscle memory that lets me pull the hot pans off the range before anything burns. I set them both on the warmer and immediately move, needing to be closer to Emma.

She sways on her feet, dazed. I don't even think before I go to her, but she's suddenly in motion. *Barreling* toward—

Knox.

Well, fuck me sideways.

I stop in my tracks. He drops whatever shit he's holding just as Emma collides with his chest. He grunts on impact, his arms automatically wrapping around her curves, head falling forward.

She buries her face in his chest, rubbing her sweet round cheeks all over his shirt. Jealousy bursts inside of me, rising to block my throat.

I'm... *devastated.*

Rejected and hurt and tortured by longing.

For this *literal stranger.*

By the look of utter dismay on Micah's face, I'd say the poor bastard is in the same boat as me. His jaw hangs open, eyes widening as he stares and clenches his fists.

I'm drifting closer. I can't *stop* myself. Knox's head snaps up —and for a moment, I think we're about to have an all-out alpha brawl over this blonde angel.

The omega notices the same second I do. To her, his angry face looks a lot like rejection. A soft whine starts in her throat and Knox visibly stiffens, thrusting her away like he's afraid he'll accidentally hurt her or something.

Which, of course, makes that whole "possible rejection" thing even worse for Emma.

The sound she makes scrapes my inner ear like a shard of glass. I instantly snap forward and bundle her into my arms, hoping to quell her fear. Needing her close for my own sanity.

Heaven.

Fucking heaven, that's what she is. This scent and her light-green eyes? My chest clenches, waiting for her to cry for the alpha she clearly wants.

Instead, her pupils expand, and her soft pink lips fall open. She leans closer to my naked chest, sniffing right between my pecs. The graze of her nose makes me harder than granite.

I groan and she gasps, practically climbing me to get to the scent of my throat. She marks hers along it, and I think I might come in my pants.

Knox's pants.

I think I might come in Knox's pants.

My body forms a cradle for hers, wrapping her long legs around my waist and tucking my arms under her ass. I palm the back of her head, pressing her mouth against my neck, growling while she licks me.

"You like that, gorgeous?" I hum, inhaling her perfume and bucking into the open air. "Fuck, you smell *divine*. What do you want, hmm? You want my knot? Tell me, baby."

She sucks on my neck and we both moan. Rearing back, she opens her mouth to bite me. I should panic—but all I can think is *yessssssssss*.

A hand lands on my shoulder, intercepting her teeth. "No," Micah scolds softly. "No, sweet girl. You can't bite Zane."

The hell she can't!

I lift my head to snarl in his face, but he shakes my shoulder, forcing my eyes to his. "Zane, man, *think*. Breathe."

Right. Fuck.

I'm in a stranger's kitchen. Holding a woman I don't know.

And she was about to soul-bond us forever and ever.

And I was about to let her.

That's my bad, guys.

But as Micah slowly eases Emma out of my arms, I'm not relieved. All I feel is loss.

Her whine starts again, and *I can't take it*. I move to scoop her back up, but Micah steps in my path, his hands rising to hold her cheeks.

Emma blinks up at him, breathtaking with her bare face and raw emotion. They stare into each other's eyes for a long minute. The connection between them is *visible*. I swear, I *see* that shit. Like a beam of pure fucking light arcing between their faces.

Micah exhales hard. "Emma," he breathes, wrapping her into a bear hug. "It's—Are you—"

Emma nods frantically into his chest, scent-marking him the same way she did with me and Knox.

"Yes," she breathes, shaking. Spring-green eyes turn to Knox, then land on me. "With all of you."

chapter
fourteen

THERE'S BEEN A HORRIBLE MISTAKE.

My wedding? My pack? The ninety five-percent scent-matches that were supposedly "perfection?"

Nope.

Nope, nope, nope, nope, nope.

There's no way that was true. Not when I'm standing here with these three men, absolutely *drowning* in the perfection of them.

Separately, together. It doesn't matter. I've never perfumed this hard before, ever. Even during my heats.

Just the thought of the word "heat" in reference to these three alphas makes a desperate whine build in my chest. Micah shudders against me, pressing an erection into my belly while he clutches me closer. "What's wrong, sweet girl? Tell me and I'll fix it."

What's wrong is I don't have any panties on so I'm currently *pouring* slick into Knox's borrowed pajama bottoms.

All of them notice. Zane closes in behind me, pressing his hot, hard chest into my back. I sigh and squirm closer, absorbing the tingles that race down my spine.

"Do you need us to get you off, baby?" he murmurs, dark and delicious. "I could hold you in my lap while Micah works these pants off. My offer stands—I'll give you my knot if you want it."

The suggestion ought to horrify me. Instead, my core cinches tight and another burst of perfume escapes. That horribly achy, empty feeling I've only ever associated with heat echoes deep inside me.

"I—I don't know what to do," I tell them, too overwhelmed to remember to be coy. "The pack I left last night were supposed to be my scent-matches, but this... this feels stronger. Almost like..."

"*Mates.*"

It's Knox, standing right where I left him. His chest heaves while intensity spins in his blue eyes. Power pours off him, every bit as thick as his pine-and-cedar musk.

My knees wobble and my vision tunnels. When I sway and he still doesn't move, my heart sinks. Another raw whine scrapes up my throat.

Micah cups my head against his chest. "It's okay, sweet girl. We'll get this figured out."

I burrow closer, practically hyperventilating. Zane presses against my back, sealing me between two walls of muscle.

This is *insane*. I don't know these men at all. Not even their last names. But their scents make me feel high—hazy and *euphoric* —while somehow *sharpening* every nerve in my body.

I keep telling myself I'll push them away. But then I *breathe,* and it's just... *right.*

I'm in the right place. Every fiber of my being believes that.

Zane seems to agree. His hips grind tight to my backside while he bends to inhale against my neck, nuzzling past my wet curls. Tension grips his body. The growl that rolls out of him feels more primal than the last.

Micah stiffens and reaches over to Zane's shoulder. "Hey. No."

Knox closes the space between us, snapping forward to bark out a strangled command. *"Take a walk, Zane. Now."*

I feel Zane's desire to rebel. His frame rattles while he restrains his urges, eventually ripping himself off my back and flinging himself toward the exit. "I'm sorry, baby," he mumbles. "I'll be right back."

Some fuzzy, hysterical part of my mind wonders if I should tell him there's a nice fake pussy upstairs. But a moment later, a door snaps open and I assume he's gone in search of fresh air.

Maybe I should follow him. My thoughts are starting to lag, my stream of consciousness buffering a bit.

Knox's nostrils flare as he watches me blink at the place where Zane used to be. The pack's most dominant alpha still looks like he's ten seconds away from roaring the roof off the place, but he grinds his jaw and nods over to their stove.

"She should eat," he grits to Micah. "She needs her strength."

Normally, I hate it when alphas talk over my head. But the bright fervor in Knox's eyes makes it less condescending and more... sincere. Protective in the purest sense—one where he doesn't want me to worry about *anything.* Not even what he's saying.

Micah nods, his broad chest and shoulders expanding on a breath that shakes as he exhales. "Right. Are you hungry, Emma?"

The earnest look on his face might be cute, if I were sane. I'm not, though. And my Omega wants to know why he's using my real name instead of the endearment he gave me before.

When I make a pitiful sound, he sweeps me off my feet and sets me on the nearest barstool, bending his big body low to put us eye-to-eye. I flutter my lashes, trying to focus.

It's way harder than it should be—this man is *unfairly sexy* in a classic tall, dark, and handsome sort of way. A perfect fantasy fireman.

I have to keep breathing, I remind myself, remembering my friends' cautionary tales of passing out the first time they met their mates. *I can't look any weaker or more ridiculous than I already do.*

With a stiffness to his gait that wasn't there before, Knox rounds the kitchen island and goes to their gas range, pulling breakfast off the warming section. Micah watches him, dark eyes wary in a way I don't understand.

Maybe they aren't close? Or they've had a fight recently? Or they're a new pack?

It seems as good a question as any to distract myself from the magical, snowy sweetness rising off Micah's throat.

"How long have you guys been a pack?" I ask, skirting my eyes to Knox.

The flannel-clad alpha snaps his gaze up, past me, to Micah. There's an odd beat of thick silence before he sighs, scratching his short beard and sliding those icy irises over to me. "We aren't, omega."

A pin drops in my mind.

Which is now completely empty.

The hot firefighter cocks a rueful grin. "This is Knox's place. He and I have met a few times in town, but we aren't friends. And Zane isn't even from here. He was camping nearby when he saw smoke from the crash and called it in. I was the one who answered. Knox was walking his dog nearby and happened upon your accident."

My mouth drops open. "Y-you mean... you guys *aren't* a pack?"

They both look at one another. Knox's features harden while Micah's pull into a grimace. "Afraid not," he admits.

The instinct to huff in quick, desperate breaths finally overwhelms me. I suck both their scents into my lungs, panting hard while my thoughts tilt and spiral.

Well.

I tried.

chapter fifteen

I PASSED out once with the Dunlap Pack.

Renee liked to hike, so despite my deep dislike of sweating in the Florida heat, I bought some new boots and agreed to brave the trails with them. I remember how optimistic I was about the whole thing—how certain I felt that the day out would bond all of us.

Naturally, it didn't take long for me to make a fool of myself. I couldn't keep up with them, for one thing. And, after falling behind for the eighteenth time, I twisted my ankle and stupidly tried not to put up a fuss about it. Which meant speed-limping in the hundred-degree heat while my Omega shrieked that we were disappointing our future pack.

When I came to, I could tell I'd ruined everyone's day. I spent the rest of the afternoon watching William and Rob's noses twitch while I pumped burned cinnamon stress into their Lexus.

So imagine my shock when I pass out in this strange alpha's kitchen and come to…

In his lap?

He isn't purring, but the burly alpha, who hasn't smiled once since I met him, has my thighs hooked around his hips and my face pressed into the V of hot, woody skin at the open collar of his flannel shirt. Thick, calloused fingers lightly touch the back of my head.

Petting me?

"Shhh," he rumbles, so quiet that I might just be hearing things. "You're okay, honey."

Off to the side, someone else presses cool fingertips into my pulse. I realize it's Micah when the sharp, magical wintertime aroma of frost creeps into the air. "Heart rate is still normal, so this is just stress. Or shock," he murmurs quietly. "Poor sweet girl."

A door cracks open, and I hear panting. "What"—*gasp*—"the fuck"— *pant*—"happened?!"

My lips twitch. *Zane.*

It doesn't seem to matter that he was just outside in the cold. His chai spiciness still washes into the room like a tidal wave. The warmth of it thickens the air as his footsteps pad across the open living room.

I still have my eyes closed, clinging to some silly instinct that tells me not to let them know I can hear them yet.

Or maybe it isn't *so* silly. After all, I trusted my nose blindly last time, and look where that got us. Listening in on them for a few seconds might not be the *worst* thing…

"Emma got overwhelmed for a moment," Micah replies. "It happens all the time when omegas meet their—"

Again, the gruff man under me says the word no one else can get out. "Mates."

There's a thick swallow, but this time, Micah repeats, "Mates."

Zane doesn't say the word, but he drops to his knees behind me. A low growl starts in Knox's chest. The beautiful alpha ignores it; a second later, his big hand lands on my lower back, rubbing circles.

"I'm sorry I had to go outside, *shona*," he murmurs, leaning close enough for me to feel the heat rising off his bare chest. "I'll be better. I promise."

I hear wet snuffling and realize McKinley has crowded between Knox's legs and Zane's side. "Yeah, I know, buddy," Zane sighs. "I'm worried about her, too."

Awww!

I don't even know what that word he called me means, but how am I supposed to ignore a promise like *that*?! And with *the dog*, too? Come *on*.

Pretending to blink awake, I turn my bleary eyes in his direction. The genuine way his dark gaze lights sends my heart fluttering, even before his secretive smirk tells me he knew I was awake.

"There you are, gorgeous. Did these two bore you into a coma while I was gone?"

It's obviously a joke, but behind him, Micah grimaces and rubs at his nape. The alpha holding me grumbles something and rearranges my body, propping me up and cupping my face so he can examine it.

He's serious and intense, the thick ledge of his brow folding over laser-sharp blue eyes. "How do you feel, Emma?"

I shrink under his intent regard, my stomach squirming at the strength of the dominance rolling off him. My Omega doesn't know if she's annoyed that he didn't call us *honey* again... or too interested in presenting for him to care.

The second that image sails through my thoughts, I start shaking for a whole new reason.

Uh oh.

I know this feeling. The shivery sensation at the base of my spine, the thick pulse that starts between my legs and echoes in my neck...

It isn't a full heat because there isn't any gut-wrenching pain. But quivers of achy need shoot through my lower abdomen until I inhale sharply.

Which is a stupid mistake, of course. Because they're all *here*. Enchanted, frosty coolness; the rich earthiness of cedar; sun-warmed spice. The three scents curl in my lungs, caressing my chest from the inside.

My nipples harden into painful points. Cinnamon-sugar perfume leaks into the air, the thick, gooey smell expanding between the three alphas crowded around me. Knox's hands flinch, his fingertips digging into me as a low snarl rips from his throat. Zane freezes, his hands fisted at his sides.

But Micah...

"Aww, baby," he whispers, easing me off Knox into his hard body. "Does it hurt?"

I swallow thickly and bite my lower lip, resisting the urge to nod. The Dunlap Pack hated it when their plans got derailed by one of my heat-spikes.

They'd been so irritated by them that I went back on suppressants to keep from having any breakthroughs between actual heats. Now, I realize I didn't take my dose last night and might not even have my medicine with me anymore. Which is probably why this is happening at the worst possible moment.

Micah doesn't seem bothered. He reads my expression and makes a sympathetic sound, gathering me up and pushing to his feet. Our eyes meet, his hazel gaze utterly sincere. "Do you want some help? Or should we get you set up in that big bed upstairs and give you some privacy?"

Zane turns to look at Knox. "You have a fake pussy in your drawer—got any dildos?"

My cheeks burn, and Micah frowns at Zane. "Don't be a dick," he tuts, molding his cool palm to my burning face.

Those earnest gold-brown eyes meet mine. "Do you need

easing, Emma? I'm a heat-clinic volunteer—I could try to be as professional about it as possible."

The thought of any of them feeling like they *have* to ease me is suddenly the worst thing I can imagine. Rejection hits my heart in a hard stab. Tears well in my eyes, and I'm too overwrought to fight them anymore.

What is *happening*?

I'm on the edge of a heat-spike, in a strange house, with alphas who have never met *each other* before, let alone me. I've never heard of an omega finding a collection of mates who aren't in the same pack, but I feel a connection to their scents that makes my "scientifically-matched" exes seem like a joke. And, yet, there's a deep throb in my middle, too—the sensation that something vital is still missing.

Is my Omega trying to tell me these guys aren't the ones? The way she tried to tell me the Dunlaps weren't right?

No, that can't be it. Because I'm perfuming like crazy and *dousing* these pants I borrowed from Knox.

When fresh slick pours out of my bare pussy, all three of the alphas go still, each breathing harder. "Emma," Knox finally grits, standing to complete the triangle of perfect chests surrounding me. His blue beams snag my focus, staring into me. "What do you want?"

I want...

I want—

I want to be *wanted*.

I'm so tired of being sneered at. *Tolerated*. Pushed aside and forgotten and just... insignificant. For once, I want someone to need me so much they can't fathom not having me.

Knox's eyebrows twitch as he watches the longing pass through my wet eyes. His jaw flexes twice before he nods at Zane. "She needs you."

Chai spice instantly swells to twine with my own cinnamon scent. His voice drops into a low husk. "Yeah?" he asks me, gaze burning. "Is he right? Do you need *me*, gorgeous?"

The way he's looking at me—with dark, seething hunger blazing in his bottomless eyes—is *exactly* what I need. I whine, my head bobbing before I can stop it.

Part of me expects Micah to remain calm and professional, but his voice rasps, "Can I help?"

The room starts to spin, but I whirl my head around to see his face, which has taken on a harshness that connects with the quivers warming my lower belly. "Please, sweet girl," he adds. "I want to touch you, too."

My entire body trembles, more perfume and slick gushing out of me. Micah curses and sits forward, sealing me between his abdomen and Zane's.

Knox grinds out a deep growl. "I'm watching your every move. If *either* of you does *anything* she doesn't like, you'll answer to *me*," he warns.

Oh my God. The power roiling off him is *insane.* My thighs clench, fear and white-hot want chasing one another through my veins.

When I loll my head in his direction, his rough hand sifts through the hair on the top of my head, but falls away.

Things have slurred into a haze. I only understand that this alpha doesn't want to touch me like the others do. A sharp whine snags behind my sternum, throwing the other two into high gear.

"Her clothes. They'll chafe her," Micah mutters, tugging gently at the hem of the large sweatshirt I have on.

He's right. The scratch of the fabric against my skin *hurts.* It rasps over my raw nerves while my pulse pounds in a desperate drumbeat to match the one throbbing between my thighs.

"Have you ever done this before?" the one with dark, hypnotic eyes asks.

The taller, wider one grunts, "Yes, at the clinic. I've never been with an omega anywhere else."

The other makes an odd sound, muttering, "I've been with omegas, but never during a heat or a spike."

They look at each other for a long moment and seem to reach

some silent agreement. "Here, baby," the one with the swirling gaze whispers. "Let Micah take you. He's going to show me what to do."

He's leaving me? He doesn't want me, now? Is it because he took my shirt off and saw me? I whimper, trying to reach for him. The flash of red material being whipped off the second alpha distracts me, though.

Oh.

Oh.

His body is the most amazing thing I've ever seen. Stacked with rippling muscles, all under perfect brown skin. I whine louder and his teeth flash white while he chuckles. "You like that, sweet girl?"

I try desperately to get closer to him, but the other alpha—the pretty one behind me—grips my chin and turns my head to him. The smirk on his face doesn't match his eyes, but I can't think long enough to figure out why.

He's still wearing something over his lap, covering *everything* I want. When I tug at the cloth and whine, a spark ignites in his fathomless depths. "Mmm. Greedy girl, huh? You want us *both* naked?"

Is he... kidding?

I shouldn't be able to tell. My haze is so strong I can barely *see.* And there have been others—alphas whose names I don't remember right now—who told me how irrational I am when I'm like this.

But the way *this* alpha teases me feels warm. All of the instincts begging for flesh-on-flesh closeness sink into that intimacy. My whines drop to whimpers while I bounce on my knees, desperate to fill the aching emptiness carved into my core.

Compassion fills his face. "*Shona,*" he says softly, framing my face with his big, soft palms. "Settle for me. *Settle.*"

The soft bark soothes more of the restlessness raging in my blood. His gaze drops to my chest, skimming slow circles over each of my tingling breasts.

"So beautiful," he adds, his full, dusky lips quirking up. "Can I kiss you before I kiss this perfect little pussy? Or should we let Micah do that part?"

chapter
sixteen

KNOX

I COULD LIST a hundred reasons why this entire situation is *wrong*.

I have three strangers in my living room. Which is three more than I've ever had here before.

Because I hate other people. Most especially when they're loud, entitled, and lazy like this Zane character.

And—more importantly—*all* of these people are now naked.

I'm too old for this shit.

Which is the next issue. The pretty little omega writhing and perfuming in the middle of my living room? She's too young for me.

Too innocent and sweet. Softness and beauty, all wrapped in

silky skin and blonde curls. Much too pure and perfect for a hard, jaded man like me.

That's the biggest problem. This *has* to be some sort of mistake.

God and I gave up on each other a long time ago—so who sent *me* a mate like *this*?

Is it a trick? Or a dream?

Do I want to wake up?

No, I decide, watching Emma's topless body stretch between Micah and Zane.

That may be the worst, most wrong thing about this: She's *not* in *my* arms.

And I want her to be.

I spent the better part of the last hour trying to deny how good she felt there. When she passed out in the kitchen, instincts I've brutally suppressed all morning came roaring to the surface.

I barely let the others touch her while she was unconscious. I *couldn't*. It was already difficult when we found her. But once my Alpha got a beat on her scent and locked in?

The thought of allowing anyone access to her when she was vulnerable *enraged* me. In that state, I wouldn't let *anyone* touch her but me. Because *I knew* I would keep her safe.

And now? I can't look away for the same reason.

Even though part of me—the piece that wants to cling to solitude for all our sakes—begs to walk away. I can't do it. Because that would mean leaving her unprotected.

And I'd *never* do that.

I watch as Emma whines quietly, bucking against Micah's lap. Zane's long fingers weave into her mussed curls, pulling her flushed face closer to his. Their lips brush and slip together, eliciting a small, ragged moan from the omega and a low growl from the alpha.

Micah takes advantage of the fact that they're distracted and rolls Emma's borrowed sweats off. He tosses them in my direction, and I catch them on instinct, hoarding the slick-soaked fabric against my chest.

Her regular scent is heavenly. Gooey, soft, and warm. Now that she's aroused? My mouth *waters*.

The cinnamon is richer, her vanilla-sugar sweetness slicing down my throat while I huff deeply and lock my muscles into stillness.

I've never been this hard for this long. After damn-near two hours, the throbbing erection still presses insistently into the seam of my hiking pants, twitching while I watch her hands tug at Zane's overly coiffed hair.

When he finally breaks their kiss, Micah has gotten everyone's clothes off. His dick stands at attention, his balls already full, the knot at the base of his shaft starting to swell.

Unsurprisingly, Zane has different ideas. He kicks the furry briefs off, and Emma gasps, instantly trying to lunge for his wide, veiny erection.

There's desperation in every line of her face, but he murmurs sweetly to her. "I know, gorgeous," he says, rubbing his cheek into hers, scent-marking her.

Sweet thing that she is, she nuzzles him right back.

And he pauses.

I watch his chest heave—leaner than mine and waxed smooth. It expands on harsh breaths while the rest of him freezes.

His dark eyes gaze up at her face. She whimpers, trying to wriggle out of Micah's grip on her hips and go for his groin again.

But Zane swallows, the motion thick with hesitation. My eyes narrow.

People don't often surprise me. Right now, though? He is.

I thought he'd shove right in the second he could. He's clearly fucked plenty of omegas. I'm sure being a famous influencer or whatever he is gets him laid plenty.

Why does he suddenly look lost?

And what will it do to Emma if she notices?

I can't allow anything to hurt her. The very thought has my

fists clenching tighter. I meet Micah's eyes and give a hard nod toward them, along with a flex of my dominance.

Zane feels it and snaps back to attention. Whatever tripped him up must not have anything to do with how he feels about her because his free hand tenderly pets her hair as he leans away. "Be my good girl and go to Micah, baby," he rasps. "I want to lick this pussy."

Emma fusses, clearly distressed about all the delays. My body braces, muscles thrumming with the urge to stalk over and fix everything for her.

But that would mean fucking her myself.

And if I do that, I won't ever be able to let her *leave*.

It only takes a second for Micah to lift Emma up and place her face-out on his lap. Her soft, creamy thighs bracket his quad muscles, the blush-pink lips of her spread pussy a perfect contrast to his dark cock.

He doesn't tease her, but I never expected him to. I may only know him in passing, but he's clearly a good alpha and the kind of person who always strives to do the right thing. He'd never edge an omega in a heat-spike.

Unlike some people.

Back on his game, Zane tosses Emma a sly grin. He kneels between Micah's legs and blatantly watches him sink the omega onto his dick.

She lets out a keen that makes my knot pound. Micah groans. Zane's jaw falls slack for a moment as he keeps staring.

Can't say I blame him.

It's just about the prettiest damn thing I've ever seen, too.

A long, deep growl rumbles in the bottom of my lungs as her sweet, cinnamon slick gushes around Micah's cock, slipping down his knot and balls. Micah's head falls back on a strangled groan. Zane moans, too, snapping forward and lapping at the top of her folds.

Fuck. She smells so incredible and looks even better. Blonde curls bounce around her shoulders while she bobs on Micah's girth, pounding it into her pussy as much as she can while also grinding forward, slicking Zane's face.

The alpha on his knees grips her hips and starts to help, lifting and rolling her body against his mouth while Micah pants out praises. "You feel so damn good, Emma. Is this what you need, sweet girl? You like this big alpha cock?"

She nods frantically, hazy green eyes searching for his face. She can't see him behind her, though, and Zane has his mouth pressed right against her pussy, looping his tongue over her clit.

A tiny whimper eeks out of her as her brows crease. The expression—so full of honest *sadness*—smashes whatever logic I'm clinging to. Her body wants release, but Emma...

What does she *want?*

Is it something as simple as... connection?

All I know is, I can't accept that look on her face. I sit forward, bracing my forearms on my knees. "Here, omega," I say, catching her eye with my gentlest bark. "*Look at me.*"

Our gazes clash, hers smoky with lust and wide with fear. *Poor little thing.* This must be so fucking confusing for her and her Omega.

I grit my teeth against the urge to shove Zane out of the way and taste her for myself, focusing enough to send her a wave of approval and reassurance. When the line between her brows softens and vulnerability floods her face, I feel an answering tug in my gut.

Fucking hell.

Why does this fucked-up moment feel so *right*?

I can't think straight long enough to figure it out. Instead, I let that sensation seep into my bones, filling the room with another wave of calm dominance as I mutter, "You're okay, honey. I'm right here. Just look at me. Look at me while you come."

And, goddamn it, she *does*. Those pretty jade eyes lock right onto mine as her back bows and her thighs clench. Micah shouts, latching his lips at her neck, bucking up into her body, sending them both over the edge.

Zane gives a serrated groan, lapping up the literal *burst* of slick that propels out of her body as she squirms on Micah's lap.

Good God.

Did this innocent little omega just squirt creamy cinnamon cum all over my floor?

Yes. And I want *more.*

My body moves, snapping me to my feet and over to her side before I can even register the motion. By the time I realize what I'm doing, I have a clump of her curls in my fist, tugging her head back to sink my mouth against hers.

Just once, I tell myself. *Only a taste.*

chapter
seventeen

THIS IS STARTING to feel like some sort of bad dream.

One of those nightmares where nothing obviously horrifying happens. At first. But as you go along through a fuzzy, indistinct reality... stuff gets weird.

Then things get *wrong*.

Pretty sure this is where someone stabs me and buries me under the porch.

There's a lot of room under there, I bet.

Even with dozens of pro-athlete friends and their extra-giant houses, this compound is easily the largest I've ever stepped foot on.

Well. Trespassed on, technically.

I leave my Jeep behind the snow-crusted Ram parked crookedly at the base of the enormous stone slab propping up the front of the—cabin?

No, it's way too fucking big to be called a cabin. But also way too rustic to be a mansion. This home is one huge A-frame, made entirely of stained timber and natural stone.

It's December, and this place is surrounded by pine trees, but I don't see any wreaths or decorations. Not a great sign, right? I mean, I'm a hopeless bachelor without a bathmat and even *I* have a wreath.

As I trudge up the front porch steps, I note a few other quirks. Like the fact that there's only *one* rocking chair out here, despite the multiple sets of footprints I found back at the abandoned car.

What the hell kind of pack only has *one* chair on their porch?

It makes no sense.

Out here, in the freezing cold, it's hard to get any scents—though, I'm pretty sure there's a woody alpha aroma in the mix. Maybe something spiced, too?

The closer I get to the front door, the more I pick up. Including the mind-bending perfection of fresh, warm cinnamon—

My feet plant on the wood planks beneath me. I blink at the closed doors, gasping again.

Holy shit.

Mate. My Alpha shoves me so hard that I feel my teeth rattle. *This is our mate.*

Not Lucy, then? But *her sister*?! The one I've never met who was about to get *married*?

Unless...

Is it possible the girl I met at Theo's *wasn't* Lucy? Was it *Emma*? And was *she* the perfect dessert I couldn't stand to walk away from at the venue earlier?

...

Fuck. Me.

Emma *was the one in that car tonight, not Lucy.* Emma *is the one they found and brought here.*

The girl I met last year... wasn't Lucy. It was Emma.

My mind reels, calling up my hazy, drunken memories. *I called her Lucy a couple of times... but did she ever* confirm *that was her name?*

Of course not.

Because *this is Emma.*

...the one I called Theo's "other sister."

Oh God. I'm an *idiot.*

I have to be sure. So, closing my eyes, I take a deep, purposeful breath.

And everything inside of me snaps.

Holy FUCK.

My brain blurs white as I stuff her scent into my lungs, feeding a deep, tingling pull as my body sucks the sweet oxygen into my blood. Veins humming, my cock hardens against my inseam, knot growing as my teeth gnash into a snarl.

My canines ache almost as much as my dick, pulsing with the need to sink deep into that scent and *bite.* Saliva wells. Protective, possessive instincts swarm my body. I go right for the door, peering in through the glass embedded in the oak slab.

My omega.

I spot her right away—the woman from last year's party, looking just as damp and lovely as she did in the pool. Her blonde curls are dark, her lashes fanned over round cheeks as she—

Rides another alpha?

While a second one licks her pussy, and a third stands, charging right toward her bared body and wide-eyed face and—

Hell no.

With a roar that could shatter the windows, I throw my weight at the door and bust it open. The toe of my shoe catches on the doorframe, and I stagger into the house, wind and snow blustering at my back.

Everyone goes entirely still except for their dog, who barks until he's close enough for me to touch him, then decides he's cool with me after all. While he weaves between my calves, my eyes bulge out of my head and my hands curl into claws at my sides.

I'm too late.

That one thought sails through my blank mind—now just as barren and chaotic as the weather raging outside.

In here, though, I have my proof; I waited too long to go after the sweet, beautiful omega. She almost got *married* this weekend. And now *another pack* has claimed her.

Thoroughly, by the looks of it.

Part of me is surprised. The shy girl from Theo's lanai didn't seem like she had a ton of experience. I've spent the last twelve months smiling to myself every time I recalled how her green eyes bugged out when she scented my throat... and the way they somehow got even *bigger* when she started perfuming.

I never would have expected that timid little thing to make the list now burning through my shirt pocket like a hot coal, either.

But this woman? Spread over one alpha's fat cock, her fingers twisted in the glossy hair of the one on his knees who, I swear to God, I've seen on TikTok?

Right now, she doesn't seem shy or awkward at all. She looks like a naughty little goddess. One of those nymphs from Greek mythology—innocent, but bursting with light, glowing sensuality.

Joy.

That's what she looks like.

And, fuck me. I *want* it.

Actually, I think I might *need* it. The dark, hollow space under my ribs suddenly aches, as if it's finally remembered I used to have a soul there. The same place that's been numb since the day I lost my mom—and then, in a different sense, my dad, too.

Now that I can feel it again, I don't know how I'll go back to cold, empty dark.

My body reacts to the desperation emanating from my Alpha —and my own damn *self*. Before I can think, my feet move, carrying me halfway into the huge living room, arrowing right for the omega who has me in a chokehold—

"*No.*"

The older alpha's bark is *vicious.* Just one word, but that single syllable proves more than enough to clobber me where I stand, pinning my feet to the light-wood planks underneath my snow-crusted dress shoes. Instantly, everyone else in the room goes utterly still.

With a flash of his menacing blue eyes, the only other guy with clothes on stalks across the room and grabs my arms. I only struggle for a moment before he barks again, forcing me to stop and demanding to know who I am and why I'm there.

"I came from the wedding," I manage, trying to break free. "Everyone is out looking for Emma!"

When I say her name—the correct one, this time—she squeaks a small, scared sound that snaps the two naked dudes out of their stupors. The one she's impaled on instantly snaps her body into his chest and covers her with his bulging arms. The guy on his knees lunges for a throw blanket and bundles the omega between them, murmuring low reassurances while he tucks the fabric around her.

My Alpha practically harrumphs when I see the way she gazes at the man's model-like face. I have to begrudgingly admit there's something there between them... *and* the dude behind her, who cups her jaw gently and turns her head toward him.

He looks dazed, but fully entranced by her. When he scent-marks her cheek and starts to purr, my jaw grinds shut.

Too late, I think again, dread curdling my gut. *I'm too late.*

She doesn't need me, clearly. And if the way she suddenly scrambles to get closer to the man purring for her is any indication, my scent isn't affecting her the way hers rips at me.

"Shh, sweet girl," the dude husks, cutting me a threatening glare while he folds her into his chest. "I've got you. We'll handle this."

The more handsome one seems to recover from whatever he

was doing between Emma's thighs and return from the new dimension it sent him to. Leaping to his feet in a languid roll of muscle, he pads over without a stitch of clothing or a single care for his nudity.

I've been an athlete long enough to know he isn't nearly as strong as he looks. Those muscles are a facade—whatever work-outs he does are geared toward *looking* cut, not actual strength.

If it were just him, I might give in to the buzzing urge to *fight*. I know I could beat him, and possibly even the guy pinning my arms behind my back.

His dominance would be a problem, but once I cut off his ability to bark, he'd have to use brawn. Being that I'm probably twenty years younger and three inches taller...

That would leave the last of them, though. And the dude cuddling Emma into his purr is easily as strong as me. If not more.

Against all three? I don't stand a chance.

Which is an insane thought, because *what the fuck is even happening right now*? Am I seriously about to try to fight off three other grown men just to get to *Theo's little sister*?

No.

I'm about to try to fight off three other grown men to get to *my mate.*

Because that word—*mate*—is the only one to describe the way my vision has tunneled, focused solely on the quivering blonde bundled into this stranger's buff brown chest. The way the whole world has narrowed to the pink button of her nose and the tears welled at the corners of her verdant eyes.

She's *scared.*

Of me?

Just in case, I let the older alpha wrestle me to my knees without complaint. As my shins hit the hardwood floor, the pretty guy's junk suddenly looms a foot away from my face.

I spend a fair bit of time in locker rooms, so I normally wouldn't notice or care—except this particular package is so *hard* it's curving upward and turning a concerning shade of purple.

Then again, if the painful pound in my pants is any indication, my own dick is probably a few minutes away from falling off, too.

"You were at the wedding?" the naked alpha asks, his black brows slanting over dark eyes. "So that would make you one of her...?"

He's asking if I'm part of the dumbass pack who barely waited two hours before ending their engagement. The thought alone is enough to tear a growl up my throat. Pissed, I struggle against the rough hands binding my wrists.

"*Fuck them*," I spit. "They didn't even go out looking for her. I'm—" My teeth gnash as the alpha behind me presses his knee on my shoulder, forcing me to stay put.

"That's Gunnar."

We all freeze again, even the guy behind me. Four pairs of eyes fly to the sad, determined look on Emma's face. The man holding her squeezes his arms to hug her.

All the fight drains out of me the second her gaze latches on to mine, shining with obvious pain. "His name is Gunnar Sinclair," she repeats. "He's my older brother's friend, not my alpha."

Those words gore into me, ruthlessly ripping the air from my lungs. Her chin trembles as she says them and dips her head, hiding her face from us all.

And, hell, I think I might be starting to develop some respect for the guy under her. Because he responds exactly the way she deserves, cuddling her closer and whispering in her ear.

Seeing the hurt in her eyes is like taking a stab to the chest. I choke on a breath, wheezing while I try to fight my way free and go to her side. The oldest alpha lets me get to my feet but keeps his iron grip on my arms when I lunge forward.

"Emma," I grit, flashing a murderous look at the middle-aged guy's equally furious face. He doesn't let me go, though, so I turn back to the omega.

"We need to talk," I rasp, desperate. "We need to call your family. They're all so worried about you."

The fingers bruising my forearms finally relent, dropping me with a shove. I stagger away, shuffling right to Emma. The alpha holding her doesn't flinch when I kneel at the side of the couch and reach over.

I'm not sure what makes me think I can touch her, but my instincts demand it. Cupping her jaw in my numb hand, I turn her face to examine it. There's a bruise over her nose, and I scowl at it.

She sniffles, wide eyes bouncing between mine. "I ran into a door."

For the first time in ages, I feel like I might laugh. My lips curl up. "I just did, too," I reply, nodding over my shoulder to where the clothed alpha kicks snow back out his front door and locks it.

I narrow my eyes at him, then the naked dude lounging indolently against the nearest wall... and the *other* naked dude under her. When I look back at her face, her embarrassed expression turns my stomach.

Poor baby. I'd never be mad at her for this—it's my own damn fault for not going after her last year. And I don't give a fuck how many alphas she sleeps with—as long as she gives me a shot to prove I should be one of them.

So I try to smile at her, even though I'm rusty. "You've been busy, huh, squirt?"

chapter
eighteen

THIS, quite simply, cannot be real.

I must have died in that car crash. Or I'm in a coma. *Something bad.* Because this *can't be my reality.*

Fading quivers of achy need echo through my lower abdomen. Right now, those trembles are the only convincing proof that this might actually be happening.

That... and the all-too real swirl of scents sinking into my lungs.

Even *that's* too good to be true, though. Enchanted mountaintops and snowy pine trees and spicy warmth. Especially now that the sweet, salty nuttiness I've dreamed about all year is woven in the mix.

Because Gunnar Sinclair is... *here*?!

Gunnar. Sinclair.

Here.

Now??

Does not compute. Cannot compute.

And maybe, probably, *should not* compute, because this has to be a hallucination.

The fingers sliding into the damp hair at my nape don't feel like a mirage. They're solid and warm, drawing gentle circles that raise the fine hairs there.

I blink at Gunnar's handsome face—his square jaw and mussed, highlighted hair—peeping the only question I can think to ask. "Are you really here?"

His warm smile pulls into something pained. "Twelve months too late," he admits. "But, yeah, I really am."

The air between us thickens. When I finally manage to drag in a gasp, the taste that skims over my tongue widens my eyes.

It hits my throat and a sharp whine shatters out of me. Because it's just... *impossible.*

Unfathomably good.

A mix of all of them. Woody and spiced and rich and fresh. My whole mind melts and twirls, blotting out the room as my core convulses with fresh need. Perfume pours out of me, infusing the alphas' world-ending aroma with cinnamon sugar.

Gunnar leans closer, raking in a breath and sloughing it back out on a ragged moan. "*Fuck*, you smell so good, Em."

My inner muscles give a wet squeeze at hearing him husk my name. The delicious salty richness pouring off his skin has me whimpering for more. A shaky exhale bursts from his sculpted lips as he crowds closer, setting his forehead against mine.

"Yeah?" he asks, gray eyes brimming with emotion. "You feel this, too?"

A thick lump wedges its way into my gullet. How is this *happening*? How can I possibly feel this way about *all* of them?

They aren't an established pack; and the match service told me the Dunlaps were my mates.

No, my Omega snaps, nearly barking at me. *These are your mates.*

I don't know *how*, but I know it's true. So I ignore the light-headed panic soaring high inside my head and nod at Gunnar. "I —I feel it."

His eyes fall shut, relief and despair tearing at his handsome features. "Did you know?" he whispers, squeezing his eyelids tighter. "That night...?"

The sting of rejection returns full-force, just as strong as it was last New Year's. My scent shifts, and Micah's purr hitches into a low growl, his muscles twitching around me protectively.

"I thought I felt it," I manage, my voice thick. "But the champagne and the de-scenter... and then you were gone, and you didn't ever come back—"

Zane interrupts, straightening and snapping forward. "This asshole *left you somewhere*?" His eyes bulge as they fly to the alpha behind me. "What are you waiting for? Kill him, Micah."

Micah frowns deeply, as if he's already considered the idea. After a tense beat spent tracing my face with his hazel gaze, he sighs. "Don't think I can. Our little omega likes him too much."

But that's the problem. I like *all* of them.

Way too much.

chapter
nineteen

I'M PRETTY MUCH an expert at embarrassing myself.

So trust me when I say: There is no humiliation quite like having a hormonal meltdown, riding one stranger's face and another's dick, then having your big brother's friend burst in and almost get beat up by the forty-something alpha whose leather sofa you just squirted slick all over.

Yeah.

So...

I think I've peaked.

"Thanks," I sniff, my eyes downcast as Knox hands me a bundle of fresh clothing from his dryer.

The warm fabric sends an answering chill down my bare back.

Or maybe that's the crushingly dominant alpha's gruff voice when he replies, "You're welcome."

Figuring there's no sense running to hide in a corner, I drop Knox's throw blanket and slip his navy sweatshirt and baggy joggers on as quickly as I can.

I notice Micah, focused on donning his own underwear, his hazel gaze never leaving the floor. He's probably horrified by me at this point.

I can't say I blame him. I've been forgettable for half my life and a hot mess the other half—but I've never done anything quite this insurmountably mortifying before.

I choke down whines any time I glance at the firefighter's tight features, my shoulders hunching lower with every passing second.

Zane—freshly dressed in clean Knox-wear—snags my gaze. Something about the playful look in his eye and the concerned crease between his brows hits my tender heart. He doesn't know what's wrong or what to do, but he's trying. Which is so much sweeter than I deserve, after essentially using him and leaving him high and dry.

He hesitates, uncertainty filling his features. "You... good?"

My teeth sink into my lower lip. "I—I don't even know what to say," I babble, hoping no one else can hear. "But I'm *so sorry*—"

Zane visibly balks, his perfect face dropping into a scowl. "Why?"

"For—for—" *Grinding mindlessly into your mouth. Using you to get off. Losing my mind in the first place.*

But I can't get any of that out, so he starts guessing. "For having the most perfect pussy I've ever seen? Or the best slick I've ever tasted?" He gives an exaggerated scoff, all sarcasm and charm. "I mean, *I guess* I can forgive you, gorgeous. Just don't let it happen again, huh? My knot might explode."

I smile despite myself, a watery giggle sticking in my throat. The second the amusement fades, though, another, deeper stab of chagrin hits.

Zane didn't want to be the one who took me, I remember, my insides curling tighter. *He gave me to Micah...*

Who won't even look at me now.

But that's okay! That's... okay? I think I'll probably live if he rejects me. Most likely.

I mean, I did when Gunnar pushed me into Theo's pool...

Maybe everything the Dunlap Pack said about me was true. Here I am, with my dumb brain and hopelessly hopeful heart, trying to turn this whole situation into something *positive.*

It's possible these guys will see how naive I am and be just as off-put as my last "mates."

Thinking this, I drop Zane's gaze, sitting on the sofa where I can reach McKinley's furry face. None of the alphas loitering around the edges of the room question me, but I sense Zane's scent burn.

Tears start gathering then. A mixture of every kind of embarrassment—a different strain for each catastrophe I've endured in the last twelve hours.

For a while, I keep the waterworks under wraps. Calling upon years of stumbling through life and swallowing what little pride I definitely don't have, I force myself to take the plate of reheated breakfast food Knox hands me.

I pick at it while the guys grunt and huff, shooting one another dirty looks. They all find places to sit around the palatial living room, stabbing at their food and eyeing each other between bites.

Gunnar doesn't sit down or take his plate, though. He whips out his phone and starts making calls while he paces.

When he finally gets ahold of Theo and tries to hand me the cell, I blink up at it. My chin wobbles when I attempt to summon the courage to face my big brother after everything I put him through. In the end, I shake my head so hard that the tears at the corners of my eyes leak out.

Frowning, Gunnar mutters, "Uhhh, actually, Theo? She just went to the bathroom. I'll have her call you on our way ba—"

With a whine, I frantically whip my head faster. Gunnar's wide-eyed look and nervous stammering might be cute if I wasn't about to burst into tears. "Aaaaaactually..." he corrects, "We might stay here for a beat. Emma's upset and—no."

His gray eyes land on me, lips quirking down. "*No*, man," he says, firmer. "She doesn't want to talk to you right now. And she doesn't want to come back. ...Yeah. Okay... I'll call you."

He hangs up, and I realize the whole room is watching me. *Again.*

Knox pins me in place from the other side of his U-shaped sofa. I'm not sure what it is about this alpha that lets him see right into my *soul*, but he does.

I can tell from the look on his face that he doesn't understand our connection either. He said he lived alone—and the *way* he said it, like it was a point of pride for him, seemed like he *enjoys* being by himself. And maybe even *likes* not getting along with most people.

So I'm not sure how he manages to look over at me and see the truth I haven't even admitted to myself.

His voice drops low. "You *aren't* going back."

My teeth nip the corner of my lip while more tears spill from my eyes. My head shake is much smaller this time. "I can't. They —It's better if I don't. They'll be..."

The last word is so hard to say, even though I know it's true. For them *and* for me.

"*Happier*," I croak. "They're happier without me."

Knox's eyes blaze, but his expression doesn't change. Gunnar's arms drop to his sides, shock sailing over his features before he shuts them down.

Zane leans over his lap and pets McKinley, turning to frown softly at me. I see the question in his dark irises.

Why?

Micah's the one who asks, though. His scent sharpens before he sets his hand on my back. "Do you want to tell us what happened, Emma?"

———— ♥ ————

EVER BEEN in a room full of strangers who all want to shred each other to bits?

Ever been in a room full of strangers who all want to shred each other to bits *and then* go kill your ex-fiancés?

McKinley huddles into my legs as I finish my sorry story, flattening his ears against his head. I can't say I blame the pup—the energy in here is *razor-sharp*.

My Omega doesn't like it, either. She paces my insides the same way Gunnar keeps pacing the raised platform leading to the front door.

He's almost slipped into the sunken living room twice. I'm starting to think he might be as clumsy as me.

Zane seems restless, too. Halfway through my tale, he gets up and starts wearing his own path into the floor; though his route is shorter, less predictable, and more lopsided.

Micah pumps out alpha aggression by the bucket-full, but his hand on my back hasn't so much as twitched. He listens with his eyes on the coffee table, blinking and squinting at all the right moments, silently telling me he's heard every single word.

But Knox...

I've never had *anyone* listen to me the way Knox is right now.

The entire time, really. While I fumbled my way through my humiliating account of the last twenty-four hours, he watched with rapt attention.

His cool eyes somehow see right through my mind, past all the chaos swirling my thoughts and anxieties, straight to the heart of me. It's steadying and terrifying, and I have no idea how to feel about it.

Or how to look away.

When I finally finish my story with the moment I woke up

here, Gunnar stops carving ovals into the hardwoods and turns to me.

They all do. Three pairs of eyes join Knox's, all staring at my tear-smeared cheeks.

Usually, I pride myself on staying positive. That part of my brain pings, telling me they're all just surprised. Surely, they don't think I'm as pathetic as I sound…

But there's another voice in my head now. One that had been dormant for a long time before everything happened yesterday. The hiss that reminds me I've never been anyone's first choice—or even their *second* choice.

I'm always the one no one remembers. The most easily-overlooked Matthews; the average omega with a boring job and far too much optimism for my own good.

This is it, she says. *This is the moment they all turn their backs on you and decide any attraction they felt isn't real. Or maybe just isn't worth the trouble.*

The room holds its breath. I blink at each of their drawn faces.

And then they're *on* me.

Zane looses a soft groan, snapping forward to crowd into my side and drop his face to my shoulder. "They were going to *use* you. Emma, *baby*, that is *so* fucked up."

Micah slides his hand around my waist, frowning mightily. "Those alphas should be ashamed of themselves." When I turn to him, his free fingers wrap around mine, squeezing softly. "How could anyone ever try to deceive you like that?"

Because I make it too easy?

I don't get a chance to answer him. Gunnar stalks into the fray, dropping to kneel in front of my quivering legs. When his palms cup the sides of my thighs, tingles race to my core.

"Fucking *what*?" he demands, gray eyes seething for a whole different reason. "Your brother *barked* at you? I'll kick his ass!"

That might actually be… hilarious. If Gunnar is as klutzy as I think, Theo isn't far behind. Watching the two of them try to beat each other up is the sort of thing that would usually have Lucy and me laughing for days.

I file the mental image away, my middle a mixture of bemusement and wistfulness. I wonder if my brother is still mad at me, and if my sister made it there in one piece.

Even if I can't bring myself to face Theo yet, I really should call Lucy, at least. And Bridget.

Just as a fresh round of dismay starts to delve into my guts, a crack of attention-grabbing, big-knot energy snaps across the room.

When I look up, I find Knox looming right behind Gunnar, thrumming with urgent alpha power that belies his solemn, calm expression. When I dare a glance into his piercing blue eyes, he sighs, releasing a tiny bit of the tension gripping his broad frame.

"Good girl," he grunts. "Most people—once they've sunk so much into something, they're too scared to walk away. I'm proud of you for leaving when you did."

His approval soothes the choking mortification squeezing my gullet. My shoulders drop as my mouth falls slack, mind reeling.

He isn't going to tell me I'm dumb for being fooled? Or silly for hoping for the best until the last possible second? Or an utter failure for losing all that money? Or a complete and total inconvenience to him—ruining his day, taking over his house, filling it with people he doesn't know when, clearly, he likes to be alone…???

Nope. He doesn't say any of that. He just keeps gazing into me like he can read the inside of my skull.

It might be unnerving if he wasn't also filling the great room with a thick, weighted blanket of serenity.

It isn't just him, actually. Micah gives off the same reassurance; though his is tinged with a fondness that has me pressing closer to his side. When his chest begins to rumble gently, I make a very obvious moaning noise that has everyone tensing.

Except for him.

Micah *tsk*s quietly, his strong arms easily lifting me into his lap. The delicious purr vibrating behind his pecs gets louder as I bury my face against it, absorbing the shivers of pleasure that skitter over my scalp and down my spine.

I wish I could help myself, but I can't. His purr is all my Omega has been begging for—and everything the Dunlaps refused to give me.

Micah seems surprised by my reaction, craning his neck and chuckling quietly while I move closer. Hazel irises trace my face for a long moment before any hint of amusement falls from his straight features.

Understanding blooms in his eyes. "Sweet girl," he whispers, "You need this, don't you?"

My voice quivers as I deliver the same promise I always made to William and Rob. "I—I just need t-two minutes."

The hard muscles wrapped around me seem to tighten and soften all at once—turning into a solid bear hug that holds me exactly where I want to be. "You could stay right here forever," he replies. "And I'd be the luckiest alpha on this whole damn mountain."

A rush of warmth washes through me. My heart leaps, so eager to believe that he means what he's saying.

But I'm trying to be *smart* now. And isn't this the same alpha who couldn't even look me in the eye twenty minutes ago? Has he changed his mind again? Or is he maybe just... shy?

Looking up at his handsome face, muddled with all my uncertainty, it hits me: I don't know any of these guys.

And they don't know each other.

It probably doesn't matter how I feel. A year ago, I would have believed that all of this must *mean* something. Now, though?

She's the neediest, naivest klutz that's ever lived.

If I really was smart, I'd just close my eyes, block out their scents and my Omega's frantic internal whines, and tell them to call my brother to come get me. Or my parents.

Then I could go home and face the music. Move back into my childhood bedroom and beg the school to give me back my old job. Hang out with Bridget when I feel lonely.

But all of that starts with getting off Micah's lap...

...which has somehow become impossible?

Especially when Zane slides right into Micah's side, totally unbothered by the other alpha's proximity. His chest buzzes on a low sound that isn't quite a purr, but the wry, beautiful smile he flashes makes up for it.

"Sorry, gorgeous, I'm a bit rusty with purring. I'll get better. You can whip me into shape," he says, winking on the last bit.

I can't help the snuffly laugh that bursts out of me. He's so ridiculously good-looking, trying not to giggle like an idiot when he looks right at me seems hopeless.

Plus, he's literally *the only* person I've ever seen pull off a wink. On Zane, the move doesn't feel cheesy or even trite. It somehow just... *works*.

A bolt of arousal snakes into my stomach, gelling the lower muscles of my belly while my heart flutters. Tittering like a moron is the only way I can cover the fact that slick and perfume slip into my second pair of borrowed pants.

Zane can tell, though. Instead of getting cockier, his grin grows completely genuine. The vibrations in his chest deepen into a real purr, and he slowly leans his forehead into mine, closing his eyes briefly.

"What are we going to do, gorgeous?" he whispers. "I don't want to leave here without you."

Micah's fingers tighten on my back just as Gunnar's latch around my legs. The mood shifts instantly. All three of them go from comforting to confrontational. Micah's purr drops into a growl, and Zane's follows suit.

Alpha tug-of-war? my Omega asks, all-too excited by that idea. I bat her aside, refusing to admit how good it feels to have these sexy men fight over me.

Knox releases a low bark, mumbled but deadly. "*Knock it off.*"

All of their growls cut off abruptly. I crack my eyelids open, chancing a peek at each of them. Knox has his head tilted back and his eyes shut—likely asking whatever God he believes in why he's been saddled with this mess.

On the floor beside Knox's booted feet, Gunnar's face has gone completely blank in a way I don't understand. It's the opposite of Micah and Zane's expressions—which are both variations of thinly-veiled aggression.

I'm embarrassed to admit... it has taken me this long to realize:

If I stay here and wait for Theo or my parents, I'll be staying *with Knox*. Which, because they aren't packed, is basically the same as telling the others to go back to their lives and forget about me.

The thought alone is a stab of panic, right between the ribs.

But... if I *don't* stay with Knox—if I leave him here—I'll have to choose one of them to go with.

I know I seem stupid, but my brain *does* work. *I know* Gunnar makes the most sense. He's the only alpha in the room that I've met before and the only one who knows my family.

I suppose, if I still had the capacity for my usual optimism, I might also notice that we're from the same city, which may give us future courting potential.

But the look on his face scares me. He seems *bleak*. Like he's completely checked out of this whole situation and no longer cares what happens.

My Omega whines at the thought, and Micah hugs me tighter. Reminding me that, so far, *he's* been the one to prove himself the best caretaker here. But, then, Zane is trying *so hard...*

Oh my God—*what is happening?!*

Am I honestly going to pick *one* of these guys? Is there another option?

All of the above, my Omega shouts, filling my head with supremely unhelpful images.

Sensing my rising panic, Knox intervenes again. I'm starting to suspect he can't help it—he clearly hates that he's become the de facto leader almost as much as he obviously loathes having company in the first place. A slight snarl mars his rugged features as he blows out an exasperated breath.

"Emma will stay here with me until her family can come get her," he decides, then flicks a look at Gunnar. "Since you know her brother, I suppose you can stay while we wait for him."

Gunnar's features don't move, aside from a tick in his jaw. Micah's crisp scent sharpens into a cold blade as he swallows hard.

But Zane *erupts.*

"You're not the boss of her!" he snaps, glaring. "I'm already heading into Asheville today—I should just take her with me!"

Micah lets a small growl slip, nodding at the back wall of windows and the chaotic blitz of white beyond. "To the *airport*? Do you honestly think *either* of you will be flying anywhere in weather like *that*?!"

"The roads aren't safe right now anyway," Gunnar grumbles, falling onto his butt and scrubbing both hands over his face. Exhaustion lines his thoughtful scowl. "Unless whoever owns that big-ass truck out there has tire chains for it."

"Of course I do," Micah grunts, rolling his eyes. "We live in the *mountains.*"

"Fucking city boys," Knox adds, shaking his head. "Neither of you are taking Emma anywhere. You couldn't navigate your way out of a wet paper bag, let alone a storm like this."

His strong jaw clenches as he skirts blue eyes to mine. "If you don't want to stay here, omega, Micah and I will drive you back to your family."

Gunnar snarls. "Over my dead body will *any* of you be alone with her again. I saw what you were doing when I got here. Absolutely fucking *not.*"

I open my mouth to defend the guys, but Zane answers with a fearsome roar. I cower from the noise while Micah wraps a hand around my head, protecting my ears.

"She was in a heat-spike, dickhead!" Zane shouts at Gunnar. "She would have been in *pain.* And where the hell would *you* have been? *Not fucking here* because you *rejected* her last year. And now you think *you* get to make orders? Get fucked, man."

That does it. The room explodes into yelling, growling, barking, and a swirling soup of alpha pheromones so strong that my head spins. McKinley and I whine, the piercing noises blurring into the high-pitched shriek that suddenly sounds in Knox's pocket.

"*Quiet!*" he barks, cutting through the commotion as he yanks out a phone and frowns at it.

Spitting a vicious curse, he tosses the device to Micah and plows both hands into his hair, spinning to stalk out of the room.

Well, then.

Micah grabs the cell and scans the screen, sighing his own, "Fuck," before falling back against the couch cushions and pinching the bridge of his nose.

"What?" Zane demands at the same time Gunnar bites out, "The hell else could be wrong now?"

Micah's hazel eyes fly open, pinning the other two alphas in place. "It's a notification from our local authorities. They have an emergency alert system."

My insides go cold, my scent plummeting as fear grips my throat. Micah feels my reaction and pulls me back into a hug. His voice loses every last edge before he murmurs, "Do you want the good news or the bad news first, sweet girl?"

Maybe I'm still too stupid to live after all, because I immediately say, "Good news."

His smile is as wry as it is handsome. "The good news is, we don't have to fight about who's leaving. Because none of us are going anywhere. The road is washed out."

I blink at him, not understanding. His brows quirk as he looks to the others and back at me, translating, "We're snowed in."

chapter twenty

UNKNOWN NUMBER HAS ADDED YOU TO A CHAT. MARK AS SPAM?

MICAH

This is Micah. I know we already exchanged numbers but I figured it would be good for us to have group text in case Emma needs anything.

GUNNAR

Makes sense.

ZANE

you can all save my name under Drop Dead Gorgeous

GUNNAR HAS CHANGED ZANE'S NAME TO DROP DEAD

GUNNAR

Got it.

ZANE HAS CHANGED GUNNAR'S NAME TO STICK UP OUR BUTTS

DROP DEAD

I might be the pain in your asses, but Gunnar's definitely the stick.

MICAH CHANGED DROP DEAD'S NAME IN THIS CHAT TO ZANE

*MICAH CHANGED STICK UP OUR BUTTS NAME
IN THIS CHAT TO GUNNAR*

MICAH

You guys are exhausting

Can we at least attempt to get along for
Emma's sake?

KNOX

How are you all texting me in the same
message?

ZANE

oh my god

he's kidding right?

RIGHT??

Knox, man, say psych right now.

GUNNAR

It's called a group text, gramps

MICAH

So we can all talk at the same time

KNOX

Follow-up question:

Why?

GUNNAR

JFC

KNOX

You're probably lucky I have no idea what that
means.

micah

"MOTHERFUCKING, DUMB-AS-SHIT, PAIN-IN-THE-ASS—"

Under different circumstances, I might laugh. Knox hasn't stopped muttering since we got in my truck and peeled out, spitting a low tirade the whole ride up to the washed-out portion of the road.

I can't tell if he's holding out hope that the path may still be passable or resigned to having all of us stranded at his place. If the feverish feeling blooming under my skin is any indication, I'm *relieved* none of us can get very far.

Being away from Emma for this twenty-minute excursion is making me almost as crazy as knowing that I left her back at another alpha's house with two strangers. The need to return to her beats alongside my pulse, filling my blood with urgency that edges my scent.

Knox shoots me a murderous look when he notices, and I snort. "This is *my* truck." I laugh, the sound flat. "If you wanted to be in charge, you should have stayed back at your compound."

His face says it all: he *doesn't* want to be in charge.

He doesn't want *any* of this.

Which is a shame, because he's the only one I trust around Emma and the only one I could conceivably form a pack with.

That fact that my thoughts continue to flicker back to that place—along with the way it felt to be inside her earlier—tells me what I need to know. This omega is *mine*. The notion of letting Zane or Gunnar disappear with her guts me.

There's a chance she'd prefer them, though. After the way I nearly knotted her and then lost my nerve when Gunnar showed up... I probably made her feel every bit as rejected as that stupid hockey player did. Or—*worse*—the pack she just ran away from.

Knox senses my darkening mood and stops muttering long enough to shoot me some side-eye. "Worrying won't help," he grumbles. "She's going to choose whichever one of you her Omega tells her to."

I raise a brow. "One of *us*? So, not you?"

He sighs, scratching at his beard. "What the hell would a sweet little thing like her want with me? I'm old as dirt compared to all of you. And she's clearly a social woman who's used to a big family. Being stuck up here with me and my damn dog isn't much of a life for a little miss like her."

Emma hasn't had the chance to give a lot of details, but she did manage to drop tidbits about coming from a big family, her siblings and friends, and her former job as an elementary school guidance counselor. All those things align with the picture Knox paints—a vibrant, upbeat person who enjoys the company of others and likes to be around children.

"You could have kids," I mumble, imagining it.

Emma would look so damn pretty pregnant. I've only seen her smile a few times, but somehow, it feels natural to picture her round and glowing with happiness.

The thought enriches my scent for a whole different reason. I can't help but notice that Knox's woody aroma is thicker, too. He likes the idea of breeding the cute, kind-hearted omega as much as I do.

The realization helps me clear my throat and add the piece I've been waiting to mention, "Or you could find some packmates."

At first, he chuffs a dismissive scoff, scowling at the windshield as white flakes pile onto my truck's hood. When I don't go on, his gaze snaps over the center console.

"Or *you* could," he returns. "It'd be easy for you. You work with half a dozen unbonded alphas. Take Emma into town and see if she likes any of them."

I'm not sure why his suggestion puts a frown on my face. Possibly because it feels ridiculous, when I know for a fact there are three other alphas she's already attracted to.

"If I wanted to be in a pack with any of the other alphas in town, I probably wouldn't have waited so long," I muse. "Most of the guys at the station are younger than me. Not ready to settle and all that."

"Mm." It's hard to tell if he's disapproving or contemplative. "Zane strikes me as one of those."

God, *that* guy. He's a hot mess.

Very hot, apparently, if the way Emma stares at him is any indication.

Still, he hung in with me during her heat-spike. I don't understand why he froze up instead of taking her himself, but he did a decent enough job of getting her off while her perfect, wet pussy *strangled my cock.*

I wince, rearranging the crotch of my pants and trying not to full-on cringe when I recall the way I reacted after it was over. The truth isn't macho or flattering, but I honestly felt like she'd snatched my soul straight out of my body when she came around me and covered me in her slick.

Having her scramble away so quickly, hearing that another alpha had driven through the night to find her and essentially rescue her *from me* was devastating. I didn't know how to react until I realized that being in my head was making her feel insecure.

The way her needs have already—automatically—started to feel like my own is another sign.

What do I *do*?

If she even picks me out of the group vying for her attention... we live in different states.

Maybe I ask her to stay? Or I offer to go with her? I can work as a firefighter anywhere. I'd miss my brother a lot, but we could visit...

Shit.

I've known her for *hours* and this is the way my thoughts are turning? If Zane and Gunnar feel the same way, it may not matter how dedicated either of them are to remaining bachelors. They might not have a choice anymore.

There's a chance none of us do.

"Zane's not so bad," I allow, swallowing the wad of dread in my throat. When Knox shoots me a look, I grimace. Needing to convince myself as much as him, I add, "Your dog likes him, anyway."

The older alpha grunts. "There is that. He likes Emma, too. And that Gunnar kid."

I try for a smile. "Maybe he isn't such a good judge of character after all."

With another shake of his head, Knox replies, "Gunnar seems protective of her. Didn't let her brother upset her and didn't promise to bring her back against her will. I guess all of that's a good sign. Although, he did leave her last year."

Silence descends 'while we both chew on that.

It's true. Gunnar did leave her. The thought of that fills me with outrage.

But, if I let Emma go... am I really any better?

I feel Knox thinking the same thing. The cab of my truck suddenly smells like a forest fire in the dead of winter—the driest, most frigid frost and smoldering tinder.

The washed-out portion of the road comes into view. I jerk my truck to a stop. We both sit forward, peering out into the heavy snowfall.

There's a good chance I won't *be able* to let Emma go.

Literally.

Because we're really fucking stuck.

I know we've both had the same thought for the second time in ten seconds when Knox very succinctly sighs, "Goddamn it."

chapter
twenty-one

"EMMY," my sister hisses through Gunnar's borrowed phone. "*What* is happening?"

I've never liked being called Emmy. But when a cutesy version of your name is your baby sister's first word? You sort of end up going with it. *Forever.*

Exhaling deeply, I glance over at the closed door of Knox's bedroom, then to the cracked window. He must have put sealant on it before he and Micah left, because gloopy filling now holds the pane together.

"Emmy!" Lucy snaps, still whispering. "Theo says you're at some *random alpha's cabin*? With *Gunnar Sinclair*? And you're *refusing* to come back? I'm keeping Mom from losing her shit, but I need *details*."

That, I believe. Lucy could put on a pair of porkchop panties and still tame a den of lions. It doesn't surprise me that she's managed to smooth everyone's ruffled feathers within a matter of hours.

"I told you," I groan. "I need you to get away from the others and conference call Bridget!"

Lucy huffs, but I hear her heels on the mansion's hardwoods. Lucy *lives* in heels, which might not annoy me so much if I could just *walk upright* in them.

"Fine, fine," she grouses.

A door *snick*s and the sound of her thumbs tapping at her cell comes through Gunnar's. The call clicks as it adds my best friend and switches all three of us to FaceTime.

Bridget's beautiful, rounded face appears besides my sister's slender one. Lucy's blonde hair is coiffed into a perfect half-up style while Bridget's fans around her face in a pinkish-red mane. She yawns and rubs at her blue eyes, pouting.

"Emma, it's almost five! Aren't you supposed to be in that cream puff Renee picked out?"

She means my former wedding dress. Which, yes, looked sort of like a cotton ball someone had dipped in alfredo sauce.

Renee chose it. And when I told her I probably couldn't manage a ballgown without falling, she just smirked and told me to do my best.

It's strange how utterly *wrong* all of it feels to me now. Not just the wedding details—which, honestly, never reflected my taste as much as they reflected the Dunlap Pack's need to show off— but the *whole six months* I spent courting them.

Every time I think back, I remember new details that I forced myself to accept—or forced myself to *forget*.

When Micah purred for me this afternoon without even a moment's hesitation, something inside me finally clicked. He clearly has mixed feelings about this whole horrible situation, but he still didn't skip a single beat when it came to comforting me or offering his support. Compared to the alphas who spent half a year telling me everything I wanted to hear but flinching any time I tried to go to them for reassurance, that feels like a big deal.

For the first time, I allow myself to accept the words as I say them. My voice is surprisingly calm. "I'm not going back to the Dunlap Pack. Luce, I need you to tell Mom."

Bridget's jaw drops open. Lucy's beautiful face pinches; then a look of pure *relief* passes over her features. "Oh, thank *God*. I hate those alpha-holes. Don't even worry about it, Emmy; I'll take care of everything."

My best friend sputters. "So you're—you're just—*staying* in that cabin with all those strange alphas?"

They don't *feel* strange, though. Even now, as I inhale the scent of Knox's sheets...

They feel like *my* alphas.

I stare at the two faces I know and love best; Lucy's, steeped in concern; and Bridget's, full of shock. My voice drops into a whisper. "Am I stupid if I believe I might be here with them for a reason?"

Lucy's brows crunch lower. "Like what? A Christmas miracle?"

"I don't know," I mumble back. "Maybe?"

My whole life has been a series of embarrassing mishaps and unfortunate stumbles. Is it really so crazy for me to think the universe might owe me one? That, *just maybe*—what happened to me last night doesn't mean I shouldn't trust this, but, actually, might mean that I *deserve* this?

Bridget's expression softens when she sees the desperation in my eyes. "It could be," she allows, ever the sweetheart. "As long as you feel safe and your family is staying nearby, I guess there's no harm in staying for a couple of days to figure things out."

She bites her full bottom lip, fretting around it. "But... isn't your heat coming, Em? I know you and I made that silly list of things for your old pack to try. Didn't you plan your honeymoon around it?"

Only because my heats were the only times William and Rob would have sex with me… and they never seemed to know what to do apart from the obvious.

I wince at the memories. "I don't think I have the list anymore. But my heat should be in, like, three weeks?"

Lucy gives a huffing laugh. "Uh, don't bet on it, Emmy," she chortles. "If you're telling us you actually found four *mates* who feel like stronger matches than the ones you had, I'd say your heat is probably going to get there *waaaaaay* before the big guy in the red suit stuffs himself down anyone's chimney."

chapter
twenty-two

PEOPLE ALWAYS ASK me how I started cooking.

They're not polite about it, either.

They don't ask with innocent interest or admiration or even fascination. It's usually more of a drawling, smirking sort of thing where they look me up and down and say, "How did *you* start *cooking*?"

Implying, I guess, that I should just be on a mattress somewhere? Fucking for a camera?

I mean, that sounds *fun*...

Normally, when I'm questioned, I make some sort of joke to that effect. I tell people I started cooking because I'm so hot, I didn't even need an oven... or some other shit.

The real answer is too personal. I don't even let *myself* think about it most days.

But today is different. It has been since I saw the smoke rising outside my window this morning.

While I stand over Knox's fancy gas range, heating a cast-iron skillet, I stare down at the flame. A familiar squeeze grips my throat. I let my eyes fall shut and breathe, knowing it will pass. Hopefully, before Emma comes downstairs or Micah and Knox barrel back in here.

After the fireman called his station and confirmed where the road had washed out—whatever the fuck *that* means—Emma borrowed Hockey Boy's phone to call her sister. She took McKinley upstairs with her while the two mountain-dwellers went to figure out exactly how stuck we are.

I hope we're *really* fucking stuck.

I shake my head at myself for having the thought. Two days ago, if you'd told me I'd be entertaining the idea of a *mate*, let alone an *entire pack of strangers*, I would have fallen over laughing.

But I'm pretty sure that's exactly what I'm doing here.

I could have left a while ago. Knox said my glamping site is within walking distance. Granted, "walking distance" probably means something different to Grizzly Adams than it would to a normal person, but still. I work out. I could have hiked back there before this storm got so shitty.

I didn't *want* to.

I've been traveling without a permanent address for three years, and canceling a flight has never felt so good. I made short work of it, returning my ticket and hovering my thumb over the button to rebook...

Only to tap out of the app entirely.

In the living room, Gunnar tries to stay awake, sitting on the portion of the sofa closest to the stairs like he's the omega's body-guard. I roll my eyes and swipe over to Spotify for some jazz. I let it play while I scroll my socials, telling my followers I'll be out of range for a couple days.

Hockey Boy is snoring within minutes, leaving me free to decide what to make as an afternoon meal. Easier said than done, since Knox apparently seasons all his food with the same five spices. Not to mention—I don't know what any of these people like to eat.

When scouring Knox's pantry doesn't help quiet my mind, I know it's bad. Food has always been the easiest way to shut off my mind. It's *connection*, for me. To others, to all the things I never had and *always* wanted. The fact that moving through this luxury kitchen doesn't get the image of Emma's face out of my mind *means* something.

Restlessness prickles the back of my neck, and I glance up at the ceiling, wishing I could somehow develop x-ray eyes.

Stupid. She's fine up there. I know that.

But I hated the way she looked when she shuffled upstairs earlier. So uncertain and confused. Her whole world has been flipped upside-down at least six times in the last twenty-four hours. I don't blame her for not knowing which way is up anymore.

I'm just shocked at how much it's *killing* me.

Pain pinches deep in my chest, the pang radiating into my stomach. My fingers curl around the wooden cabinet doors while I glance up again.

I can't... go to her, can I?

And do what? Fuck her? How the hell would that *help?*

I'm angry at myself for even having the thought. That nonsense is the last thing she needs right now.

Plus, I already tried, remember? But then she looked me right in the eye with those big, trusting green beacons... and *scent-marked* me.

I can still feel the tingle along the underside of my cheekbone. The place where she left a swath of cinnamon sweetness seems especially warm, even now.

I don't have a word for how it makes me feel. Awe comes

close, but it doesn't quite capture the deep, smoldering *pride*. The *gratitude*.

And fear.

Yeah, there's a lot of that shit, too.

Because, in one moment, I knew my whole life had changed.

I battle my way through anxious hopes and squirming nerves while I pull a few things off the bare shelves. Knox has decent salt, at least, and some dried basil. A few cans of stewed tomatoes. I see a second onion and more bacon in the fridge.

Italian it is.

I'll call it "Spaghetti alla Desperation."

Once I have the bacon rendering in the skillet, I move on to dicing the onion, along with—*score*—the half-head of garlic I find at the back of the veggie crisper.

Spotify changes to a low house song. My body automatically rolls with the music, all-too used to flexing my abs and spinning my knife in time.

I'm about to add aromatics to the pan when I feel someone watching me. My insides seize as Emma's curly head pokes around the corner. Before I can think about how to react, a grin stretches over my face.

"Hey, *shona*. How's your sister?"

Damn. It's the second time I've said that. I wonder what she would think if she found out I was calling her "precious treasure."

Probably some form of *chill all the way out, bro.*

Fuck, but she's so cute. Her front teeth press into her lower lip as she shuffles through the archway. Cinnamon-sugar warmth winds into my lungs, tickling them until I give in to the rusty purr that wants to rattle there.

The way Emma's eyes round and gleam when she hears the sound... I instantly shove my skillet off the heat and open my arms.

How did I know that I should do that?

I have no clue, but the little omega *flies* at me. So fast that I chuckle as I catch her in my arms.

The humor is short-lived, though. When she nuzzles her cheek into my chest, another hard lump lodges in my throat. My head falls forward, curling my frame around her smaller body.

"This is crazy," I whisper.

Cool fingers clutch my bare back, holding me tight as she breathes, "Good crazy or bad crazy?"

The instinct to comfort is every bit as strong as my need to protect her. Pleasure her. Make her happy. My biceps flex, hugging harder. "*Best* crazy," I reply.

She leans back to grace me with a small smile. Spring green beams up at me. "Really?"

Fuck me.

How am I supposed to avoid falling in love with her when she looks at me like *that*?

Impossible, I realize. *Even more impossible than somehow turning four strangers into a pack.*

Which pretty much means I'm fucked.

I hate the disbelief in her expression. Why doesn't she think that finding out she's my mate is the best thing to ever happen to me?

Look at her! And the sweet way she's stroking circles down my spine? The fuck else could a man want?!

"Really," I promise, tucking her head under my chin. "Come here."

She's already pressed about as close as she can be with clothes on, but she doesn't complain. Her rounded cheek rubs over my chest, leaving more cinnamon warmth on top of my spiciness.

A deep vein of contentment carves a canyon in my middle. The rush of fulfillment is enough to sap all the tension out of my muscles.

Until her scent starts to singe.

"I'm sorry about earlier," Emma mumbles, shyly skirting her gaze up to mine and then down to the floor. "I didn't mean to use you or pressure you into anything."

The swell in my throat expands while guilt floods my gut.

"Baby, no," I murmur, drawing her back into my arms. "It wasn't like that. I just—when you scent-marked me, I could *feel* how real all of this is. And I lost my shit for a minute."

Remembering the way her skin felt against mine, her mind-blowing taste... my body stiffens for her instantly. When I press my lower half into her soft belly, she gasps.

"Trust me," I add, rumbling, "I fucking *want you*. More than I ever have with anyone. You'll see when you let me have you."

Her scent somehow warms and sweetens, until it's *so good*, I could moan. When I look at Emma to see what emotion has caused this earth-shattering *perfection*, I find the smallest, most hopeful smile playing on her plump pink lips.

Happiness. That's all it is.

And seeing the emotion on her face sends an answering echo right through me.

"So you're... staying?" she asks.

Fuck, this is going to take some practice. Flirting and jokes and knowing my angles? Yeah, sure. But earnest, heart-felt conversations?

I'm way out of my depth.

Hell, I'm out of my pool altogether. Thrown right in the middle of the fucking *ocean*.

But then I *look* at her and—*fuck it*. Someone hand me some water wings.

I nod, my voice rasping a bit. "Yeah, I think I am."

Beautiful light gilds her eyes. True, pure excitement. The innocent kind I haven't felt in a long-ass time.

"Yay!" she chimes, glowing. "I—I know it sounds crazy, but I really feel like something important is happening here, and I just —I hope—I want everyone to get along."

She's so genuine; my heart hurts. When was the last time I met someone who told me *anything* real? Let alone *everything* they're honestly feeling?

"I know you do," I whisper, bending to rub my forehead against hers. Scent-marking—because I can't *not*. The swell of masculine satisfaction that pours through me when I put my mark on her is enough to edge my voice in a rumble. "We'll get these assholes in line, huh?"

I'm not exactly sure how. But, hell, I'll figure it out. Though, there's a chance Knox will make me sleep in the snow once he finds out what I do for a living.

Maybe we should start with getting the stick out of his ass. Hockey Boy needs a good branch-removal, too. Not sure what he has to be so bent out of shape about—he's literally famous, rich, and *he* wasted an entire year to have Emma to himself.

So, yeah, all his moping seems pretty stupid to me. I don't have much sympathy for the bastard, but we probably need to ask him what his problem is, at some point.

Should I do that before or after I show them the viral reels of me spanking sides of pork belly?

My phone buzzes on the counter. Emma glances at it, then widens her eyes when she sees hundreds of notifications stacked on the screen.

Oops.

I guess I'm doing this now?

With a not-quite casual shrug, I admit, "My phone is pretty much non-stop. I don't usually look at it."

Her sweet blend of curiosity and excitement swells in those green eyes. "Ooh! Are you on call? Like a doctor?"

HA. I chuckle awkwardly, running my hand through my hair. "Not quite, gorgeous."

Her answer smile is kind and teasing. "Then, what? Are you, like, famous?"

I feel my features crease into a cringe. She clocks the expression, her mouth dropping open. I quickly backtrack. "I mean, not really. But... sorta? Maybe *internet*-famous? Depends on your definition."

Emma blinks, but there's no judgment or greed in her expression. "Well... do you have a lot of followers?"

Twenty-four million.

I nod, my stomach turning. It's strange to be nervous. Ordinarily, this is my hook when I'm interested in someone. Hell, most of those people just slide into my DMs. I'm not used to wondering if I should *hide* my account.

Remembering the way Emma laid out every painful detail of her disastrous night, I know I can't lie to her. The very thought takes me from queasy to full-on sick. Which means there's only one option.

I swipe my screen, navigating to my Instagram account. She leans over the counter to squint at my handle. "The Knotty Chef," she reads out loud.

And she *giggles.*

It isn't a condescending sound at all. It's just as bright and sweet as her scent. "That's so cute!" she trills, scrolling down.

I brace myself, knowing she's about to see a whole lot of my naked chest... and legs... and arms... and back...

Not to mention the *comments.*

Oof.

Didn't think about those.

Mercifully, she taps one of my tamer reels. In it, I had an open white button-down on, along with a pair of gorgeous Armani slacks. I made a seafood risotto followed by homemade almond cookies and espresso gelato. I'd been going for a "fantasy date night" sort of vibe—and my followers went *wild* for it, despite me not having as much skin on display as usual.

Emma seems to like it, too.

Her eyes flicker wide when my body rolls for the camera. A close-up of my folded sleeves and forearms has her biting her lower lip. And when I lick a drop of white wine off my thumb? She *perfumes.*

Of the two reactions an omega could have—outraged disgust or carnal interest—I suppose this *is* the better option. So, why does my gut clench harder?

Regret trickles into my middle as I realize: I shouldn't have shown her this. Not yet. Now, she'll just think I'm a piece of meat. Or a slut.

I mean, traditionally, I *am* both of those things.

But the idea of Emma thinking so makes it hard to breathe.

Something incredible happens, though. Just when I think I've fucked this all to hell—within minutes, no less—she straightens. Her blonde brows fold into a befuddled look. Worry puts a sour edge on her perfume.

"Oh no!" she gasps. "Zane, you don't have any of your equipment here to film, and we're snowed in!"

I—

I don't even know how to react. My mind trips and tumbles.

She's... worried about me*? Me?! Not how jealous she needs to be? Or what a hoe I am? Or how she's going to pressure me into a respectable career so I can be worthy of her?*

Guileless concern lines her pretty face. "Oh, this is all my fault, Zane. Is there something I can do to help? Could I hold the camera or—maybe one of the guys grabbed my suitcase and you can borrow my laptop? Or we can walk back to my car to get it?"

She really is worried about me.

My body moves, snatching her up into my chest and hugging her *hard*. "Fuck," I whisper, afraid my normal volume will give away just how ragged my breathing is. "Gorgeous, you are so damn sweet. How did I get so lucky, huh?"

Her palms press into my pecs—soothing. Not even copping a feel. She laughs lightly. "What do you mean?! *I'm* the reason you're in this mess! Please let me help. I feel *terrible*."

She really does. I can scent it on her.

My purr revs to life, needing to comfort her. "It's all good, baby. It's about time I take a holiday break. I worked Thanksgiving."

That's true. I spent the holiday filming "stuffing v. fisting" videos at a vacation rental in Mesa, Arizona. By the end of the day, I was so grossed out by the sight of sage stuffing and roasted turkey that I wound up ordering Chinese. Hardly a festive vibe.

That's the dark side of this career I fell into. Endless validation without any real connection.

But not this. Not now.

Because as this earnest, kind-hearted omega stares up at me, I feel a tether sprout between us. Binding the ache at the bottom of my heart straight to *her*.

I brush her lopsided curls back from her forehead, bending to put our faces inches apart. "What do you think, gorgeous?"

I don't know what I'm even asking about. Me taking a break from my socials? Her being the reason why? The fact that our lips are about to touch? Or this whole fucked-up situation?

She wobbles a bit as she stretches onto her toes, settling her mouth against mine.

It's graceless in the best way. Shy and so damn innocent, I feel a new lump fill my throat while I gather her close and take over, sliding my lips between hers while my purr ratchets up.

Her fingers twitch against my chest, scrabbling like she wants desperately to hold on to the sound there. She had a similar reaction to Micah when he purred for her; and it breaks my fucking heart to think she's been needing this—*us*—and we weren't there for her yet.

Tender pain pierces me while pleasure swirls down to pull at my base. God, she tastes *incredible*. It makes me hard and happy and so goddamn hopeful. Especially when she tentatively strokes her tongue along mine.

Fuck. I'm *done for*.

I've kissed hundreds of people, but I've never felt like *this*. So aroused, I swear I could come just from pressing my hard groin into her soft hip. So connected to her that it *hurts*. Never wanting to stop slicking my tongue against hers, or holding her, or making sure my purr sinks into both of her big, peaked breasts.

No surprise she's the one who has to pull away first.

The timid smile she gives me eases the clutching sensation in my stomach. She nibbles on her lip, speaking slowly. "We're all stuck here, anyway... maybe we could... try to see what this would be like? All of us?" She blinks up at me, her eyes beseeching. "W-would you be okay with that?"

Only if we all agree to spoil the absolute hell *out of her.*

But that's a conversation for me to have with these other assholes.

For the moment, I love being her co-conspirator. It puts a wide grin on my face as I wink at her. "Great plan, gorgeous. Is Gunnar still snoring out there? You could work on him while I talk Scrooge into being a decent host."

Her giggle hits like a bolt of lightning, electrifying my chest, chasing the lingering ache away. She leans back, her cheeks turning the cutest damn shade of pink. "Gunnar went upstairs to shower."

Mm. She must like the idea of Hockey Boy in the shower, because the luscious sweetness in the air gets thicker. When I toss her a flirtatious smirk, she winces.

"I guess I'll... go talk to him?"

If she came looking for me, smelling like that, we wouldn't be *talking.* But I release her with a firm slap to her gorgeous ass. "Sure thing, baby. Tell him I said, 'You're welcome.'"

chapter
twenty-three

I SCURRY UP THE STAIRS, hope sparkling in my chest.

Zane is making the other guys dinner. That has to mean *something, right?*

I can't help the way my heart floats as I scamper toward Knox's room. The patter of the shower is audible in the hallway, but the door is open. I peek in, finding the room empty. The door to the bathroom is barely cracked, so I step over the threshold and call his name.

"Gunnar?"

There's no answer, which makes sense. Knox might live in the middle of nowhere, but this house is insane. Everything—from his furniture to the water pressure—is top-of-the-line.

"Gunnar?" I try again, shuffling further into the room. He still doesn't reply, but I'm grateful for that a second later when I spy his clothes lying in a rumpled heap on Knox's leather chair.

A thought occurs to me. Remi is a perfect homemaker, and her alphas adore her. *I better try to get myself into gear if I'm going to turn any of this into something real...*

My feet move, carrying me to the discarded suit and bringing Gunnar's worn dress shirt to my face. I inhale the scent of roasting pecans and my lungs stutter.

Finally, my Omega huffs, annoyed. *I've been trying to tell you for __months__ that we needed our mate.*

I roll my eyes internally, remembering all the times I'd felt so squirmy around the Dunlaps and how she usually just chanted one word over and over. *You could have said something more instructional than "mate, mate, mate."*

She sends me more exasperation. *As if you didn't already know, deep down, that this alpha was the one. But what the hell is __his__ excuse? Does he really think he can just come back after putting us through all of this and we'll forgive him?*

I __have__ forgiven him, I tell her. *He __apologized__!*

Well, tell his Alpha that I said to go kick rocks. The other alphas all want me the way they __should__.

Which is so *not* helpful. Especially when she starts firing me images of Zane's kisses... Knox holding me earlier... Micah's hands all over me...

When my fingers reflexively clutch Gunnar's shirt tighter, a paper crinkles in his front pocket.

A... purple piece of paper?

With little hearts on the—

Oh.

My.

God.

Oh my God.

OH. MY. GOD.

Did Gunnar Sinclair find the list Bridget and I made after two pitchers of margaritas?

And then he *read* it? *And kept it?!*

I will die. In fact, I think I *have* died—until a loud *clang* sounds from inside the bathroom.

My heart restarts with a lurch. The note falls to the floor as I whirl toward the door, hesitating.

It sounds like he fell. Which, I'll be honest, seems like something he would do. Knox's shower is beautiful, but the all-stone floor makes it slippery. With just a floating glass partition to shield it, there aren't any bars to hold on to. And Gunnar was up all night.

I might have slipped in there earlier.

But I was totally fine.

What if Gunnar isn't?

My Omega is frantic at the thought of him being hurt. She's already worried about him after the way he shut down before—and the deep, earnest exhaustion I saw all over his face.

When I hear a pained groan, my instincts snap forward. I race across the wood floor, sliding on my borrowed socks and nearly barreling into the bathroom door.

Which is right around the time I realize I'm not necessarily hearing a man *in pain*.

Sort of... the opposite?

The one brief glimpse I allow myself reveals a whole lot more than I imagined.

For one: Gunnar does *not* seem to be in any near-death predicaments.

Two: He somehow looks bigger naked? I'm not even sure how he fit into that slim black suit, because the body behind the fogged glass shower partition is larger and broader than any man has a right to be.

Third: he's *wet*. And *covered* in muscle.

Cinched abs, straining quads, bulging pectorals, and heaving shoulders. Not to mention the grapefruit-sized masses of his biceps and the veins roped along his—

Oh. Holy. Night.

As my gaze traces the masculine lines of his forearm, I realize his hand is between his legs. Cupping his very hard, very noticeable cock.

No.

Stroking it.

The sound that tears out of his throat resembles the one I heard before. A long moan, tortured and tight. Only, this time, he says something else, too.

My name.

"*Emma.*"

Goosebumps scatter down my spine while my lungs stop working. I go completely still, certain he's spotted me and he hates me and he's going to yell at me to get out—or bark, like Theo did.

Seconds tick by, and he continues gliding his fist up and down his bobbing length, grunting. When I realize he hasn't seen me, the truth sinks in.

He's... thinking about me? While he...???

Before I can control my body, a *deluge* of perfume pours off of me. It rises into the thick, steamy air, mingling with his salty, roasted scent.

When the mixture hits him, he groans again. Deeper and more urgent. His fingers tighten, his wrist snaps faster, his—

Gunnar's eyes snap open and fly to the doorway. To me, standing in the doorway.

Oh, sugar.

A thunderous look rolls over his square features as he bellows my name, dropping his erection and lunging out of the shower to shut the bathroom door. I step back automatically, squealing while I cover my eyes.

Still, when he slips on the edge of the wet stone floor and goes careening into a half-split, I totally see it through the crack between my fingers.

He straightens up almost as quickly as he went down, ripping a towel off the nearby rack and snapping it around his hips before he stalks toward me.

"What are you *doing* in here?" he hisses. "Jesus, Em! You thought you could just scratch number thirteen off your list? You almost gave me a fucking heart attack!"

Lord, he really looks mad. And, you know, *gorgeous*.

His wide jaw ticks. Thick blond-brown brows furrow over his eyes, setting off the gold streaked through those gray irises. His outrage isn't anything like the blankness I saw there before—in a lot of ways, it's better. He looks so much more *alive* like this.

Alive and *pissed*.

"I'm sorry!" I squeak, true remorse and mortification swamping my stomach as my sense returns. "Zane is making us all food, and I came up to tell you it's time to eat, but then I heard you make a noise, so..." I swallow hard, shrinking back a bit. "S-sorry."

He exhales hard through his nose, nostrils flaring while he grinds his teeth and fidgets with the towel wrapped around his lower half. I recognize his energy immediately since it's one I'm very familiar with.

He's *embarrassed*.

Why is that *so* adorable?

And sort of... hot?

I don't know, but the lower muscles in my abdomen clench and gel. Slick slips down my thighs, and I bite my lip.

Crap.

Maybe Lucy has a point about my heat...

Gunnar doesn't notice. He's too busy dropping his eyes, muttering, "What were you *doing*? Just standing around the bedroom?"

"No," I rush to explain, "I was—"

Holding my sex list.

The one he stole.

And wait—

WAIT.

Did he just ask me if I thought I could *scratch off number thirteen???!!!*

I shriek again, this time in complete horror. My hands fly to my cheeks, making me a silent-but-decent dupe for that one famous painting of the guy screaming his head off.

"You *pig*!" I accuse, gasping.

His eyes go wide. "*Me? What did I do?"*

I feel faint. Literally dizzy. Like my head might detach from my body and drift into the atmosphere to orbit the Earth. Just a big, really stupid satellite.

"You read my list!" I shriek, pointing. "You read my list, and you *memorized it*?!"

It's Gunnar's turn to panic. He holds up his palms in a placating gesture and starts to ramble. "I didn't know it was yours! Or, well, I didn't know you were *you*. I mean, I knew it was *yours* because I saw it fall out of your purse, but then I didn't know *you* —the bride—was also *you*—the girl I met at that party. So I didn't *really know*, you know?"

Part of me wants to laugh, and another wants to cry. Some weird half-sob-snort comes out instead.

Gunnar winces. "I didn't mean to memorize it, but it's memorable, okay? I—shit, Em, don't cry."

Am I? I guess those *are* tears streaming down my cheeks. I swipe at them and force a smile. "Sorry. I'm fine. It's just humiliating, and I... I've pretty much gotten used to being a joke to everyone, but there's something about you guys that makes me wish I could be—"

Important.
Taken seriously.
Considered.
Cherished.

"—something else."

All of the anger slumps out of his posture. "Em," he rumbles, stepping closer. "You aren't *a joke*. I've *never* thought that."

I sniffle miserably. "Not even when I fell in the pool?"

"No," he laughs softly, reaching for my hand, folding my chilled fingers in his water-heated ones.

"Or when you found out I drove into a snowbank?"

His smile disappears, replaced by a small frown that's all honest concern and maybe a little heartbreak. "No, squirt," he murmurs, totally sincere. "Not even a little bit."

I snuff loudly. More tears fall. "Or when you walked in on me and the guys today?"

That one trips him up for a moment. He pauses, then clears his throat...

And comes even *closer*.

His free hand reaches for my hip, settling my belly against his hard groin. Those gray eyes blaze with dark, swirling desire, but he still gulps like he's nervous.

"*Especially* not then," he husks. "What did you think I was picturing just now in the shower?"

My eyes round. "R-really?"

He huffs out a quiet chuckle, his cheeks turning light pink as he grimaces. "Maybe some other stuff, too. That list of yours is pretty, uh, comprehensive."

I cover my face with the hand that isn't wrapped around his, moaning. When I drop my face to hide my shame, my forehead lands on his wide, damp chest.

He slips his touch from my hip to the back of my neck, hesitating for a brief second before sinking his fingertips against my nape and kneading sweetly. My arm wraps around his cut waist, hugging him while I have the opportunity.

"I'm sorry," I whisper again. "I shouldn't have come in here."

Gunnar hums a grumble. "We can call it even, squirt. I shouldn't have read your list once I realized what it was."

His scent takes a sudden, sharp plummet from roasted nuttiness to burning charcoal. "I can't believe how stupid those other alphas were. You guys did all of the shit on that list, and they didn't even try to go after you when you left?"

For a second, I consider letting him think that's what happened. It's almost less mortifying than the truth. But the last time I let him run with an incorrect assumption, I ended up ringing in the New Year with mascara running down my face.

"No," I admit, barely whispering. "They—We were only, um, intimate during my heat a few months ago. I don't remember much of it, but my knees were really sore for a few weeks, so I think it was pretty much a presenting-only situation. They said they didn't want to do other stuff until after we were bonded. Now, I realize they just didn't want *me*."

Gunnar's scent swells, pressing closer. My Omega loves it, but she's still decidedly pissy about *him*. I wince slightly, biting my lip as I add, "I should probably tell you... I'm okay with what happened last year, but my Omega still has a lot of... feelings about it."

There's a long beat of silence, punctuated by the patter of the shower and the hiss of steam filling the air. Gunnar's chest expands faster and harder as he slips his palm around my neck and uses his thumb to tilt my chin back.

Gray eyes meet mine. "You tell her that she can take all the time she needs. I'll be right here. Every day."

The solid warmth in his voice is enough to make me slick my thighs again. Gunnar notices, pressing closer and dropping his forehead to mine. "You really haven't done any of the things on your list?"

Items fly through my head. Phrases like *cockwarming, spit-roasting, DVP...* Honestly, as the margaritas got stronger, the ideas only got wilder.

And what *was* number thirteen?

Oh, right, I remember, swallowing hard. *Voyeurism.*

Technically, Bridget wrote, *"Watch an alpha jack his knot."*

But, you know, semantics.

I shake my head, hoping to clear some of the arousal and nerves blurring my thoughts. Gunnar's scent lightens by the second, edging back into sweet, salted heaven.

"It's like a wishlist?" he asks.

I nod again. Gunnar's jaw flexes as he slowly walks me backward, until I'm pressed into the blank wall beside the bathroom door.

He presses his forearm over my head, his intense stare swirling while he grips my face in his strong fingers and growls, "You really shouldn't have told me that, squirt."

And then he kisses me.

chapter
twenty-four

KISSING EMMA IS TEN-THOUSAND VOLTS, electrifying my blood.

It's remembering what it's like to *want*. And wish. And maybe, for a second, *believe*.

The last six months have felt like trying to swim through quicksand. Just an endless, impossible slog. Exhausting; and so fucking *futile*. Everything worth doing just felt infuriating.

But... *Emma*.

Emma is every last good thing left in the world, all rolled together and wrapped up in blonde curls and guileless green eyes.

Our kiss starts out urgent but softens into something sweeter the second I feel her little hands rubbing my lower back. *Hugging me, I realize.*

No one's done that since...

My mom.

That one thought has my chest shuddering. Emma feels it and makes a reassuring sound, scent-marking my forehead while she squeezes me.

Tenderness bleeds behind my sternum. My hands go from clutching at her to smoothing down her curves, exploring every dip and relishing the give of her body.

She feels like everything I'm not—a soft place for all the hard, sharpened edges I've honed over the last year. They've been effective at keeping everyone else away from me.

But not Emma.

She absorbs them effortlessly, opening up for me. Like I'm just a man. And not a big thorny tangle poised to poke her.

We break apart, both of us panting. The muscles of her face flinch against my fingertips as she winces. "I should probably tell you," she whispers. "I kissed Zane, like, twenty minutes ago."

The honest trepidation in her eyes hits my heart head-on, but the way she cringes makes me want to laugh. Just like her questions did earlier.

She's *funny*—and so innocently honest about everything.

Who she is; what she thinks. Even things that embarrass her.

It almost seems like it doesn't *occur* to her to lie. Which is fucking adorable in the sweetest damn way.

My mouth curls into a half-smile, reassuring her with a gentle nuzzle along her cheek. When I pull back, I quirk a wry look. "Zane, huh?"

Her teeth nip her plump lip, sending a bolt of heat to my hard cock. "Yeah," she admits. "Is that—I mean, I don't—"

My hand wanders back to Emma's hip, tracing its perfect fullness all the way to her ass. Which is a *handful* in the *best* possible way.

Goddamn.

Imagining her all up on Zane does strange things to my body. My Alpha rages and roars, jealous and possessive beyond all reason. But the images make me just as hard as the ones I was slobbering over in the shower.

She looked hot as fuck with her pretty pussy spread over Micah's big cock. And the way she squirted on the floor when Zane hit the right spot with his tongue?

Fuck.

I may want her all to myself. But I can't deny that, during my suspension from the team, I've missed this feeling.

The rush of determination, the thrill of a worthy opponent.

A growl slips up my throat as my lips spread into a sharp grin. "Em," I warn, crowding closer. "You're forgetting one important thing."

Her beautiful features blink in surprise. "What?"

"I'm a pro hockey player, baby." My hands drop down to the backs of her thighs, grasping them easily and lifting her into my body. She squeaks as I set her on the nearby counter and lean down, putting us eye-to-eye.

"Competition doesn't scare me. It makes me *fucking hard*."

Sucking in a loud breath, Emma practically leaps at me. Which would be cute if my knot wasn't about to explode.

I wrap my arms around her, snarling softly when my torso presses into the pine-scented fabric of Knox's sweatshirt and not Emma's bare skin. But I wasn't kidding—having other alphas all over her makes my cock *ache*.

Her hands drop to the edge of the towel wrapped around me while our tongues glide together. My mind reels, awash in a haze of fantasies, along with all the ideas from her list.

A lot of them actually *require* one of these other assholes. Spit-roasting, DVP, something about watching two alphas jack each other off.

Half either have location limitations—like exhibitionism—or imply a longer stretch of time. Cockwarming could take *hours*...

There *was* one thing, though. I think it was number four.

Panting, I break our kiss to skim my lips down her neck, leaving gentle bites behind. "You wanted to learn how to juice a knot?"

I remember those words very specifically. *Juice a knot.* I'd probably be snickering if she didn't look so heartrendingly excited about it.

"I've tried before, but..." She swallows thickly, her scent burning at the edges. "I think I did it wrong."

I can't imagine *that.* "Why?"

The cinnamon singes even more. Her voice sounds small as she peeps, "They... they never liked anything I tried to do."

I've never wanted to punch someone I haven't met until now. What a bunch of dick-headed doorknobs. They had this beautiful angel of an omega willing to learn how to touch them, and they *criticized* her?

My heart flops. *This is my fault. If I hadn't run off that night...*

"Fuck, Em. I'm so sorry about leaving like that. I swear I didn't mean to reject you. Honestly, I didn't even *scent* you; I just saw you start to perfume and panicked."

Her features screw up, then crack into a sudden snort. "You *panicked*? Aren't you supposed to be some famous playboy?!"

If she wasn't so amused, I'd probably feel like a total fraud. Instead, it's just a pinch of embarrassment. "I've dated a lot, but, uh..."

There are reasons I'm still single, and most of them have to do with being exactly the sort of oaf who would accidentally knock his mate into a swimming pool. With a grimace, I stumble for a more artful explanation. One that's just as true, but definitely not as humiliating.

"Theo," I grumble. "I saw you react to me, and you were already so fucking pretty and warm and—shit." I shake my head, remembering. "I figured I better get out of there before I wound up mauling my buddy's baby sister."

She arches an eyebrow, grinning as she calls me out. "It didn't have anything to do with sending me into the deep end?"

Busted. I flinch into a wince. "Well, that wasn't *great...*"

Emma huffs another giggle, hugging me again. "I forgive you, Hot Shot. Trust me, no one understands embarrassing yourself and then freaking out about it better than I do."

Her easy forgiveness and that nickname make my chest clench. The ache there doubles when I recall what she admitted about her old pack.

A purr rumbles behind my ribs, and Emma moans quietly, falling against it. My cock kicks, trying to reach her through the towel. When she notices, perfume swells into the most incredible, gooey cinnamon.

My voice rasps as I nod at our bodies. "Do you want me to show you what *I* like?"

I expect more embarrassment, but instead, genuine delight beams from her green eyes. "Really? No one's ever *shown* me what I'm supposed to do! Is there more than one way?"

God, she's sweet. *So full of light*, I think, staring down at her.

A deep jolt of affection has me smiling again. "There are lots of ways," I confirm, kissing her cheek with my grin. "I'm sure the others will show you their own—if you ask them."

"That wouldn't... bother you?" she breathes, fluttering her lashes. It's clear she's nervous, but her expression stays open and attentive. Truly *listening*—caring about how I would feel.

It puts a warm stone in my throat. "Denying you something you need would bother me," I rough out.

My vulnerability is so fucking worth it. The fear falls off her face. She licks her lips, glancing at my towel with pointed interest. It's so goddamn adorable, I'm still grinning when she flashes me a shy look. "Will you show me?"

I don't even have to think. I rip my towel off in one tug.

Cinnamon sugar warms the steamy air swirling between us as she perfumes, scooting to the edge of the countertop and spreading her legs to make space for my naked body. Her eyes drop directly to my straining cock.

I've had puck bunnies cooing over me for *years*. I've made winning goals, had my picture on magazine covers. But nothing —*nothing*— has ever made me feel quite as tall as the way Emma gapes at my package.

"Fuck me, you're so *cute*," I grunt, cradling her face between my palms and kissing her again. "Stop looking at me like that, or I'll end up coming all over your lap."

Emma giggles, the sound rushing right to the blank space where my soul used to be. It lights up and glows as she makes a little space between our bodies and floats her hands to my hips.

"Like this," I murmur, guiding them around the base of my shaft. She curls her fingers lightly, her breath catching when I twitch in her grasp.

A pearl of pre-cum beads at the buzzing head. I feel the pressure of her fingertips like separate pulses, each point pounding as my blood beats in desperate throbs.

She skims her touch along my length. A low growl vibrates out of me.

"Want to know what I was thinking about?" I ask, distracting her as I rearrange the fit of her fingers and smooth out her glides with my hand wrapped over hers.

"What?" she gasps, watching more creamy wetness seep from the head.

"Your pretty pink pussy, gushing all over Micah's big-ass knot," I grunt, dragging her touch down my entire shaft, showing her how to make a ring with her fingers and pop it over the hot, swollen mass at the base.

Fuck, it feels so *good*. So much better than my own hands, even if hers are hesitant and infinitely more gentle than mine.

This little omega has good instincts, though. As soon as I release my hold on her, she goes to town. Stroking my throbbing knot, working both palms up to slick themselves with my pre-cum. When she glides one to my tingling head and slides the other to pop over my knot at the same time, I forget to breathe.

She repeats the motion easily, moaning softly when my head falls back on a groan. "You're going to make me come so hard," I tell her, widening my stance and bearing down, thrusting into her slippery fists. "Fuck, Emma. Make me stop, or I'm going to—"

For a moment, I think she's obeying. Her grip releases me for half a breath—just long enough to yank her own pants off, presenting me with the soft roll of her belly and the bare perfection of her glistening pink cunt.

My mouth drops open. Sensation cracks down my spine and draws my balls up. When she stacks her closed hands around my cock and tugs from the bottom of my knot to the wide, ruddy head, I lose it.

Ropes of cum erupt across smooth skin, melding into her pale, naked stomach, her luscious thighs, and that goddamned *gorgeous* pussy.

I watch it all drip down her abdomen, my Alpha shoving impulses at me. "Are you on birth control?" I ask.

Before she finishes nodding, I scoop my release onto my fingers, painting it over the swollen bud begging for attention at the top of her plump folds.

It's like an out-of-body experience. Utterly fixated, I rub my essence over her thrumming clit, memorizing the way she mewls.

"Did stroking my cock make you wet, Em?" I purr, skimming my touch over her soaked slit.

She chokes on another moan, clutching my forearms. A burst of perfumed slick dribbles from her hot, clenching core. I press two fingers to her opening and roll her clit with my thumb, ensuring my cum covers the entire—

"Gunnar!" she cries.

Her pussy sucks at my fingers, pulling me into her as she comes all over my hand. And the floor.

Squirting all over.

We both look down at the hot mess we've just made. *Mate,*

my Alpha chuffs, nodding at the sight of her cream mixed into mine. As if that's some sort of cosmic proof.

It isn't. I know that.

But a moment later, when we both gape at one another and start laughing at the exact same second...

Maybe *that* is.

chapter
twenty-five

BRIDGET

attached video

I'm sorry. Is this man... whipping cream... with the mixer positioned where his PENIS should be?

LUCY

He's whipping something totally different in this one:

attached video

BRIDGET

Holy shit. Did you see the one where he spanks the pork belly?

LUCY

I'm watching him jack off a carrot. Hold on.

Ope.

There it is.

BRIDGET

Kneading that bread dough.... 😍

EMMA

WHAT ARE YOU HORNY HIPPOS DOING IN HERE?!

BRIDGET

Checking out your new mans.

His butt is my screensaver, btw.

The one with the apron on and nothing else.

LUCY

Has he fingered you like he does with this papaya yet? *Attached video*

EMMA

...no

LUCY

...but???

EMMA

☺ Gunnar did.

LUCY

WHAT???

BRIDGET

ALREADY!

EMMA

LEAVE ME ALONE OK

And stopppppp creeping on Zane. Or at least telling me about it.

Especially you, Luce

LUCY

ok, ok

BRIDGET

fiiiiiine

LUCY

…

Jesus.

Look at his TONGUE.

micah

I'VE ALWAYS TRIED to be honest. With other people, of course, but mostly with myself.

And honestly?

I cannot imagine a more perfect mate than Emma.

I spend our entire dinner watching her, absorbing tiny details and her more general personality traits, too. Those are pretty easy to spot—positivity, curiosity, a good sense of humor, and absolutely zero self-importance.

All of that would appeal to me on a soul-deep level, even if she didn't smell so perfect or look like she belonged at the top of Knox's nonexistent Christmas tree.

But it's the little things that press the solid weight of certainty deeper and deeper, anchoring it into my stomach by the time our meal is done.

Like the way she giggles every time Zane tries to make her laugh—even when she's clearly feeling shy or uncertain. Or how she looks for little things to link each of us—pointing out that Gunnar and I both like to work out, Zane and Gunnar have both traveled a lot, Knox and Gunnar both follow most major sports.

There are also random things. She eats two-and-a-half bowls of pasta with zero shame, and I love that. She coos adoringly over the dog every time he presses his nose into her lap. Her cheeks turn pink the second she has to answer any questions about herself.

I don't think she *dislikes* sharing; it mostly seems like she isn't used to being asked. Which is odd for an omega with such a large family and so many friends. Not to mention her former pack.

Do people not ask about *her*?

Why not?

She is adorable *and* smart. An ultra-endearing combination I've rarely encountered. Most sharp people like to *act* sharp. Emma is soft through-and-through, despite being so intelligent. Almost as if she's never noticed that she is.

She grins easily as she describes her guidance counselor work with elementary-aged children, giggling about their antics and obliviously dipping into her well of child psychology knowledge. Talking about how goofy it is to Chicken Dance for a living before casually mentioning that her *master's degree* is in a frame that she let some five-year-old smother in Elmer's and macaroni.

There's simply no pretense about her whatsoever. To the point where I wonder if she's ever noticed how impressive she is.

I doubt it. She's clearly beautiful, caring, hard-working, and smart—but she's also the punchline to all of her own jokes.

As if she thinks *she's* the joke.

I hear it again when Gunnar grumbles his own series of questions, asking how she wound up engaged over the past year and why they decided to have their bonding ceremony here. His shitty attitude—which, c'mon, dude, as if this whole mess isn't *your own damn fault*—notwithstanding, I find I'm rapt to hear her answers.

Helping children understand their feelings, being the glue that holds her high-achieving siblings together, speaking about all of her friends and her sister-in-law with empathy, despite the fact they all essentially left her to deal with the bonding ceremony alone...

Emma obviously has tons of emotional intelligence—how did she end up with alphas who were going to *use* her?

When she doesn't answer Gunnar right away, his roasted pecan-and-chestnut scent darkens into something burnt. He's been hovering near her protectively ever since they came downstairs. Given how his essence is all over her—covering *mine*—I think I can guess why.

But his arm drops from the back of her chair while his face pales. "It was me, wasn't it?" he asks, clearly pained. "Because your Omega felt rejected by me?"

Somehow, I smother the growl vibrating at the base of my lungs. I've seen him apologize, and obviously, he and Emma came to some sort of understanding upstairs...

But still.

Who the hell does this guy think he is?

Rejecting *my omega*?

My *mate*.

Because, God help me, but that's what she is. Every word out of her mouth, every giggle and sigh and twitch of her blonde brows. Even her love of children and desire to have a big family— it all feels tailor-made, just for me.

And, apparently, three other strangers.

Jesus. This is a mess.

I've never heard of anything like this happening before. Omegas who have partners or a pack and then meet another alpha they want to add? Yes. But *this*?

I can't seem to wrap my head around how this will work. It's not as if any of us will be able to bond with her while we're here— unless *all* of us do, but that would be insane. Willingly inviting *three people you don't know* to literally access your innermost thoughts?

Not to mention the sharing aspect. Even if we somehow got it together to bond her separately, without a pack leader to form a central pack bond for us... she'd be torn four ways. Forever. Juggling four alphas who each want her all to themselves.

Simply going through a heat with her would be a trial for each of us. It's one thing when I volunteer at the clinic and the omegas are as anonymous as the other alphas in the nest. More often than not, I'm only marginally attracted to them or their scents.

But with Emma? She smiles, and my *soul* snaps to attention. She laughs, and my lungs stop working. Not to mention her *perfume*... which would only be *stronger* during a heat.

How would we keep from ripping each other to shreds?

Bonding with her on the spot?

Accidentally tangling ourselves together for the rest of our lives?

My Alpha isn't as hopeless as I am, though. He has me turn my head, taking in each of their faces before I settle on the way Emma chews her lip.

Mate, he thinks. And it's a resigned, indulgent sort of thing. As if he's saying, *anything she needs...*

Even if it's these guys.

Which I think may be the case.

They're as enamored with her as I am. Even Knox, who won't admit it to himself. He doesn't need to—I feel the way he leans in, listening closely as she answers Gunnar's sorry ass.

"After that night, my Omega was in a really bad way," she admits, mumbling to her lap. "My sister's friends had all used a matching service before. I thought maybe, if I did, too, the pack they put me with would actually, um." Emma swallows. "Want me?"

She's in my arms before I can even breathe through the pain lancing my lungs. It puts a serrated edge on my purr, but my omega dives for the sound anyway.

"Sweet girl," I murmur, my throat tight as I cup a hand around her head and urge her closer. "I'm so sorry for everything they put you through. So sorry I wasn't *there*, God."

She burrows into my throat, whining softly. Zane's own

rumble revs up, much smoother than mine. I meet his dark eyes across the table, and we both snap our gazes over to Gunnar, joining Knox in his murderous glare.

It's sort of difficult to threaten a man who looks this lost, though. His skin seems so ashen it's almost gray enough to match his eyes. Those are rimmed in red and full of misery. He watches Emma press her face into my chest like it's ice for a burn. Balm for her broken heart.

My arms flex around her as I turn my gaze back where it belongs. Emma's eyelashes twitch as she exhales deeply, not bothering to pretend she doesn't enjoy the attention. My mouth curls up in a grim smile she can't see.

Really, I should be thrilled that Gunnar's such a fuck-up. It strengthens my case, surely—and I am all-too happy to provide anything he failed to.

The fact that I only feel disappointment toward the guy and utter dismay about him leaving Emma means something I'm not sure I'm ready to accept yet.

If ever.

Knowing we all need a subject change, I give her a little bounce on my lap and whisper, "So, you like it up here in the snow? That's why you wanted to have your ceremony here?"

To my delight, she doesn't even attempt to hide her massive cringe. "Um, no. Not exactly."

When she sits up a little, Knox wordlessly pushes his own bowl of noodles closer so I can feed her. Zane flashes our girl a smile I can only describe as "dazzling," even if I'm not the one dazed by it.

Ignoring her wide-eyed reaction to his grin, the smooth bastard asks, "Did your mom choose it? Is she a Momzilla?"

Emma giggles. "No, no, nothing like that! I like this area! We used to vacation up here in the summer when I was a kid and always loved it. With the wildflowers and the fireflies and the pretty sunsets. Doing it this time of year wasn't ever my idea. It was the, um, beta in the pack, actually. A white Christmas in the mountains was *her* dream wedding."

And, of course, my sweet girl wanted her new pack to be happy, even if it cost Emma her own dreams. I doubt she even noticed that part until everything went sideways.

I don't love that. But maybe I *would* enjoy planting my fist in the faces of the alphas she left behind last night. *Fucking assholes.*

That has to be the one thing all four of us have in common. I hear the others choke down growls the same way I do, silencing our rage so Emma can continue defending the horrible woman who encouraged her alphas to use our omega.

"It actually wasn't bad timing!" she chimes, still kind as ever. "My heat is coming in a couple of weeks, so—"

Her *heat*?

Oh God.

The image I had earlier—of the four of us ripping each other apart to get to her—flashes through my thoughts. Zane's mouth drops, his features slack. Gunnar's eyes bulge. But Knox...

A very low, ominous growl hisses out of him. Emma's heart accelerates into a sprint as he pins her with an intense look and roughs out, "*What?*"

She shivers. I guide her face back to my throat and fold my hand around her head, purring more while I pin him with a glower.

"She said," I repeat, slow and even, "that her heat is coming in a couple weeks."

There's no reason for anyone to be angry or panic. She has no control over her body's cycles, and I refuse to let anyone make her feel bad about it.

My brain snaps pieces together as I snuggle her closer. "That's probably why you had that spike earlier, baby. I'm so sorry—if I had known, I would have given you my knot right away."

Gunnar surprises me when he nearly falls out of his chair to kneel by my side, lifting his hand to her cheek. "Are you okay now, Em? Does it still hurt? Do you need more?"

Her answering smile is as shy as it is lovely. "I'm okay now." She flicks a nervous glance at Knox, who still looks pissed, his nostrils flaring. "I-I don't want to be an imposition."

Whatever he sees on her face helps him marshal himself. He slowly sits back in his seat, gaze fixed on Emma's profile. She turns to Gunnar, reassuring him with a squeeze to his wrist.

"I promise I'm okay. There isn't anything we can do about it right now, since we're stuck here. I'm sure the road will be fixed way before I need to leave to get to"—she stumbles over herself, then sniffs—"a clinic, I guess."

Because her home is gone. She doesn't even have her own nest.

Tension pulls tight between all four of us—the stirrings of that competitive aggression I was worried about. We each want to be with her for her heat. All of us except maybe Knox—who's looking at her like she's a foreign creature he doesn't quite understand. Or maybe some riddle the universe sent for him to solve.

It's clear the intuitive omega senses trouble ahead. With a nervous shiver, she wiggles out of my arms and starts to stack our bowls. Zane shoots up, swooping in to kiss her cheek and snatch the dishes out of her hands.

"Nice try, gorgeous," he grins. "You go get comfy, huh? Use the blanket on the couch; it's cold in here."

Knox seems to take that personally, snapping out of his stupor to flash a baleful look at Zane's bare chest. "A shirt might help."

Zane rolls his eyes good-naturedly and shrugs. "Shirts aren't really my brand, Grinch."

I can tell Knox wants to argue, but his gaze skirts over to Emma's fretful face, and he sighs. Muttering under his breath, he shoves to his feet and trudges to the thermostat.

Gunnar watches him go, frowning warily at his flannel-covered back, then down at the nearly matching borrowed shirt he has rolled up to his forearms. With a minute shake of his head, he turns to me.

"So."

I cross my arms and sit back, testing the aggression rolling off him. "So."

Our alphas clash. He flexes his dominance, and I shove my own right back, both of us upping the ante until Knox comes stalking back in.

He pauses between us, turning from my face to Gunnar's, then pointing his eyes at Emma's trembling shoulders.

Oh. *Shit.*

His hands fly out, knocking each of us on the backs of our skulls. His own—more potent—brand of power washes over the room while he snaps, "Enough," and reaches his hand out to Emma.

She blinks at it before accepting with one of her beaming smiles.

Gunnar rubs the side of his neck, but his scowl morphs into begrudging fondness while we watch the little omega follow Knox's lead every bit as eagerly as McKinley does. If she had a tail, it would be wagging.

I chuckle, bemused. This situation might be impossible, but I've already smiled more today than I have in weeks.

"I'm not going anywhere," I realize out loud, leveling my gaze at Gunnar. "So, you'll have to get used to me if you plan to stick around this time."

An angry V forms between his eyebrows. "I'm *not* leaving her again."

I have questions about that, but a dishtowel lands in the middle of the table. We both whip our attention to Zane, who leans over the island with a shit-eating grin on his face. "None of us *can* leave, you idiots. And it seems to *me*, as long as we're all stuck here together, trying to win Emma over, this is prime time for some serious courting."

Damn it. Of course.

He's right. This is exactly why courting exists. To show an omega their options and allow them the opportunity to see who can meet their needs.

Maybe it will only be one of us.

Maybe it will be *all* of us.

God. My mind spins out again, trying to imagine the impossible. How the hell is this going to *work*?

Zane seems alarmingly unbothered. He gestures at the dinner he made and the fact that he's currently the only one cleaning up. One of his groomed eyebrows arches. "Not to brag, but if this turns into a *real* competition because you fuckers can't play nice, I'm pretty sure I got a head start."

Zane smirks at the way we scramble to our feet. He tosses a second towel over. "Good boys. No reason we can't wash a few dishes while we measure our dicks, right?"

chapter
twenty-six

EMMA

Hey, Theo. I don't know if Lucy told you that I called her on Gunnar's phone before, but I have my cell back and charged now.

THEO

EMMY

HOLY FUCK

I've been freaking out.

I'm so so sorry I lost my shit last night.

Are you ok??

LUCY

Oh she's more than ok...

EMMA

Luce!

THEO

Hell

Don't tell me THAT 😳

But, seriously, Emmy, I'm really fucking sorry.

EMMA

It's okay. Meg was really upset... is she alright?

THEO

All good. She just feels terrible about running you off.

Wants to know how many Christmas gifts will make it up to you lol

EMMA

Well, for the time being, I'm stuck here.

So she might not need to get me any at all!

THEO

I'm just going to do the Big Brother thing for a sec:

Are you safe?

Do you need me to come get you?

Blink twice if you want Ronan to send a chopper.

EMMA

actually... I think Knox has his own helicopter.

THEO

...so that's a no?

EMMA

LOL that's a no.

They're all being very sweet to me.

Knox even gave me the only bed in the house.

LUCY

Then where are all those alphas sleeping?!

EMMA

Um

Well...

KNOX

"WELL," Zane chirps, smirking, "This is cozy."

Micah stands between us, holding a pillow and cringing. "There really isn't anywhere else to sleep, Knox?"

Unfortunately, no.

I scratch my beard and shake my head. Gunnar chuffs, "An entire *compound* with God-knows-how-many rooms, and you only have one sofa and one bed?"

The fact is, I almost didn't buy the sofa. I had my eye on a recliner.

Micah reads my expression and snorts. "Figures."

With a grunt, I shuffle toward the couch and shove one of the cushions off to make more room. "It's the couch or the floor," I admit. "If you want to freeze your ass off on the hardwoods, be my guest."

"Such hospitality," Gunnar mutters, tossing the extra pillow I gave him onto the opposite end of the U-shaped sectional.

Releasing a deep sigh, Micah snatches two more leather cushions off the back of the sofa and lines them up on the floor to form a makeshift cot. "I've been camping since I was two. I'll take the floor."

Zane looks from me to Gunnar and back again. "So *I* have to decide whose feet will be in my face all night?" He eyes my socks and then the other alphas'. "Easy," he declares. "Hockey Boy it is."

He's been insulting me all night long—all day, really. Something about the way he does it that makes it feel less like a true threat, and more like a form of camaraderie. Granted, it's been a while since I spent any time around other alphas.

We all shuffle into our places for the night, silently maneuvering around each other until Zane breaks the silence again. "How long does it usually take you mountain-dwellers to fix your roads?"

"A few days," Micah replies, pounding a fist into his cushion and lying back on it. "They can't start until the snow stops, though."

Everyone turns to look out the wall of windows at the back of the room. An insistent deluge falls from the sky, creating freshly fluffed piles all over the back porch.

Goddamn it.

Gunnar grunts. "What do we do if we need stuff?"

Zane chortles. "If? Mountain Man only has one bed, and his taste in groceries is appalling. We *definitely* need stuff."

Micah hums thoughtfully. "Especially if Emma starts nesting."

Right. Her heat.

My teeth grit on a smothered growl. *How the hell am I going to send her away if she's about to go into heat? Or, worse—what will I do if it happens early?*

"When I was checking the bump on her head before she went to bed," Micah goes on, solemn and quiet. "Her forehead felt warm, and she mentioned that being around all of us might speed things up for her."

Low-grade panic thrums under my skin as a possessive rush

rears up in my chest. I fight both down, repeating all the facts I've chanted to myself since the moment Micah pulled Emma out of her car.

She can't stay.

She doesn't belong here.

She doesn't belong to me.

I don't have anything to offer her.

And she deserves *everything.*

I may not know much about Emma, but I already know that. The little omega we rescued is kind, with more love than most and a stunning willingness to share it. I've never seen anything like it—never met anyone so confoundingly *open.*

She should have a pack of generous, protective alphas who can meet all of her needs when she goes into heat. Not some flashy, shallow asshole like Zane. Or someone as lost as Gunnar.

Or me. Even if I weren't ten years too old for her, I'd still be all wrong. Rough and hardened and just... better off alone.

Of all of us, Micah might be the only one here I could stomach for her. But she would still need other knots. And *a goddamned nest.*

Fuck. I'm barely holding my Alpha back as it is. If she goes into heat while we're stuck here, will I be able to force myself to leave? I already feel less than three heartbeats away from bending her over the nearest hard surface every time she drifts too close.

I could snap into a rut and terrify her.

I've seen that happen before. And knowing I put even an ounce of fear on that sweet little thing's face would smash the hardened remnants of my heart to bits.

"She can't stay here," I snarl, low. "I'm not equipped for an omega in heat."

Gunnar tosses me a look. "Yeah, no shit. You don't even have a Christmas tree."

"What does that have to do with anything?"

Zane makes a ponderous sound. "Omegas like homey shit.

Blankets and pillows and twinkle lights. You know, Knox, *if* you wanted in on this whole courting thing, I bet Emma would love a big tree and stockings and a few garlands—"

"*Enough,*" I bark, unable to stand the odd, seething stomach flip his words invoke. "I don't decorate. Because I don't *have* an omega. Or a pack. I'm sure as hell not going to get a bunch of Christmas stuff airlifted in with our groceries. You're all leaving the minute the road is fixed."

Thick silence pulls taut between all of us.

Micah finally clears his throat. "Actually…" he says, "I don't know what any of your plans are, but I don't want to be away from Emma. I was planning to call the station tomorrow and take some leave. I want to offer to stay with her for her heat, if she'll have me."

My insides coil tighter, envy burning bright. Zane rolls up onto his side, looking down at Micah through the dark. "Oh, she would. She told me she wants to see what this would be like. As in all of us—together. You know, *if* we can do the whole courting thing and still get along, somehow."

But that's not possible.

None of this is. The courting, the heat. These guys.

I can't have a pack. I've proven as much.

Even if I could, I wouldn't want three strangers in my head. And I wouldn't want to share my omega with outsiders, either.

That's the way bonds *work*, though. If Emma wanted all of us, we would have to bond with her individually because we aren't a pack. If we did that, she would be split between the four of us forever.

No, I correct myself, *the three of* them.

I'll never trust myself to be alone with her. The very thought of what might happen is unacceptable. I refuse. She deserves so much *better*.

"Court her if you want to," I practically growl, flexing all of my control. Needing it in order to hold my Alpha down while he thrashes against the painful reality unfolding under my own damn roof. "But don't make her choose one of you before her heat. She's going to need more than one alpha. So you all need to figure out how to share, at least temporarily."

Gunnar grunts his thoughts about sharing with a terse, "Goddamn it. I really am stuck with you fuckers, aren't I?"

Another thick beat of shock echoes through the room, while my Alpha's rage gathers. Zane finally sighs, "Guess so, Hockey Boy. I know *I* can't say no to her. Have you seen her *face*?"

He has a point. How *will* I say no to her if she asks? Telling these guys is one thing, but looking into those big, hopeful green eyes? Telling her all the reasons I could never do right by her?

Damn it all to hell.

When I can't come up with one single solution, I tell myself I must be too tired to think straight. It's late, and it's been a hell of a day. I'm sure the fact that all of my blood has been circulating through my dick instead of my brain for the last twelve hours isn't helping.

Nothing I can do about that now. God knows I can never use that masturbator again without reliving Emma's horrified giggles.

Sighing, I lie back and try to force my eyes shut. The rest of the room falls into silence reminiscent of a bunk room at summer camp. I hear Zane rolling from one shoulder to the other. Micah breathing deeper, Gunnar rearranging his blanket.

None of us have anything left to say.

I tell myself it isn't my problem what any of these guys choose to do, but as minutes slide past, I find myself clocking everyone's breathing, paying attention to who falls asleep first, second, and third.

Gunnar is last. My restless mind wonders what kept him up so long... and if a certain omega upstairs might be having the same issue.

When my Alpha abruptly stops pacing my middle and settles with an exasperated huff, I get the sinking feeling I'm only at peace because everyone else finally is.

I'm not sure what to make of that, but I know I don't like it.

THERE'S a thin band of pink light on the horizon when I open my eyes. The pale sun burns my retinas while I restart my thoughts. For a second, I don't remember why the fuck I'm in my living room.

Then, Zane snores.

With a grumble, I push myself upright and rub my crusted eyelids.

I slept like shit the first half of the night, then dropped into the deepest slumber I've ever had. The others seem to be in the same state, each of them knocked out cold.

Except for my dog. He comes sniffing at my hand, licking the knuckles.

"What are you doing down here, traitor?" I tease, ruffling the fur between his ears. "I thought you were all about the little miss upstairs now."

He chuffs at me, clearly expecting to go out for our usual walk despite giving me the cold shoulder all day yesterday. I start to roll my eyes, but they catch on a tartan-wrapped bundle wedged between Micah's big body and Zane's spot on the sofa.

Emma.

She must have wandered down here in the middle of the night and brought my only throw blanket with her.

Is that why I finally got some rest? Did my Alpha hold out until she was nearby?

More importantly: did she have such a hard time being away from us that she couldn't sleep either?

McKinley whines softly, nosing at Emma's blonde curls. I wave him back to my side, petting his head. "That's why you're here," I realize. "You came down with her?"

He leans into my leg, looking back at the omega with an intent expression; because he wants *her* to come on our walk, too. I exhale hard, bending to pull the blanket away from her face, pausing to brush her hair back before I even know what I'm doing.

The silky strands sift through my fingertips, and for just a moment, I let myself stare.

It's something I avoided at all costs yesterday. Even when my instincts insisted I hold her in my lap after she passed out... I did everything I could *not* to look at her face too closely.

But now, in the buttery morning light, with my mind at half-speed, it suddenly doesn't seem so dangerous.

It suddenly seems... *necessary*.

She really is beautiful.

So much softness and light. Her bright hair and brows, the rounded apples of her cheeks. Her sloping little nose. The chin that wobbles between tears and giggles in the most endearing ways.

The word I can't allow myself to accept bubbles back up. I said it twice yesterday, lost to the heat of her haze. Then, I vowed to myself that I was wrong.

I had to be.

This is clearly a mistake. Because I don't deserve her, and I can't take care of her. She's already been through so much. The universe wouldn't be so cruel to someone so kind.

But the word reverberates through the very core of me. Louder with every step I take in retreat.

Over to the closet where I keep my outerwear.

Out the back door.

Across the fresh field of snow sprawled over my property.
Mate.
Mate.
Mate.

chapter
twenty-seven

KNOX IS GOING to get some serious forehead wrinkles if he keeps scowling at me like this.

"Where the hell did you find *sprinkles*?"

I smirk across the kitchen island, eyeing his omnipresent flannel shirt. So far, he's worn a different color every day. Red, green. Today's is blue, which might be a good color on him, if I could see the matching shade of his irises under that faded hat.

"Your neighbor," I tell him, grinning as I remember the way the little old lady *two miles* up the road balked when she opened her door and found me on the other side. "I got the sense she doesn't get many visitors."

Knox blinks, clearly surprised to find he's not the only human living in this mountain's ass-crack. "Huh."

I thought courting Emma would be complicated, but it's actually been shockingly easy. Or rather, she *makes* it easy by being so open and endearing. Her enthusiasm is contagious; every time we talk, she gives me half a dozen ideas for things I could do or get for her.

She also loves food and devours every meal I make, which has been way more fun for me than her. It's been a long time since I had someone to share my love of cooking with. The way she oohs and ahhs over every bite is as good for my ego as taking care of her is for my sanity.

I nod at Knox, hiding another grin. "Had to freeze my dick off to get there and back before Emma woke up this morning, but it will be worth it. She's wanted to bake Christmas cookies all week. Can't have Christmas cookies without sprinkles. And icing."

I tilt the mixing bowl in front of me so he can see the royal icing I've whipped up. Luckily, once the neighbor realized I wasn't there to rob her, she was thrilled to help me woo my omega. Three of her granddaughters are omegas, apparently. She gushed about how sweet I was while loading a bag full of confectioner's sugar, food coloring, and all sorts of other goodies.

"By the way," I say, remembering, "Mrs. Henderson needs you to shovel her sidewalk. Today."

Knox's woody musk smolders. He grits his teeth. "*Me?*"

"Didn't you read the group text?" I ask, knowing damn well he didn't. I offer a chipper, innocent smile. "Of course, you! The big, strong mountain-man alpha! Who else would help his little old neighbor with her snowy sidewalk? Oh—and her driveway."

The grumpy hermit flexes his fists on the top of the island. "And why," he grinds, "don't *you* do it?"

I wave my hands around his kitchen. "Because *I'm* courting an omega! And cooking meals for five! No time for manual labor. Oh, Gunnar's out, too. He has to set up his little travel goals and do drills on your pond or something? I wasn't listening. But

Micah said he'd help! Guess he wants to give the rest of us a fighting chance today."

It's no secret that Micah's been killing it in the courting department. He has a sixth sense for how to be helpful in the exact right ways. Combined with his seemingly endless patience— the guy's a natural.

Maybe being a fireman gave him superhuman powers of cooperation. He's always looking for ways to chip in, offering help without a speck of hesitation. Micah is a do-gooder in the truest sense... one more thing he and Emma have in common.

I swear, he's the greenest of green flags.

Unlike the alpha across from me.

I don't get it. Even now, just sitting there seething, I can tell Knox clearly *wants* to court Emma. His alpha energy may be leashed tight, but it still *claws* at mine. Plus, in the moments when he lets himself relax a little, he doesn't take his eyes off the sweet omega traipsing around his house.

Can't blame him there. Our girl is *hot*.

My balls are going to turn to stone if they get any more backed-up. I've been walking around with a constant erection for more than two days.

The whole slumber-party situation we have going on doesn't exactly make it easy to relieve myself. But that *definitely* hasn't stopped the others, if the swirl of pheromones in Knox's shower is any indication. As embarrassing as it is, that ache anchored to the bottom of my heart tugs taut every time I think about jacking off to the many filthy Emma fantasies I've conjured up.

I want *her*. And the first time I come for her, I want to be *inside* her.

I know, right? That's some romantic shit.

Who knew I had it in me?

Not me, but there's no denying the way my stomach flips when Emma comes bouncing into the room.

Gunnar rescued her suitcase from the rental car Knox took care of, so she has all her cute clothes. Today's outfit is my favorite by far—a loose pink sweater with sparkly thread and white tights that hug her perfect ass. She put on knee-high snowman socks, too. Their googley eyes have me grinning as she jumps into my open arms with an exuberant squeal.

I press kisses over her cheeks, chuckling while I lift her onto the counter. "Hi, gorgeous. Ready for our date?"

Emma smiles, her scent brightening into sugar-and-spice perfection that lights up my soul. Apparently, it's too much for Knox, because he grumbles something about shoveling that walkway and clips out of the kitchen.

Our girl flinches when the door to the garage shuts behind him. I swoop in and plant my lips over hers as a distraction, purring automatically.

She's slowly getting used to us doing that for her. Mostly because Micah pretty much never stops. And Gunnar has taken that as some sort of challenge. He likes to compete, and his competitive nature seems to turn Emma on.

It definitely hasn't escaped any of our notice that his scent is almost always entwined with hers. Whenever they get a moment alone, they're all over each other.

It makes sense that he's the one she's most comfortable with; she knew him before this whole scenario unfolded. I expected to be more jealous, but so far, I'm all for it—Emma needs easing, and Gunnar caring for her might help her Omega come around to him faster.

Plus, more cuddles for our girl means more of this *insanely good* perfume.

Emma feels me lock up when she crosses her ankles around the backs of my thighs. She hesitates for a moment, probably thinking she's done something wrong.

Embarrassment is her default setting, and I hate that for her. Scent-marking her neck with my cheek, I deepen my purr to reassure her.

"You smell so good; it's making me crazy," I murmur against

her pulse. "It's not fair. I'm trying this new thing where I *attempt* to act like a gentleman."

"Act like?" she titters. "You mean you're not really a giant softy?!"

My face pulls into a wince as I flex my hips, pressing the hard length of my cock against her core. "Not *quite*. But I did plan something fun that doesn't require removing your clothes."

Emma smiles slowly, beaming gratitude and softness. She casts her eyes over all the cookie ingredients I've organized. Her thighs tighten around my middle while mischief dances into her gaze.

"What if I *want* you to remove my clothes?"

Fuck. Me.

I force down a swallow, leaning back to scan her features. Part of me worries I've read this all wrong. I want her to know she's so much more to me than a perfect pussy and mind-melting scent—but maybe I should have been showing her the way my body aches for her instead of holding back.

She sees my hesitation and stretches up to rub her nose along my cheek, exactly the way she did the first day we met. My heart lurches, expanding twice as fast as my knot.

I force a shaky laugh, explaining, "I didn't mean to hold out on you, gorgeous. I'm just trying to be romantic. And I'm not quite sure how to combine sex and romance, if I'm being honest. I've never tried before."

Her legs hug me again, easy acceptance filling the space around her smile. "So I get to be your first?"

My laugh feels more genuine this time. "You sure do."

A wicked gleam touches her green eyes. They roll down my naked torso before flashing back to mine. "Hmm... I wanted to paint frosting on your abs and lick it off, but that isn't exactly roman—*mmph*."

My mouth lands on hers, cutting off the rest of her tease. The second our tongues touch, my control collapses and a gravelly groan tears up my throat.

Fuck the cookies.

I'll make them for her later. While she's stretched around my knot.

My hands drop to her ass, lifting her into my body. She pulls me closer, locking her limbs around my hips and neck.

Warm curves and plush lips and handfuls of blonde curls. Goddamn, she's like a feast. I don't know where to *start*.

Her frosting comment loops through my mind as her fingers trace the bulge at the front of my sweats. I imagine her big, beautiful tits covered in icing and buck into her touch.

Oh yes.

That's happening.

Right now.

Still, I take my time working off her sweater, pressing my palms into her curves as I draw it up her body. Fuck, she feels perfect. All softness and flawless pale skin.

I hold her gaze until her shirt is off, knowing that the second I let myself look down at her bared body, I won't be able to resist. To my surprise, she flashes me a teasing look and reaches down to pluck my hands off her ribs, placing them right over her tits.

"Merry Christmas," she grins.

And honestly? Best present *ever*.

I growl, hefting their rounded weight. "Shouldn't have done that, gorgeous. Giving me free access to these is dangerous."

She shrugs, the loose gesture belying the way her eyes suddenly seem painfully earnest. "You make doing dangerous things feel *really* safe."

That maybe shouldn't make sense, but I somehow understand exactly what she means. Those alpha-holes made her feel bad about *everything*. I'm sure sex was part of that. And I'm guessing any kinks that appealed to her were squashed just as thoroughly as her other interests.

But here's the thing: those pieces of her? They *are* safe with me.

I give her breasts a gentle squeeze, smiling softly when she gasps. My forehead nuzzles hers. "You bring me whatever kinks that beautiful brain comes up with and I'll be the luckiest man on Earth."

A burst of perfume erupts between us. I groan again, pressing my face to hers more insistently. Her fingers find my sides, tracing my obliques while she stammers, "R-really?"

Shit, I'm not going to make it through another breath. So I nod, gripping her tits with more intent. Her questing touch finds my waistband. The erection pressed into it throbs.

A dozen gloriously filthy ideas fly through my mind. I pick my favorite, snapping one of my hands to the side and snatching the pastry bag I filled with green icing.

"Hold still," I husk, lifting the tip to the bare expanse of her chest. Finally letting myself look at the *glory* of her.

Holy shit.

The two creamy swells are more than a handful; each tipped in the prettiest pink nipples. They've furled tight, waiting for me.

Because she really is the most perfect present.

Licking my lips, I start to shove my joggers off. Her scent thickens into a snickerdoodle haze—cinnamon, vanilla, torched sugar.

Fuck me, I want to *lap it out of the air.*

Instead, I tug at my pulsing cock, growling on every exhale as she stares blatantly. I can tell she's gushing for me already because she shifts on the counter, wiggling her hips. Without thought, I drop my knot and reach over to press my fingers into the crotch of her tights.

They're *soaked*.

With a wolfish smirk, I grind my thumb into the wet fabric. Emma moans, but just as she starts to squirm for me, I stop, repositioning the pastry bag, tilting it against her tits just so.

"This is royal icing," I murmur, hiding a smile when the cool liquid hits her skin and she sucks in a sharp breath. "Which means it will *harden*."

And it does. The lines and curves I draw over her perfect skin start to set as soon as they hit the cool air of the kitchen.

Emma watches in wide-eyed fascination, which might be adorable if I wasn't so fucking hard. Like this, though, her awed attention gives me all sorts of wicked ideas.

I make short work of my design, scrawling her name and mine with a plus sign in between and a heart at the end. Cute, right? It probably would be—if I didn't also draw careful swirls over both of her nipples.

Her lips part, gasping little moans until we're both grinding at the open air between us. Tossing the bag back onto the counter, I go straight for her tights, ripping them down her legs at the same second she wraps both hands around my cock.

Fuuuuuuuuuck.

Every nerve sizzles and snaps as she tugs her fists down my dick. My balls draw up, tingling and aching. I snarl around my next exhale. When a burst of slick dribbles onto my fingers, something in my brain breaks.

"Fuck, Emma," I pant, dropping straight to my knees. "C'mere."

My erection smacks the cabinet, but I don't give a shit. I grip her hips and pull her forward, right into my open mouth.

Good sweet holy fucking—

I might be dead. She tastes so good that I'm either *actually* in heaven or I'm *about* to be—because I will smother myself between this woman's legs.

Yes, *please.*

Her slick coats my tongue when I slip it between her lips, licking her hot core until she gives me more. Warm cinnamon and gooey brown sugar fill my senses. A trickle of something even more sugary touches my upper lip—and I realize... she's squirted some of the cookie icing onto her mound.

She didn't even warn me. *She just covered her pretty pussy in frosting and let it drip down...*

Holy fuck.

I'm in love.

Moaning, I lap it all up like ambrosia. When I suck her clit clean, she keens, writhing as she screams my name and comes. Squirting cinnamon bun slick all over my chest—and, I swear to God, if I even *grazed* my cock right now, I would go off like a firehose.

Jeeeeeesus.

Before I can embarrass myself, I lunge to my feet. Emma doesn't let me hesitate for even a second—her legs instantly draw me in, notching the head of my cock against her slit.

Gritting my teeth, I pant, "I shouldn't knot you here. On the counter."

Emma whines, scrabbling at my hips. "Alpha, *please!*"

What—am I supposed to say *no?*

chapter
twenty-eight

IF I WASN'T HALFWAY to combusting, watching Zane scramble like this might be a little funny.

He's so effortlessly sensual all the time—seeing him stare down at my body like he doesn't even know where to begin is as entertaining as it is flattering.

Also *painful*. Because, you know, he needs to *get in me right now.*

My second whine snaps him out of his stupor. A choked snarl catches behind his heaving chest, dark eyes flashing as he rearranges me. Gently pushing until I balance on my elbows; then, clutching at my thighs, pulling me toward him as he slides home.

"Emma, baby," he gasps, "*Fuck*."

Rock-hard heat spears into my aching muscles. They scream and sigh, frantically twitching around the throbbing warmth of his shaft.

I whine and thrash, wanting him to *pound me*—but he pins my hips with his big hands and bends over my torso. His head dips, those soft lips and that talented tongue finding the tip of my breast. He licks at the pattern he drew there, sending a dart of need straight to my clenching core.

It must taste as good as it feels, because he hums and sucks my entire nipple into his mouth. I moan, and he matches the sound, snapping a hand up to cup the full weight of my breast in his palm while he *sucks* me.

A sharp cry jolts out of me, my body mirroring his ravenous draws with pulls of its own. The inner walls tug at his girth as my pussy gushes around the heavy length. Zane feels me slick his cock, curses under his breath, and starts to *move*.

Oh. Holy. NIGHT.

I probably shouldn't be surprised after watching all of his videos a dozen times... but this alpha knows *exactly* how to fuck a woman right out of her mind.

His body *rolls*, the motion of his hips powerful and fluid in a way that's still somehow *filthy*. Every ripple presses his hard knot against me, and the undulating motions stroke his hot, swollen flesh over my slick, buzzing clit.

With a desperate sound, he leaves my clean nipple tingling and switches to the other. I whine once more, pumping my hips into his rhythm, already so close to the edge that it's embarrassing.

"Zane!" I squirm against him, frantic need building in my middle. "I—I—"

I want his knot, but I can't bring myself to ask for it. No one's ever knotted me outside of my heat because no one has ever wanted to. Besides, am I *really* going to ask an alpha *this* beautiful if he wants to be locked inside of me for an hour? Or two...?

When I can't finish my request, he pulls off my nipple and

slants his glittering gaze up at me. Whatever look I have on my face turns his perfect, rolling thrusts into shallow flexes of his hips.

The hand holding my tits floats up to my cheek. He frowns. "What is it, *shona*? Too much?"

I shake my head, swallowing the urge to cry.

He's just so *perfect*. Sweet and sensitive and fun. And *look at him*! What the heck is he doing with *me*?

Watching him straighten doesn't help. It just offers me a glimpse of his full glory.

The muscles stacked over his quads, the ladder of his abdominals, all the cut lines of his sides, and the grooves carved over his groin. Not to mention the thick, solid weight expanding at the base of his shaft, spreading my pussy lips wide.

I want it, I want it, I want it.

"Mm," he murmurs, automatically pistoning into me with more purpose while we both watch. "You want my knot, gorgeous? Right here?"

The shrill whine that shatters out of me is almost as desperate as the way my body closes down on his. Zane's head falls back on a pant.

"You do," he growls, thrusting faster. "I can *feel* it. Fuck. Tell me, baby. Tell me you want my knot."

My words get choked by a scream when he changes angles, grinding the base of that full, perfect swell into the clutch of my opening. I shake and buck, fighting to get closer, but I can't overcome the deep-seated fear that asking out loud will elicit a "no."

It always has. And if this alpha turned me down... I just don't think my heart could take it.

Zane lifts his head to look at me, his brows creasing as he slows again. "Emma," he murmurs, much softer. "Hey, come here."

Within seconds, he has me off my elbows and in his arms, the length of his torso pressed into mine as he kisses my face and purrs. The vibration smears the icing between his smooth chest and mine, but he doesn't seem to notice, scent-marking my fore-head with a gentle hum.

"You feel so good," he whispers. "Perfect, *shona*. I want to knot you and stay inside you all afternoon. Is that okay?"

I still can't say anything, but I nod as hard as I can without head-butting him.

Well, without head-butting him *much*...

"Goddamn it," Zane breathes, grinning as his gaze sinks into mine. "I don't know what I did to deserve you, but I know I'll do *anything* to keep you."

His words unlock mine. The tears gathered at the corners of my eyes spill over. I ignore them, smiling back and wrapping my arms around his neck.

"Knot me, Alpha? Please?"

Zane's fingers weave into the hair at the nape of my neck while his other hand drops to my hip. He holds me steady, keeping our eyes locked as he pushes the thick swell of hot flesh past the opening of my pussy.

Never having taken a knot outside of a heat haze, I brace for pain or pleasure or maybe something in the middle.

I'm not *at all* prepared for the whole world to end in a flash of glittering white.

That's how it feels, though. He shoves that wide warmth inside of me and it pops right against a thousand different nerves I didn't know I had. They all sing and shriek and snap, spasming around his smooth width in slick ripples.

"Fuck, Emma. *Yes*. Just like that. I'm going to come so damn hard in this sweet pussy. I want to last longer, but you feel *so good*. You want it, baby? You want my cum in you? *Fuuuuuck,* squeeze me. *Just. Like. That.*"

I shatter before I can even catch my breath, screeching out a moan while Zane curses again, rolling his hips into mine even though we're already locked together.

The tiny tugs send one climax cascading directly into another.

He fumbles to get his hand between our bodies, stroking the top of my clit until I collapse into a third and take him with me.

His groan reverberates through my bones as his teeth find my shoulder, nearly breaking my skin. His knot explodes, hot washes of cum glaze the deepest parts of my pussy. I feel myself release again, squirting slick until my vision blurs.

When I blink my eyes open again, we're on the floor. Zane sits directly on the cold tile, but he has my legs wrapped around the small of his back and a nearby apron dropped over my body. A slow, soothing purr rumbles behind his decorated chest.

For a long moment, I'm embarrassed. But then I feel him nudge my temple with his forehead and see his soft smile.

"There you are," he murmurs. "I was sure you passed out on purpose to avoid me after that disastrous performance."

He's too sweet to be referring to me. And when he gestures at the mess he made of both our bodies—not to mention the countertop—chagrin fills the lines of his features.

He shakes his head, cringing. "I swear, I'm usually much smoother than that."

A giggle snags in my throat. "Well I'm *never* smooth, so."

It's impossible to feel anything apart from joy when Zane grins so widely. "You're the sexiest, sweetest woman in the world. No smoothness needed."

He nuzzles my nose as my eyes wander to the sprinkles scattered across the floor. *Oops.*

"Don't worry about it," the alpha shrugs. "I'll tell Knox it was my fault. I've never made Christmas cookies before—there was bound to be some sort of mess."

My fingers find the silky black hair at his nape, combing through it. I think back over all of his Knotty Chef videos, recalling the hundreds of dishes he's perfected. A furrow creases my brow. "You've really never baked Christmas cookies before?"

He sighs, slumping into the cabinets. "Nope. I was an only child from a single-parent household with a workaholic dad. The holidays were pretty bleak."

Snuggling closer, I breathe the toasted edge of his scent and note the unfocused way he stares at the oven, remembering. "I'm sorry," I whisper. "Did it ever get any better?"

Zane scoffs lightly. "Nah. I tried to get his approval and his attention for a long time. Eventually, I accepted that I'd never be what he wanted me to be and started cooking. He thought being a chef was a bogus career; once he found out about the uh, *style* of my videos, he cut off all contact. I haven't heard from him in years."

My pitiful omega purr starts up, shaking the tears at the corners of my eyes loose. "Zane," I whisper, touching the perfect planes of his face. "I'm *so sorry*."

Pain flashes through his answering smile while sadness dulls his dark eyes. "It is what it is. But I'm here now, with you. Any chance you have a kick-ass family I could get in on, gorgeous?"

I nod, emphatic. "Oh yeah. My family is very big on holidays."

Zane smirks at my discarded googley-eyed snowman socks. "I never would have guessed."

When I laugh, it tightens the way our bodies are locked together. I gasp and Zane groans, the ragged sound rolling into a purr that draws my face to his chest. He cuddles me into the vibrating rumble, kissing the top of my head.

I close my eyes, thinking back over all the holidays I've celebrated with my parents and siblings. It looks like this year will be different—and part of me will definitely miss some of our traditions. Like Mom's famous roast beef and Theo's absolutely atrocious gift-wrapping. Lucy's off-key singing voice. My dads fighting over who gets to kiss my mother's first kiss under the mistletoe.

Nuzzling closer, I offer, "There are some traditions I can teach you while we're here. Just in case..."

In case you're still with me next year.

Zane envelopes me in a hug, banishing any hint of doubt as he husks back, "I would love that, *shona*."

I tip my chin up, catching his gaze. "What does that mean? *Shona?*"

He truly is the most beautiful man alive, especially with that soft smile curving his lips. "It's Hindi," he replies. "The literal translation is 'gold,' but it can mean different things. 'Precious.' Or sometimes, 'treasure.'"

I already feel like I may swoon back into unconsciousness— then he bends to scent-mark my forehead with his. Tingles skitter over my skin, my core clamping around his knot.

Zane only smiles wider, radiating pure contentment as his eyes fall shut. "The name seemed fitting," he adds, "for the best gift I've ever gotten."

chapter
twenty-nine

DO I feel bad for turning Knox's dog into my accomplice?

Sort of.

But using him as an alarm clock has been the best way to sneak downstairs and sleep curled up between the couch and Micah's cot.

McKinley doesn't wake the others—he just comes over and gives my face a good lick when the sun starts to come up. Though, one of the alphas must be on to me. I've found a random pillow and an extra blanket waiting for me the last couple of nights.

I crack one eye open when a cold nose sniffs my hair, McKinley's silky fur brushing my ear. With a near-silent giggle, I reach up to pet his head. "Hey, boy."

He makes a pitiful sound in his throat, and I pop my head up, looking around the living room where three alphas are still crashed out.

Three...

Because Knox is already gone.

Zane has his mouth hanging open and his arm dangling off the edge of the sofa. Without his sly smirks and sexy winks, he looks boyish and sweet while he snores.

Micah is sprawled beside me, his large, brawny body stretched in all directions. Gunnar is the cutest, though, snuggled under three different blankets like a true Florida boy, and pouting in his dreams.

McKinley boops my leg, clearly wanting me to get up and let him out. I figure it's fine since the snow *finally* stopped falling after dinner last night. Micah said we would all be able to get outside more today, even if we still can't drive anywhere.

While McKinley loops around the room in excited circles, I go searching for some shoes. Zane's furry boots are way too big, but they're the first ones I find, so I lace them as tightly as I can and throw my body weight into opening the sliding glass door at the back of the enormous A-frame living space.

Whoa.

This place is *beautiful*!

It's a literal *winter wonderland*—gleaming snow drifts, distant mountain peaks, golden morning mist, and towering pine trees.

There's a frozen pond fifty yards off in one direction and the entrance to a hiking path on the opposite side of the field.

Fresh white powder has covered the whole expanse like pristine velvet, tucked snuggly over the cliff outlined by a low log fence.

For a second, I breathe deep, smiling to myself when the frosty, wooded scent reminds me of being wedged between Micah and Knox.

Off in the distance, a pair of songbirds warble to each other.

There's also a distant thumping sound that pricks McKinley's ears.

He must be used to whatever it is because instead of investigating, he loses interest and trots back to the house. When I see he has a doggy door he could have used instead of waking me up, I snort a laugh.

Oh well. I slept most of the day away yesterday, recovering from Zane blowing my mind to smithereens.

And today? I really need to figure out how to approach this whole four-separate-mates thing.

Well.

Three.

Apart from holding me after I fainted and a few vague concerns about my well-being, Knox hasn't exactly made his intentions clear. I guess none of them have *said* anything explicit, apart from insisting they aren't leaving here without me.

Even if he wanted to, Knox *can't* leave. He lives here, and we're all intruding.

I don't know if I understood the appeal of his place before this moment. But as I look out at the crystal landscape, something in my chest catches.

Whatever he did to make all this money... wherever he came from before... he left it all behind to come here and have some peace.

Shame curls in my middle while I consider that. Really, we've all barged into his home without any apologies. The man clearly built his life so he could be alone—we're ruining his solitude, and none of us have even said thank you.

Not to mention the way I've bombarded him with my scent and the connection I feel toward his Alpha.

Another *thwack* rings out over the stillness, followed by two more. I assume it must be the reclusive alpha since his dog seemed so used to the noise. When I follow it around the side of the big, empty cabin, all the air hisses out of my lungs.

Oh.

Holy.

Night.

It's the mountain man, all right. With his red flannel shirt rolled over his brawny forearms and hanging open around his glistening chest. And his tan baseball cap, sitting atop thick brown hair. Backward.

He plants his feet, the thick soles of his leather boots crunching snow as he arches his body back—*holy flapjacks, he has* muscles—and swings the tool gripped his fists straight down.

Thwack.

The log positioned on a larger stump cracks, splitting into two pieces of dry timber.

Oh. *Firewood.*

Knox bends to pick up the logs, tossing them onto a big tarp he has spread beside him. He already has quite a stack there— meaning he's been at this for a while.

...which would explain why he wedges his axe into the stump and shrugs his shirt off, pausing to wipe down his dark chest hair and the tight thickness of his abdomen. He turns to toss the shirt aside, flashing a glimpse of his wide, chiseled back.

This time, when he sets up another log, I see every tiny twitch of muscle as he rears back and swings down.

Lord. He's... magnificent.

Handsome and strong and rugged, of course. But there's something so attractive about how capable he is, too. The no-nonsense way he moves, knowing exactly *what* to do and *how* to do it.

His thick scent—cedar and pine needles—swirls into the cold air, tickling my lungs when I gasp. My core clenches as my own scent swells up to meet his. Knox's shoulders go stiff when he senses it. The axe dangles from his hand as his head snaps in my direction.

For a moment, everything is still. Without the thwack of his blade or the sound of the birds. Even the wind holds its breath while our gazes connect.

Something thick and hot bolts down my throat, settling into the tender place at the bottom of my ribs. It expands and thrums; the energy so intense and palpable, I can't inhale around it.

He feels it, too. I know he does because his blue gaze sparks, smoldering with want and warmth, and something that almost looks like bewilderment.

After a long pause, his thick brows lower over those piercing eyes. "You shouldn't be out here while I'm working," he gruffs. "It isn't safe for a little thing like you."

He's called me that a few times. *Little thing. Little miss.* The sorts of names that would make Lucy scrunch her nose in outrage.

I'd probably hate it more if not for the fact that I've always considered myself a bit too big for an omega. Taller and thicker than my sister or Meg, for sure. To a strapping man like Knox, though... I *am* little.

I still ignore his patronizing and try for a bright smile. "I can help! Just show me what to do."

I swear he blanches. "Over my dead body," he grumbles, swinging the axe into the stump and leaving it there, standing upright. My stomach flips as he starts toward me, bending to snatch something off the ground.

A coat.

His coat, judging by the woodsy musk clinging to it.

Knox drapes the thick material around my body, frowning down at me. "You'll get cold again," he says, quiet.

He fusses with the back of the heavy collar, pulling my curls free and smoothing them back. When he catches me gaping at him, he sighs.

The oddest sort of pained resignation pulls the faint lines at the corners of his eyes. I can't tell if it's from wanting to turn me away but not being able to...

...or the opposite.

Knox looks right into me for the dozenth time, reading my

questions and answering in a low timbre, "Go back inside, little miss. This is no place for you."

His hand is still curled into my loose hair, his calloused fingers woven into the blonde disarray. And I know I should know better —really, guys, *I know*—but some silly, hopeful piece of me believes that his actions mean more than his words.

My hands shake as I raise them to his chest. Cool sweat mists his skin, but the muscles underneath warm my chilled fingers. I feel his heart lurch, the throb behind his pecs reaching out to touch me back.

Calloused fingertips graze my scalp as his hand flexes, nostrils flaring on an audible exhale. "Damn it, Emma," Knox growls, but steps closer. "You need to *go*."

He has more dormant dominance than any other alpha I know. Ordinarily, a force this powerful would send me scrambling to escape, but this is a riptide, drawing me closer.

I'm not scared of him. He doesn't seem angry. More... afraid?

"Why?" I ask, staring up into his blue eyes while I whisper. "Why do I need to go?"

Because I suddenly understand—he isn't just saying I need to go *inside*. He knows as well as I do that standing out here while he works is perfectly safe. That he would never let anything happen to me—hypothermia included.

He's saying that I need to *leave*.

Leave *him*.

Pain carves dark grooves in the ice of his irises, a scrape that echoes through my own chest.

Does he live out here all alone because he wants to? Or because he thinks he should?

The thought cleaves my heart in two, just like one of his logs. "Knox," I say softly, stepping closer. "Why do you think I need to go?"

He grits his teeth, obviously warring with himself, but never drops my gaze. "It isn't safe here," he repeats, beseeching me with every blink. Begging me to understand.

I'm not sure why I do. I'm the clueless one, remember? Dumb and needy and so optimistic it's practically a liability. Yet, as I stand in the cold, clean air, breathing the burned scent of his stress, I *get* it.

"*It's* not safe for me," I say slowly, raising my brows, "or *you're* not?"

When a sharp dart of misery cracks across his face, I know I'm right. An instinctive jolt of fear streaks down my spine, arching my back and drawing a quivering gasp.

Knox's jaw sets, his eyes flashing. "I would never hurt you on purpose," he bites out. "I don't *want* to hurt anyone. I'm just—"

Strong.

He doesn't say the word, but he flexes that indomitable power, carefully squeezing the air from my lungs just to show that he can. A display of everything he has buried under his stoic silences and intense stares.

"It isn't *right*," he finally roughs out. "The way I am. It isn't fair to other alphas. Or to an omega."

I see what he means. If this is just a taste of his potency, Knox would definitely be too powerful for any other alphas to disobey him... which means he could *clobber* me if he wanted to.

I've never been much good at shutting up, but my mouth stays closed as I watch him roll his lips together, his chest heaving fast on deep breaths while he continues, "If I formed a pack with anyone, it wouldn't be a *pack*. It would be me overpowering everyone else at every turn."

His swallow is thick. I watch his stubbled throat work over it slowly before he admits, "I've tried. Years ago, when I was young like those guys in there. I had a group of alphas as friends. We were going to start my business together and form a pack. I didn't realize my dominance was overpowering them at every turn—I thought we all naturally agreed on things. Turns out, I was a tyrant and didn't even notice."

My whole heart aches for him, and he hasn't even gotten to

the bad part yet. But it doesn't matter. I know what it's like to think a pack wants you and find out they don't.

I slip my hands down his torso and wrap my arms around his waist, turning to press my cheek over his sternum. His body stiffens, brittle and unbending. When I rub my scent-mark at the base of his throat, he releases a shaky exhale.

"Tell me what happened," I murmur, stroking the small of his back.

"It wasn't anything big," he insists, rasping. "But remember when I told you that you were smart to leave when you did? Well, I *wasn't* smart. By the time I had the whole business set up, the others had already found *their* omega behind my back. While I was working around the clock, they were courting her.

"When I found out, I lost my shit. Tried challenging one of them to get control of the pack back. But all that did was terrify the omega they wanted to bond. Which finally convinced me to walk away—I hated that I had scared her, but I didn't *feel* anything for her. I realized, if she belonged with them, I didn't."

My eyes well and spill, imagining how much he must have hurt. Clearly, he went on to be successful anyway. But they took away something so much more important than a business.

He's spent all this time alone because he didn't trust himself to be a good alpha. Sort of the way I've been questioning my instincts every moment since I woke up in his bed.

A lump blocks my breath, squeezing more tears from my eyes. "I'm so sorry, Knox. I—I don't know if it means anything, but I don't think your Alpha is scary. I like him."

The words tangle on my tongue, but once they're out, I hear how true they are. Just remembering the way he barked my name, telling me to look at him while I came on Micah's cock...

Perfume winds into the air as slick dribbles down my thighs. Knox's entire body shudders. His eyes fall shut as his teeth grind, jaw flexing under his dark beard. When his gaze snaps back to mine, the blue *seethes*.

"You think that now," he grinds out. "But what about

during your heat, when you're vulnerable? Or if I went into a fucking rut? If I ever lost control, I wouldn't be able to stop myself from barking—and you wouldn't be able to tell me no."

Well, I guess we've officially confirmed that there is something *very* wrong with me—because the thought of Knox losing his mind, barking me into submission, and rutting me through his headboard doesn't scare me at all. It only makes a thicker stream of slick slip from my core.

Scenting my arousal, the bare-chested alpha growls low. "Emma," he rasps, cheek muscles clenching even as his eyes soften. "Honey, that can never happen. It would fucking kill me, do you understand? If you were going to stay here, we would need the others to keep an eye on me. And even that wouldn't be enough."

Because he would bark, and they would back down. Although, Gunnar fought him pretty hard when he came barging in. And Micah's never had an issue meeting this alpha's steely blue gaze in challenge when he wants to.

Zane works differently. He might not step up to Knox directly, but he holds his own with his quick mind and his charm. He wouldn't necessarily need physical strength or big-knot energy to assert himself.

And what about me? I bite my lip, considering, while we stare at each other.

Knox has told me to go inside. Multiple times. And I'm still here.

Honestly, though? Even if I *couldn't* resist his dominance, I don't know if I believe he'd ever use it for anything other than keeping me safe.

When he barked on that first day, he only did it to keep Gunnar—who he thought was a stranger—away from me. And, before that, to make sure I felt secure during my heat-spike.

He didn't bark when I broke his window. Or cried about it. He still isn't, now.

This is the part where I'm supposed to doubt the swelling certainty engulfing my gut.

That's what a *smart* person would do. Someone who isn't naive.

I can't question this, though. I've never felt anything so solid or *real*.

This alpha is my *mate,* and he's been *hurt.*

That look in his eyes? The haunted, resigned one? It's *loneliness.*

My chest rumbles, a pitiful omega purr rattling beneath my breasts. Knox snaps his eyes down, his tight mouth falling open in shock.

Which is sort of adorable.

I skim my touch up his back muscles, leaning up on my tiptoes to kiss the slash of his jaw.

"I'm not afraid of you, Alpha," I whisper around my purr. "I think you're good. And I think everything you want is good, too."

His answers with an unsteady exhale. I nuzzle my cheek into his beard, leaving my scent there.

"That other pack was wrong not to communicate with you," I tell him. "If they had, you would have listened. They should have known that. I've only been with you for a short time, and I already believe you just want the best for everyone."

Fire snaps back into his gaze. He opens his mouth to argue, but I press gentle fingers to his lips.

"Think about it, Knox. You've been in self-imposed exile. All because you didn't trust yourself not to wield some sort of undue influence over other people. That's a good person. With good intentions."

I try for a small smile. "Besides, McKinley is obviously a brilliant judge of character, and he *loves* you."

Knox huffs a surprised laugh, but his eyes turn soft again. One big, rough palm floats up to cup my face. "He might love you more, little miss. I've never seen him take to anyone like he has to you."

This time, the nickname makes me wrinkle my nose. Remembering what I said about his old pack and communication, I cock my head at him.

"Are we totally set on the whole 'little miss' thing? Because it sort of makes me feel like I should be calling you 'Daddy'."

An Earth-melting wave of cedar musk rolls off him, betraying how much he likes the sound of that.

I'm... *surprised.*

The big, grumpy mountain man... wants me to call him Daddy?

I mean...

Yes, please?

Still, it's so unlike him that I find myself smiling again. His thick eyebrow arches as he scans my expression. "Something funny, little miss?"

The solid weight of his influence presses into my diaphragm until I'm short of breath. "Not funny," I titter, "I just... I've never called anyone that."

His free hand clamps around the place where my backside meets my thigh, the touch as inherently possessive as his fingers wrapped into the hair at my nape.

"That's because no one has ever taken proper care of you," he husks. "Not the way I would if I was your alpha."

If?! my Omega shrieks.

When I whine with want, perfuming harder than before, his lips quirk up slightly at the corners.

"You should go back inside," he says, softly this time. "Give one of those lucky bastards the wake-up of a lifetime."

He's selfless by nature. Turning me on and willingly sending me to one of the other guys.

Not even considering that *he* could have me.

It solidifies all the certainty inside of me, until my grin hurts my face. "I don't know, Daddy. I think I need *you* to take care of me. Maybe you should show the others how to—*eep!*"

Can confirm—the magical landscape looks just as pretty hanging upside-down over a mountain man's shoulder.

chapter
thirty

THIS IS everything I was afraid of.

And all the things I wanted, back when I let myself think I could have pack life.

The simple fact is—I can't control myself. I can't turn down what Emma's offering. Even if it's the *only* taste I'll ever get.

God knows what my scent is like at this moment. I assume the tension gripping my chest isn't quite burning the woody aroma to ash, though, because the little omega draped over my shoulder doesn't seem the least bit distressed.

Only delicious as hell.

She giggles sweetly while I stomp around the back of the house, leaving gooey cinnamon perfume in our wake. I flex my arm around her thighs, appreciating how thick and curved they feel.

Mate, my Alpha chuffs, full of gruff pride.

Mate, I think back, fitting the word around all the things I just told her and the way she reacted like she was tailor-made for me.

Sent like a hand-picked present. Some magical mixture of compassion and submission and strength.

I ignore the optimistic thoughts. Because there's a hell of a long way to go before I have *any* business throwing my hat into the ring. And three other alphas are jockeying for position.

But, hell—the solid weight of her is as perfect as her scent. It reassures some primal part of me, knowing that she isn't frail or underfed.

Still, it's cold here. She could use some feeding up.

When we step into the house, my eyes fly to the kitchen. I shove back the desire to set her in my lap and force her to eat breakfast.

Last night, at dinner, I very nearly did just that. Then she ate two bowls of chili along with a small stack of cornbread biscuits, and my Alpha practically swooned.

I noticed the way she covered herself up after riding Micah through her heat-spike, though. We might love how she looks and feels, but she seems self-conscious.

That will be my first priority when I have her naked.

If I don't scare her off before we get that far.

Gunnar and Zane won't be any help. They're both passed out. Micah is the only one sitting up, rubbing at his hazel eyes.

The second he sees us and scents Emma, he lumbers to his feet and shoots me an accusatory look that connects with the self-doubt sloshing in my gut. For a second, I question if any of this is *good* for Emma—

—then she leans around my hip and gives him an upside-down grin. "Hi, Hazels!"

All traces of concern fall off Micah's features. He chuckles as he strides over. "Good morning, sweet girl. Did you go outside and bag a bear?" He smirks at me. "Or did Knox bag you?"

"No one's bagged anyone," I grumble, setting Emma on her feet.

"*Yet*," she adds, smiling widely again.

Micah grins right back. "Hmm. Well, if you're going upstairs for some one-on-one time, I can run interference when these jackasses wake up."

Emma touches his chest and glances up at me, letting me choose if I want her alone or if I would feel better having someone there for backup.

Her open, submissive expression sparks some deep, burning instinct that smolders under my center. It's been a long time since I intentionally accessed that place, but the impulses come effortlessly.

I *know* what's best for her and ache to provide it. There's a deep-seated pleasure in that.

"My little miss needs a bath," I decide out loud, squeezing her nape as I guide her toward the stairs and toss a look back at Micah. "You're going to watch."

THERE ARE layers to being a natural-born alpha.

On one level, I know what Emma needs to get off. I also know what she needs to be safe.

There are selfish impulses—the obsessive urge to hoard her to myself and fight off the alpha at my back. The growl that snaps out of my lungs when I sense Gunnar's scent twined with hers in *my* bathroom.

But then there are others, too.

I want to test Micah to some degree. Weigh how trustworthy he would be as a packmate and—more importantly—what he has to offer this omega.

Because she's at the center of every last instinct raging through me.

Protecting her. Pleasuring her. Making sure she's clean and fed and *happy*.

Emma makes that last one too easy. She's already beaming at me like I hung the moon in the sky, and I haven't done one damn thing to deserve it.

Yet.

I sling Emma back over my shoulder, relishing her giggly squeal as I charge past my bedroom. Micah casts me a questioning look, but I curl my free hand, indicating he should follow us.

It's been years since I walked all the way down this hall. The local team of no-nonsense grandmothers I pay to come and clean all the empty parts of the house have kept the floors dust-free and the walls de-cobwebbed, but other than that, I'm not sure anyone else has ever set foot in here.

I tried to, once, but it tied my stomach into a tangle. I also tried to convince my architect to omit it altogether, but the alpha woman refused, claiming not having a proper Omega Suite in a house of this size would kill any future property value. The investor in me couldn't argue, so I wound up with a sealed-off suite and two carved wooden doors I never even let myself look at.

Neither of them comment as we shove in, but I find myself sweeping the room, remembering things I'd purposefully forgotten. Like how this portion of the upstairs is built into the mountain, with a deck stretching from the wall of window sliders. Or how it faces the distant blue-misted peaks, where golden sunrise spills into the sky at this time of day.

Emma cranes her neck to look around and I feel a beat of anxious pride. She clearly likes the room, but I'm wary of letting her get attached to it. Or me.

If it would be better for her to move on without either, that's what she's going to do.

But we won't know until we try. And the way she reacted to my story brought me closer to hope than I have been in years.

Micah catches on quickly, cutting across the wide wood floor to the open bathroom door. He goes right for the tub, pausing to check it for dust before he turns on the tap.

It's a bare-ass room, though, and he notices. Tossing me a slightly exasperated look, he asks, "Towels?"

"Hall closet," I rough out, gently setting Emma on her feet. I realize then that she's wearing Zane's boots, probably because she didn't want to come up here to find her own before following me earlier.

I'm about to ask Micah to go grab her a clean set of clothes when I hear his footsteps head for the bedroom.

Huh.

He's doing it himself.

Emma doesn't notice my surprise; she's too preoccupied with her own. Turning in a slow circle, her wide green eyes drink in the rustic design — light wood walls, an enormous trough-style sink with four faucets, and an enclosed shower-slash-sauna.

With a teasing smile, she accuses, "You've been holding out on us!"

I palm the back of my neck, grumbling. Truth is, I'd forgotten this bathroom is basically something straight out of a posh ski resort; otherwise, I would have suggested she use it when she got here.

The light in her eyes makes her next taunt even sweeter. "Do you also have a home theater hidden somewhere?"

She clocks the way my features freeze up, her lashes fluttering wide. "You do!" she laughs, bouncing in place. "Ooh, can we watch *Home Alone*? No, wait, *The Grinch*?"

I remember Gunnar's lament the first night he spent with us. And, hell, I can't say no to Emma's beaming, hope-filled face, either.

I grip handfuls of her borrowed sweatshirt and shove it out of my way, finding the warm, bare skin of her sides as I step closer and stare down my nose. "If you're a good girl for me, you can have just about anything you want, little miss."

She nips her lower lip, shy and gorgeous as all hell. "I'll be good."

When she hesitates, my fingers tug gently on her curls. Big eyes fly to mine, absorbing the thick beat of potency my Alpha projects.

"Say it."

It's not normal to want this, I'm sure. Zane will probably laugh his ass off when he hears what I'm asking the sweet little omega to call me. But I can't help myself. When she said it earlier, my blood *roared*. Deep down, it feels right in a way I can't quite describe.

I just *know* what she needs. And my Alpha knows that being what she needs is the most important thing now.

"D-daddy," she stutters, adorably uncertain. I huff a grunt, bending to scent-mark her forehead in reassurance. My fingers return to stroking her curved sides.

"That's okay," I husk, staring into her as I inject sincerity into every word. "I'm here, and I'm listening to you. Try it again, honey. Tell me who's going to take care of you."

I feel more than see her chest shudder as cinnamon sweetness creeps into the air. My cock and scent both rise up to meet her arousal while she breathes, "You are, Daddy."

"That's right," I praise, skimming my palms to her ribs. "Daddy will take care of his baby girl."

Her skin feels so soft against my calloused fingers. I trace one down the line of her spine while the other draws a curve under her breast. I feel the weight of those big, natural tits pressed into the top of my abdomen. My dick kicks against my jeans, throbbing at her belly.

With my eyes on hers, I slip her sweatshirt off. In my periphery, I clock her gorgeous, pink-tipped peaks bouncing into view, but there's something more important going on here. Some door inside her soul that I'm unlocking, just by offering her my complete, undivided attention.

"I'm here," I say again, lower, "I'm listening. Tell me what you want, honey."

She quivers against me. Somewhere in the attached bedroom, I hear Micah rejoin us. He doesn't interrupt, though, even when Emma can't manage to form words.

Turns out, I don't need them.

This is what she wants. To be the center of our attention. Our absolute focus.

Done.

chapter
thirty-one

THE WHOLE TIME Knox strips off my clothes and guides me into the tub, his intense gaze never leaves my face. Micah watches, too, his full lips hanging open like he's in a trance.

Because of *me*?

For a second, I can't believe it. I even start to glance over my shoulder, sure that the neighboring mountain framed in the window behind the tub must be crumbling or something.

Knox doesn't allow that. His big, rough palm molds under my chin, pulling my attention back to him. His brow ticks up.

"Good girls keep their eyes on their alphas."

That blue, blue gaze sees so much more than it should. His gruff voice takes on a soft, growly edge. "And you *want* to be good for me," he says slowly, as if piecing my thoughts together, "don't you, baby?"

If I were cooler or smarter, I'd find some way to stop the desperate whine that eeks out of my throat. But the idea of being exactly what these men want—*who* they want—is too much for me to resist.

I've never been *anyone's* first choice or their focus.

And maybe it makes me the naive, needy girl the Dunlaps accused me of being, but I want to please Knox more than I've ever wanted anything else.

The rugged alpha's lips curl slightly when he hears my whimper, soft satisfaction streaking his irises. "I know you do, honey," he murmurs. "Daddy knows. I'm going to make it real easy for you this first time, I promise."

He doesn't have endless, hypnotic eyes like Zane, but Knox's dominance is almost more potent. Like a drug, numbing the edges of my self-consciousness and filling my belly with languid flutters.

His thumb skims my lower lip, pulling it from my teeth as he tosses a casual command over to Micah. "Her pants. We need to get her warmed up."

My hazel-eyed fireman smiles as he approaches, pausing to nuzzle my bare shoulder sweetly before he settles his long-fingered hands on my hips. "Mm, sweet girl. You're so fucking pretty for us, aren't you?"

His compliment puts a sharp lump in my throat. When Knox sees my dismayed blink at the other alpha, he growls quietly, dropping his heated gaze over my exposed skin. "You're goddamn *beautiful*, baby. My knot's been aching since you took your top off—*days ago*."

Micah hums as he works my sweats down, leaving my body completely bare. His lips find my pulse and suck it gently. "She feels like a fucking dream, Knox. I can't stop thinking about the way she rode me." He groans to himself. "So *perfect*."

Every word soaks into my center, warming my blood and

gelling the muscles clenched in my core. Slick starts to slip down my thighs, the scent of cinnamon a spicy, toasted burst of heat.

Micah moans louder as he tugs at his own clothes, gold-green eyes blazing. "Fuck, sweet girl. You gonna squirt some more for us?"

Knox feels the jolt of mortification that jams its way into me. He freezes, scanning my face before a more sinister snarl starts in his chest.

"Did they tell you there was something wrong with that? Your other alphas?"

I hate that he's called them that—and I hate that he's right. When I shrink back a bit, his features pull into a deep frown.

Micah crowds into my back, purring smoothly and hugging me around the waist as Knox steps into my front, holding my head between his hands.

"Pay close attention, baby girl, because Daddy will be mad if you don't listen," he roughs. "I *want* your sweet slick all over me, Micah, *and* this tub. So when you come, this pretty pussy better gush for us. Or I'll be spanking it, you hear?"

Holy night.

I feel like I'm *made* of slick at this point. Melting into a drippy puddle as I nod breathlessly. "Yes, Alpha."

Knox's cedar scent takes on a sweetness I never would have expected, especially when his brow arches sternly. I swallow, correcting myself, "I mean, yes, Daddy."

Tension leaves his shoulders on a deep exhale. I think I understand—most pack alphas like it when omegas give them the "Alpha" designation, but after everything he went through, he's scared to take that title from me.

Knox confirms my musings when he mumbles, "That's better." He nods at the steaming water and pulsing jets. "Into the tub, little miss."

Micah chuffs at my nape. "I think you actually tamed Knox, sweet girl. That didn't take long."

The other alpha looses a sound that makes the fine hairs on

my arms stand up, but Micah only pauses for half a breath before laughing, the snicker just a bit strained.

"Okay, okay," he replies, kissing my shoulder one final time before casting Knox a look. "If you wanted her all to yourself, what did you drag me up here for?"

My chest tightens, the urge to reach back and clutch Micah nearly overwhelming. Knox makes a reassuring noise, petting my hair. "Emma wants you here," he tells my other alpha. "And I need backup."

I already know Micah is the best of us. He's been the kindest, most-selfless alpha I've ever met since the second I opened my eyes and found him staring back at me. But the way he nods without a speck of judgment and solemnly promises, "Then I'm here."

How is he possibly real?

I turn without thinking, jumping into his arms. He catches me in a big hug, kissing me between chuckles. "Hi, baby. You like it when we get along, huh?"

Before I can ask myself if that's a good thing, Knox brushes my hair back, nodding with steely approval. "That's a *gift*, omega. Your instinct to bring people together is *exactly* what a pack needs."

They aren't a pack, though. And that fact dangles between us, even as they work together to get me into the hot water.

A moment later, I can't care anymore. Because Micah kneels at my back while Knox shucks his jeans and boots, leaving himself naked and poised for my perusal.

Oh.

Sweet.

Lord.

His *knot*. It's *huge*.

My pussy clenches at the sight, fluttering in anticipation. Perfume fills the warm room, and Knox's hard cock jumps... before his knot fills even *more*.

I don't think.

I *lunge*.

And I would probably fall face-first into the edge of the whirlpool tub, but Micah's forearm hooks around my waist, keeping me upright while I bend forward to suck Knox right into my mouth.

I have no idea what I'm doing, but he doesn't seem to care. The alpha chokes on a gasped growl, snapping his brawny hands to my head and holding me steady.

"Fuck, *Emma*," he grits, watching me try to fit him in my mouth.

He tastes delicious, somehow. That sweet cedar musk heady enough to make me dizzy as I attempt to take him into my throat without gagging.

When I don't make it very far, I brace for a stern correction. Or even a taunt. The one time I tried to do this for Rob, he *laughed*.

I wince, remembering, and Knox's fingers loosen. A spark of fondness lights his eyes as he strokes my cheek with his roughened thumb.

"Here, baby," he whispers, adjusting the jut of my chin. "Like this, all right? Breathe through your nose and open your throat so I can fill it up."

When I follow his directions, the whole arrangement gets much more comfortable. He gathers my hair, thrusting against my tongue, letting me feel his smooth skin and firm girth as it teases the back of my throat.

My core pulses, slick slipping into the whirling water that laps at my hips. Micah rises higher on his knees, pressing his own erection into my backside, scraping his teeth along my nape.

His hands curl under my breasts, hefting them in his grip while he exhales against my neck. "Fuck me, Emma, you look so pretty sucking his cock."

My fingers scrabble against Knox's thick, flexing thighs. Micah cups my tits and thumbs my nipples, husking, "Try touching him at the same time, sweet girl. I bet he would love your hands on his knot."

I scramble to obey, sliding my hands inward until they're spread over Knox's knot the way Gunnar taught me. He groans, the noise deep and serrated. When I glance up, a mask of prideful lust covers his face.

Possession.

My Omega and I whine, lapping up the way his eyes blaze, locked on my face like I'm all he can see. When he hears the sound, Micah bites my neck softly, his hardness twitching against my back.

"Good girl, Emma," he murmurs. "Look how much he likes that."

"Too much." Knox's jaw flexes. His nostrils flare, inhaling my perfume. "Need you to stop," he snarls, his alpha power whipping me into stillness.

My insides start to curl as I rear back into Micah, but Knox flexes a soothing beat of reassurance, holding my face every bit as reverently as he has this whole time.

His eyes flash, begging me to understand. "I need to mark you, omega. Put my cum deep inside you. Will you let me?"

chapter
thirty-two

I WAKE up with Gunnar's feet in my face.

I mean, it could be worse.

They could be Knox's.

But still.

Grousing, I haul myself up and realize we must have slept in, by Mountain Man standards. Micah is long gone and so is Knox. The plaid blanket wadded up between my spot on the couch and Micah's makeshift cot smells just like Emma, too.

Was she here? Did I miss her?

Shit.

I hop from foot to foot, cursing the freezing floor while I

hobble to the one armchair shoved into the corner of the room, where we all left our shit last night.

I don't remember which pair of Knox's Costco-couture black sweats were mine, and I'm in too much of a rush to care. Plucking up the first pair I see, I spit more insults at the floorboards while I shimmy them on. Patting the pockets, hoping to find my phone around here, somewhere—

Hmm. What's this?

It's a piece of purple notebook paper. I unfold it, smiling at the tiny hearts inked along the margins.

Emma.

I don't need to sniff it or read the name at the top to know it's hers. The bubbly handwriting *looks* like Emma. The words she's written out, however...

I blink at them, shock unhinging my jaw. *Holy motherfucking—*

My girl is a *freak.*

Double penetration, voyeurism, spit-roasting—

HELL. YES.

Until I read all the dirty, filthy ideas on her list, I didn't notice there's been a part of me, deep inside, bracing. The sex we had yesterday was incredible, but I still wondered how she would feel once she realizes just how sexual I am.

But *look* at this beautiful collection of kinky ideas my little mate *wrote down.* In *fine detail.*

Hot damn, gorgeous, say less.

I need to find her.

Like *now.*

A groggy growl interrupts my train of thought. Gunnar's nutty smell burns, warning me that he's awake the same second I hear his heavy footsteps behind me.

I whirl, baring my teeth in reply. Not because I really want to fight the guy—more because he needs to cool his shit all the way down.

Our omega wants us to get along. She wants us to *try*, anyway.

So, instead of shoving him away, I hide the note behind my back and bounce my brows at him. "You got a problem, Hockey Boy? Or are you just not a morning person?"

With a roar, he reaches around me and snatches the list out of my hand. His eyes flare—and, I swear, the guy practically foams at the mouth as he spits, "The fuck do you think you're doing?!"

I scoff, crossing my arms. "Other than falling even more madly in love with our dirty girl? Knox has no sense of style, and all his fucking pants look the same. I grabbed yours by mistake."

Gunnar glares, his blondish brows folded over bleary gray eyes. He holds the charming expression for a long moment before sloughing out a breath, his wide shoulders falling forward. "Fuck. She's going to be embarrassed."

"About being my literal wet dream?" I smirk, but the feeling drains away as I imagine her sweet face covered in shame. My voice drops into a more solemn tone. "I'll make sure she's not embarrassed. Did she tell you what the list is? Her favorite things or...?"

For a long second, he debates not telling me. In the end, he blows out another sigh. "They're things she wants to try. She wrote it for the honeymoon she never got to go on."

Ah fuck. My heart catches, aching at the thought of how sad their lies must've been for her. I hope we've helped her feel better, at least a little bit. I don't ever want her to be upset.

Gunnar looks as contemplative as I feel, frowning at the crinkled purple paper in his grasp. "It surprised me, too," he allows. "She wasn't sure if she should show you guys. She thought you might judge her."

Fuck, I hate how much I get that. How familiar that fear is for me.

I shrug. "Not judging at all"—*drooling like a damn dog, maybe*—"Where the heck is our sweet little omega anyway? Did the mountain men carry her off into the hills? I need to make her pancakes and tell her how gorgeous she is."

Gunnar looks mildly mollified by that. He crosses his arms and shrugs. "I thought I heard people go upstairs a while ago."

I look down at the list hanging from the hand tucked under his left elbow, scanning the first set of words I see.

Watch two alphas jack each other off.

I swear to God, I'm going to marry this woman.

"So, wait," I say slowly, snapping my eyes to his. "You're telling me those two knot-heads are upstairs with her *right now*?"

Gunnar nods.

I throw my arms out to the side. "And you and I are *standing around down here*?!"

There's a long pause, both of us turning our heads toward the stairs and back to one another.

And then we're running.

chapter
thirty-three

ZANE and I race to the double doors at the end of Knox's upstairs hallway, shoving one another as we burst into the large, round bedroom.

He lands an elbow to my ribs and forces his way past me. A snarl builds in my chest. The sound dies when a high, desperate keen spills from the attached bathroom.

Fucking *fuck*.

Whatever Micah and Knox are doing in there must be right up her alley because this whole empty room is *soaked* in cinnamon and sex.

Given the fact that there's water running... if she's in it, we shouldn't even be able to scent her out here. But every breath is a burst of warm sweetness, rolling over my tongue.

Zane's waxed, deep-tan chest heaves. His dark eyes flash, locking on the open doors across the suite.

"You know her better than I do," he grinds out. "Do you think she would care if we walked in?"

I'm pretty sure she would *like* it. The piece of paper clutched in my fist has a lot of group activities on it—and I know Emma has always dreamed of pack life, just like me.

Probably because we both came from such happy families.

I stuff down the bitterness that tries to creep up at the thought of my dad and his bullshit. Or big, burly Theo, barking at *my* omega.

Zane mistakes the sudden singeing of my scent for aggression. He scoffs, rolling his eyes. "Chill, I'm not going to fight you, Hockey Boy. I think we're both too late to get to her first, anyway."

He has a point. My dick jerks in my boxers as another loud moan echoes off the bathroom walls.

It's too much for me. There's a steel cord anchored in the aching place where good things used to reside. It pulls me over, my feet shuffling across the barren floorboards.

Hooooooly—

It's like I've stepped into the hottest, wettest fantasy my fucked-up brain could muster. Micah sits on the wide ledge of the tub with his legs spread, Emma's blonde head bobbing over his long, dark thickness.

His hands are all over her, one supporting the back of her neck while the other cups her swinging, pink-tipped tits. He murmurs directions and praises her, working his hips into the fingers she has wrapped around his knot.

Pride simmers in my stomach. *I taught her that.*

That knowledge quells a bit of the sting when I see Knox nearly balls-deep in her pussy.

Just a bit.

But still.

He's being gentle, rocking his cock into her pretty pink center while he pets her hips and strokes the line of her spine.

"So beautiful," he grunts. "Taking two cocks like Daddy's *good fucking girl*."

Jesus Christ.

I slept in for an *extra thirty minutes* and now Knox is *Daddy*?! I can't turn my back for two seconds around these fuckers.

Sparks snap in Zane's gaze as he watches, his jaw ajar. He starts to step closer, but his foot finds a discarded pair of sweats... with a scrap of blue lace tangled in the legs.

He inhales sharply, muttering, "You thinking what I'm thinking?"

There's no way I am. My jaw clicks. "I'm thinking I want to fight you," I growl. "And hold you down while I come all over *my* omega's panties. To show you who she belongs to."

And *now* I'm thinking maybe there's something wrong with this other alpha. Or something *right*.

Because he groans, a waft of spice filling the space between us. When it mingles with Emma's perfume, a moan of my own snags in my throat.

Shit. Her scent really is melting my mind.

I shake the thought off, loosing an outraged growl when Zane bends to snap up the panties. A rush froths through my middle, the roil of competition mixed with my Alpha's insistent need to possess every piece of Em. Even her blue panties.

"If you don't give me those," I warn. "You're going to *have* to fight me."

Micah's strained laugh interrupts us. "Would you two"—he chokes, his head falling back—"*shut up*?"

Knox fucks Emma faster. When she pops off Micah's dick to whine, his expression softens. Gathering her hair into a ponytail, he gently turns her head in our direction.

"Look," he murmurs to her. "Those two are so hard for you; they're about to fight for your underwear, omega."

Molten desire flares in Emma's green eyes—and it's *so hot,* I can't fucking breathe.

...but it's the *surprise* I see there that rips the air out of me. She seems *shocked* that we could actually want to watch her like this.

What the hell did that other pack do to make her feel like this? Am I really going to let her walk around with this doubt?

My Alpha roars, raging. *I don't fucking think so.*

I've already let her think I didn't want her once before. I will *never* let that shit happen again.

So I pin her gaze with mine and shuck my underwear.

Her brows curve, those plush lips falling open even further. Micah takes advantage, using his knuckle to collect pre-cum from the shining head of his cock and feed it to her at the same moment I drop my fist to my knot.

It's *screaming*—hot and swollen, throbbing for the tight suction Knox is pounding into. He growls, a low sound that pauses me and my Alpha completely.

He turns his intensity from Zane and me to Emma's slack features. "Can they watch, honey? Is that something you want?"

The tidal wave of cinnamon-sugar perfection that crests in the air is enough for all of us to pant. "Okay," Knox roughs out, working his hips faster. "They can watch you take Daddy's cock."

"Maybe you should punch me," Zane croaks. "I think I might be dreaming. Or dead."

With an obliging shrug, I throw my fist into his arm.

That does it. Zane bares his perfect teeth in a snarl. "Hockey Boy, if you want to keep your dick, you better—"

I snatch the panties right out of his grasp, wrapping the silken blue material over my pulsing knot, making sure it cups my balls, too. Until her cinnamon slick is soaking into my whole package.

"I better what?" I taunt, stroking myself. "Let you have these without a fight? Not a fucking chance."

His brows crouch. "I saw them first. You can wait."

But my Alpha isn't going to let that slide. And this pumped-up high I get from competing for Emma's favor is the closest I've come to feeling alive in a long time.

A glint of mischief moves over Zane's—admittedly—handsome face. "We could share them," he suggests, shucking his sweats and stepping closer to me. "She wanted to watch two alphas jack each other off."

That's true. Besides, at this point, if the fucker wants to try to take these panties, he's going to *have* to rip them off my dick.

Micah growls while Emma licks the underside of his bobbing erection. His hazel eyes slide over to us, narrating for her. "Zane and Gunnar are going juice each other's knots. Let me come for you, sweet girl. Then Knox can turn you around so you can watch."

Her shriek is desperate enough for all of us to rumble in reply. She takes Micah deep into her throat—*okay, I did* not *teach her* that—and he pulls her ponytail, arching her neck for us to watch as he comes in her mouth.

Holy fucking—

Emma drinks him down, moaning. Knox mumbles soothing praises, effortlessly looping his thick arm under her tits and pivoting her in our direction.

Micah swallows hard, his chest still rising and falling too fast as he sinks into the bubbling water and slinks to her side, dropping grateful kisses along the side of her head. I don't miss the way he offers his forearm to pad her elbows against the hard edge of the tub, either.

Hell.

Do I *approve* of these guys?

I think I might.

Just as well, since one of them is about to wrap his hand around my dick.

"*Fuck*," Zane grunts, stepping up beside me. "I am rapidly devolving into an absolute simp."

Same, bro.

Emma's round, glorious tits are on full display, jiggling as

Knox rails her from behind. I grit my teeth, riveted to the sight of her throwing her head back, her puffy lips ringed in an "O" as she moans.

Zane's hand snaps over to my groin, going right for the panties wrapped around my thickening knot. The edges of my vision start to blur as he plucks one of the leg holes off me, hooking it around his own cock.

I've always thought of myself as pretty well-groomed, but this guy's shit makes me look like Tarzan. He is *waxed*—entirely smooth, with every vein standing out in sharp relief. Even his balls look unwrinkled, tight and full. The whole damn thing shines like it's been oiled.

Who the hell *is* this guy?

When he catches my mouth falling open, he shoots me a smirk. "Problem, Hockey Boy? I figured this way, we can race. You jack me off, and I'll touch you—whoever comes first gets to paint the crotch of these pretty blue panties. Get their scent all mixed in with our omega's."

Ah hell.

The smug light in Zane's dark eyes tells me he knows he's got me. My dick twitches, swelling thicker, until the material stretched between us is taut.

Because it's Zane, I expect another cocky tease. But he surprises me with a rough, solid tone that sends a tingle down my spine. "That's a good boy."

Okay.

Fuck.

Guess we're learning a lot of shit about ourselves.

My stomach drops, freefalling, until the bastard's mouth quirks back up. He's used his grip on my shaft to re-align us, turning so Emma can see most of my front and most of his back, while still having a perfect view of the sliver of space between us... where her panties span the gap.

"This is my good side," he explains, shrugging. "Angles are half the battle, babe."

Before I can decide whether to growl or laugh at him, he tightens his fist and *tugs*.

It's nothing like Emma's soft hands, but something about the savage way he goes for it makes me snarl. I rut into his fingers, circling the smooth base of his hard length, feeling it fill and stretch.

Emma cries out, watching. *Fuck, she's so perfect.* Looking like a goddamn dream while she lets Knox fuck her raw. Smelling so sweet and warm and just—

Zane uses his free hand to cup my balls.

Then he squeezes.

I gasp, my cock buzzing as pain and pleasure shred through my core. The fingers milking my length speed up, chasing the tingle that pounds along the hardness.

Fucking fuck.

I've never done anything like this with another alpha. The instinct to fight swarms my blood, clouding my mind.

With a menacing flash of my teeth, I use my left hand to grip his knot and balls, cupping both just as hard as he's holding me. The swollen mass at the bottom is hard *as fuck*.

When a pained moan rips from his throat and his head falls back, his cock gets *harder*. "*Shit*," he pants, wide eyes dropping to watch as his dick drips chai-spiced pre-cum, begging for more. "I just had her yesterday. I didn't realize I was already so—"

He's fucking *throbbing* is what he is. His balls are so full, I can barely keep them curled in my fingers while they pulse and draw up. They're nearly as solid as his knot, which is insane, considering I can feel it getting firmer with every breathless second.

"You're hard up," I grumble, releasing a bit of the pressure I applied. "This must hurt."

I see the way he winces, darting his gaze down to look at his angry dick and then over at the sight of Emma licking her lips.

Fuuuuuuuck.

He moans again, his knuckles kneading my panty-wrapped knot. My own fingers tighten in reflexive retribution, and his hips kick, thrusting into the pressure. His brow creases as he focuses on the glide of my hand and the panties between his skin and mine.

He hisses just as a particularly loud keen echoes from the bathtub. Knox has Emma's legs spread wider now, his head tipped back, and his legs half-submerged in the hot water while he holds her ass against his groin and grinds the edge of his knot over her clit.

Just imagining her slick core, gushing around his dick, has my cock jerking. Zane's does the same, twitching within my grasp.

I take advantage of the glorious visual we have and start stroking him firmer and faster. He sucks in a deep breath, his chest vibrating on a growl while his jaw clenches. "*Fuck.*"

I almost laugh, but then he twists his wrist, working the plump, purple head of my cock more directly. The tip is swollen enough to ache. And the feeling of his hot palm rubbing underneath is enough for my balls to pull up.

Shit.

I'm not sure I can hold out, which was the whole point. *I wanted to paint her panties.* But this motherfucker must be melting off my competitive edge with his hot hands because I suddenly want nothing more than to prove I can make him lose his shit before I do.

It isn't difficult, actually. Within a minute, Zane's neck arches, his head dropping back on a long groan, his dick pounding into my fist like he's rutting Emma's sweet little pussy.

It's nowhere near as good as that, I know, but feeling him tense and grunt next to me is its own sort of reward. *That's right,* I think, remembering the way he called me good boy. *Come for me, you smug bastard.*

As if he hears my taunt, his black eyes flare with aggression—then smolder with lust when he flings them to our beautiful omega. I stare, too, losing track of where I am and what's happening. Only caring about the firm glide of the silk-covered hand around my cock and the sight of Emma thrusting back onto the other alpha's dick.

Micah reaches under her body to rub her clit, sucking soft bites into her shoulder while she screams.

Matching moans of desperation tumble out of Zane and me as we jack each other harder and faster, watching Emma roll into her own climax. When I hear Knox's vicious curse and Micah's hoarse cry, I know she's squirted all over them the way she came on the bathroom floor for me.

Fuck.

FUCK.

"Come here."

I yank Zane closer. He must be as crazed as I am because he doesn't even hesitate. Understanding flashes through his eyes, and then he's stepping so close, his knee goes between mine.

I don't care. If I don't come, I'm going to die.

We both move with more urgency, paying no mind to the way our knots brush and our balls swing into each other. If anything, the small jolts of sensation just make this better.

Zane bites his lip, bending his knees to bear down against my palm as he starts to lose control. I growl at the thought of him painting Emma's underwear before I can and fuck his fist harder, imagining the walls of her wet pussy fluttering around my cock.

"Fuck, Gunnar," he mutters, hunching closer as his mouth drops open. "*Yes.*"

Cum erupts from his cock, the warm white spilling over both of us. It lubricates his hand, giving me the perfect slip to rut into. Within seconds, I pull back just far enough to cover his release with mine. Until the soaked blue fabric stretched between us *drips.*

Holy shit.

We blink at each other. And I feel my stomach clench... until Zane cocks a grin at me, exactly the way Emma did our first night here.

"Correct me if I'm wrong, Hot Shot, but did you just *lose*?"

The tightness in my middle dissipates as I snarl at him, releasing my half of the blue panties so they snap wetly into his groin.

He just laughs, flickering an affectionate look over to our omega. She's all wrapped up against Knox's chest while he buries his face against her shoulder and tries to piece his brain back together.

Same, bro, I think again.

Same.

chapter
thirty-four

ZANE'S SMILE really ought to be illegal.

Combined with the fact that I've literally *never* seen him wear a shirt, the beautiful flash of his perfect teeth is lethal to my brain cells.

Well, the two brain cells I have left after what happened in the bathroom.

I still can't decide what my favorite part was—the feel of Knox's fingertips digging into my hips, Micah's nuzzles and kisses, or watching Zane and Gunnar race each other to orgasm.

Having all of them naked at the same time essentially turned me into a moron. Maybe that's why I agreed to Gunnar and Zane's insane suggestion.

Now, Micah and Knox are both standing at the corner of the kitchen island, staring down at the tattered scrap of purple paper.

Gaping, really.

My scent singes a bit as I back into Gunnar's protective embrace. His arms are thick and strong, snuggling me while he scent-marks my neck with his forehead.

He's been so affectionate since I got out of the bath, barely letting me out of his sight when we all shuffled off to find another round of clean clothes. Thankfully, I have my luggage—including my own yoga pants, a red Christmas sweatshirt, and fuzzy, light-up reindeer socks.

I probably should have quit while I was ahead—I mean, *seriously?* Pro hockey's most handsome player still wants to snuggle with me while I'm makeup-less and wearing a sweatshirt with a giant Santa face on it? But then the guys pulled me aside to sheepishly confess that Zane had found my list hidden in Gunnar's pants.

The way they both husked and growled about how hot it is convinced me they might have a point. Besides, they might still see each other as competition, but my Omega hates the idea of creating division among any of these alphas. It wouldn't be fair for only half of them to know about it.

I want them all to get along. Especially if we're staying together for my heat. When Zane pointed out that a literal *list* of common goals would be good for that purpose, I had to admit he had a point.

How better to get them all on the *same page?*

Pun absolutely intended.

It all seemed fairly simple, then, but watching Knox scowl and Micah's eyes widen while they each scan over the paper practically leaves me vibrating in place.

It's hard to be *too* regretful when Zane grins at me again.

"*Shona,*" he says softly, cupping his hands around my face and dropping a warm kiss to my lips. "You must be hungry, huh? I want to make you something good."

He's been cooking non-stop for days. When I can't resist his offer of maple bacon and fresh pancakes for brunch, I insist on making dinner sometime in the next few days.

He agrees with one of those silken winks, nodding at Knox and Micah. "Of course, gorgeous. Assuming those knot-heads haven't died from shock." He leans closer, muttering out of the side of his mouth, "Is Micah even breathing?"

I turn into Zane, laughing, and his dark eyes melt. "Beautiful, happy girl," he praises, rubbing my cheek with his.

Gunnar hums his agreement, breathing deeply as my scent sweetens. Behind me, the thump of his heart starts to slow.

Knowing I can relax him actually relaxes me, too. And—stupid, *I know,* but—I think I'm starting to feel safe with him. Like he really does want me and like me.

Or maybe even *needs* me?

The soft kisses he places against the slope of my shoulder make all of that seem remarkably possible. Especially when he purrs and whispers, "You feel so good, Em. I think I've been missing you since before I even met you."

My Omega still has a lot of feelings about that, but even she starts to soften as he purrs for me. His vibrating chest breaks up the last of the tension locked around my lungs, turning me into mush while I watch Knox step back from my list and raise his piercing gaze to mine.

Whatever he sees on my face tightens his. He speaks in his rough timbre. "Come here, little omega."

Without releasing me, Gunnar walks us forward, putting me between two powerful walls of alpha muscle. Knox nods at him in acknowledgment before grasping my hips and lifting me onto the countertop beside Micah.

The fireman pushes my list to the side and takes advantage of being a step closer than Knox, swooping in for a hot, wet kiss. By the time he breaks away, we're both panting.

"Sweet girl," he breathes, "you surprise me in all the best ways."

Knox grunts in *agreement*, stroking my hair back.

He's not angry or annoyed? Or even disapproving?

He's... *possessive*.

That same lustful pride I saw all over his face earlier blazes back to life. "I love your list, little miss, but I hate that any other alphas have seen it."

His absolute attention settles into me like a key sliding into a lock. It unlatches my voice and words just pour out of me.

"None of them wanted to look at it. So you guys are the only ones who have seen it."

Collective anger stretches taut across the room. My gaze falls to my lap, but I feel them all turn to look at one another.

Zane's buttery purr starts up. Gunnar's hand slips lower, rubbing the small of my back as Micah touches the space between my shoulder blades. But Knox flexes that weighted blanket of reassurance he has.

"I don't want to *look* at it," he says, growling. "I want to *destroy* it. Scratch every last thing off. Twice."

Zane appears behind the alpha, flashing a grin while he claps Knox on the back. "I'm with the Grinch."

Gunnar's purr replaces Zane's, pressing into my arm while Micah cocks his head, musing, "We've already ticked a handful of things off."

The hockey hot shot flashes his rare smile, hooking his arm around me tighter. "Dibs on number eight."

chapter
thirty-five

TOTALLY NOT SPAM

MICAH

Zane, man

There's no easy way to say this but...

I found a video of you spanking bacon.

GUNNAR

uh

what?

ZANE

yeah...

About that...

KNOX

"Spanking bacon" as a literal thing or a figure of speech?

GUNNAR

I'm actually not sure which one is worse.

ZANE

It's ACTUAL BACON

MICAH

attached video

It really is.

KNOX

what the hell am I watching?

GUNNAR

ZANE WHAT THE FUCK

MY EYES

ZANE

yes, it is difficult to take in my physical perfection all at once.

You managed just fine the other day, though.

MICAH

Are you seriously trying to change the subject

As if I'm going to forget I've seen this*:

Attached video

KNOX

Are you fingering a coconut?

Dear God. Is this what you meant by "influencer"?

ZANE

Yup!

MICAH

He's pretty good, actually. 24 million followers. And... whatever this is: *attached video*

GUNNAR

Is that a carrot?!

ZANE

Mm. Not as good as the one with the sausage imo

MICAH

yeah I have that one too. And the one where you lick all that whipped cream off that one drink.

GUNNAR

WHERE ARE YOU FINDING THESE?

ZANE

Be a good boy, Hot Shot, and I'll send you my handle.

But how *did* you find them, Micah?

MICAH

My brother sent them to me. He recognized your name.

Btw he wants you to sign his ass.

ZANE

Shit, I don't have my Ass Sharpie with me up here.

Got one I could borrow, Daddy K?

KNOX HAS LEFT THIS GROUP CHAT

LET ME TELL YOU SOMETHING. Training to become a firefighter wasn't exactly a walk in the park. There were burns, smoke inhalation, bruises, scrapes, and scars.

But nothing—*nothing*—I dealt with could have prepared me for *this*.

"What *is* it?" I mutter, poking my fork at the vaguely meat-like substance floating in a dark-orange sauce. Or, bobbing, more like.

Zane swallows hard, his dark gaze skirting from the omega humming at the stove to the table between us. When he winces, I empathize completely; everything is laid out so beautifully that it clenches my gut.

Emma spent two days planning this dinner. She worked so hard, scrolling through recipes while we all orbited around her, doing our best to keep her happy and entertained. Most of yesterday consisted of lounging on the couch for her favorite Christmas movies, watching cooking tutorials on YouTube.

She also spent most of today shooing us all out of the kitchen before excitedly calling us back in several hours later. Now, none of us can tell what, exactly, she's served.

Thankfully, our sweetheart is oblivious to the strained hush looming over us. She bops along to the Christmas music playing through her phone's speaker while she plates up one last item.

Knox's eyes go from soft to squinting as he turns from her smiling profile to the dish in front of him. He cocks his head, considering in his stoic, silent way.

Gunnar touches the tines of his own fork to the saucy mass on his plate, gnashing his teeth in a grimace. "She said she was making Zane's favorite."

Zane's eyes bug out of his model-like face—a surprisingly ugly look I'll have to remember to chuckle about later. "This is supposed to be *Swedish meatballs*?"

I look back down at the gloopy orange sauce, my eyes rounding. "Oh, boy."

I've only had Swedish meatballs at Ikea, but this looks *nothing* like that. For one, our little omega made five giant meatballs instead of giving each of us several small ones. And then there's the color... and the consistency... and—*oh, shit.*

"What are those black flecks floating in the sauce?"

Ever the competitor, Gunnar's the only one who's forced himself to take a bite. He's also turned a white-gray color. "Something charred," he coughs, covering his mouth. "*Fuck*."

Knox chances another glance at Emma before shoving his mega-meat-mound to the side of his plate, revealing the white gloop underneath. He scoops some up and shoves it into his mouth while she has her back turned.

"And potatoes." He manages to turn his choking gag into a throat-clearing cough. "I think."

The music abruptly cuts off. Emma whirls, catching all of us with our forks poised to poke at the meatballs some more. The sweet, trusting girl doesn't even notice, though. Her brows fold over her green gaze before bouncing back up excitedly.

"My sister is calling!"

Knox, God bless him, sends her a steely beat of alpha power. "Go talk to her, honey. We'll wait for you."

It's impossible not to smile at the way she jumps and scuttles out of the room, slipping on her fuzzy reindeer socks while she swipes the call on. We all watch her leave...

And fly into motion.

"Holy fuck," Gunnar groans, scrambling to the kitchen trash can and spitting into it repeatedly.

Zane snatches his dish and mine, nodding at the others while he hisses, "Hurry! I can make sure they're cooked through, but we don't have much time!"

I jump up to help him hustle to the stove. We both frantically unload the meat mountains into the dirty pan Emma left out. Gunnar makes another retching noise, the sound almost drowning out—

Holy shit.

Is Knox *laughing*?

chapter thirty-six

I ADMIT, begrudgingly, that I owe Zane.

It took a little longer than I expected to get all my hockey gear out of my Jeep and shlep it around Knox's big-ass house. It took even longer not to trip in the snow every six steps.

Now that I'm back on ice, with my beloved skates strapped to my ankles and the two travel goals I brought with me to keep my game sharp, I feel more like myself than I have in days.

Trudging around in frozen muck might not be my forte, but on my blades? I move like a totally different person.

That was one of the reasons I fell in love with the game. My mom used to smirk at me after pee-wee practices and fondly asserted that I should have been born on two skates instead of two feet.

Maybe that's why I'm out here in the freezing cold, hoping Emma will play with me. It started out as an apology—one of a hundred I hope I'll be paying back for a very long time. But now that I have a stick in one hand and the brand-new women's skates I brought all the way from Florida in the other...

Am I doing this to say I'm sorry? Or show her that I'm not always such a pathetic grouch with balance issues?

Can it be both?

When I text Zane to tell him everything is in place, he answers within a minute. I mentally put more points in his column; although when he leads our omega out of the house, and I sense his chai scent *all over her*, he definitely loses at least half a tally.

His wolfish smirk says just how sorry he is.

Or *isn't*. At all.

Emma might smell like some decadently spicy version of a classic cinnamon bun, but she's also smiling. Despite having Zane's hands clapped over the top half of her face while he guides her through the snow.

"Careful here, gorgeous," he mumbles, directing her around a branch. He places a reassuring kiss and a nuzzle against her temple. "Just a few more steps."

Jesus. He's... sweet?

I shake off the strange squirm in my stomach. Which is pretty easy to do since, ten seconds later, the guy winks and offers me an even bigger shit-eating grin. "I have a delivery for you, Hot Shot."

With a roll of my eyes, I glide forward, coming to the edge of Knox's frozen pond. "Thanks," I mutter, taking Emma's mittened hands. "Now beat it."

He smiles wider. "With pleasure. Our girl's tuckered me out. I need a nap."

Her cheeks glow pink, but he drops his face to her neck, scent-marking her with a whisper I don't quite catch. Whatever he says has her beaming as he takes his palms off her eyes and starts making his way back to the cabin.

Emma blinks a few times, her eyes refocusing in the late-morning light. I watch her, mesmerized. It feels like my first time seeing the sunrise, drinking in every stray beam of light that catches in her curls or soaks into her jade-green irises.

She's so fucking beautiful, I almost forget I'm in the middle of a romantic gesture here. With a swallow, I lift my left hand to show her the skates dangling from my fingers.

When I packed an extra set for this trip up, I scoffed at myself. It was a stupidly hopeful thing to do—why would the girl I'd accidentally pushed into the pool want to come skating with me?

I had to train, but she didn't. And why did I think she'd want anything to do with me at all, let alone skating drills?

I couldn't explain the impulse to plan for something that, surely, would remain an insane pipe dream. Yet here I am, on my own well-loved set of blades, offering the new pair to Emma.

Might as well be my heart on a freakin' silver platter.

I've spent enough years using hockey to pull chicks—so I'm fairly sure I'm about to get one of two reactions. She'll either squeal like I've splattered her in pig's blood and pretend she needs me to teach her how to skate... Or she'll act coy and bat her lashes as some sort of tease.

Honestly? With Emma? I don't think I'll mind either way.

Instead, she completely surprises me.

Her chiming laugh breaks the tranquility around us. A heart-stopping flash of competitive fire burns across her gaze as she lunges forward to snatch the laces right out of my hand.

"Oh, you're going *down*, Hot Shot."

IT SEEMS, in all my angst about lusting after Theo's little sister, I forgot that she's—

Well.

Theo's little sister.

She trash-talks like a *pro.* Bounds head-first into dangerous maneuvers with zero hesitation. And laughs her way through every slip and skid.

Emma clearly sucks at skating, in general, and hockey, specifically. She can barely turn in a circle and has to use her borrowed stick to keep herself from unintentionally sinking into splits, but she has so much *fun* that it's impossible for me not to have fun, too.

My skating drills are a lot more limited than usual with the pond's forty-foot diameter. She cheerfully heckles me through all of them, anyway.

"Is that all you got, Sinclair?"

"My grandmother shoots better than that!"

"Once I figure out how to hold this stick and balance at the same time, it's *over* for you!"

All her banter would amuse me anyway, but the fact that her voice is chipper and she alternates her taunts with genuine cheers has me laughing until I'm breathless.

When I finally chuck my stick and loop around her in a smooth circle, she drops hers, too, falling hard against my chest. I catch her with another chuckle. "I don't get it—are you cheering me on or insulting me?"

She shrugs, smiling wide. "Both, I think. My Omega likes insulting you; I like cheering you on. This seemed like a good time to combine the two."

"Mm," I hum dryly, tucking my lips into a thin line. "You gave her my message?"

She nods, suddenly serious. "No luck."

My lip quirks up. "Guess I'll have to try harder."

Still as solemn as our sweet, silly girl can get, Emma nods again. "Afraid so."

It's odd, but suddenly, I'm not afraid. This whole day—setting up the goals, sharpening the skates—I've felt nervous and out of my depth. Now, as I gaze into Emma's eyes and see the hurt swirling there, I just feel the steady weight of determination.

I cup my hands around her chilled cheeks. "Hold still."

She does, clinging to my hips to keep herself upright while I hunch to murmur to the shapeless-but-very-real instincts that make up her essence. "I'm still here, Omega. Not going anywhere without you again." A bleak smile flickers across my face. "Happy to grovel on my knees anytime."

For once, Emma doesn't laugh. Her small, wool-covered hands brush my dirty-blond hair back. When I glance at her face, I find her lower lip wobbling.

Fuck. Folding her into my chest, I squeeze her close. "I promise, Em, I'm going to make this up to you if it's the last thing I do. I can't even tell you how fucking sorry I am. I've been—"

Lost.

Grieving.

A black hole.

She trembles slightly, her gaze wide and earnest as it skirts up to mine. My heart cracks, staring down into that vulnerability. Every instinct I have rears back from burdening her.

"It was a really long, really hard year," I finally rasp out. "But, please, give me a chance to prove I can do this. Let me stay with you for your heat. And every other heat. I want to show your Omega I'll never abandon her again."

Emma's answering exhale quivers. "Sh-she says, 'bring it on, Alpha.'"

My face splits into a smile. "That's my girl."

Her hands wander down the small of my back, reminding me that I have one last surprise in my back pocket.

Extracting the dark green sprig from my sweats, I hook its red ribbon around my forefinger and hold it between us. Her face lights up, sending a fresh pang through my chest.

"Mistletoe! Ooh!"

Before I can make a move, she bounces up, planting her lips over mine in a kiss that's all enthusiasm and zero finesse.

My little sunbeam.

Heart swelling, I clutch her closer, fisting her coat with my free hand and sealing our lips together. She whimpers into my mouth, gliding her tongue along mine until we're both breathless.

The scent of warm, gooey cinnamon buns winds into the frigid air. When she shifts her weight, pressing her thighs together, my Alpha snarls.

When she senses the shift in my mood, mischief glints in my omega's eyes. She leans back, reaching to take the mistletoe from my fingers.

"Did you say you were happy to grovel on your knees?" she asks, cocking a sunny smirk.

I nod. "More than happy."

"Hmm." Emma arches a blonde brow, slowly bringing the bundled leaves between our bodies. Until she's holding it over the apex of her thighs.

Getting on my knees to kiss her pussy? Oh fuck *yeah.*

"You sure?" she teases, tilting her head in a coquettish gesture. "The ground out here is pretty co—"

She doesn't get to finish her last taunt because I'm on her before she can blink. And as I scoop my girl into my arms and skate to the edge of the pond, I know with absolute certainty:

My heart might be a shredded mess, but it's beating. Bursting. Bleeding.

For her.

chapter
thirty-seven

KNOX

THE WONDERFUL, dangerous thing about Emma is her contagious *spirit*.

She's just so damn hopeful... after a week or so, I started feeling like all my concerns could melt off my back. As though, maybe, she was right to be so positive and optimistic.

I really should have known better.

I *did* know better, damn it. But the omega's big green eyes and the guys' encouragement had me questioning my judgment.

I feel it the second I wake up, though.

The sensation of someone tugging at the edges of my sanity. Swiping it away, strip by strip. My blood ticks under my skin, buzzing in my dick and pounding at my pulse points.

Fucking hell.

A rut.

I haven't had one in years. Back then, I rode them out alone, with that damn sex toy Emma found. I barely remember the last one, but afterward my bedroom was ripped half to shreds. I must have made a hell of a ruckus, too, because McKinley was in his crate downstairs and he *still* wouldn't look at me for two days.

Remembering my own dog, unable to look at me, gores a corkscrew into my gut. I don't want Emma to avoid my gaze or tremble when I come near her.

And I would *never* let myself rut her.

I told the guys as much last night. They all seemed convinced that they could handle me if it happened during Emma's heat, but this is *exactly why* I can't commit to being there.

My instincts are too demanding. My Alpha is too strong. And if I don't get the hell out of here, I'm going to end up hunting the little omega down and—

No.

Go.

The force expanding in my center fights me on every step. Somehow, I wrench myself forward, following familiar steps by rote.

Front closet.

Boots.

Coat.

I can't pause. Can't let myself think about the cinnamon soaked into the room or the purple paper with her list on it. Especially can't let myself remember one of the lines on there.

Have an alpha during a rut.

Fuck.

Go, go, go.

I don't have much time. The soles of my feet tingle, every cell vibrating in protest when I don't turn for the stairs. The edges of my vision have already melted into a blur. My teeth *ache* to sink into the omega's thin skin.

Painful hardness throbs against the press of my sweatpants, an answering jolt of discomfort lodged into my core. My knot is already solid and thick, begging for the press of Emma's sweet, slick heat—

Fuck.

Go.

The bracing mountain air helps for a moment. Long enough for me to haul myself away from my house, heading for a familiar hiking path.

Maybe, as long as I'm in a place I know well, I won't wander too far.

It's worth a shot. I refuse to be anywhere in the house when I'm like this. Not with Emma there, where she could see me or hear me or—worse—somehow get barked into doing whatever my Alpha is about to demand.

The thought makes my blood run cold. It's a strange sensation, with my skin burning while my core smolders like a furnace.

Every staggered step is another slip of the knife in my chest. More proof that I can't do this. Handle this. Not without turning into a beast and imposing my whims on the others.

And Emma.

God, I would strangle myself on my own leash before I ever dreamed of touching her when I'm—

"Slow," a distant voice chirps, panting. "Down!"

I freeze, fresh horror contorting my middle.

The sweet, innocent little miss trailing behind me uses the opportunity to scurry closer, until I can make out the gleam of her wide, trusting smile.

"Sheesh," she huffs, "For someone with fifteen years on me, you can really move. We'll have to tell Zane that 'gramps' isn't a good nickname. Grinch probably still works, though."

Hearing her happy musings, inhaling the light, creeping scent of her joy... Fear free-falls into the pit of my stomach and hits bottom, exploding in a gruesome splatter that has me wheeling on my booted heel, snarling.

"You need to *leave me alone!*"

Fuck.

Her face.

A thousand arrows soaked in alcohol would sting less than the way her chin wobbles when her mouth starts to tremble. And *ten-*thousand stab wounds would be better than the honest hurt that flashes through her eyes.

My Alpha roars, shoving me even closer to the edge, snapping at the reins. He thinks *he* can fix this, the stupid, senseless bastard. He thinks *I'm* the problem, keeping him from showing this omega how much we want her and care about her.

Jesus.

Is he right?

Emma shrinks back a step, her rosy lips furling closed like a rosebud trying to shield itself from the elements. "O-oh," she stammers, small. "All right. I—I'm sorry. I saw you walk out from the window in your bedroom, and I just thought we could—"

She thought I'd want to spend time with her. Give her my full attention, the way she seems to crave so fiercely. My poor, sweet little thing.

If walking away before felt wrong, this feels impossible. My instincts sense my weakness and lunge, nearly ripping my control away.

But her *scent.*

It drops past singed, or even burned. Into an absolutely horrifying... something. More burned than tinder, more sour than vinegar. Sad and embarrassed and so heartrendingly *surprised.* Then, ashamed.

It's *rejection.*

I don't get to think before I move. My brain blinks off until I feel her skin under my fingertips, cupping her cool hands inside the heat of mine.

"It isn't you," I rough out, half-growling. "I woke up on the edge of a rut. I'll take care of it—but, please, you need to go back to the house."

Hell and damnation, but she's the *single sweetest person* in the world.

The notion of me rutting her into oblivion doesn't even make her *flinch*. Instead, true eagerness fills her face while she makes a soft sound of sympathy.

"Knox," she whispers, glancing down at the ram-pole in my pants. "That must *hurt*. Are you *okay*? Do you want me to—"

I snap my palm up to cover her mouth, glaring. I don't mean to, but some part of me knows that if I hear her offer anything specific, I won't be able to walk away.

"No," I rasp, swallowing painfully. "No, honey, I don't want you to stay. It would fucking kill me if I hurt you or made you do anything you didn't want to do. I don't trust my Alpha like this. He could bark at you, and you wouldn't have a choice. I'll never allow that."

Emma gazes up at me with all sorts of things swirling in her green eyes. Affection and trust and worry. Arousal, too, God help me.

Her pupils dilate; the faintest traces of perfume leaking through her tight leggings and tiptoeing into the frigid air. I'm thankful for the thick fabric and the way this weather suppresses her scent. Almost as relieved as I am when she steps back again.

She doesn't go, though. Instead, her head tilts slightly, sending blonde curls over the shoulder of her pink sweatshirt. "You want to rut me?" she says slowly, "but you don't trust yourself?"

Patience. She's going to leave, and we can go.

"Right," I bite out.

She rolls her lips together, the smell of her arousal flaring into something richer and warmer. *Good fucking God.*

"You *want* to chase me," she breathes, "pin me down, and rut me... but you won't let yourself?"

"Yes," I practically roar, my chest heaving. "Now, you need to—"

She takes off.

Just... *runs*.

Not toward the house and the safety of the others. But right past me, into the thick forest surrounding us. The one that's blanketed by freezing snow and full of places for her to trip and get hurt. Full of animals, too, who could scent her and come looking for cinnamon buns for breakfast.

My brain registers the danger while my body reacts to her disobedience, getting harder and hotter. The instincts chained in my center let out a war cry, snapping the binds like dental floss.

Until I turn and chase.

chapter
thirty-eight

LOOK, I'm not going to defend myself here.

Clearly, I'm too stupid to live in the most literal of fashions.

Charging head-long into the actual wilderness, dodging tree stumps, and tripping over snow-covered roots while I scramble away in some sort of insane attempt at baiting Knox's Alpha?

It is *dumb*.

I know that.

But is it really my fault that so many reckless, unintelligent things appeal to my Omega?

Well, in this case, it's more than just an appeal, I guess. More like an imperative.

She straight-up needs this alpha to rut us.

Mostly, I suspect, because *he* needs it.

The pack he almost formed all those years ago had no right to make him feel like the villain in their story. If they couldn't step up to a man as dominant as him, or if they didn't want to, then fine. But making him feel like some sort of heinous monster who would hold people against their will?

That isn't Knox.

Everything I've seen in the last week has shown me who he really is. And he isn't a beast.

His Alpha, on the other hand...

The deep *roar* that echoes behind me sends a flock of birds flying for their lives. Can't blame them there—I *want* to be chased and the sound still makes *my* blood race.

I zip into the trees, my feet moving faster than I thought they could. I'm still me, though. So, a lot of tripping contributes to the momentum I gain while throwing myself down the sloping, slippery landscape.

Footsteps pound behind me, gaining. My pussy clenches in answer, slick sliding into my panties, perfume curling behind me.

Another growl shatters the peaceful forest, impaling my throat with a bolt of wanton want. The thick throb of my pulse echoes between my thighs, my need thickening when Knox finally gets close enough for me to smell his concentrated cedar musk.

It fits, out here. Almost like the whole dang mountain exists just to suit him. And me. And this.

Which, turns out, does not make him any less intimidating.

He snarls, only a few meters behind me now. My nipples pebble at the sound, and it's like he *knows*—because the second they prick up, he tackles me into the snow.

Tackles.

Me.

A bright burst of happiness lights my chest. Enjoying our game, I start to laugh, squirming away from him. A sharp whine follows my giggles when he clamps his huge, warm hand around my shoulder and flips me.

The world rolls in a swirl of magical white and panty-melting pine. When I blink, I find myself on top of Knox's broad body, pressing my palms into his pulsing chest.

His eyes are wild, the blue a thin band around his blown pupils. He glares up at me with a snarl. The grip on my thighs tweak a smidge too tight, and I wince, automatically reaching for his face.

When I smooth my fingertips along the corner of his mouth, touching his dark beard, he goes from angry lust to pained longing.

My poor alpha.

"It hurts," I say again, trailing my other hand down to his pants, hunting for his waistband. "Let me make you feel better, Alpha."

His chest heaves. Confused indecision splits his expression— those burning eyes that want to devour me and the grimace on his lips that tells me Knox is still in there, somewhere, fighting his instincts with every ragged breath.

"I *want* you to rut me," I confess, the muscles of my inner thighs flexing under his fingertips. "I'm soaked in slick *for you*. Do you want to see?"

That does it. Whatever thin tether he had to sanity snaps.

And the Alpha emerges.

Knox's black eyes spark. He bellows, lunging upright. I squeak as one calloused hand tugs my hair, baring my throat to his mouth while his free fingers rip at my clothes.

The scrape of his teeth over my pulse sends a skitter down my spine. I gasp, falling into his rough touches, relishing the drugging submission that thickens my blood.

It feels so good to let him do whatever he wants with me. Almost as good as feeling his desperation—the burning need that has him biting bruises into the thin skin of my neck and ripping buttons off his own shirt.

My hands slip into the open fabric, skimming his sides, feeling the purr that rattles under his endless growls. That sensation sinks into me, too. I moan softly and press my aching core against his hardness.

With an animalistic snarl, Knox yanks my leggings down as far as he can with my thighs spread. His muscles bulge as he lifts me high enough to wrestle the pants to my ankles, then lays my lower back on his hard thighs and raises my hips in the air.

What the—

His hungry expression makes complete sense a second later as he bends my knees around his head and *dives* for my pussy.

Oh holy *night.*

This big, vicious alpha is locked in his first rut in *years...* and he wants to *eat my pussy*?!

Plot twist.

I barely have time to be surprised before he's there, opening his hot mouth over my spread lips, groaning. I whine as he finds my slippery core, delving his thick tongue into my squelching heat.

When I tremble around him, one of his enormous hands spreads over the top of my mound, covering my lower belly. He hums—a still-growly but definitely-sweet sound.

Comfort.

His Alpha is trying to comfort me.

Wetness glazes my eyes while more slick seeps from my slit. He moans again, the palms spread over my stomach and under my ass pressing tighter and maneuvering me even closer.

I drop my head back against his shins, crying out when he noses at my clit. It isn't intentional, which just makes it hotter, somehow? Because literally *all* this man currently cares about is lapping up the taste of me.

The thought has me perfuming more, gushing against his open lips. Slick dribbles down his beard, and he bucks under me, rubbing his cock against his seam.

Oh. Right.

The whole point of this is definitely *him.*

I whine, putting a little extra oomph into it, knowing it will snap his attention up from my pussy. When his hazy eyes meet mine, I lick my lips. "Can I present for you, Alpha?" I ask breathily. "Please?"

He wants it. I see the way his bleary gaze suddenly snaps with fire. But when he starts to roar out a reply, he suddenly chokes himself into silence.

I swear, something pained passes over his eyes. Because he doesn't want me to present? Or because he wants it so badly that he feels wrong opening his mouth and essentially making me?

If I know Knox, it's the second one. Which is silly, because I'm obviously offering.

He's spent a long time telling himself he couldn't have any of the things he used to want, all for the sake of never accidentally hurting or scaring anyone.

How does he not see how good that makes him?

He's perfect! my Omega squees, hearts throbbing in her eyes. *Take his knot and tell him to bite you!*

The thought alone has me slicking right in front of his face. When his gaze snaps to the evidence of how much I want him, a low, dangerous rumble shakes his chest.

"*Omega. Present.*"

Hooooooooly fu—

Okay.

OKAY.

He wasn't exaggerating. Not even a little bit. Because the second the bark hits me, I blink and find that I'm already on my knees.

Which would be great, except I had the stupid idea to go running into the woods like a lunatic, and it is *cold* out here, guys.

Fiddlesticks.

My palms burn as they sink against the snow. Not ideal, but nowhere near as bad as my knees. Probably because my lower half is so much larger than the top—

Oof!

A hand lands a hard slap to my rear. Then another.

He wants my attention.

My heart melts, and I look over my shoulder to reassure him. Knox is as handsome as he is intimidating—a big, barrel chest covered in coarse, dark hair. Every muscle and line on his face pulled taut. His pants torn down, and that world-ending knot ticking fuller by the second.

He's *magnificent.* The sort of alpha any omega would die to be on their knees for.

I reach back to stroke his wrist. "It isn't you, Alpha," I explain. "I'm just chilly. But I want you to rut me now. Please?"

His jaw ticks. Without a word, he bends and tugs my leggings back to my knees, bunching them under my bare skin. He nods at the towering sycamore tree in front of us, barking roughly. "*Hands up, omega.*"

I don't get to realize what a brilliant idea it is until I'm in position. My brain just glitches. One second, I'm on all-fours, and the next time I open my eyes, I'm stretched between the wide warmth of the hands on my hips and the not-quite-as-cold wooden trunk.

A growly purr fills the still air between us. I feel his eyes on my backside... and everything below it.

"*Wider.*"

I love his commands. His power. I don't have to think at all. He tells me what to do, and my instincts do the rest.

When I obey, pumping out more cinnamon-sugar perfume, his purr drops lower and grows louder. One of his hands floats up to trace my spine.

"My omega," he grunts. "So good. You're going to take my knot."

I am, I am, I AM.

Everything inside of me screams, and I keen, shoving my hips back, trying to follow his order.

"*Yes,*" he mutters, almost to himself. And then he slides in.

All. The. Way. In.

I take his thick cock and huge knot with a breathless sob, my inner walls slipping and squeezing in frantic clenches. He gives another of those soul-deep war cries, sinking against my ass until there's no space left between us. Nothing else for him to give me.

Then he moves.

Every sizzling nerve inside of me sparks against the thick friction. His knot catches right where I want it, pulsing and tugging at the pleasure points ringed around it. More slick gushes around us, the sound wet and filthy as he pounds his hips, relentless.

The forest around me melts and swirls while I mewl. This is a rut. No hesitation or thought. Just him, mindless with need, shoving in and out of me as much as he can with this glorious knot trying to seal us together.

And—*oh my God*—I'm not gonna make it.

Guys. *I'm not gonna make it.*

I'm going to die when this orgasm hits me because nothing can possibly feel this good without killing you, right?

He growls and bellows every time I tweak tighter around his girth. The hand on my spine snaps up to fist my hair, turning my head. When I feel his wild eyes graze my face, my core starts to convulse.

"*Omega,*" he hisses, his thrusts growing sloppy and desperate. "*Come. Come on this knot. Never stop.*"

And I do.

I am.

I come and come and *I can't stop.* The pleasure doesn't end; it's a mindless spiral that sucks me into its vortex and then keeps right on spinning.

I'm vaguely aware of the hoarse bellow behind me. The fingertips bruising my sides while the alpha jets hot streams of cum into me. So *much*—it glazes my insides until wetness leaks around his knot and starts to slip down my thighs, along with my slick and the release I'm squirting all over both of us.

Still.

Because I really can't stop.

A hard twinge of pained pleasure tweaks around him,

squeezing in frantic pulses until he barks again, much softer, "*Enough, honey.* You'll hurt yourself. *Enough.*"

My palms slip against the sycamore tree; my eyes blur as they fall shut. And my last thought is that the rutting alpha I want more than anything sounds just like the man I'm falling in love with.

chapter
thirty-nine

I WAKE up sore and stiff in the oddest places.

My memories are hazy and halting, but mostly, I remember pine and snow and Knox's rough hands and rougher voice.

He knotted me, I recall, feeling something thick and firm wedged up in me. *A while ago, I think...*

When I open my eyes, I see that it has, in fact, been a while. The picture window above the jetted tub shows a wide, twilight swath of sky.

I blink up at it, letting myself float in a daze while I remember Knox rutting me up against half the trees we passed. Then, carrying me, still knotted, up the house... where he spent the rest of the day inside me.

Now, it appears we're taking a bath.

My mind moves sluggishly, piecing everything together. Whatever rut blockers he normally takes must have worked somewhat because he had brief lucid moments throughout the rut.

I sensed him in there, too. The man worrying about me, holding his Alpha back from issuing as many commands as he could.

When I feel the way Knox's fingers trace gentle circles on my scalp, I know he's back to being himself. The purr rattling under my cheek isn't unfamiliar, after the way his Alpha rumbled for me —but it *is* new for me and *Knox*. I press my ear into his chest, curling closer in his embrace.

"You awake, little miss?" His voice is hoarse from all his roaring, but I get the feeling he's quiet for another reason.

Did I upset him? Or disappoint him?

Maybe he's angry that I ran?

He shifts us, arching his neck to peer down at me with intense blue eyes. "Tell me," he says, rougher than before. "How bad is it?"

How... *bad*?

"W-what do you mean?" I ask, my own voice raspier than usual.

Knox frowns ferociously. His hold on my torso tightens slightly—and I feel what he's referring to. Because all that time I spent? Knotted on his cock and being carried through the woods with his rock-solid forearms bracing under my belly?

My middle maaaaaay be a little sore for a while.

Not to mention my slightly battered pussy.

When I think about it, a small quiver runs through my inner walls. They twitch around his length, letting me know that, yes, they are sore—and, also, yes, we would like some more.

I feel my cheeks heat when Knox groans, the noise pained. "We're already going to be locked together until morning, little miss," he husks out, grinding his jaw. "Best not make it any harder, hmm?"

Normally, I'd make a joke about that—I mean, *"make it any harder"*? Come on.

But his blazing blues snap back to my face. His features settle into a stony mask. "Tell me," he urges again. "How much did I hurt you?"

He's *scared*.

That's what this look is, this smoldering wood scent. The second I recognize it, I twist at the waist, reaching for his handsome face with the one hand that can reach.

"You *didn't*, Knox. You didn't hurt me. I'm *fine*."

His eyes squeeze shut, and he huffs a breath out of his nose. He turns into my palm, kissing it before he nudges it with his nose as if to say *See? Look.*

Okay, okay, *fine*. There are a few superficial scratches from holding onto tree bark, but nothing *painful*. The same sensation in my core and abdomen—the sense that my body's been used and has used someone else's. *Thoroughly.*

"It really doesn't hurt very much at all," I promise, flexing my fingers for him.

He pins me in place with his gaze, solemn. "It didn't *have* to hurt at all, honey."

Hearing that somehow feels worse than any of the bumps or bruises littered across my pale skin. When I whine and turn away, he wraps his arms around me again, hugging me to his purring chest.

"I never wanted you to see me like that," he whispers. "I barked so many times. You didn't have any say—"

His voice breaks off as my scent swells—sweetness swirling into the smoldering cinnamon. I feel his breath catch behind me as I hang my head, hiding the way my face flames. "I—I liked that. Not having to think. It was..."

Freeing. Invigorating. Comforting.

I felt so desired. Needed, even. And then, also, completely cared for. To the point where I didn't even have to *think*.

Knox doesn't answer, though I feel him staring at me. After a couple long minutes, I finally glance up and peep, "Are you mad?"

Our eyes meet. And I know—*I know*—he sees everything. The desperation to please him. The totally humiliating need to gain his approval. The fear, too, because he isn't the first alpha I've tried to please, and if I failed today... then, well, that wouldn't be a first, either.

Knox sighs, his muscles flexing protectively around me. "No, baby girl," he murmurs, dropping a stubbled kiss to my shoulder. "Daddy isn't mad at you at all. Come here, hm?"

His knot is finally loose enough for me to gently turn around. The second I do, he wraps me tight into his damp chest and guides my face to his throat, purring louder than ever. His fingers go back to massaging my scalp.

"I don't know what I did," he mutters, relaxing incrementally.

Honestly, it's all a blur to me, too. I wonder which part he can't remember. "In the woods?"

He shakes his head, turning to plant a kiss on my forehead. "No, honey. I don't know what I did to deserve you."

My heart catches, its pulse snagging over the impossible words.

Him? Deserve... *me*?

When he has all of this wealth and power and alpha energy... when he literally rescued me...

I throw my arms around his neck, hugging him hard. "Knox," I choke, crying. "Does this mean—will you stay with me? For my heat?"

Knox holds me so tenderly, more tears gather in my eyes. He scent-marks my cheek with his, nuzzling our faces together with a soft groan.

"Fucking hell," he grouses, serious as ever despite the fact that his scent is practically glowing right now. His voice drops into a whisper against my lips. "Yes, baby girl. I'll stay with you for your heat."

My face splits into a sobbing, beaming grin. I rear back, ready to kiss-attack his scruffy face—

—when all three of my other alphas burst into the bathroom.

With Zane leading the charge. Naturally.

"Daddy's *in*?!" he whoops, grinning with his trademark exuberance.

Micah rolls his eyes and smiles at Zane before shooting us a wince. "Sorry. I tried to keep them out of here, but they were"— Gunnar shoves past the others, crashing to his knees beside the tub and frantically reaching for me—"climbing the walls," Micah finishes, sighing.

Gunnar ignores them all; his gaze locked on my face while he glides his touch down my back and my arm. "Hey, squirt," he mumbles, clearly stressed. "You okay? Do I need to kick some alpha ass?"

Knox harrumphs, and I giggle. "You could *try*," I tease, darting an affectionate look at Knox. "But you'd risk breaking your winning streak, Hot Shot."

"Too late," Zane crows, clearly still pleased with himself. "I did that already, remember?"

I feel the man under me stiffen and cuddle closer to him again. "Besides, Knox was perfect."

Zane laughs, the sound warm and musical. "Oh yes. A perfect, rutting *gentleman*."

Micah rubs the back of his head, still grimacing. "We... might have overheard. A bit. A lot. It—We were just trying to ensure Emma was safe, Knox."

The alpha holding me releases a deep breath under his purr. He brings his hand up to cup the back of my head while Gunnar scowls at the faint pink lines on my hand.

"Thank you," Knox roughs out. "I hope you'll be willing to do it again during Emma's heat."

Micah is so kind; it makes my heart swell. He offers Knox a true smile, totally devoid of any judgment or annoyance, and nods. "Yeah, man. No problem."

Everything inside of me tightens and *sings*. Because—*oh my God*—is this really happening?! Are they all getting along, and... are they all *staying*?

Zane catches my bewildered disbelief and offers the soft smile he reserves just for me. With much more grace than my clumsy hockey player, he sinks to his knees beside Gunnar and kisses my nose.

"Mm, *shona*. Cinnamon and pine needles. You smell like a Christmas tree."

Gunnar's folded brows un-quirk long enough for him to slide Zane a look I can't quite decipher. "Maybe we should get one," he mumbles, sheepish. "A Christmas tree."

Zane's answering grin *dazzles*. He loves that idea as much as I do. I reach over and touch his cheek, letting him leave his spicy scent-mark on the back of my knuckles.

Micah shrugs, looking to Knox. "I could help chop one down. You only have about two thousand out there."

Knox glowers, but his scent is fresher and more wonderful than ever as he hugs me tighter, examining my eager expression. His lips almost flick up before he sets his features into their usual sternness, casting me a very *Daddy* look.

"We'll see, little miss," he allows, tucking me closer to his purr. "We'll see."

chapter
forty

I REALLY WANT to be better than this.

This seethe in my gut. The way my eyes slide toward the stairs or the ceiling—or, now, the back door—every few minutes.

Micah finishes restoring the couch to its proper order. He seems to be the self-appointed guy-who-keeps-everything-together. Which is probably a good thing because Zane is oblivious to messes, and I'm...

Useless.

Depressed.

Stuck under the dark cloud that's followed me for months. The one that colors everything around me in these mottled shades of gray I loathe so much.

I thought I had army-crawled out of this barbed-wire cage. It has been a few days since I felt the spike sinking into my skin.

But now? They're back.

I hate this. Before the mind-fuck of this year, I knew who I was. What I wanted and what I thought about shit. Now, it all seems hopelessly layered and also, somehow, completely meaningless.

Except for Emma.

Which makes today a problem.

"It's only been one day," Micah reminds me. "This is normal pack-alpha stuff."

But the irrational anger and swirling helplessness thickening my throat aren't appeased by the knowledge that ultra-dominant alphas often "hoard" their omegas after knotting them for the first time. Not even a little bit.

"We aren't a pack," I snap back.

At the same second Zane calls from the kitchen, "Who made *him* the pack alpha?"

Micah chuffs, rolling his eyes as he falls back onto the sofa. "You guys are kidding me, right? Knox could put any of us on our asses. Of course, he'd be the pack alpha. Fighting that would be like trying to fight the sun."

Sunshine.

Emma.

Everything feels so dismal without her here. How the fuck am I supposed to go back to real life when her heat is over? What am I going to do if she doesn't come with me?

Am I really even willing to leave if she wants to stay here?

What about my career? My apartment? Her whole family, back home?

Zane mutters some shit under his breath, balancing three plates and three mugs of coffee between his bare arms and his naked chest while he saunters into the living room.

I reach for the closest cup, and he kicks at my shin, frowning.

He juggles everything to hand me a different coffee. "This one is yours, Hot Shot."

I look down into the dark liquid, confused, until the scent of hazelnuts hits me. Zane finishes laying the plates out and cocks a glossy black brow at me. "You *like* hazelnut, right?"

I do. It's my favorite.

When I nod, he shrugs and sits between me and Micah, spreading his thighs to lean between them and start on his breakfast. "Then you're welcome, Hockey Boy."

He shovels two bites into his mouth before realizing Micah and I are staring at the back door. "They still out there?" he asks around some toast.

I grunt, and Micah nods. Zane doesn't seem all that bothered —maybe just slightly tweaked if the way his muscles swell is any indication—until he really *looks* at me. I feel his dark eyes on my face, my hands, the slump of my spine.

"Well, fuck." He mimes, punching his own hand, setting his modelesque face into a menacing snarl. "Let's go kill him."

For a second, I gape. But the motherfucker is committed to the bit, glaring like he's some sort of mercenary and not a half-naked half-chef wearing truly ridiculous fur booties.

Before I know what's happening, I laugh. Just a chuckle, at first, until Micah guffaws and joins in. Zane's face drops back into his easy grin as he reaches over and squeezes my knee. Only for a second, because in the next breath, he's on his feet, stretching his exposed torso into a lean arch of deeply tanned muscle.

"Seriously, though," he says, gesturing toward the doors. "Fuck it. Let's go out there and say good morning. He can't hog her forever."

He and Micah exchange a glance that tells me everything I need to know—*they* can stand this, but they know *I* can't.

And right now?

I think I'm too pathetic to care that they're only pretending to be as bothered as I am.

We leave our food behind, each of us stumbling into our

outerwear. Well, I stumble, at least. Micah can get his on and off in three seconds, probably because he's used to doing it with a fire alarm blaring. And Zane, of course, has no shirt on. Just a big-ass pimp coat made of the same fur lining his feet.

Jesus.

What is my life?

Knox and Emma took the dog for a walk, so we know they're nearby when we step out onto the back porch and McKinley comes wagging over. Zane drops right to his knees and smiles widely, cooing at the dog the same way Emma would.

McKinley's tail goes wild, his whole rump wiggling while he licks the model's face. And, fuck, it's almost enough for me to smile.

Until Micah sighs, the sound deeply exasperated. "Looks like they're busy."

I squint across the gleaming white landscape and spot Knox and Emma wrapped up together against the trunk of a nearby maple tree. Jealousy floods my gut, tightening around my insides like a choking vine. My Alpha bucks and roars, urging me to fight and claim and—

"Hey."

It's Zane, rising back to his full height and frowning at me. I open my mouth to try to explain, but I don't know how to tell him that the little omega currently too wrapped up in another alpha is the first thing that's made me feel good in months. I can't find words for how irrational I know I'm being... and how much I really, actually *can't help myself.*

He stares for a long moment, those dark eyes examining. So much deeper than I gave him credit for. Deeper than he gives *himself* credit for, maybe.

But simple, too.

Because instead of questioning me, he jaunts down off the porch and bends to a snow drift that's built up against the side of the house. He scoops up a big ball of snow, rolling it tightly between his bare palms, winds his arm... and lobs it straight at Knox's head.

My mouth drops open.

"Oh fuck," Micah snorts.

Knox freezes, huddled over our omega, then very slowly turns his head. Furious and definitely shocked, too. I'm sure it's been a minute since anyone stepped to him.

Even from across the huge yard, I see his shoulders bunch. Murder flashing in his blue eyes.

But Emma *laughs*.

A bright, peeling sound. As pretty as any bell and completely infectious.

Micah starts chortling, and Zane joins in. When Knox scowls at our little omega and she giggles louder, I find myself chuckling, too.

Adorable mischief lights her green eyes while she skirts them to mine, leaning up on her tiptoes to whisper something to Knox. The big, lumberjack-looking fucker softens, his broad back relaxing...

Until another snowball hits him between the shoulder blades.

This time, Micah's the one who straightens and shrugs. "Looked like fun."

"Give us back our omega!" Zane calls, lobbing another.

Knox lifts his arm and the snowball explodes against his forearm. "You fuckers will have to come take her," he growls, to Emma's obvious delight. She throws her head back, blonde curls bouncing and shimmering in the morning sunlight.

Sunshine.

That's what she is to me.

Even just standing here, looking at her, I feel warmer. I can *see* clearly, too. Things aren't a dark swirl of gray anymore.

Drawn to her, I make my own snowball and start to cross the expanse between us. Knox sees me coming and throws a wad of slush, aiming for my face. While I'm dodging that, another one hits my side.

Gaping, I turn and find that Emma has snuck out from Knox's clutches. And now she's ducking behind some shrubbery, laughing maniacally.

Fucking *cute*.

"Is that funny, squirt?" I call, tossing a much smaller snowball her way. "You think you can beat all of us?"

Micah throws one at her, and she squeals, laughing more. Zane joins in, his own musical laugh layered over hers. "Of course she can! That's my girl!"

My Alpha chuffs at that, but I resist the urge to turn this into a pissing match. Emma is having *fun*. And the way she glows when she's happy fills places inside me that I thought were dead.

Trudging through the half-foot of snow on the ground, I somehow manage to avoid her snowballs and not fall on my ass. I trip twice, but still.

When I crash onto the ground beside her, she instantly jumps into my arms, hugging me tight around the neck. "I missed you," she breathes.

I'm grateful my scent is back to its usual nutty sweetness. I don't want to burden her with my shit. And she doesn't deserve to feel guilty about helping Knox through his rut or how possessive he's been since knotting her.

Zane is taking care of that, I'd say. Thrashing the older alpha with snowball after snowball, shouting nonsense taunts while he dances from foot to foot, only narrowly avoiding getting nailed in return.

Having grown up nearby, Micah is clearly the only one around here with any snowball fight experience. He dives behind a different shrub and gestures to the two of us, silently urging us over to join him.

Emma's bright, beaming smile has me on my hands and knees, shuffling behind her until we reach her hazel-eyed alpha. He has way more chill than me, for sure. With a contented smile, he scent-marks her forehead, murmuring his nickname for her. "Sweet girl, you look happy."

When she nods wholeheartedly, Micah grins. "Should we let Gunnar help us, or is it every man for himself?"

Emma tucks her hands behind her back and shrugs, still smiling that goofy, wide grin. "I guess you two can form an alliance if you want... but I'm taking you all down!"

With that, she reaches out with two handfuls of snow and shoves one down each of our collars. Freezing muck hits my spine, and I curse, falling onto my front while she gives an evil villain cackle and scurries away.

Micah follows her, pausing long enough to haul me up. "On your feet, man! This is war!"

But it isn't. It's... *fun*.

We all run around the yard like idiots, slipping and flinging snowballs at each other. We fall into clusters sometimes, but betrayal runs rampant. Emma is the worst of all, sidling up to each of us in turn and giving hugs until she decides it's more fun to smush snow on our heads.

We chase her and swing her around. Tackle her and roll her under us. McKinley even joins, running after each of us and nipping at our heels when we try to capture his beloved omega.

Micah builds snow forts with alarming efficiency. Zane kicks them down. Knox can take any hit without even flinching, but I have the best arm and the best aim, lobbing Hail Marys that land more often than not.

Emma is deeply terrible at every aspect of this game. The fact that she doesn't give a shit and somehow has a better time than anyone else is exactly why I love her.

Laughter and insults and *more* laughter ring over the side of the mountain. Until we're all dizzy and breathless, collapsing into the middle of the yard.

Knox goes down first, and Micah follows, flopping beside him. Zane slinks next to the older alpha, leaving one blank space for me.

Emma crashes onto my chest and I catch her with a huff, snuggling her cold body close. She buries her nose against my neck, humming happily. Something deep inside me clicks back together—tension I didn't realize I was holding seeps out of my lungs.

When I exhale and turn my head, I find Zane watching the two of us with a fond look on his face. He reaches his hand over and pets Emma's mussed curls into place...

...then he lifts his palm and ruffles my hair, too.

"Good boy," he mouths, doing that wink thing that he always —don't ask me how—pulls off.

I glower at him, rolling my eyes, but that only cracks his grin wider. He leaves his hand in the snow next to my crown, and Micah reaches backward to slap it in a high-five. "Great work, Z. Solid snowball fight."

Knox watches all of us with his sharp eyes, taking in every little detail of each exchange. I know he doesn't necessarily like other people, but I have to say, for a self-professed hermit, the guy has crazy insight into other people.

He probably *would* make a great pack alpha—though, whatever he thinks he's seeing when he narrows his eyes at Zane's hand flips my stomach into a somersault.

A buzz interrupts us all trying to catch our breath. Micah pulls his phone out of his pocket. The light, airy scent of mint and frost immediately plummets into something sharp and *cold*.

Emma lifts her head from my chest, eyes wide. "What is it?"

Micah frowns at the screen. "It's the road. They fixed it. We're all free to go."

chapter
forty-one

AM I proud of the way I had a whining panic attack in the middle of the backyard?

No.

Does being snuggled between Micah and Zane on the couch make the whole ordeal worth the mortification?

Yes.

Which I am also not proud of.

Zane's spiced skin is like a tranquilizer. I snuggle my cheek into his pectoral, and he presses kisses over my forehead. "My poor gorgeous girl," he murmurs. "No one is leaving you. I promise, I promise."

They've *all* promised, repeatedly. And I believe them. No matter how naive or needy that makes me, I really do.

My Omega is frantic, though. She wants us to bite them and bond them *right now*. To be sure that none of them would *ever* leave us.

When I quiver, Zane cups my chin and tilts my head back. His hypnotic gaze swallows mine. "*Settle*, baby. I'm here. *Settle*."

The oh-so-gentle bark winds through me like novocaine, numbing the anxiety vibrating around my lungs. Micah presses his purring chest into my back, nuzzling at my nape. "I'm so sorry, sweet girl. I didn't mean to panic you. No one wants to leave."

Gunnar is positioned on the table across from us, his thighs spread, and his elbows on his knees. He watches me with worry in his gray eyes and creases pulling at his lips.

After a long moment, he looks at Micah. "Did you say there was a town up the mountain?"

My fireman nods. "Yeah. My hometown. Why?"

Gunnar shoots a quick glance over his shoulder at Knox and suggests, "Let's go into town. Zane can get all the fancy groceries he's been clamoring for, and we can buy some Christmas decorations."

My Omega practically spasms at the thought of leaving this house. Partly because, deep down, this all still feels like a dream.

If we go out into the real world, will they all wake up?

Look over at me and realize I'm not their mate?

That this was all a big, situational case of group insanity?

What if we come across a better omega—or one they wouldn't have to share?

Maybe some pretty, hometown omega will catch Micah's eye.

Or another traveler for Zane.

Or—

Gunnar gives a distressed grunt, dropping to the floor between Zane's legs and rubbing my back while he holds my face with his free hand. "We don't have to go anywhere, sunshine," he says, soft. "We'll all stay right here and snuggle you all day long."

My chest snags on a ragged breath. "S-sunshine?"

He doesn't explain. He just nods emphatically and kisses my hand, murmuring, "*My* sunshine."

Something about those words, combined with the steady weight of his gaze and Zane's drugging scent... More of my tension unwinds. My mind processes what everyone just said without the fuzzy, vibrating lens of panic, hearing things I didn't before.

My head whips to the side. "Micah, did you say your *hometown*? Like where you went to high school and had your first kiss and learned to ride a bike and *everything*?"

He flashes a mildly sheepish smile, rubbing the back of his buzzed hair. "Yeah. I, uh, never left."

I never left my hometown either. My parents eventually moved to a cooler climate, but my brother and I both loved Florida too much.

Thinking of Theo puts a lump in my throat. He texted a few days ago to tell me that they all made it home. Their football team lost a home game yesterday, but he didn't care. Meg seemed closer to labor every day and I could practically feel his excitement vibrating through his messages.

Lucy has also been in touch. She texted to tell me the "whole wedding situation" was "handled." Which is very Olivia Pope and totally on-brand for my boss-babe sister. She also told me that my parents are worried about me, but she "had them under control."

I'm telling you, I really came from the shallow end of that gene pool.

Micah's soft hazel eyes land on mine, beaming pure warmth at me. "My brother might be around. I know he would love to meet you." His full lips quirk as he tosses a look at Zane. "And you."

Zane grins, so unbelievably beautiful it *hurts*. Part of me is a jealous psycho who hates the idea of letting Micah's omega brother meet my hot-chef alpha. Which is so crazy because Micah's brother is bonded and—you know—*his literal brother*.

In the sweetest moment of indulgent understanding ever,

Zane frowns mildly at my expression before telling Micah, "Maybe next time, eh?"

My firefighter catches up quickly, empathy filling his features. "Of course. Whatever you're comfortable with, Emma."

They're *perfect*. And I'm *crazy*.

My Omega needs to *chill*.

Maybe my heat really *is* coming early, like Lucy suggested.

I actually do need a few things if I'm really going to stay here for all of that. Knox's bed will probably be fine, but I'll need some extra pillows to make it feel nest-y enough...and we'll have to figure out how the heck I'll make a pillow retaining wall and still have room for four grown men, but that sounds like a Tomorrow Emma problem.

It will be fine!

I can do this!

Daddy has to say yes first, though. Especially since I have no money.

When I chance a glance across the room, I find Knox scowling at his phone for the first time ever. He's on it so little that I almost forgot he had one.

As soon as he feels me watching, he looks over and nods. "You can go into town, little miss," he gruffs. "I keep accounts open at the local shops. Just tell them to put whatever you all need on my tab."

My heart sinks. "You don't want to come?"

A grimace pulls at his bearded mouth. "Not today." He flicks a stern look at Gunnar. "And don't get any Christmas shit. Food and nesting supplies only."

Suddenly, the air in the living room feels tighter. Is he not planning for us to be *here* for Christmas? Is that why he won't decorate? He wants us to leave right after my heat?

I thought yesterday—showing him I could handle his Alpha and the guys showing they could stay alert to monitor his rut—changed things. I thought, maybe, he'd started to believe we could really work. As a pack.

But he doesn't look at me now. His eyes drop back to his screen, and he nods toward the front door, putting just enough bark into his next command to make it impossible for all of us to ignore. "Y'all go on. Get out of here."

chapter
forty-two

EMMA HAS to be one of the most resilient people I've ever met.

I turn my head every few moments to watch the way she gazes out the window of my truck with the sweetest half-smile on her face. Even after getting her spirits crushed by Knox, she somehow finds a silver lining to trace.

She loves this wintery landscape. That's the other thing I admire about her—she never hides how she feels or pretends to be "too cool."

Her awe is written all over her features, turning the soft curves into something so open and lovely... I'll remember the way she looks right now for the rest of my life.

Gunnar and Zane jostle each other in the back seat. We made quick pit stops at both of the places they were staying before we got snowed in, picking up their stuff so we could move it into the cabin.

That was Zane's idea. He claimed he needed skincare supplies, but I suspect he knew the gesture of "moving in" would help ease some of Emma's anxiety about being abandoned.

My poor, sweet girl. On some level, she still doesn't believe we all want her.

Knox certainly didn't help by refusing to come with us. I know the guy is a hermit—hell, before this whole clusterfuck, I'd probably seen him around town a handful of times in the past five *years*. But he could have swallowed his issues to make this a little easier on her.

Staring at her face, noting the vulnerability in her crystalline eyes, I resolve to talk to the alpha when we get back. Maybe he just doesn't know what to do and needs some help.

There's a lot to think about with this not-a-pack situation. Especially since we have something so precious to protect and care for.

Emma's giddy joy makes it all worthwhile by a mile. When she sees the holiday garlands strung up over the entrance to town, the iron gate all trimmed in shimmering silver, she bounces in her seat.

"Look at the bells!" she cries, leaning over the dashboard. "And the sleigh! Oh my God—*is that Santa*?!"

"Oh boy," Zane chuckles, affection all over his face. "Why do I feel like Emma's about to end up in Santa's lap?"

Gunnar snarls. "She won't be in *anyone else's* lap."

Emma giggles at his grumpiness as Zane cocks a smirk at him. "What if *I* sit in Santa's lap and Emma sits on mine?"

The hockey player grunts, dropping his gray eyes and fidgeting with his matching T-shirt. "Fine."

I pull into a parking spot along the main drag—a wide brick-paved street between two rows of historic stone buildings. They all have the same rustic wood and wrought-iron accents the rest of the hamlet has—and everything is gilded in twinkle lights and greenery.

Emma's excitement is palpable. In her sweet scent, for one, but also the way she leaps out of my truck and practically twirls to the sidewalk.

The three of us smile while we follow her. Zane gets there first, taking her hand in a real dance move, spinning her into a dip and kissing her soundly.

When they break apart, he rubs his cheek against hers. "You're the prettiest, happiest girl, gorgeous. I love it."

The way she gazes at him is enough to break my heart. God. She just gives and gives, opening herself up for all of us without missing a beat.

"You do?" she asks. "I'm not... annoying you guys?"

A record scratches in my head. "*Annoying* us?" I ask, sure I misheard.

Gunnar pushes past me to snap her in a bear hug. "Never, sunshine," he vows. "We love when you're happy like this."

When he sees me looming at his shoulder, he turns and lets me wrap my arms around her, too. She lifts her face to look into my eyes, biting her plush lower lip. "I don't want to embarrass you."

Fuck.

I snap her into my arms, yanking her up so fast, her feet leave the ground and come to wrap around my torso. My palms frame her face as she clings to my neck.

"You are *not* embarrassing," I tell her, so firmly it's almost a bark. "None of us will ever be anything but grateful to be out with you."

The hope that sparkles in her eyes is enough to gut me. I can't imagine how cruel her previous pack was to make her so unsure of herself and her worth. This girl is resilient, like I said. Which means they must have been truly abusive to get to her.

I kiss her gently, nuzzling my face against hers. "Sweet girl," I whisper. "You're never more beautiful to me than you are when something gives you joy. I've been thinking that all day."

"Me too," Gunnar agrees.

Zane adds an insistent nod. "Me three."

I see Knox's name form on her lips, but she doesn't say it. I rest my forehead against hers, wishing we were bonded so I could reassure her, even in her thoughts. Wishing I was bonded to Knox's dumb ass so I could show him her face at this precise moment.

As always, Zane is the one who knows how to lighten her mood. He leans around my shoulder to smile at her. "I have an idea, *shona*. How about more Christmas cookies? We'll *destroy* Knox's kitchen and get sprinkles *everywhere*. He'll hate it."

Our omega nods, smiling but distinctly shyer than before. Zane's expression softens. "What about dinner, baby? I'll make anything you want."

"I can cook," she murmurs. "I probably should be doing it more—"

"No!" we all blurt.

Her eyes widen. Zane recovers first, shaking his head with a slick grin. "Nuh-uhh, gorgeous. You're the only one who enjoys my pretty face, so I have to find some other way to contribute to this pack. Besides, I haven't gotten to show off what I can really do yet. Now that I have access to actual groceries and not just what I have borrowed from the neighbors, prepare to have your panties melted off by my mad skills."

Emma's scent lifted as soon as he said "pack." *Sweet girl.* She looks a bit brighter when she smiles back. "Oh, okay. How about... tacos? Or macaroni and cheese? You can't make me choose; those are literally the two best foods in the world."

Zane scoffs. "Piece of cake. I'll even make them go together." He reaches over and grabs Gunnar by his coat collar. "Come on, Hot Shot. You're pushing the cart."

"I'm taking Emma," I decide, petting her hair back as my purr rattles. "I have something to show her."

———————— ♥ ————————

I CARRY my omega the whole way up the hill, just because I can. After spending the last day missing her, it feels so good to bury my face against her warmth and listen to her talk.

She loves the little town as much as I do. Maybe more, actually. She notices *everything*. Right down to the way I cringe when we pass the firehouse.

"My stuff is in there, so we'll have to stop on our way back," I explain. "My chief will want to meet you, too."

Emma's blonde brows bounce up. "Me? Why?"

I shrug. Darryl's known me and my family since I was born. When I called to beg for this odd stretch of pre-heat leave, he whooped and hollered about me finally having an omega of my own instead of "loaning myself out" like I used to at the local heat clinic.

"You're *my* omega," I tell her simply. "This is a small town. *Everyone* is gonna want to meet you."

She gazes up at me with her heart in her eyes. "Then I want to meet everyone."

Rewarding her with a series of kisses, I keep one eye on the path we're treading. When we reach the end, Emma squeals in excitement.

"Oh, Micah!" she gasps. "It's beautiful!"

The gazebo has been here for more than a hundred years, tucked up on a slope that overlooks the town. Every year, the most recent crop of high school seniors decorate it with any crazy Christmas decor they can find.

What started as a prank has become a tradition. One of my personal favorites.

This year, fat multicolored bulbs line every beam. Uneven clumps of rainbow tinsel cover all four corners. And laminated hand-cut snowflakes—all right, maybe a few dong shapes, too—dangle from every available bit of ceiling space over us.

A few of them brush the top of my head and I smirk, seating us on the bench that faces the main street, turning Emma so she can admire the view.

My body forms a cradle for hers while I wrap my forearms over her soft belly and set my chin on her shoulder. For a long moment, we're both quiet, staring out.

"Hey, Hazels?"

I turn to look at her face, seeing the small smile on her lips and the tears gathering in her eyes. She goes on without prompting.

"This is so pretty. No one's ever brought me somewhere romantic like this before. I—I really love it." She turns and nestles her cheek into mine, just in time for me to feel a tear leak over her pale skin. "Thank you, Alpha."

I'm in love.

I already was before, but now I *know* I am. There's just no one else like her on Earth. With a huge heart she gives pieces of to everyone she meets.

I love her.

"You're so welcome, love," I whisper. "Come here."

She kisses me, sliding those perfect pink lips between mine and melting against my chest. The second my tongue skims hers, a burst of cinnamon-bun warmth perfumes the chilly air around us. My cock kicks in my jeans, trying to punch its way out to her.

Emma feels me harden for her and moans, scraping her nails against my nape while our tongues glide together faster. Her scent deepens, plunging from light sweetness to dark, gooey perfection in two heartbeats.

The next sound she makes is desperate. I rear back and catch her bleary eyes, noting the way her pupils have yawned wide. "Are you okay, sweet girl?"

She bites her lip again while she glances down at my lap. "I think I'm having a pre-heat-spike. I'm sorry."

I shake my head, gathering her closer. "Don't be sorry. Your body is just getting you ready for us. I love it. Let me take care of you, okay?"

She hesitates for half a second before nodding. My mind reels, trying to come up with a private place to take her. *My apartment is on the other side of town, and the firehouse definitely won't be empty...*

Besides, it doesn't seem like time is on my side here. Emma's gaze has lost all focus by the time she turns in my lap and goes for my pants.

Shit.

I look around to ensure we're the only ones up on the ridge, thinking.

Exhibitionism was on her list. I think she actually wrote, "bang in public," but whatever. This would qualify.

"You want me right here, love?" I rumble, my purr kicking in. "Where anyone could see? You can ride my cock and rub your sweet little clit on my knot until it fills you too full to move. Or I could take you home first."

She whines, whether at the mention of "home" or because she just can't wait another moment, I'm not sure. Either way, I lift my hips long enough for her to free my throbbing dick and the partial swell at its base.

The second she sees it, her eyes light up, and I smile, my heart aching. I just... *adore* her. So much that every little expression on her face has me falling harder.

I help her strip her leggings past her knees, leaving her black panties on just in case. I'm happy to indulge her and make sure she has what she needs, but I'll be damned if anyone from town sees her pretty ass.

Fuck, but the crotch of her underwear is *soaked* in slick. When I tug it to the side for her, she instantly glazes my fingers with cinnamon sweetness.

I growl over my purr, snapping her hips forward. If she wants to play with the lines of propriety and feel like she's at risk of exposure, I'll make it my mission to give her that rush—even if I know she's totally safe up here with me.

"Do you think anyone will see me sink into this perfect pussy?" I ask, growling into the sensitive hollow under her ear. "If they do, I bet they'll be jealous. I would be, watching someone else fill you with their cum."

She keens and bobs her body, trying to find the head of my dick to slide down. I gentle her, grabbing a fistful of her curls and holding her steady while I guide her onto my erection.

Fucking hell.

Slippery heat strangles my pulsing length, her slick bathing my knot and balls as she sinks all the way to the hilt. When she writhes and bucks, her core clenches, tugging every electrified nerve buzzing under my skin.

My knot expands, filling to tug at the lips of Emma's pussy every time she pulls off of me. I pant, my head falling back while I fight not to come inside her just from that alone.

Her soft whine doesn't sound any different from the ones she makes when she likes what we're doing, so I'm not sure how I know something is wrong.

I just *do.* The second it hits my ears, I straighten immediately, searching for the source of her distress.

Emma rides me harder than before, but her unfocused eyes dart around the space between us. Like she can't find—

Me.

She's looking for me.

"Hey, hey," I husk, reaching for her jaw with both hands. "I'm here, love. I'm right here with you."

She slows as I nuzzle my nose against hers, holding on to her gaze until I see a distant sort of recognition sail through it. "Alpha," she says, her scent instantly brightening. "You're here."

My heart cracks. "Right here, love." I drop my hands to settle her torso against mine, holding her close while I grind up into her heat, vowing, "Never leaving you. Might never leave this pussy either. Going to fill it up and lock my knot in, keep all my cum inside. I want you to soak it up."

Let me breed you.

I know it won't do much now because she's protected by her implant—but fucking *hell*, the thought of marking her in such a primal way puts me right on the edge. I want to absolutely *glaze* her depths, until her little pussy is *stuffed full*. Then, I want to make sure none of it ever slips out.

My thrusts get more frantic. Emma cries out, diving for my throat. Her blunt teeth scrape my pulse and I snarl louder.

"Everyone's going to hear us, omega. They'll all wonder who's up here, making you moan, marking you with their cum. They'll all wish *they* were the ones sinking into this perfect body, feeling your slick all over their laps."

Emma's hips start churning, pulling at my pounding cock more urgently. Hissing, I tilt her pelvis to grind the edge of my knot against her swollen clit until it pops into place.

Holy fuck—goddamn it.

My roar is loud enough to scare anyone off. Surely loud enough for people down on the main drag to hear.

But I don't care.

I don't think I'll *ever* care about *anything* ever again.

Pure ecstasy echoes through my abdomen while Emma's body clutches at my cock and knot, milking them with rhythmic squeezes. The silken heat glides and throbs over me, drawing out my release almost instantly.

An erotic whine shatters the air as she starts to come, gripping me in a slippery vise that has my eyes rolling back. I jet cum into her core, working her hips in a circle to make sure she feels every inch of me pressed where she needs my knot. With one final, earth-shattering clench, we're both spent and locked together.

Emma hugs herself closer, tucking her thighs around my hips. I can tell her mini-haze has burned off the second she murmurs my name, exactly the way she did before. "Hey, Micah?"

I pet her hair, panting into it while I scent-mark. "Mm-hmm?"

She pulls back just long enough to show me her clear, brilliant eyes. "I love you."

chapter
forty-three

HOCKEY BOY IS TRULY a terrible sport.

Which is hella ironic.

"You know who you look like?" I ask conversationally, adding more chicken stock to our cart. "Grumpy Cat."

His glower intensifies, which just makes my statement more true. He denies it, though. "I do *not*."

"Sure do," I chip, counting limes. "You know, tacos aren't very festive for Christmas. We should get a ham. And some heavy cream. I'll make an actual holiday meal at some point."

Gunnar shuffles behind me, shrugging and sighing, but never outright complaining. I suspect he wants Emma to have a nice holiday, even if he hates this stuff.

"So, tell me," I go on, still aiming for casual. "What's the bah-humbug up your butt?" I inspect a truly beautiful beef tenderloin before chucking it into the cart. "Did you have an ex cheat on you at the company Christmas party or something? Wait. Do hockey teams have company Christmas parties?"

His brows lower even further. The guy's going to get crow's feet like Knox if he keeps scowling like this, I swear.

"No," he huffs. And I think that's it; until I see the way he swallows hard.

I stop, turning and giving him a pointed look. "Then what's your problem?"

Gunnar is actually really good-looking—but when he *glares*, it's pretty fucking scary. I hold my ground, though, invested.

We'll never be able to form the pack Emma deserves if we can't sort our shit out. Given that she's about to go into heat, he needs to exorcise whatever holiday demons are perched on his shoulders.

The longer we stare at each other, the less resolved he seems. Eventually, with a heaving sigh, he flings his eyes away and mutters, "My mom died this year, okay? And it's just weird. Doing Christmas stuff and knowing I won't—I won't see her again."

Fuck.

I drop the box of breadcrumbs in my left hand and lurch forward, dragging him into a hug. "Shit," I spit, guilt and worry washing through me. "Gunnar, man, I'm so fucking sorry. That —I had no idea."

He's stiff against me, but I don't let go. I'm going to hug this guy, damn it. He's clearly in hell and hasn't even told *any* of us. So, he's just been... alone in this? *The whole time?*

The longer I hold on, the more his muscles loosen. "When did it happen?" I ask.

His posture falls slack, swaying closer to me. "In June."

My eyes squeeze on a vicarious jolt of pain. "I'm sorry,

Gunnar," I say again, speaking over the lump in my throat. "I'll stop giving you shit for—"

I almost say "being an ass." But, really, he *isn't* being an ass. He's *grieving*.

His arms flinch, then slowly move to hug me back. *Holding on to me*, actually. "Don't," he mumbles. "I think it's actually helping."

I hold him right back, confused by the rattle at the base of my lungs. *The fuck am I purring for? And is he... reciprocating?*

Our bodies seem more comfortable with each other than we are. We sort of sink together in a way I've never experienced with another alpha.

He feels good, though. When I tuck my chin over his shoulder and he turns his face into my neck, I have the sneaking suspicion he agrees.

This big, grumpy hockey player enjoying a simple hug so much sends a pang through my chest. It's also sort of amusing, in a pleasant-surprise sort of way.

I laugh quietly, giving him one final squeeze before I step away, winking. "I'll keep fucking with you then. Emma can help me come up with some new material."

His cheeks are pink as he steps back, but he smiles to himself. "She'll like that."

I push our cart forward, distracting myself with the various brands of baker's chocolate lined up on the nearest shelf. I grab two of my favorite kind and realize, "You haven't told Emma yet, have you?"

He sighs at his feet. "No. I didn't want to ruin her holiday. And it feels like a piss-poor excuse for where I've been all year."

My brows arch because I personally can't think of a better excuse for falling off the face of the Earth. Emma would totally understand.

"I think you should tell her," I suggest. "I can help if you want."

Gunnar looks at me for a long moment. "Yeah," he finally says, like he's testing the taste of the word. "Maybe."

THE TOWN'S only nesting store is pretty... uh... sparse.

I wince while we wander the aisles, all three of us trailing behind Emma while she parses her limited options. This might be something for me to think about. If I'm going to try to stay with Emma, and Emma is staying *here*?

Well, I better start earning cashback on international shipping or something.

By the time we check out, I'm antsy and unhappy in a way I didn't anticipate. I like nice things, that's no secret—but it's more than that.

This is about Emma.

She deserves better than the four flat pillows and two threadbare blankets this place has in stock. I can tell her selections have stressed her out, too.

When I reach around her and hand the guy behind the counter my credit card—because Knox can *suck my dick* if he thinks he's getting credit for her nesting supplies without actually coming to the damn store—she says "thank you" in her small, uncertain voice. The one *I hate* because it means something is wrong and she doesn't know how to tell us.

I hug her from behind. "Don't worry, *shona*. I'll take you into the city before your heat starts, and we can get anything you want."

Gunnar slides my card back to me and puts his down. "Or we can order stuff," he points out, plucking up her hand to kiss her palm. "Whatever you want, squirt."

Micah drops his own credit card into the mix, as if he doesn't make a firefighter's salary. I snort and shove it back at him. Gunnar takes advantage and wins our squabble by tapping the keypad first.

"Dick," I chip cheerfully, per his request that I keep giving him shit.

He rolls his eyes with a smile while Micah snatches Emma away from me. "Hey!" I protest, whirling. "You already got your time!"

That was clear the second we saw them. His frosty scent and her warmth were mingled into a very festive blend. Then our excited omega told us they'd scratched exhibitionism off her list.

Honestly? Good for Micah. I didn't know the noble, nice guy had it in him.

Whatever they did left the biggest smile on the guy's face. Every time he looks at her, he practically melts.

I mean... *same*.

Emma sort of loves it when we fight over her. She tries to bite down on the sly little smile that crosses her face, but I love it enough to keep up our tug-of-war all the way to the truck.

Micah finally wins because he has to drive this monstrosity, and our princess gets shotgun, of course. Still, the way he buckles her in and then pauses to make out with her for two minutes is just rude. *Way to rub my nose in it.*

"All right, all right," I grouse, slamming the truck bed shut and rounding the car, leaving all my precious groceries in the back. "Let's get back to Daddy. He said we needed to be home before dark because of the roads."

Micah pulls back just as Emma's scent burns slightly. The fireman closes her door and shoots me a look. As if it's *my* fault that Knox had his head up his ass earlier.

Gunnar looks between the two of us and gruffs out a grunt. "Maybe Daddy needs an ass-kicking for Christmas."

chapter
forty-four

I'M TIRED.

There, I said it.

I generally try to be upbeat and stay positive, but having four alphas who aren't even in the same pack is *hard*.

I'm not sure why, but it feels worse today than it did at first. Perhaps because I thought it would all be settled by now. It *felt* settled this morning when we were all playing together. But now...

The uncertainty of it starting to wear on me, I think as Micah's truck rumbles down Knox's lane. *And going "home" to a place that isn't really my "home" because I don't have one isn't going to help much.*

I want a nest, dang it. And my blankets. I don't even have my favorite Christmas pillow with the dancing Santas on it.

Zane chatters on about the dinner he's going to make, no doubt sensing my stress and trying to cheer me up. It only makes me feel worse, though, and more insecure.

If I can't get a grip on all these feelings, will the guys even want me anymore?

That one thought is enough to fling me from self-doubt right into *despair*. Micah tenses at my side, then jerks his truck off the road, throwing it into park.

"Sweet girl," he croons, turning just in time to catch me bursting into tears.

Gunnar and Zane gape at me, then at each other, before both of them jockey for space to lean over the center console. I'm already being unbuckled and dragged into Micah's lap when Gunnar's hand brushes tear tracks off my cheek. "Em," he rasps, "baby, what's wrong?"

But I can't tell them the real reason because it's *crazy*. Just absolutely butt-ass *bonkers*. Like me, apparently.

"Oh, God," I cry, overwrought. "You guys must be so *sick* of me!"

There's a long beat of horrible silence. And then they all bellow, "*WHAT?!*"

"I've ruined all your plans! I literally crashed into all of your lives, and you've all dropped everything to stay with me for my heat and—and—"

It's not enough.

I want them all forever. And *this isn't enough.*

Or, rather, *I'm* not. There's no way I can possibly hold the attention of men like this for the rest of my life. They're all *so wonderful,* and I'm the omega no one's ever wanted for longer than the span of a heat.

I've put off talk of bonding for days, partly to keep myself optimistic and partly because I hoped one of them might bring it up. It makes sense that they haven't offered, though—bonding with me as a group means being bonded to one another.

Of course none of them would want that, which only leaves individual bonding on the table. The thought alone devastates my Omega. It's her job to bring these alphas together and make them happier. If they don't want to form a proper pack bond, she's *failed*.

I try frantically to talk her down from the ledge, knowing the last thing this situation needs is a hormonal meltdown. But she has a point—this is *hopeless*.

And I'm in love with *all four of them*.

I can't even offer her platitudes about individual bonds because every time I try to think about it, I feel dizzy. They would all, presumably, want to be there for my heats if we had solo bonds... but where *is* "there"?

Gunnar has to live in Florida to keep his job, Zane's never stayed anywhere for longer than a month in his adult life, Micah's whole family is in Knotty Hollow, and Knox prefers his peaceful, silent wilderness over any sort of company.

How would we make this work?

The fact that they all got along so well today somehow just makes my despair worse. This morning, while we all played in the snow, forming a real pack seemed like an actual *possibility*. And now that the image of all of us, bonded and happy, has lodged itself in my brain like a splinter...

This isn't enough.

That unacceptable thought is the only coherent one I have, so instead of speaking, I drop my face to my hands and sob.

Micah starts to purr and the others follow suit, until the cab of the truck practically vibrates. "Emma, love," he whispers, "*None* of us are sick of you."

"Knox is," I cry, my heart twisting. "He spent one day with me and practically barked me out of his house! And I can't even blame him! I'm needy and naive and stupid an—"

Gunnar looses a truly scary snarl that stops me cold. I blink over at his furious face, trembling.

"You are *not* stupid, Em," he grits. "Why would you *ever* think that?"

She's the neediest, naivest klutz that's ever lived. And <u>dumb</u>.

When I sniffle miserably, Zane tsks softly, threading his warm hand into my hair and drawing gentle circles on my crown. "Oh, baby. Did they tell you that? The other alphas?"

I've already told them the story, but I purposely left out the specific things Rob and William said. At the time, I was too embarrassed. And as the days went on... I didn't want to tip any of them off to just how mediocre I am.

My chin falls forward in a defeated nod. Micah's arms tighten around me. "Emma, none of us think you're dumb *at all*."

"I must be," I wail. "Otherwise, I wouldn't be thinking all of this could somehow work out! And I definitely wouldn't be so needy and clumsy and just—*embarrassing* around you guys."

Micah's purr revs louder. "Sweetheart, you aren't needy."

How can he say that after the way I *literally climbed him* in public today? With a snort, I cast them all a look. "I suppose next you're going to tell me I'm not clumsy, either."

Damning silence fills the car. Until Zane sighs. "Hell, gorgeous, Gunnar is *way* clumsier than you'll ever be."

My hockey star winces at me, then smirks at Zane. "That's fair. I'll take that one."

Micah kisses my forehead. "*Needing* us doesn't make you *needy,* and being clumsy is just one of the things I love about you. Your exuberance and the fact that you don't put on airs or try to come off like you're above anything or anyone is so damn sweet."

Zane nods in agreement, his eyes big and earnest. "Seriously, *shona*. I've been thinking the same thing all week. You lose your balance or drop stuff because you get *excited*. I *love* that."

Gunnar's mouth ticks up at the corner. "Damn. What's my excuse?"

Zane slaps his back. "You're just a klutz, Hot Shot."

Gunnar's eye roll is definitely good-natured that time. Micah bounces me a little. "See? We're all getting along just fine, love. And we'll figure everything out. Because we have the most important thing in common: *you*."

The silence that now fills the cab is different from the last, and it's enough to make me look up again. When I do, I find the three of them gazing back at me, their expressions solemn but settled.

They... mean it? They're really okay with all of this? With *each other*? Because of *me*?

It's amazing. Wonderful, really. My dream... but with one very obvious missing piece. A fissure splits my heart, sending a pang of pain through my chest as I whisper, "What about Knox?"

I can tell none of them know what to say. A note of helplessness rings through the cab before Gunnar finally says, "What *about* Knox, squirt? He already agreed to let us all stay for your heat. And being there with you."

And... this is where it ends. This is where I blurt the one question that's been boring a hole in my middle for days. Because I can't lie to them, and I can't hold things in.

Especially when Gunnar frowns like the tears tracking down my face are more serious than world peace. Or when Micah's purr sounds a little breathless because he hates inhaling the scent of my stress. Or the way Zane *looks* like me with his dark, searching eyes.

Fiddlesticks.

I shrink lower on Micah's lap. "What about after my heat?"

I brace for another beat of collective uncertainty, but instead, I look up to find them all giving each other solid, brusque nods. Zane's the one who finally bends forward, pressing a soft kiss to my mouth before murmuring, "We're all ready to talk about that whenever you are, *shona*."

The spark of hope in my chest is enough to get me back into my own seat. I cling to it desperately as Micah drives on, knowing my bubble of optimism a fragile, fleeting thing. Because as soon as I see the look on Knox's face when I ask them all to talk about this later...

Wait.

What is *that*?

We're still a little way down the snowy dirt driveway—and, granted, it's getting dark out here. But... I'm pretty darn sure that's a wreath.

A wreath I can *see* because *there are Christmas lights on the cabin.*

...

There are Christmas lights on the cabin?!

Zane sees me and Micah gaping at the windshield and leans forward, barking a laugh before he says exactly what I'm thinking.

"Oh holy night! Did Knox *decorate*?"

KNOX *DID* DECORATE.

And—even more shocking—my mountain man did a *beautiful* job.

The house looks like a modern, enormous take on a fairytale Christmas cabin. Soft white lights line every edge and each window. Festive greenery covered in holly berries and red ribbons frame the doorway and the porch's front eave.

The porch that used to have only one rocking chair, but now has...

Five.

Micah stops his truck right at the mouth of the circular drive, just as the front door opens and a set of big, gold bells attached to the wreath chimes.

Knox steps into view, his usual flannel shirt rolled to his elbows and his hands in front pockets. Looking adorably sheepish because there is a *Santa hat on his head.*

With a sob of pure, stunned amazement stuck in my throat, I fling myself out of the truck and race over to the porch, managing only to slip on the last step.

Knox catches me, chuckling as he swings me into his arms and holds me close. "I wanted to surprise you. Figured your trip into town was my best shot."

He did surprise me. So much that I'm choking on disbelief. "But I—I thought—"

He scent-marks my forehead and then presses a kiss there. "This house has always been nice, but it was never intended for all this. After yesterday, I had to fix that. Turn it into a home."

Oh great, now I'm blubbering.

You know what?

Who cares?

"A—a home?" I gasp out.

He nods firmly as my other alphas bound up the porch steps to join us. Knox drops a kiss on my lips, murmuring, "Welcome home, baby girl."

chapter forty-five

DEFINITELY NOT SPAM

ZANE

I'm about to do a face mask. Anyone want one?

KNOX

A face mask? Like from hockey?

MICAH

lol pretty sure it's a skincare thing, Knox.

ZANE

it has collagen in it. AND peptides.

GUNNAR

You have a photoshoot we don't know about?

ZANE

hate all you want, but I've gotta make sure our girl has a nice seat.

throne, really.

MICAH

...

Fine, I'll take one.

GUNNAR

JFC

What is my life?

Make it two.

ZANE

😊 good boy

Daddy?

KNOX HAS LEFT THIS GROUP CHAT

MICAH

Not again.

"I CANNOT BELIEVE you got a whole winter-freaking-wonderland but didn't buy a second mattress," Gunnar snaps.

Some things—like the outdoor decorations, the throw pillows, and the blankets—were easy to get here within hours. Other things, however...

"You honestly gonna tell me that any of us would *volunteer* to sleep in a different room?" I reply. "I got a *bigger* mattress that will fit us all, but it won't be here until tomorrow."

Same with Emma's final surprise—a state-of-the-art nest pod that will fit on the big balcony of the Omega Suite. That's going to require a crane and some installation, but it should be good to go well before her heat next week.

Zane tosses his pillow in the air and fluffs it. "So, we're doing this, then? One bed? Booktok would go *wild*."

I have no idea what that means, but I shoot him an annoyed look anyway. Those are typically a pretty safe bet in reply to anything Zane says that ends in "-tok."

We all fall silent as we look over at Emma, asleep in the middle of the mattress. I honestly suspect she passed out from sheer excitement. All evening, she never once stopped grinning or bouncing around to look at all the things I had airlifted in to make the house more suitable for her. She and McKinley even rolled around in the new blankets I left on the couch.

"Who gets to be next to her?" Gunnar asks, puffing up like he's ready to wrestle for it.

I snort a smirk. He really is a competitive klutz. "Since it's my damn bed, I think I'll claim at least one of the spots."

"I'll take the other one," Gunnar decides.

Micah laughs tersely. "Oh, *will you*?"

Zane isn't having it either. He scoffs. "Nuh-uhh. Rock, paper, scissors, Hot Shot."

My dog chuffs while he trots right between our legs, leaping onto the mattress and settling along Emma's left side.

All four of us stare for a beat before laughing. "Fuck," Micah chuckles. "That's a smart dog."

"Too smart," I agree, scratching at my beard before I bark my pet's name softly. He makes a low groaning noise and sighs at me like I'm exasperating. When I motion toward his dog bed, I swear he rolls his eyes before he hops down.

Gunnar jumps at the spot before the others can. Micah shakes his head but doesn't argue, walking around to the other side of the bed and settling as close to the edge of the mattress as he can.

Zane chortles. "Fine, fine. But tomorrow night, we switch."

I ignore the territorial impulse that says I don't want to have to share...and find it's getting easier and easier to do.

Because this? This is what *Emma* needs. And that makes it more important.

I still grumble while I shuffle in between Micah and my baby girl, though. Can't let these assholes think I'm going soft.

Or soft*er*, given I just redecorated my whole damn house simply to see the look on Emma's face.

And, *fuck me*, it did not disappoint.

We all shift around, trying to fit without overlapping. Micah manages to balance on his side and give me enough space to curl around Emma. We still have a sliver of space between us, but Zane sidles right up to Gunnar's back. His body goes stiff.

"Look," the chef smirks, unbothered, "It's either my chest near your back or we can bump butts all night. You know I don't mind either way, Hockey Boy."

Gunnar makes a long-suffering sound, but I catch the way his mouth twitches up. "Whatever, Magic Mike, just keep it in your pants."

Zane shrugs, snuggling closer with a yawn. "I make no promises."

Micah reaches his long arm out to hit the bedside lamp. Darkness swells through the room—the pure, perfect kind you can only get out in the mountains. No light pollution or neighbors or streetlamps. Downstairs, the light from the damn internet router drove me crazy because I'm used to *this*.

Maybe the lack of light is good for us all, because the silence that falls seems a lot less tense than it has on other nights. I'm getting used to the way Zane has to rock back and forth to settle in. How Micah always stretches his legs twice before going still. I guess they're probably getting accustomed to my habit of clearing my throat as I close my eyes.

Once all those ticks are appeased, I wait to see who's going to take the bullet and speak first. For a second, it seems like we might all just fall asleep like normal people.

But then Micah murmurs, "Emma told me she loves me today."

For a long second, no one so much as *breathes*. Gunnar's the one who finally breaks, an exhale quivering out of him. "She—she did?"

I hear Micah's swallow. "Yeah. We were—We scratched something off her list. And after, I was holding her, and she just... said it."

I blink in the deep darkness, barely making out the curve of Emma's cheek. Of course she said it first. Our sweet, open-hearted girl would never hold something like that back.

I stroke one knuckle down the side of her face, unable to care about the jealousy stinging my stomach. Not when I have to know if she got what she needed in return.

"Did you say it back?" I ask, my voice low.

Micah sounds like he's smiling. "Yeah. I did."

"Good for you, man," Zane replies, blowing out a loud breath. "I never thought I'd be such a chickenshit. But I've known that I'm in love with her for days, and I haven't said anything."

Gunnar's gray eyes are nearly invisible as they follow the same trail mine have, looking at Emma's face. When he finally glances over at me, I see his feelings before he sets his jaw and says, "I'm in love with her, too."

My head nods, but I'm not sure if I'm agreeing or approving. It seems to calm him somewhat, though, because he stops gritting his teeth and asks, "What about you, Knox?"

I shift a bit, lying on my back and not caring that my shoulder grazes Micah's spine. Who fucking cares? What I'm about to say is going to change all of this anyway.

"I think I've loved her since the first second she looked into my eyes."

I can still picture her in this very bed, wrapped up in my tartan blanket, blinking those big green eyes up at me. She was scared, and she'd been crying, but I'd never seen anyone so beautiful in all my life. I think that was the moment some hardened, hurting part of me sunk into her, craving all her softness. All her light.

Zane interrupts my musings. For the first time since we met, he sounds small. "What do we do?"

Fucking hell.

I'm done questioning why, but my Alpha really fucking hates it when any of these guys struggle. I breathe through the instinctive jolt of dominance that answers my jag of concern, making sure I don't put any command into my words.

"We tell her."

Gunnar hums. "Together?"

That idea rings through the room and slowly sinks in, feeling more and more right with every moment. "I think she would like that," Micah finally answers. "Feeling like we're all..."

"Together," Gunnar says again.

An answer, this time. Not a question.

Because that's the thing.

None of this is a question anymore.

chapter
forty-six

THIS WAS MY IDEA, but I'll never admit it.

For one, Gunnar looks like he's ready to murder me already. And now that I see an axe in his clumsy clutches... I'm starting to rethink my strategy.

Originally, I tried to be casual when I pointed out that Gunnar and I were both required to be super fit for our jobs—it only made sense that we would be out here, chopping down the Christmas tree our omega wants to decorate tonight.

Technically, none of it is untrue. And Knox needs to be home this morning to deal with the delivery of Emma's furnishings. I just happened to leave out the part where I think it's smart for the

alphas in this non-pack who currently don't get along to spend
some extra time together.

Hence, me out here, in the snow, trudging along beside
grumpy Gunnar and the axe he definitely doesn't know how to
hold properly.

Knox and Zane stayed behind to bake cookies with Emma.
Between Zane and me... I'm not sure who got the surlier alpha to
deal with.

Although, Zane seems to have charmed Gunnar somehow.
He can probably do the same to Knox, but, uh, I think the *way*
Zane is charming Gunnar may not be something he'd offer to just
anyone.

I saw it this morning over breakfast. Gunnar looks at Zane in
some bemused, indulgent way that *almost* seems fond. When I
point this out, the hockey player grumbles, "What are you talking
about? He's another alpha."

I shrug, my mouth curling at the corner. "So? That happens
in packs all the time."

Gunnar grunts. "In case you need a TLDR, bro, the whole
issue is that we *aren't* a pack."

I don't point out the fact that we're acting like one. This
approach I've been taking—being a team player, subtly encour-
aging everyone to get along—only works if I let them think things
are *their* idea.

Instead, I say, "We're all going to do her heat together."

Gunnar's nutty scent gets saltier. "That's true," he sighs. His
eyes scan over our work before his vice drops into something
quieter. "Emma may not like us fucking around, though."

I can't picture Emma *ever* having negative feelings about two
people making each other happy. Even two alphas. Even two of
her alphas.

Hell, if the way she reacted to watching them touch each
other was any indication, she'd *love* it.

"Emma doesn't seem like the jealous type to me," I reply carefully, eyeing his profile.

He cringes. "No. But she's insecure. Those assholes made her feel like no one wanted her. And I didn't help, running off the night we met. Her Omega still hasn't forgiven me."

Hmm. That *is* a problem.

"What if she took it as some sort of..." Gunnar trails off, huffing a frustrated breath. "Preference?"

My brows spike. "Is it?"

He laughs. "No. I could never prefer *anything* or *anyone* to her. She's like... the fucking *sun*. The light of my whole existence. It was so—" He swallows. "It was dark. Before her."

His face glitches several times before he admits, "We don't make any sense without her. She's the thing we have in common. Any bond we might have... she's at the center."

His brows pinch harder. "It's like... the things about him that appeal to me? It's *all* from watching him with her. The way he makes her smile, how comfortable he makes her with her body. How he dotes on her and cooks for her. That's where I started to respect him."

I can't help but smile. The feeling he's describing—watching Zane with Emma and developing a sense of respect for him—is one I know well. It's how I feel about all of them.

I just... don't happen to notice how any of them look naked.

I shrug, still going for casual. "I don't think you need to make any decisions. You both have Emma as your number one priority. Whatever other feelings develop will just take time. If we make a pack—with or without a bond—no one says we need to have our pack dynamics figured out immediately. And those dynamics don't necessarily have to be all-or-nothing."

Gunnar pauses to listen, some tension leaving the space between his brows. "I guess you're right. My mom used to tell me I was an Ansel Adams."

When he sees my face, he laughs again, but not unkindly. "Ansel Adams was a photographer. Only shot in black-and-white." Sadness passes over his features. "My mom was an art professor."

Was.

His tone—and the loss there—is, unfortunately, very familiar. The fingers I have resting on his shoulder curl, squeezing. "I'm really sorry, man. When did you lose her?"

Pain spasms over his features. "Like six months ago."

Fucking *hell.* I've been judging his shitty attitude since he got here... but this is his first Christmas without his *mom*?

I remember my first few years slogging through the holidays without my mother. It was hell. The memory alone tightens my throat and my voice as I reply, "My mom died when I was in high school. It's the hardest thing I've ever lived through."

His nose twitches, drawing attention to his glassy eyes. "But you did?"

I give him another squeeze. "Yeah, I did. And after a while... Now, I just feel grateful, for the most part. I had a great mom who loved me. She's at peace, and I'm still here. I get to do the things she didn't—and make choices that would make her proud."

I drop my gaze, embarrassed about blurting out more than I intended. Surprise pinches my lungs when Gunnar *answers.*

"She would have wanted that, I think," he rasps. "For you to be grateful. And have adventures. And make her proud."

Grief is odd. After ten years, I know it never goes away. There are still moments like this, every once in a while. I had one when Emma sang that song in the shower, the day we found her. My mother loved to hum the tune from The Sound of Music, warbling her own nonsense versions about whiskers on kittens and mittens or whatever. She had a jewelry box that played it, and I used to sit at her feet as child to listen.

Hearing the tune still makes me sad, but, looking back, that was also the moment I knew there was something special about Emma.

Maybe my mom sent her here, somehow.

Maybe Gunnar's helped.

When I look back at him, I choose not to hide the fact that my nose is stinging and my eyes are wet. He deserves to know—this is normal. The remembering, the sadness. It's just respect for the person you loved and nothing to be ashamed of.

Besides, you can't go around it.

But you *can* go through it.

"I think your mom would have wanted the same," I tell him. "The way you talk about her, I think she would have liked Emma. And maybe Zane, too."

Gunnar laughs. The sound is watery, but it's also genuine. And one I've only heard him make when he's with Emma. "Oh, man, she would have *loved* Emma. And Zane, too, with the way he's constantly on my ass."

I smirk, and he slaps me away, returning to his grumpy scowl. "Not like *that*. Jesus."

I shrug again, unbothered and back to smiling. "Like I said; we've got time."

chapter
forty-seven

IF I THOUGHT Zane was sexy before, I was nowhere near prepared for the sight of him in all his well-coiffed glory.

Now that he has all his belongings, I've realized the outrageously handsome version of Zane I've seen over the last couple of weeks was just the acoustic version.

With his glossy black hair raked into a perfect pompadour and his skin freshly washed, buffed, and moisturized, he might as well be a god. Especially when he wears the designer threads he's so fond of.

Unlike Lucy, I've never been much for labels—but after just a day and a half, I'm realizing the couture loungewear is sexy in a way I never knew sweats and sweaters could be.

My most ostentatious alpha also has a way of somehow turning ordinary items into the sexiest accessories. Like the Clark-Kent-style glasses currently perched on the straight blade of his nose.

They're for blocking blue light, he informed us when Gunnar teased him about them yesterday. And—sure enough, Zane wears them while he bends over his MacBook, frowning in puzzlement at whatever content he's working on.

I hope it's the reel he shot this morning. Wearing only a pair of tight red boxer briefs and an open flannel shirt he stole from Knox, Zane shot a whole series of campfire breakfast videos.

I was a perfuming mess just watching him from the back porch. Micah chuckled as he rocked me in one of our new chairs, snuggling his face into my neck and murmuring filth about "fucking me full" while his hands roamed inside my panties until I came.

I've definitely been needier today after finally sharing a bed with all of them last night. Lucy and Bridget are convinced I'll go into heat early, since I'm now steeped in alpha pheromones while I sleep, but I'm keeping the faith. I've already derailed all their holiday plans—I *really* don't want us to be stuck in my nest on Christmas Day.

The nest that *finally exists*!

Knox is currently down the hall in the Omega Suite, making sure the delivery and installation guys don't do anything he doesn't approve of. Or, as Micah chuckled, "Putting his scary Alpha to good use, for once."

He and Gunnar left a couple hours ago to find us a proper Christmas tree. The two of them set off with saws and a big roll of twine, McKinley barking happily while he raced after them. It only took me half of a Hallmark Christmas movie to come looking for my fourth alpha, all-too happy to find him already shirtless and in the bed we've all been sharing.

He taps at his trackpad and I watch him work, my heart glowing steadily brighter with every passing second. Eventually, my perfume winds its way to him. His full, dusky lips twitch into a panty-melting grin before he even slides his eyes up from his screen.

When he sees me lingering in the doorway, biting my lip, he starts to purr, shoving his stuff aside to open his arms, "Come here, gorgeous."

I'm surprised by the relief I feel as I scamper over and crawl into his arms. Zane hums, cradling me against the spicy skin of his bare chest. "They'll all be gone soon, hmm? You're safe here with me, *shona*."

I don't realize until he says something, but he's right. I don't like having the delivery men in the house, and I feel nervous. Zane's purr revs louder, soothing the tightness behind my breasts.

"My pretty baby," he adds, kissing my forehead. "I know we need to get your room sorted, but I hate that you're stressed. How can I help?"

I don't know, but the way he's holding me is enough to let my eyes fall shut on a deep exhale. His chai scent deepens as he leans closer to my ear. "I could knot you. It might help your Omega feel safe if we're connected."

The uncertainty in his voice is so unlike him, I lean back and frown slightly. His beautiful smile turns sheepish. "You make me nervous. It's nice, actually. My stomach flips and flutters every time I come on to you."

I smile at my beautiful alpha, my heart melting. He's been with his fair share of other people, but knowing I'm the only one he ever cared enough to get butterflies for is thrilling.

He senses the shift in my scent and purrs louder, his hands skimming my body with more intent. "Let me knot you," he whispers, husky but without any of usual flirtatiousness. "Keep you safe all wrapped around me."

I sink into his embrace immediately, marking his chest with my cheek. I love that his cock jerks in reply, answering my neediness with desire, just like he always has.

From the first moment, on that first day, Zane has chosen me.

And all of the stuff that's made me unlovable to other alphas in the past? Those are his *favorite* parts.

With one of his silky-smooth motions, he has me pinned underneath him in a languid roll of dark-tan muscle. His hot mouth latches onto my throat, skimming my pulse with flicks of his tongue as his hands make short work of my joggers.

Dang, he works *fast*. Before I know what's hit me, we're both down to our skivvies. When he sees my mouth drop in shock, he flashes his most beautiful grin. "I told you I was smooth, gorgeous."

As if to prove his point, he kneels up to give me the full effect of his drool-worthy physique. My gaze traces every chiseled line and flexed muscle stretched over his six-foot frame. Cinnamon perfume rises off me in a rush when my focus snags on his ultra-tight crimson briefs and the erection prodding at them. Zane groans, his head falling forward.

"Fuck, baby," he laughs, breathless, as he lowers himself onto his stomach and buries his face against the curve of my belly. "I guess it's a good thing you like me. Because all my moves go out the window the second I scent you..."

He kisses the spot just below my navel. "And feel you..." His lips brush my hip bone. His tongue nudges my panties lower while he slants a look up to my face. "And *look* at you. *Damn* it."

I flash a teasing smirk and shrug, knowing it will bounce my boobs for him. "You should just flip me over. Might improve your game—*ooh*!"

With another of his seamless moves, he flips me to my front, guiding my hips up until I balance on my elbows. Chai deliciousness warms the air as I glance back at the wicked grin spreading over his face.

"You know," he husks, his palms gliding in from my hips to squeeze my backside. "I couldn't help but notice that your list had double penetration on it... a couple of times. Along with some other very naughty ideas for this pretty ass."

An unfortunate memory flickers into my mind. It's my

former alpha, William's, face when we met at the matching center. I watched him scan my file, and when he got to the section about sexual preferences—specifically, butt stuff—his mouth twisted into a sour pucker.

After that, I never had the nerve to ask any of them about it. Although, Renee made sure to mention that they "had to" use a toy on me "there" during my heat to "get me to quiet down."

Okay, so—maybe there *were* a few red flags.

Yikes.

Thinking about it now, with the way these men have treated me since I met them, it all feels even more shameful and devastating than before. How did I not see how horrible the Dunlaps were? Why did I think they wanted me?

Zane underscores the difference between those clowns and the alphas in this house when he immediately picks up on my hesitation. I tense slightly and his purr starts up.

His voice softens into something tender while his thumb carefully traces between my cheeks. "Do you like that, *shona*? Is it something I could give you?"

I bite my lip, glad he can't see me cringe at the headboard. "Um... only if—only if you do."

"Mm," he hums. "It would be damn-near impossible for you to find something I don't want to do to you, gorgeous. But this isn't about me. I'm asking *you*. Do you like playing back here?"

My chagrin doubles as I recall the wide variety of plugs and toys I left back in Florida. "Yeah," I whisper. "I—I *really* do."

He could make a sly comment or say something flirtatious, but instead, Zane stretches over me, planting his hands beside my elbows. His hard heat presses into my ass as he nuzzles my nape sweetly.

"Good girl, telling me what you like. You want me to do it now? We need to get you all ready for your heat, and I was thinking—this needs prep."

Just like that day in the kitchen, I can tell he truly has thought about this. Sex might be effortless for him, but *I'm* not. He truly cares about me and puts consideration into every interaction we have.

It doesn't surprise me at all—Zane only acts shallow to keep things light for his followers. It's a persona. But I know his heart now. And it might even be as soft as mine.

His forehead rubs my shoulder before he drops a kiss there. "You know," he murmurs, "If we had another one of these knot-heads handy, we could both fuck you at the same time."

I moan before I can help myself, a rush of slick pouring out of my pussy. Dousing the muscled thigh Zane has wedged between mine.

His purr rolls into a growl, even as a smile brushes the top of my spine. "Dirty girl. You're perfect for me, aren't you?"

chapter
forty-eight

GOOD. Sweet. Lord.

I barely lasted ten minutes inside Emma's tight little cunt, last time. How am I supposed to last *half a breath* inside her even tighter ass?

She whines, dribbling more wetness. I feel it slip down my knot and balls while I press myself tight against the back of her thighs, working fingers in and out of her.

It's clear she likes this enough to do it for herself at home— whatever I give her, she takes, moaning loud enough to make my blood roar.

Fuck, *yes*.

My omega is so goddamn perfect for me.

The purr rattling inside my chest stutters on a gasp when I fit the head of my cock against her puckered opening. Her delicious cinnamon-bun slick lets me shove right in, the plush heat *strangling* me.

Oh shit. Fuck. I swear to God, this woman. I'm already right on the edge of—

A knock at the door interrupts my first thrust into glorious tightness.

Then, a *crash* at the door.

"Ow. Fuck." Gunnar's muffled voice comes from the other side of the slab. When he hears Emma's alarmed whine, he bursts into the room, hopping on one foot and only narrowly avoiding going to the ground.

After having stubbed his toe, somehow?

I don't know if I'm closer to laughing at him or kicking his ass.

Emma starts to giggle the second she sees him, but her muscles relax just enough to give me space to push deeper. Gunnar's already frozen on the threshold, but his jaw falls when I don't stop, rocking my hips to start up a rhythm.

Jesus, she feels incredible. I grit my teeth and glide deeper, relishing the pressure clasping at my throbbing cock. "Could you —" I grind out, rolling my hips to push the last inch in, eliciting a filthy keen from Emma. "—close the fucking door?"

Gunnar jumps, slamming the door shut. "Sorry. Shit. I was trying to hear if there was any reason for me not to come in, and then I tripped on—"

"The air?" I pant. Emma thrusts her hips back, loving the feel of my cock stuffed into her back hole. I reach down and press my palm into her clit, groaning when she gushes slick.

"Fuck, baby, you like being watched. And you like this big dick in your ass. You take every single inch of me, don't you?"

Emma's spine arches, her pussy convulsing. My hand winds around her hair on instinct, holding her in the pretty pose she's struck for me.

And maybe showing off a little bit.

Gunnar's reaction is worth it. He bites his lower lip, blatantly staring at the way I drill into our omega's ass. She turns to look at him, whining softly.

The sound visibly hits him, right in the heart. All his tension leeches away. He slants me a glance, silently asking permission before he closes the distance between us.

Emma whimpers when his hand cups her cheek. He traces her features tenderly before giving her a true smile—one of his rare, beautiful ones.

Fuck.

Why can't I *breathe*?

"Hey, squirt." He keeps smirking as he raises a brow. "Does he feel good?"

I relax my grip on her curls so she can nod. Gunnar's gaze flashes to my fist, then up to my face. A dark, heated intensity gilds his grey eyes. His voice drops into a low rumble. "How does she feel?"

The hand I have between our girl's thighs works a bit faster, matching my thrusts. Emma douses my fingers, and I groan, replying through gnashed teeth. "*So fucking good.*"

His brow arches higher. "Want to share?"

Oh *God*.

Emma's pussy *pours* slick down my wrist. She keens, the whining moan as desperate as her scent is sweet. My head falls back as I try to fill my lungs.

"What do you think, baby?" he murmurs to our omega. "You want to taste my cum? Or feel me in your pussy while Zane fills your ass?"

Jesus, Hot Shot. You're killing my game.

He feels my wide eyes on his face and flips me a wry smile. "I assume you're good with that, Pretty Boy?"

Am I good with the way having him in her pussy will make the clench of her heat twice as intense? I have to slow my hips to keep from blowing my load just from the thought.

"Probably better to save your mouth for another time," I pant to Emma, rubbing my hand down her spine. "Or my knot will be too full to press into you."

Emma balances on one arm, going for Gunnar's jeans with her usual fumbling eagerness. We both grin while she tears at his fly, chuckling to one another. Which feels... nice. Grounding.

I release a slow breath and block out the glorious snugness squeezing me so I can help our girl balance on her knees. The change in angle seats me even deeper in her ass. I growl against her neck while her head thrashes into the wide curve of my shoulder.

Gunnar slips his shirt off in one pull, leaving all his athleticism on full display. When he shucks his boxers, Emma isn't the only one who stares at the thick erection stretching up to the lace of his abs.

Goddamn, he's hard. Roped in veins that visibly pulse blue under his pale skin.

The guy may not be waxed bare like I am, but he's groomed. Even more than he was the last time I saw him, if I'm not mistaken...

At the questioning bounce my brow, he cuts me a glower. I shrug. "It looks good. Well-coiffed."

"Shut up." He huffs a breathless laugh, shuffling into position at Emma's front. She instantly grabs for him.

"*Both of you* shut up," she whines.

Gunnar scent-marks her cheek, his chest thrumming with a quiet purr. "Impatient, sunshine?"

She nods, beaming those brilliant green eyes at him. "Please, Alpha. I want you both to knot me."

I watch him swallow thickly and remember he hasn't been tied to her yet. If the way his cock twitches is any indication, he's dying to. But he still presses their foreheads together, asking, "You sure?"

Her head bobs on another enthusiastic jerk. Gunnar's lips quirk softly as he slides his hand down to knock mine away and stroke his knuckles over her buzzing clit. When she whines, he smiles for real.

"And what about your Omega? How does she feel about it?"

Emma's fingers dig into his sides, yanking him closer as she gasps, "She says you better give her your knot right now."

His salty sweetness grows more intense. "Mm. Is she listening?"

Some of Emma's curls fly close to my face when she nods again. Gunnar snaps his hand up, cupping it around her jaw while he stares into her eyes. "I'll give you this knot anytime you want it, baby," he vows, rough and solemn. "Any part of me you want. It's all yours. *Forever.*"

I feel the moment everything inside of her relaxes, her inner muscles gelling around my ticking erection. She makes a small noise, moving to throw herself into his arms. While he hugs her to his purring chest, an odd sort of warmth spreads through mine.

I set my hand on his bicep, skimming a path to his bulging shoulder. Gray eyes flicker to mine, more vulnerable than I've seen them since that moment we had in the grocery store.

I'm not used to being the solid one—but something about him and Emma... They bring out a steadiness I didn't know I had. A protective peace that fills my Alpha with possession for our omega.

And for Gunnar? I think it's *pride.*

Without overthinking it, I follow my impulse to pull him closer, sealing Emma between our bodies. He takes my lead, positioning his forearms under hers. I grip her hips, lifting her until she starts to glide up my pulsing dick.

Our perfect girl reaches for Gunnar, arranging him against her wet heat, dragging in a sharp breath as soon as he's in position. We both lower her slowly, all three of us gasping and groaning while her body slowly stretches around two rock-hard cocks.

Holy fucking *shit.* I can feel Gunnar through the thin wall separating us. His blood is pounding hard enough for me to sense his pulse and hers. My blood races, my vision tunneling while I grasp at Gunnar's sides, tugging him closer.

"Like this," I grit, angling my hips until I'm as straight as I can get underneath her. Hockey Boy follows suit, pressing his slicked-up balls and knot right into mine.

Fuuuuuuuck.

Emma screams, the position allowing her to sink all the way onto us. "Oh my—oh—oh my God, I'm so full!"

Gunnar snarls, clamping his brawny hold around one of her thighs, helping her ride us both in fast, deep plunges. I growl right back, gripping the back of his hair for balance while I pump up and forward, grinding my knot into his the same way his dick rubs at the underside of mine through the slick, clenching wall of Emma's pussy.

We're both soaked already. His full balls and knot glide fast against mine when Emma whines and starts to writhe, looking for more.

I slip my hand between his groin and hers, tugging harder at his nape as I start to stroke the swollen bud of her clit.

Gunnar roughs out a torn, panted version of my name. One of his hands lands on my hip and pulls me closer. "Don't stop," he begs, picking up speed. "Fuck, Emma, you feel like heaven when you're about to come, baby."

They *both* feel *incredible*. Her plush, snug heat. His strong, thick thrusts.

"Gotta knot you, *shona*," I growl. "Not going to last much longer before I fill this perfect ass."

Emma's body responds before she even manages to moan, clenching rhythmically. Milking Gunnar and pulling me in as deep as I can go without popping my knot into place.

He moves fast, taking her weight so I can shove everything she needs right where she wants it. Emma keens, already coming. I sling my arm around her waist and balance her for Gunnar to push all the way in, too.

My knot explodes, bumping his through the ecstatic ripples of her orgasm, both of us filling her to bursting. She squirms and gasps our names. Gunnar curses, sinking his teeth into her neck. The image has me spurting hot cum into her depths while I suck at her pulse.

Mine, my Alpha rasps, absorbing the feel of our omega, clutching Gunnar and me tighter. Bringing us closer. Showing the instincts embedded in my middle that she's what we've been missing.

And this other alpha? He's hers.

Which makes him *ours*.

chapter
forty-nine

IT'S EMBARRASSING how much I needed this.

Not the sex or even the knotting. But her. Emma.

And...

And *him*.

Zane has Emma tucked against the front of his body; his smooth forearm locked at the narrowest point of her soft waist. I watch the way he nuzzles into her neck, scraping his teeth along the thin skin and murmuring praises to her in two languages.

Emma seems to understand everything he says, even if the words elude her. She turns her pretty, bare face into his cheek and kisses him quietly, listening. They both smile to themselves, neither able to see the other's expressions.

And something deep inside of me breaks.

The collapse of the dam feels familiar. How many times has Emma busted through the shitty barriers I tried to build around my grief?

Zane has done it a few times, too. Each time, I hated the way it felt.

Like cracking. Crumbling. *Failing*.

But here in the quiet of Knox's vanquished solitude, with all of our scents layered into the sheets and a silent snow falling outside the window...

The barricades break.

And I'm *relieved*.

Because, for the first time, I'm not the flimsy, fracturing wall.

I'm the water.

Moving. Flowing.

Washing over all the brokenness. Finally free to flow *through* and settle somewhere new. A tender, terrible, transformative place. One that will take me a long time to figure out.

But it's peaceful here.

It hurts, but it feels like a place where I can rest. Maybe even a place I was always meant to find. One where I'm *allowed* to hurt. Because I can finally *let* the loss ache without festering—knowing that the people across from me in this bed will be there whenever I'm ready to leave the pain behind for a while.

I just need to ask them to wait for me.

Zane's gaze slides up to mine, catching the way my eyes have filled. The arm slung over the pillows behind us automatically curls toward me, his free hand landing on my head.

For once, he doesn't have anything cocky or cutting to say. No grins or winks or teases. His dark eyes are solid and serious while he sifts my hair back.

And this time? I don't bat him away or play it off. I lean into his fingers, letting him stroke my scalp in his sinuous, knowing way.

Concern creases his brow. The purr rattling against Emma's

spine cranks up. Bliss drifts over Emma's face and my own rumble revs louder.

I move closer to them, until the leg I have thrown over Emma's thigh is touching Zane, too. He curves his hand around my crown, bending to put our foreheads together while Emma snuggles happily between us, her scent brightening when she cracks her green gaze open and glances up.

A cute little smile tugs at her lips. She shakes her head and rolls her eyes like we're so adorable and amusing. "Boys."

Zane's laugh sounds a little breathless. He looks down at her and over at me, then back again. "You have us all figured out, huh, *shona*?"

She giggles, sweet and genuine. "I don't think *you* have it all figured out yet. But I was hoping this would happen."

The relief on Zane's face echoes through my chest. "You were?" I ask.

She gazes up at me with earnest eyes, utterly guileless. "He makes you smile more," she whispers, reaching over to trace my cheekbone. "I love that, Gunnar."

For a moment, we all gather each other closer. Then—of course—Zane pumps his hips against her ass, smirking. "And what do *I* get out of this?" he jokes.

Emma tosses him a sly smile over her shoulder. "A very good boy?"

Zane's fingers flex in my hair as we both growl reflexively. His chai scent thickens the air between the three of us, and Emma whines when mine responds.

Slick gushes over my knot, sending a tingle of pleasure into my groin. When Zane pants against her nape, I know he feels it, too. Which just makes me *harder*. And Emma *wetter*. And *Zane*—

With a dazed blink, Em offers me a goofy grin, nodding at the place where we're all entangled. "Well, we know what *I* get out of this."

The swell of love that floods my middle makes me think I'm

getting a hell of a lot more than I ever expected to have. Definitely more than I deserve.

Emma senses the burned edge to my scent seconds before Zane does. She blinks up at me, suddenly looking uncertain. Which is when I realize—all this pulling away I've done? Trying to protect her and keep my darkness from staining her sunbeams?

She doesn't understand it.

She thinks it's her fault.

All this time, I've been worried about the other ways I might accidentally hurt or reject her again. It never occurred to me that putting walls up to keep her *safe* also kept her *out*.

I don't want that. I want her to be as close to me as she wants. It's a fucking *privilege* that she wants to be close to me at all. But I also need her to be happy, and my instincts revolt against taking any of her joy away.

I swallow, the motion thick and sticky as my eyes meet Zane's. His fingers slow in my hair while he gazes back, reading my hesitation. With a tiny nod, he nuzzles back into her hair and settles, acting as an anchor but not interjecting.

"Em," I sigh, dropping my face to scent-mark her forehead. "Baby... there's something I need to tell you."

chapter
fifty

THIS IS IRONIC.

I lived for silence. It was my solace, up here, alone.

At least it's quiet, I used to think, staring at all the blankness.

Now, there's not one empty corner in this living room. But the guys are quieter than they have been in the last couple of weeks.

And—*fucking hell*—I think I *hate* it.

It might not be so bad if I didn't understand it so keenly. Because these guys aren't the only ones in their own heads. I've been sitting here for thirty minutes, trying to puzzle out how the fuck this will work in the long run.

Last night changed something.

And today? Having Emma's new nest and her bedroom all arranged... sitting down to the magazine-worthy meal Zane made for all of us? Laughing and talking about Christmas, making plans for how we can all get gifts in town tomorrow without giving them away? The series of phone calls I made this afternoon?

Today changed *every*thing.

I keep waiting for the panic. The sensation of a runaway steam engine careening off its tracks.

All I get is the serenity of soft snow, falling soundlessly outside. Almost like nature is going out of its way to show me just how peaceful this could be.

McKinley senses my contemplative mood, jumping up to settle with his head in my lap. I drop my hand to his silky ears, observing how each of the alphas in my living room move around one another.

Gunnar's sitting in the middle of the floor, trying to assemble a light-up Christmas village for the mantle. He frowns at the painted houses, the ledge of his brow lowering by degrees as the moments tick past.

His mood makes sense. After spending half the day locked in my room—and our omega—with Zane, he came down and told me he wanted to talk.

Neither of us are great conversationalists, but he managed to tell me about his mom, and I listened, gathering the bottom line —he's still in the worst, earliest parts of grief. And he doesn't feel like he has a family of his own anymore.

By the time we all sat down to eat dinner, I had a better understanding of Gunnar than I did before. Greater respect for Zane, too, when he paused to check in with the hockey player and pulled him into a long hug.

Zane is unexpectedly patient, in general. I noticed it with Emma, of course, but also the way he works in the kitchen. He gives things the time they need to turn out however he wants them and doesn't seem disturbed by it at all.

Even now, he kneels at the edge of the Christmas tree, trying to get the last, lowest layer of lights strung properly. When a branch keeps catching, he calmly unstrings it and tries again.

Micah gathers up discarded boxes and packaging, scanning the room, checking for ways he can help or small tasks to finish up. He ducks into the kitchen and returns with a measuring cup full of water for the freshly cut tree.

Zane sees him coming and shuffles aside, holding up the bottom branches for him. Gunnar watches for a long moment before smiling slightly. He crawls to the other side of the eight-foot pine now positioned between the fireplace and the window, reaching around the back to plug the lights in.

My throat tightens. Absolute certainty—as heavy as it is serene—sinks into my stomach.

"I think we need to talk."

The guys all turn, looking at me and then each other. Zane swallows audibly, nodding. Gunnar's expression turns intense, but his scent actually lightens. Micah claps his shoulder briefly and calmly agrees, "Yeah, okay."

They all settle where they sit, and I lean forward, steepling my hands between my knees.

"Bonds."

The word is hard to say, but only because my Alpha wants to growl it.

None of them are surprised. No one's face so much as flinches. Which means we really have been on the same wavelength, each of us mulling this over while we worked.

Zane looks down at his hands, flexing them while he murmurs, "Without an established pack and a pack alpha, they'll be individual, right?"

Micah sighs. "Right. I've been—I was thinking about getting a different apartment, down in Orlando. I could try to figure out a system where I work down there for half the year and come back up here for the other half. As long as Knox would be okay with me crashing here."

Gunnar frowns. "So, you'd be coming to Florida for..."

"Your season," Micah shrugs. "I figure that whatever gives Emma access to all of us as often as possible is probably for the best. If I can do seasonal work for two stations, I'll be able to help her transition between being down there with you and being up here with Knox."

Zane's brows draw up, the expression hopeful. "I could—could I go in on the apartment with you, Micah? I can work from anywhere, and I don't want to be away from Emma at all. Especially not if we're bonded."

Gunnar grunts. "Hell, me either. I wish I didn't have to go back down there at all, but my suspension is up in three weeks. I really like my team, and I'm under contract for the next couple of years..."

He frowns at Micah, scratching the back of his head. "You guys don't need to get a separate place there, though. My loft has three bedrooms."

There's a bitter, broken part of me that hears how easily all of this works without me. Just like the last time I tried to have a pack—it all seems so much easier if I'm not a factor. These younger alphas, all living in Gunnar's bachelor pad...

What would they want me around for?

But Gunnar turns without hesitation. "What do you think, Knox?"

Zane half-smirks. "Yeah, Daddy, could you sleep on someone else's couch for a change?"

My lungs unclench. Relieved, I chuckle before I can stop myself. "What if I buy my own bed?"

"Or we could just share one like we do here," Gunnar mutters, rolling his eyes. When Zane shoots him a teasing look, he huffs, "What?! Is sleeping next to me so bad, Pretty Boy?"

Zane shakes his head slowly, looking oddly serious. "It's not bad at all."

Micah glances at them, then at me. "So... we'd pretty much

keep the same arrangement we have up here, but we would all have individual bonds."

The thought is maddening. Like an itch I can't quite scratch. What's the alternative, though?

Forming a pack? Letting these guys into my bond with Emma?

It kind of sounds like they're going to be there anyway. As long as we go with this plan...

Heavy silence descends, each of us holding back the one thing left to say. It beats in the air—so tangible I wonder if I even need to speak the words.

But the guys all turn to me. Counting on me.

"What if"—I stop to clear my throat, ensuring none of my Alpha's dominance influences the question—"we made a real pack?"

Gunnar's brows crunch lower. "With like... a *pack* bond?"

His question dangles over us, rapidly sucking all the air out of the room.

Until a happy hum approaches from the back of the house.

Smiling ear-to-ear, Emma walks in with a pile of stockings slung over her left arm and my Santa hat balanced on top of her head. Ever oblivious and upbeat, our girl bounces right into the middle of our all-too serious conversation, only pausing long enough to set my hat on McKinley's crown.

Her humming gets louder and peppier as she bustles to the mantle. I notice I'm not the only one who can't keep the stupid grin off my face as we watch her wobble on her tiptoes, stretching to hang the felt stockings.

Lights from the tree catch on glitter letters scrawled over the fuzzy cuffs of the oversized socks. Leaning closer, I see that they each have a name on them. *Our* names, written in Emma's bubbly handwriting.

My heart swells, cracking the crumbling remnants of its cage. It's a painful, awe-inspiring feeling, unlike anything else. But I think I know three other people who might understand why I suddenly have to work to keep my eyes dry.

I turn back to the guys and find their gazes just as glossy as mine. Slowly, they each look at one another, then me.

And I feel what no one says: Anything with this wondrous woman at the center? Would be the best thing to ever happen to any of us.

chapter fifty-one

MICAH HAS NAMED THIS CONVERSATION PACK GROUP CHAT

ZANE

Micah, man, we really need to work on your branding skills.

GUNNAR

Give the guy a break. We were all awake until like 3am

KNOX

We had a lot of shit to figure out.

ZANE

Annnnnd now we need to figure out a group chat name

Because this is just embarrassing.

MICAH

You come up with a better name, then, Knotty Chef

ZANE

I thought you'd never ask

ZANE CHANGED THE NAME OF THIS CHAT TO "EMMA'S KNOTTY LIST"

ZANE

you're welcome

GUNNAR

Well, fuck.

MICAH

Gotta give the man his due

He's good.

KNOX

Unrelated:

How do I mute a group chat?

GUNNAR

no chance gramps

MICAH

yeah it's too late for any of that

ZANE

no one can help you now muahaha

KNOX

God help me

I actually understood that.

IT'S BEEN two days since Knox made his house into a fairytale Christmas cabin.

Buuuuut having all the decorations we could possibly want didn't stop him from announcing we'd be going into town again.

Actually, they all *insisted*. Which works well enough for me, considering I have a bunch of secret stuff to pick up.

Knox drives, loading us all into his monstrous black pickup truck for the first time. To spare three of the guys smooshing into the back, I ride between Micah and Gunnar while Zane claims shotgun.

In a cream sweater that sets off his dark features, he looks extra-supremely handsome today. Every time I find myself lingering on his profile for a second too long, Micah chuckles and nudges me, nodding in Gunnar's direction to point out that my hockey star is staring at my chef quite a bit, too.

I swear, they are *so cute* I can hardly stand it.

Being shared by them yesterday was everything I ever imagined pack life could be. The way they both made me their sole focus and somehow got closer to *each other* in the process still has me floating on cloud nine.

If I weren't already madly in love with both of them, I would have been after that. Watching the way Zane stood steady as a rock for Gunnar while he was vulnerable? And how Gunnar looked to Zane for help instead of folding in on himself?

They're both amazing men. Just as incredible as Micah and Knox.

I still can't believe I got so lucky. Even if they never want to bond with me or form a real pack... these are my mates. How could anyone ask for anything more?

Um, because we *need* *them to* *bite* *us?* my Omega whines.

I give her the internal equivalent of a pat on the hand. *Give it time. They've all been getting along great, and today, they told me they want us to talk tonight. Maybe that's—*

Not soon enough, she replies.

Almost as evidence, my lower abdomen tenses.

Uh-oh.

Micah senses the way my shoulders stiffen. The arm draped

behind them slides down to hug me into his side. His lips graze my forehead and he hums. "You're warm, sweet girl. Do you feel okay?"

Staring up into his gorgeous hazel eyes, taking in the handsome planes of his face... *I feel* like I'm about to douse my panties for literally no reason.

Aside from, you know. Being surrounded by my ridiculously attractive mates.

But if I make so much as a peep about the twinge of pain twisting my core, they'll rush me home. And keep me there, curled up in the new nest, until my heat starts. If that happens, I may never get their gifts sorted.

Still, gazing right into Micah's eyes makes it hard to shake my head. I manage, but my heart pinches when some of the concern falls off his face, replaced by genuine joy.

Just from... looking at me?

My throat thickens as he bends to press his forehead into mine, scent-marking me thoroughly. A dizzy rush prickles over my scalp and down my spine, landing in a big belly flop.

I don't know what I did to deserve you.

Knox's whispered words after his rut have stuck with me because they're everything I feel when I remember I'm here, with all of them.

While I try to keep my giddy gratitude and small, crampy twinges in check, our truck lumbers into town. Everything is just as magical as I remember. A bit of my worry floats away when I spy the fat, colorful bulbs hanging over the whole stretch of Main Street.

My phone buzzes in the back pocket of my jeans, but I can't check it with Micah still holding me. He has no idea Zane helped me steal his brother's number from his contacts—or why.

Being a fellow omega, the youngest Patterson, Patrick, totally understood my obsession with getting them all perfect gifts for our first Christmas as—

Well.

Whatever we are.

I'm pretty sure I'll find out tonight... if my stupid heat cramps hold out that long.

They totally will, though. I'm not due until next week. Everything will be <u>fine</u>.

Once Knox parks, Gunnar is the first one out, offering his hand to help me down. Zane laughs when our hot shot ends up losing his balance two seconds before I set my palm against his. Knox steps in, righting Gunnar with an arm around his middle before reaching into the cab and lifting me down to the icy cobblestones.

He grumbles something to Gunnar about "proper boots" and drops a kiss on the top of my head before meeting Micah around the back of the tailgate. While they plan which stores to hit first, I surreptitiously check my iPhone and reply to Patrick's message.

Micah's little brother might be altogether sassier than his big brother—a lot like Lucy and me, honestly—but he's also just as sweet. He spent hours looking for exactly what I needed last night, and he went out of his way this morning to drop it off at the local pawn shop I called. Lucky for me, they have someone there who tinkers with broken items and dabbles in woodworking.

My perfectly coiffed alpha approaches from the front of the car, sweeping me into his arms and hugging me soundly. "Ready to go, gorgeous?"

When I told Zane I needed to stop at the pawn shop once we arrived, he didn't press me about why, but he agreed to walk me down. Apparently, he has his eye on something there, too, though he mimed locking his lips when I tried to squeeze details out of him.

I nod against his shoulder, flashing Gunnar a smile. "You coming with us, Hot Shot?"

Gunnar shuffles his feet and mutters something about needing to hit a different shop to grab new socks. It's so obviously untrue that Zane and I grin at each other in delight.

"You're getting us presents!" I accuse, bouncing.

"And you're a *terrible* liar," Zane adds, wrapping his arms around my front and setting his chin on my shoulder to raise his brows at Gunnar. "Abysmal, really."

"Be nice," I chide, giggling as I turn to face him. Zane casts a mischievous look at our hockey star and then smirks, "I think he prefers it when I'm *not* nice."

Gunnar's answering growl is enough to confirm. The throaty, sensual sound has slick seeping into my panties as perfume spins into the chilly air.

Zane chokes. Gunnar *groans*. And my body takes that as a green light, instantly pumping out *more* arousal.

Oh sugar cookies.

I can tell they sense something different about my scent. Before either of them can comment, I dance out of their grasps, turning for the pawn shop on the distant street corner. They mumble to each other but don't press the issue.

As Gunnar turns toward Micah and Knox, Zane starts to follow—

—only to run right into my back.

Because my legs have stopped working.

My *brain* has stopped working.

Across the sleepy street, a flip of auburn hair catches the late morning sun. Without many people around, I see all of them at once.

William, Rob, and Renee.

She scowls as Rob waves a shopping bag in her face. William laughs at them both, his eyes creasing while he slings his arms around their waists and pulls them into a hug.

My heart twists while my throat dries. *How many times did I wish William would pull me into one of those group hugs? How many times did they exclude me so blatantly? Why didn't I ever notice?*

What was *wrong* with me?

The neediest, naivest klutz who ever lived. And dumb.

My ears ring as the memory swirls through my mind. I brace

for the pain that used to come with those words—the horrible moment of realization when I have to admit just how accurate they are.

Except... it doesn't come.

Sure, it still hurts a little. But those criticisms hit me with a brief sting, then slide down my front like a fried egg off Teflon.

Because maybe I *am* needy.

But Micah *loves* to be needed. Every time I curl into his chest for comfort, I can *feel* his fulfillment. His... satisfaction.

He *needs* to be my protector and provider as much as I *need* his comfort. Would I ever call him "*needy*" for that?

No. Never.

And, yes, I'm naive sometimes. But I *like* to believe in good things—in the very best part of the people. I didn't realize how healing that could be for others until I met Zane.

When I meet new people, I *don't* see what everyone else sees—and that's exactly why I was able to see Zane for who he *really* is. The Knotty Chef, but so much *more*, too.

Klutz, though...

Klutz is a mean word, for sure. It should definitely sting. But when I think of it now, I just think of Gunnar falling out of the shower. And accidentally crashing into the bedroom yesterday.

Have I ever thought less of him for stumbling? I think it's only ever made me love him *more*. The same way the guys all claim they like how clumsy I can be—because they love how *excited* I get.

And dumb.

Those were the words that hurt the most, back when Rob said them. Probably since I've always thought of myself as a bit too ditzy for my own good.

Now, though?

It was dumb to drive up a mountain at night. Stupid to trust a group of strange alphas just because my instincts told me to. And downright *reckless* to run from a powerful alpha on the cusp of a *rut*...

But that was how I proved to Knox that I could handle his Alpha.

And now, here I am.

With four mates who I wouldn't trade for anything.

So, am I *dumb*? Or am I someone who follows their heart when other people would chicken out?

Actually, come to think of it, the last "smart" thing I did was sign up for a matching service... I spent *months* talking myself into it. Scientific results, a sterile environment, guaranteed results. All of that made perfect sense.

But it was also *all wrong*. For all of us.

If I'd listened to my "dumb" intuition, I could have avoided the whole painful ordeal.

Now, a new tingle of instinct creeps in as I watch the Dunlap pack laugh together:

I never belonged with them.

They never belonged with me.

But if I don't go tell them off for trying to use me? I'll regret it.

"Hey, guys?" I murmur, straightening. "I'll be right back, okay?" My alphas start to reply, but I move before I lose my nerve, darting across the street.

The Dunlaps spot me right before I reach them. All three rear back, shock freezing their faces.

Instead of whining or bursting into tears, I offer a half-smile. "Hi."

It's pretty funny, actually, watching them react. They each look at one another, mouths gaping. William is the first to recover, his blond features furrowing into a mask of anger.

"Emma, what are you *doing* here?"

I shrug, inhaling a burst of cool air. "I've been here. Staying in a cabin near town."

"*Seriously?*" Rob barks and puffs up into an aggressive stance. "Are you *seriously* walking up to us on the street? Acting like you didn't do anything wrong when you *left us at the altar*?!"

Oh boy.

He *really* shouldn't have barked.

I feel Knox before I hear him. A knee-buckling beat of dominance that would take me to the ground if Micah's arm didn't appear around my waist a second later.

All of my alphas are at my back, each of them just as jacked up as Rob but definitely angrier. Even Zane has a completely terrifying expression on his face.

"This is them, isn't it?" Gunnar guesses. "I recognize them from that night." He glances at the other guys. "These are the assholes who were going to use Emma like a fucking roundabout."

Micah releases a truly menacing snarl, and Zane starts to speak. Knox cuts them all off with a terse exhale—the tide of his dominance cresting over all our heads.

"Get behind me, baby girl," he bites out, strangling his own bark, leaving me as much freedom as he can.

My body flinches, wanting to obey anyway. But when I turn my head and meet his gaze, beseeching, some of the tension leaves his shoulders.

"I just need a minute. Please, Alpha?"

I hear the Dunlaps sputter. Knox cuts them a deadly look over my head but reaches up to rub his thumb over my cheek. "This face is too damn cute for your own good," he mutters. "Say what you need to say, honey. But we're staying here with you."

I like that compromise. With a bouncy nod, I turn back around and face the opened-mouthed pack across from us.

"I just—"

When I have to take a moment to gather my words, Gunnar grasps my hand and squeezes. Along with the protective angle of Zane's stance and the way Micah has his arm locked around my middle, I feel steadier by the second.

I soak in that sensation and exhale, pushing words out with my breath. "I wanted to tell you; what you did to me was wrong."

Renee makes a shrieking sound. "What *we* did to *you*—"

But I'm not interested in her phony outrage. "Yeah," I interrupt, louder than I meant to. But whatever. "I heard you talking the night I left. I heard what you *all* said about me. How you didn't want me and never had. You were using me to make yourselves a bond.

"And I was going to let it go without ever confronting any of you about it, but then I saw you here..." I gasp in another breath and blow it out. "What you tried to do to me was wrong. I didn't deserve it. I just wanted to tell you while I had the chance."

Gunnar's fingers slowly wind into mine. I hold Renee's stunned gaze, but I don't have to look at my alpha to feel how proud he is. How sorry he is that any of this ever happened because of something he did.

My Omega has already forgiven him. But having him here with me for this moment? Feeling his support and approval and pride? She practically *preens*.

I guess all is forgiven?

She nudges me hard. *Not now! We're telling this bitch off!*

The sour look on Renee's face informs me that we're pretty much done. She doesn't have anything to say now that all her nastiness has been exposed.

Rob does, though.

He booms an unkind laugh. "We don't give a shit about your hurt feelings. We got what we wanted most, anyway. Your trust fund will get us another omega within a month—"

Zane starts to lunge for him, and I *bark*.

"*No.*"

Every alpha around me goes still. I grab at the sleeve of Zane's sweater, pulling him close so he doesn't think I'm angry while I go on. "*No more.* I said what I wanted to. We can go now."

I think about all the money I lost, my shoulders rounding slightly as guilt worms its way into my guts. "There's nothing we can do about the trust fund," I add, murmuring to my alphas. "Just let them go."

Even though I know it's killing them, my alphas let the

Dunlaps slink off. They hustle up the street to the main drag and get into their rental car. Only after they've pulled out does Knox release a deep sigh.

"Idiots."

We all turn to him. His eyes still hold intense hostility, following their car into the distance, but his voice is calm. "Gunnar and I spoke with Ronan Ash yesterday. The contract you signed didn't guarantee them any money unless you *completed* your bonds. Theo very specifically had Ronan write that into the deal; they just didn't *mention* it to the Dunlaps. I guess they didn't read the fine print."

My pulse stutters, disbelief and relief flooding my lungs. "H-he did?"

Knox nods, brow still furrowed. "To protect you, little miss. Gunnar said he doubted Theo would ever agree to such a risky arrangement, and he was correct. The Ash Pack didn't lose anything. But even if they had? I would have paid it all back for you and set up a new fund. In fact, we're going to set up a new one for you that all of us can contribute to, anyway. We discussed it last night."

The beat in my chest gets louder, pounding my ribs with renewed ferocity. "B-but why would you do that?"

Knox looks around at the others, all nodding to each other—as if they all *really* talked about this. *Together.*

Like... a team. Or a...

Micah's protective arm-bar softens into a true hug while Gunnar takes my hand and brings it to his lips. Zane does the same, only he adds a small bite to my other palm.

But Knox holds my gaze, his blue eyes burning. "Because we love you, Emma. And we want to be your alphas. As a *pack*."

chapter
fifty-two

THE FOUR OF us surround Emma, holding our breath while she skirts those big, green eyes between our faces.

"Y-You—" she stammers, finally spinning back to Knox. "What?"

Our pack alpha steps into her space, framing her face with his calloused hands. "*We love you, Emma*. All of us discussed how we should tell you, and we thought doing it together would be best. To show you—we're in this together, now. *Because of you*. We *love* you, and we want to be your alphas. Your *pack*. If you'll have us."

Relief slips into my tight lungs, ballooning until they expand.

I've never had a pack of my own or a pack leader before, but in this moment? I *get* it.

Knox is steady and calm as he speaks for us, saying the words no one else could manage. I may have told Emma I loved her, but I'm not sure if I could have gotten the rest out. Certainly not with the soothing certainty the older alpha drapes over our group like a thick, weighted blanket.

"I— y-you do?" Emma whimpers, and all of us automatically draw closer.

"Of course we do," Gunnar asserts, his voice as fierce as his expression. He brings her fingers back up to his mouth, brushing his lips over her knuckles again. "You're our—"

He struggles for the word so Zane rasps it, his dark eyes floating from Gunnar's profile to Emma's green gaze. "Everything."

The word—and the truth of it—sinks into my center as I watch it soak into Emma. Pressing my front to her back, I hug her waist and murmur, "They're right. I know it must be hard to believe after the way those assholes treated you, but you really are *everything* to us, love."

With a thick swallow, I raise my eyes to Knox. He nods almost imperceptibly.

"We want to show you," I add, cuddling closer. "Through bonds, so you'll be able to feel it for yourself. Will you let us?"

For one brief, beautiful moment, her whole body goes lax. It seems a lot like the relief I just experienced—until she starts to stiffen a second later.

With my arms crossed over her diaphragm and a hand spread between her hips, I actually *feel* the cramp. A deep tweak that tightens the muscles and tendons under her thin sweater and my tingling fingertips.

"Baby," I mumble, disapproval and concern crowding my voice as I drop my forehead to scent-mark her shoulder so she knows I'm not angry. "Have you had cramps like this all day? Why didn't you tell me?"

She trembles in my embrace, wetness gleaming on her gaze as she turns to Knox with a pleading look. "I'm sorry! I was going to tell you all tonight that the heat cramps had started, but I needed to get all your Christmas presents first! And wrap them and—"

Knox cuts her off with a low, almost *soft* growl. "That was naughty, little miss. You always tell me when you're in pain. Especially this kind of pain."

He steps into her front, ignoring my arms folded between us to cup Emma's head in his hands once more, whispering so quietly I wonder if the others even hear him ask, "How is Daddy supposed to fix it if I don't know it hurts, baby?"

Her lips wobble while she turns to Gunnar and Zane, each positioned on either side of our pack leader. "I'm sorry—" she starts, but Gunnar makes a low sound, and Zane's face creases.

"No, gorgeous, *I'm* sorry," he replies, muscling closer. "I thought your scent was even more divine than usual in the car. I should have asked more questions."

When Gunnar offers a solid nod of agreement, Emma lets her weight fall against me. My stomach spins when her scent winds into the chilled air around us.

Fucking hell, she really *is* divine in the truest sense of the word. So heavenly, it almost *hurts*—the delicious thread of cinnamon sweetness slicing down my throat, a blade nicking my heart as it explodes to five times its usual size.

She *needs* me.

I feel the pull deep in my soul, even before she turns her face into mine and nuzzles my cheek. Heat sears my skin, sending a boulder tumbling through my torso.

Oh *shit*.

"We need to go," I rough out, ignoring the way my cock jumps to attention. When a second breath of her sweetness has my teeth grinding and my knot half-full, I drop into a protective bark. "*Now*."

Knox's eyes glint, the blue brighter than usual. He doesn't take kindly to me barking at him, but I think he might also be proud—he likes that I'm overprotective of our omega and have been since the day we found her unconscious in the snow.

"Back in the truck," he directs.

"But my gifts!" Emma cries, her voice already weaker than it was moments ago. "They're all ready and waiting and—"

Zane starts to purr, gathering her into his chest as best he can with my arms locked around her middle. "I know, *shona*," he hums, nestling his face into her hair and providing the empathy we nearly hurtled over in our panic. "It's important to you that we all have our presents, huh? And your Omega?"

When Emma nods so hard that her curls bounce, a hard lump settles in my gullet.

God. I love this sweet girl so much.

How did we get so *lucky*?

I know Gunnar is thinking the same thing when he reaches over to pet her hair, frowning softly in concern. Knox's brows fold down, his gaze snapping to the various shops and general holiday bustle just up the street. A scowl pulls at his mouth.

He's right to be wary. This is a safe place, but I still don't think it's a good idea to parade our perfuming omega around a crowd. Not to mention, she's already in a lot of pain.

My mind snaps a plan together. Knowing my brother is in town and has his own alphas to help him, I start to make a mental list of errands.

It isn't perfect—Patrick hasn't even gotten to meet any of these people yet, and asking him to run around on our behalf feels rude. Not to mention, he may be able to pick up Emma's gifts for us, but we don't have any for her.

Still, it's better than endangering her or letting her Omega stress unnecessarily.

"You leave it with me, baby," I whisper. "I'll get your gifts to the house, okay? They'll be waiting for you whenever you're ready for them. And I'll make sure McKinley is taken care of, too."

Hell, the dog will probably weigh five pounds more by the time Patrick and his pack are done spoiling him. But whatever. It's the holidays.

Knox's gratitude is palpable. He claps his hand on my

shoulder before hoisting Emma into his arms, carrying her with her legs wrapped at his waist and her arms around his neck.

She dives for his throat, inhaling and licking at his pulse. When her teeth flash and she nearly bites him, he stumbles. Gunnar is there at his back, though, keeping him upright.

"You should get some proper boots, alpha," the hockey player taunts, chuckling.

Zane huffs a laugh, slinging an arm around Gunnar's shoulders while he winks at Emma, his sly smirk drawing out a tiny smile of her own. "Can you believe this guy?"

I watch them all cross the street, the weight in my throat expanding.

My pack.

That's what they feel like. My own family.

So I pull out my phone and press the first contact on my Favorites list. It's a bittersweet feeling, knowing Patrick won't be at the top much longer. But it's also an incredible *gift.*

My own pack.

My own family.

And they're all waiting for me.

———————— ♥ ————————

"I KNOW, BABY, I KNOW."

My voice is rougher than I want it to be, but Emma responds anyway, her pussy clutching at my fingers in rhythmic squeezes that have me gritting my teeth.

I'm not the only one choking down growls. The entire cab of Knox's truck smells like cinnamon-sugared sex. Her scent is so fucking incredible; I've almost come from her writhing in my lap at least four times.

This is the closest call, though. With the way she bears down on a pained whine, her body demanding a knot we can't give her until she's safe in her nest.

Poor baby.

I stroke her inner walls as firmly as I can, hooking my fingers and twisting my wrist in circles. The easing technique helps, but it's not enough. She gives a broken sob and bounces on top of me, needing something thicker to fill her—and the hot lash of my cum to melt the pain away.

I want to fill her as many times as she'll let me. Until her pussy is *dripping*. Or should I say—until it *wants* to drip? Because I won't let her lose a *single drop*...

Fuck. The thought is enough to make me buck against her ass. I only barely manage not to spill, reminding myself that she needs it all inside of her. As much as all of us can give her.

The second Knox throws the truck into park, the others practically leap out. They've all been holding their breath as much as possible, trying to stave off the urge to fight me for her. I suspect they've appointed me the easing expert, given my medical training and experience with volunteering in clinics.

This is so damn different, though. Emma's heat perfume blurs my brain in a completely foreign, life-altering way. It feels like my actual body chemistry is changing—until each cell *vibrates* with the urgency to provide everything she needs.

Patrick must have raced ahead of us because McKinley doesn't greet us at the door when we step inside. Emma's presents aren't here yet, but I know he'll take care of it when he can.

And if the way my sweet girl tries to climb me as we make our way upstairs is any indication? Patrick has *plenty* of time. We're going to be busy for a *while*.

Knox leads us through Emma's cream-colored bedroom. My mind tilts as her tongue laps at my pulse, my knot screaming as I try to get my bearings.

Was it really only yesterday that he had everything delivered? The room is just as luxurious as I expected, but I can't take in any of the details. Within moments, it doesn't matter—because he guides us out onto the wide ledge of her suite's attached deck—

And the nest installed mere steps from the corner of the cabin's exterior.

With the thin layer of snow already layered over and around the large, round pod, it looks like it's been waiting for her forever.

Zane hums his approval. "This is nice, Knox. It matches the house perfectly."

Gunnar seems more tense. His shoulders twitch when the wind shifts and Emma's scent hits him in the back of the head. "Do you have the blankets she picked out in here?"

"Yeah," our alpha grunts, turning his key in the nest door's lock and casting his intense gaze over to Emma. "None of our clothes or scents, though."

My first instinct is to step in and fix it. But my arms won't unlock. The desire to be a team player is *nothing* in the face of my Alpha's roaring insistence that we *can't leave* our omega right now.

"I—" I start, struggling, "I could—"

Gunnar takes one look at my expression and slaps my arm in a gesture of camaraderie. "No, man. You always do everything for us. I'll get what we need. You stay with Emma."

Familiar gratitude—much like what I felt when Knox stepped in earlier—swells in my center. I nod brusquely, and Zane cocks a strained smile. "Besides, I'm pretty sure Daddy knows even less about nesting than I do."

Right. She needs to build her nest.

With us.

Suddenly, nothing has ever felt more right.

I carry her over the threshold and pivot to show her the room, whispering, "Look, sweet girl. Didn't your alpha get you a beautiful nest?"

It really is. The small dome is about half the size of her huge bedroom—much cozier, with only one circular window at the top of the rounded ceiling. I suspect the view of the night sky will be incredible. She'll love it—but, then, Knox probably chose it for that very reason.

He went with neutral sheets and a thick mattress to fill the nest crater in the middle of the space. Emma whines and wiggles for it, but our alpha steps up beside me and issues a gentle growl.

"Let us undress you first, baby girl. Then we'll build your nest with you."

chapter
fifty-three

THE HAZE HAS BASICALLY TAKEN over my whole body, aside from one tiny corner of my brain.

I cling to that last patch of logic, knowing I still need to—

I still need to—

Bite the alpha. Beg for his knot. Ask him for his taste and suck it down until we—

Gah! I try to take a deep breath and *think*, but I'm not great at focusing in the *best* of circumstances.

And *this*?

This is not the best.

This nest is beautiful, but it doesn't smell right. Every inhale reminds me that I'm missing things. Or a person? People?

No, pretty sure just one person and some things.

Gentle hands with rough skin rid me of my clothes. I look down at the big alpha crouched near my feet, carefully removing my shoes. It takes way too long for me to remember his name, but I finally do.

"Knox!"

It's a giddy squeal of relief and an impatient whine all at once. He likes it, though; his stern lips suddenly flick up at the corners.

"Yes, little miss?"

It feels stupid to admit that I'm just happy to be able to remember who he is. My cheeks and chest burn with a blush that softens the humor in his blue eyes.

"That's okay, honey," he husks out. "You don't have to talk if you don't want to. Or remember anything at all." With a tenderness I've never experienced during my heats, he leans forward on his knees and plants a kiss over my mound, murmuring quiet words into the curve of my belly. "I love you very much, Emma. Just remember *that*."

Memories flurry through my mind. This perfect alpha, promising me bonds and bites and a pack. Did all of that really happen? Was it a fever dream?

I whimper, and the alpha behind me lifts me right off my feet.

Oh.

I'm naked?

That makes sense, actually. There were all these *clothes* on me before—scratching and chafing. In fact, the man at my back still has his on—and *I hate it*.

With a growl, I spin and start attacking the horrible, needle-like material. Warmer, softer hands suddenly land on my shoulders, rubbing soothing circles.

"Shh, *shona*," an equally smooth voice croons, sliding against my side. A rush of perfect chai warms my nose, the sensation tingling down my body until slick slips from my center.

I sway toward the scent and those stroking hands. The third alpha's perfectly naked body presses into mine. "It's okay. Micah will take all his clothes off for you and help you build your pretty nest, hmm? Knox, too."

But someone is *missing*.

When I make a frantic sound, he shushes me sweetly, "Mm. And Gunnar. He's coming, baby. Just getting everything we need to make this space perfect for you."

The alpha in front of me strips, giving my blurry eyes something to focus on as I lean into the heat and spice enveloping me. "You want all of your alphas' scents in here, right?" he goes on, purring silkily. "Everyone all mixed together for you to roll around in? For your perfect pussy to squirt all over?"

My body convulses, slick pouring down my thighs. The way my belly flips isn't entirely comfortable, though.

The pack alpha must sense it. Now gloriously nude, he turns me toward him and holds my face in his raspy palms.

"Listen here, omega," he rumbles, edging so close to a bark that my pussy flutters in a painful squeeze. "I want your cum *all over* this nest. I want you to *gush* for us. And I never want you to worry about it for even half a second. Because we will relish *every drop* of your sweetness."

The other two growl their agreement, surrounding me with their hard bodies and delicious scents.

It still isn't *right,* though. My Omega starts to panic, bombarding me with frantic memories of the other heats we've endured.

The one who was supposed to want us never came for us, and we had to be with those alphas who didn't love us and didn't want us, and now the other alpha <u>*still*</u> *isn't here. And it's not right without him! It isn't*—

"Omega!"

It's him. His name comes easier, maybe because I've been trying desperately to recall it.

Gunnar.

He tosses a pile of sheets and clothes into the middle of the floor mattress and rips at his shirt, never breaking stride. When he reaches me, he sweeps me up into his arms and scent-marks me so thoroughly, it drowns out the strange sterile smell of the new nest.

"I'm here, omega," he pants, finding my eyes with his gray gaze. "I promised you I would be, and here I am, okay? Not leaving you ever again."

His expression shifts, and I know, somehow, that he's talking to *me*, not my omega. "I love you so damn much, sunshine. This is the only place I want to be."

The edges of my mind have started melting. Now that they're all here, in the small room, their scents nip at that little patch of logic I've been standing on.

I tremble, and Gunnar hugs me closer, managing to keep his balance as he steps down onto the recessed mattress. The others are there, waiting. They all open their arms and take turns touching me, putting their marks over Gunnar's scent.

It swirls my thoughts into soup but sharpens some other, deeper sense. My instincts lurch toward the pile of clothing, and four growly purrs rattle the scent-soaked air.

When I start to move, they all follow. I feel myself speaking, but I'm not sure what I'm *saying*.

Whatever it is, they listen. The warmth in my belly grows thicker as the pile of fabric becomes a real *nest*. With walls of pine and frost, tangles of spice, and nutty sweetness.

Chai threaded with cedar. Prickles of peppermint sprinkled about. Salty, roasted undertones woven in between.

As soon as I tuck the last pine-and-cedar pillow into place, a new sensation spirals through me. Just as strong as my frantic fears, but in the opposite direction.

Everything is *right*. *Too* right. So utterly, *perfectly*—
Ah!

My core clamps as a whine shatters the peaceful purrs filling my nest. Instinct zaps through my blood, lungs zinging on every inhale.

The others move, but I'm faster. Dropping to my hands and knees before I lower myself onto my elbows and raise my backside for them.

My Omega has the reins, but she allows me one final flicker of awareness. Showing me that the nest is done. Our alphas are here. And we're presenting for whoever wants to bite us first.

chapter
fifty-four

A HEAVY HUSH falls over the nest as our omega assumes presenting position.

I don't dare look. If I see her slick pussy raised high for the taking, I could lose my shit and start barking orders.

Gunnar, Zane, and Micah all turn to me, though.

Waiting.

Because *I'm* the pack alpha.

They trust me to run this heat. *Emma* trusts me. And her Omega does, too.

So I let all of the instincts I ordinarily keep leashed come to the surface—and the next thing I know, I'm in motion.

Making my way to the place in front of her. Not behind her.

Because I somehow know she needs my reassurance more than she needs my dick right now.

I'm her alpha. The leader of *her* pack.

I belong wherever *she* needs me.

"*Zane.*" My Alpha's voice cracks out, and I temper my dominance before continuing. "She needs a knot."

I feel the question in his eyes, but instead of asking why I'm letting him go first, he gets into position. Dropping his dark eyes to the back of her hair, he reaches one shaky hand out and smooths her curls to the side, carefully turning her head to reveal her face.

"There you are, *shona*," he whispers. "You need my knot?"

Her whines feel like metal shards scraping the inside of my skull. I grind my molars, holding in another bark.

It isn't necessary, anyway. As soon as the shrill, needful sound sails out of her, the other alpha snaps upright. His hands find her hips and knead them with rhythmic rolls as he fits the head of his long, dark cock against her opening.

A rush of perfume fills the pod, and he groans, eyes transfixed on whatever her pussy does in response to the press of his wide, purple head. She must be on the verge already—her knees quiver while her ass bucks backward, the muscles in her lower back pulling taut under her creamy curves.

Goddamn it. I hate that she's felt even a second of pain, but she's *beautiful* like this. Wanting and waiting, begging wordlessly for a knot to fill her gorgeous, gushing cunt.

I'm not the only one who thinks so. Gunnar and Micah have their hands wrapped around their erections, watching along with me. When both of them position themselves in her line of sight, I relax a fraction.

They're as amped up as I feel, but they're still thinking about *her*. They want to be sure she can see them, at least at the beginning.

She should settle as her heat goes on and she gets used to all of us tending to her. But for now? This is all new to her Omega. She needs comfort and to know *none* of us will leave her side. Especially not when she's in pain.

Zane starts pumping in steady thrusts, gasping, "Does this big cock feel good, baby? Because you feel so *fucking perfect*, I might never recover. *Fuck*, Emma. *Yes.* Pull me in *deeper.*"

Emma keens in reply. My Alpha hates that Zane works her up like this. He wants a knot in his omega *right fucking now.*

It's fine, I grit to myself, holding my urges in check while Zane pounds his shaft into Emma. *He'll knot her in a minute and she'll calm down.*

Besides, this alpha obviously knows what he's doing. It's my first time witnessing the way he moves inside of her, but he handles her body like he's been doing it for years. Knowing just when to speed up and slow down, keeping her on edge until he folds himself over her back and reaches between her thighs.

Fresh cinnamon perfection explodes as she screams her release and he roars, popping his knot into her. Chai mixes into the sweet cream squirting around his girth.

The tense lines of his face fall into a slack expression of awe, but Emma's only loosen a little before twitching right back to distress. Zane purrs, draping himself around her back while he murmurs praises and reassurances. She writhes, agitated.

"Bite," she begs, almost sobbing. "Please, Alpha. *Please.*"

Zane's rumbling chest catches as he speaks into the soft skin covering her spine. "Oh, baby, I want to. I *will*, but we have to wait, okay?"

The pitiful sound she makes in response is enough to break my fucking heart. When I hear it, I suddenly know exactly why she needed me in this position.

"Hey," I hum, stroking her hair. "Look at me, baby girl."

Glassy green eyes swing up to my face, a tear spilling over her nose. "I'm right here," I remind her, hoarse. "I'm here, and I see you, omega. I'm listening. I won't let you hurt, honey."

She blinks as she tries to absorb my words. More tears follow the first. My Alpha *rages*, but I ignore his fury and focus on the instincts underneath, carefully maneuvering her so Zane can stay knotted while her head rests on my left quad.

The second her cheek touches the sensitive skin along the inside of my thigh, I feel her heat in a whole different way. A sizzling charge races up to my groin, forcing a twitch of pre-cum from my throbbing cock.

Emma's eyes track the thick, white droplet. For a second, I'm relieved to see her signature eagerness—but she hesitates, skirting a fearful look up to me.

She's scared, I realize. *Or her Omega is.*

Which means those assholes who had her last heat with her must have been more cruel than she allowed herself to remember.

When this heat is over and I have time to make some calls... my Christmas gift to myself will be ensuring those pieces of shit never get another investor as long as they *live*.

There's no time for that now, though, so I shove my anger aside and focus on reassuring my baby girl that she has *nothing* to be afraid of.

"*Omega*," I bark softly. "That's *yours*. My cock, my knot, my cum. It's all yours, honey. You can take it whenever you want it."

Without any more delay, she scrambles closer, finding the broad, pulsing head and sucking it right into her mouth.

Fucking *hell*.

The wet heat of her lips and tongue stroke the pounding veins pumping under the thin skin. She sucks away my pre-cum with a starved moan, hugging me around the top of my hips as she bends her neck to slide further down.

Instead of sucking harder or bobbing back up, though, Emma just stays there. Zane caresses her back, running his hands over her body in soothing passes. His dark eyes meet mine in puzzlement, both of us trying to figure out what she wants.

Micah shuffles forward with Gunnar right behind him. The hockey pro seems as confused as we are, but Micah's expression turns solemn. He touches her cheek lightly, a sad smile pulling at his lips.

"She may not be doing it to make you come. She might just like the feeling of having you so close. Some omegas like to suckle their alphas' cocks for comfort during heats," he explains, leaning away to give me space as he frowns again. "She may have been afraid to ask us or tell us before because of... past experiences."

I feel like my chest is being cleaved in two when I turn back to Emma. The skittish twinge of her brow, the uncertainty in her hazy gaze, the way her fingers tremble as they cling to my back.

"Oh, sweetheart," I rasp, dragging my palm to her nape and squeezing to capture her full attention. "You want to have me in your mouth while you have Zane's knot in your pussy?"

Her answering nod is timid. My throat thickens.

"You're perfect," I assure her. "It feels so good, baby girl. I love it. You can suck on my cock as long as you want. And swallow anything I give you, hmm?"

Relief shines through her murky eyes. She huddles a little closer, settling in with her cheek pressed to my abdomen and my hard shaft softly sealed between her lips. When her eyes close in contentment, I nearly break.

Her trust is *everything* to me. I didn't realize how much I craved it until this moment.

It's going to be nearly impossible to wait to bond with her. I want the connection *now*. So she can feel with every breath exactly how much I love her.

And how *incredible* this is.

It's a level of intimacy that I never dreamed of. Unhurried, with no drive for any sort of result aside from closeness.

I want her to know how goddamn *good* that feels.

Her tongue laps against the underside of my cock while velvet warmth surrounds the top. Her full lips shift every few breaths, dragging up, sinking back down. Each time she swallows, there's a sudden clutch of heat that makes me want to groan.

Speaking over a lump, I work to keep my voice steady. "That's my girl. You make me so proud, you know that? No one has a better omega than our pack. *No one.*"

She whimpers and scoots closer.

"I'm right here," I rumble, purring louder. "I'm right here, and Zane is still in you, baby. He's been purring for you this whole time. I bet you feel it in your pussy, hmm?"

When Zane hisses, I know she's clamped down on his deflating knot. He glances over to the others, telling them they need to get ready. I hear them discuss it among themselves, but it feels like Emma and I are in our own little bubble.

I push her hair off her face again, massaging her scalp until her eyelids flutter. "You and I are going to do this all the time," I promise. "Anytime you need comfort, you're going to tell Daddy you want to suck this cock."

Zane disengages just as Emma moans, perfume and slick pouring out of her in a spice-tinged rush. Gunnar's head falls back on a sobbed groan. He grips the base of his thick erection with white-knuckled force. "*Fuuuuuck.*"

Something has snapped into place—for me and my Alpha. Because before her next whine even leaves her lips, I know what she needs.

"Gunnar," I grunt. "She needs more than one of us."

With a louder purr and some gentle shushing, I pull her mouth off me and lift her into my body. She only has time to rub her soaked slit down my abdomen once before I've positioned her over my throbbing dick and yanked her hips down.

Fucking—

Her cunt is mind-melting. Hotter than ever before, searing my cock with her slick, clenching core. It tugs me all the way in, until my knot slaps the underside of her swollen clit with every jerky bounce of her hips.

Shit.

I loose a growl, digging my fingertips into her plush waist. Sinking into her softness in every way. *Relishing* it.

Gunnar wastes no time, moving into position and reaching down to gather her arousal without thinking twice about how much he has to touch my knot in the process. While he works his fingers into her ass, Micah comes around my shoulder where Emma will still be able to see him.

"Did you hear your alpha, sweet girl?" he whispers, nuzzling his forehead against hers. "You're doing so good. He's so proud of you. We *all* are."

God. My lungs tweak tighter with every word. Then stutter entirely when Zane appears at my other side and puts one of our extra pillows behind my shoulders, ensuring Emma can ride me as hard as she wants without anyone needing to move.

I've had sex as part of a pack before, but it never felt like *this*. Like we're all helping each other—building up one another's relationships with our girl as much as we bolster our own.

Because they care, I realize. *About her and all of us.*

Even me.

Gunnar waits for me to look at him before he starts fitting his own cock into her. She's already strangling the cum out of me, but she must be even tighter back there because he only gets a third of the way in before he's panting.

"Fuck, Em," he growls, "Beautiful, dirty omega. I *love* seeing you skewered on two alpha cocks. Makes my knot so *fucking hard*."

Our omega gushes around me, soaking us both. His knot slips against mine, and I feel release barrel down my spine, lighting each vertebra on fire while I pound my hips up harder.

She takes it deeper, her pussy pulling in hungry squelches that suck my knot past the tight ring of her opening. It jolts into place, pressing into all the secret spots where she needs me most. Rubbing and tugging against her bucking thrusts and Gunnar's maddening pumps into her ass.

Her body locks down on us both, forcing a shout from Gunnar and a serrated snarl out of me. My vision flashes white as she squeezes us both, hiding her face in my shoulder, writhing and moaning.

Another beautiful burst of slick squirts out of her cunt, dribbling down my balls and Gunnar's pulsing knot. When he feels it, I sense his body tense, jetting into her ass.

Dragging in a loud breath, he falls against her, rubbing his face between her shoulder blades while I support their weight.

But as he settles there, his purr rattling to comfort our girl, I don't feel smothered. Not even when Micah settles beside one of my thighs and Zane the other, both of them reaching into our tangle to stroke Emma's arms and help her come down from her orgasm.

No.

I only feel... pride. Satisfaction.

And the swooping knowledge that this is just the beginning.

chapter
fifty-five

"GORGEOUS," I growl, hiding a grin. "Open up."

Emma tosses her head back and forth. When the low light coming through the ceiling's round window hits her, she really *does* look gorgeous.

Soft gold gilds her blonde curls as they bounce around her bare face. I'm taking *all* the credit for her hair after this heat. I've been making sure it's clean and putting oil in it whenever I find time to comb it out.

Our nest pod has a very small attached bathroom, but she hates it—probably because the limited space means only one of us can be in the shower with her at a time. The first night we tried washing her, she got so upset Micah wound up knotting her over the vanity just to keep her from accidentally hurting herself.

We got her into the shower after that, but I had to stand on the toilet lid and reach over the curtain to wash her hair since Micah had to use his arms to hold her against his body while I did it.

So, *yeah.*

Maybe we need a bigger shower.

Otherwise, apart from the mind-bending perfection of servicing Emma every hour or two, things have been calm. We've talked and not talked and slept whenever we can.

In terms of rest, I think Knox currently has the biggest deficit. He's been taking calls whenever he can, making all the arrangements we discussed before her heat and adjusting them as we think of new things.

If I ever wondered how I would feel about having a pack alpha, now I know how much we all *need* him. Yeah, Knox's dominance is way stronger than the average leader, but he wields it precisely—and takes care of shit I would never even *think* of.

Micah's been his usual green-flag self. He helps every chance he gets and says the sweetest damn things to Emma. She glows when he speaks to her—and I know his words soak right into the piece of her soul those other assholes stomped on.

My Hot Shot, on the other hand, has stamina to rival all of us put together. Anytime one of us is too depleted to go on, he taps in without hesitation.

And I get to watch, so...

I think I'm pretty much the luckiest alpha on the planet.

I've had the thought several times over the last five days, but most especially in moments like these, with Emma's hazy eyes beaming mischief at me.

She's so fucking cute, *oh my* God.

It took nearly two days of steadfast attentiveness, but by the third morning of her heat, our girl woke up from one of her mini-naps with a bright, lopsided *smile.*

She's been that way ever since—happy and excited. Trying to *play* with us, even though she isn't coherent. So much like *our Emma*, it makes us a little misty at times.

Hopefully, her haze will clear soon. She's been having more frequent moments like this, where her cramps are at bay and she just wants us for comfort and pleasure.

When she isn't in pain, her need goes from a wild stampede to more of a sweet, beseeching energy. If she needs us, she whines and climbs over to whoever she wants.

I love that there's no longer any fear on her face when she does that. She knows each of us will open for her. She feels like she can be herself.

She knows she's *ours*.

Waiting to *make* her ours has been fucking *torture...*

But at least her attempts at baiting us into biting her have gone from frantic to bratty. Now, when one of us gently scolds her for trying to take matters into her own hands, we just get a little snort and a pissy eye-roll.

See? *So. Fucking. Cute.*

We're currently in the middle of one of her brat attacks. The others are trying to catch some sleep while I feed her, but her Omega is totally goading me—refusing to take the last bite of her meal because she *knows* it makes my Alpha crazy when she doesn't eat properly.

Little does this naughty minx know, I've been sneaking extra veggies and protein into *everything* I slip away to make for her.

Still, a visceral part of me just wants her to *finish this damn bite...*

She shakes her head again, giving me a put-on pout that I totally know is fake... but it tugs at my heartstrings all the same.

My shoulders slump forward, a pout of my own pulling at my lips.

Gunnar shakes off his doze and crawls over, chuckling, "Let it go, Pretty Boy. It looks like she's eaten a good amount."

He reaches my side and settles close. We've been doing that more and more during the heat. Just... relaxing near each other.

His hip presses into my thigh while he sits, petting Emma's perfect curls and smiling at her. "You're trouble tonight, squirt."

Her answering grin is *dazzling*. Gunnar's pupils dilate while he absorbs it. His scent lightens; the sweet, salty smell so familiar now that I swear it feels like a part of hers. Or my own.

He cocks a brow at her, which only elicits a soft whine. I snort when it softens him instantly, smirking as he lifts her off my lap and tucks her into his purring chest. When she starts licking his throat, he simply bends his head and lets her.

"You're worse than me!" I laugh.

With a wince, he guides her face into the crook of his neck and rests his cheek against her crown. After a peaceful moment passes, our gazes catch and hold.

The current running between us ramps up every time that happens. Rising higher and crackling louder.

I watch an idea form behind his brow. Suddenly, the nuttiness in the air grows so rich, even Micah stirs. Knox must truly be exhausted because he keeps sleeping—although, as the days wear on, his Alpha has trusted us more and more on our own.

I shrug, deciding to take his quiet snores as a compliment. Then I sit forward, tilting my head at Gunnar. "What are you thinking?"

Micah yawns and rubs at his eyes, glancing over just in time to catch Gunnar's answering shrug. "I was thinking—if our omega needs to *eat* more, we need to *feed* her."

"We?" I repeat.

He holds my eyes, nodding slowly. "Yeah. We."

Oh, fuck.

I told you Hot Shot was murder for my game.

But I can't have him forgetting who's the good boy around here. Because it definitely isn't *me*.

"How would we do that?" I ask, narrowing my eyes. "You want to race? Or..."

Micah gives a good-natured snort as he approaches. He drops a kiss to the back of Emma's head and whispers to her, then looks between Gunnar and me with wry amusement.

"Can you two stop flirting and pick a position? Because I'd like to know where to put myself in order to lick our omega's pussy," Micah half-jokes.

Emma whines, scrambling up with a hopeful look in her bleary eyes. Micah flashes his kind smile at her, holding his arms open so she can leap right into them.

"Yeah? You like that idea, sweet girl?" When she whines and sucks at his pulse, he groans, "Guys? Hurry up."

"What do you want to do?" I ask Hockey Boy again. "One at a time or...?"

He bites his lip and looks down at the way I've hardened into stone. "Together," he roughs out.

This stuff is still a big deal to him. Knowing that softens the edges of my grin as I stand, reaching down to help him to his feet and sliding my hand up his arm to steady him. I leave my palm spread over his shoulder, meeting his eyes again.

"Together, then."

Zap.

Was that lightning?

No, just whatever is happening here between me and Hockey Boy.

Emma keens, and Micah kisses her as he holds her in his lap. Giving us time, I suspect, to work this out with as much privacy as he can possibly offer.

Gunnar watches them for a moment before turning to me. Showing me that flash of vulnerability so few ever get to see.

"Come here," I murmur. "I know what to do."

He listens, moving closer to let me position his body with mine in a way I know will work. He's a little taller, so when I fit the front of his left hip against the front of my right, his cock bobs just over mine.

The arrangement I have in mind won't necessarily be the most natural one, but his dick already leans slightly to his right, so bending it a bit to get us lined up won't be that different.

"Trust me?" I ask, glancing over for his approval. When he gives it, I grasp us both, only squeezing slightly as I fit his dick over mine and stroke to my left, aligning us to face Emma.

Which is as far as I get before I'm ready to burst.

Fuck, Gunnar is *scorching hot* and so damn *thick*. His girth bathes the top of my shaft in pulsing heat as he fidgets slightly, finding that the most comfortable place for his left arm is across my back. At first, his hand hovers near my side, but after a beat, he presses his palm there purposefully and... starts stroking.

Oh, damn. I like that.

"Good boy," I mutter, snaking my own free hand behind him to rub the small of his back. "You'll need to hold on for this."

Before he can reply, I fist both of us—my fingers stretching to reach halfway around—and tug.

This time, he growls, kicking his hip into mine. I rub the heads of our dicks together, slowly squeezing them until the pre-cum leaking from his slit wets the top of my tip. The next time I roll my fingers, we both groan at the slick friction.

Emma turns at the sound, her eyes burning even brighter. If I weren't so focused on chasing the pound in my knot, I might even laugh at the way she stares, her mouth open.

Our girls *loves* watching me jack Gunnar off. I knew it the first time it happened, but her heat has confirmed beyond a shadow of a doubt. Anytime we need to mesmerize her, this is the way to do it.

And her *perfume*.

Good, sweet *Lord*.

She wets her lips, the motion absent, and starts to crawl for us. Micah follows with a grin, letting her get up onto her knees between Gunnar's leg and mine. Once she's there, watching me rub our cockheads together, the firefighter lies down facing the other direction and nestles his head between her thighs.

"Sit right here, love," he husks, petting her ass with both

hands to guide her into place. "Fuck, you're soaked. Watching your alphas touch each other turns you on so much, doesn't it?"

Emma's answering whine is helpless and a little dazed. Gunnar threads his hand into her hair, his fingers tracing soothing circles. "We love it, omega," he assures her. "And we love *you*."

He really is sweet to her. The hand I have at his back dips lower, wanting to show him how grateful I am for that. When I cup one of his muscular ass cheeks with my palm, goosebumps prickle his skin.

Huh.

We'll definitely be looking into *that* later, but for now, I have to help my gorgeous girl fit two cocks into her mouth.

Gunnar's already on it, taking advantage of Micah's good work and Emma's open-mouthed gasps to rub her parted lips against us. One brush over my leaking slit has me salivating.

Emma, too, apparently, because she sucks at us both, humming in ecstasy while her eyes fall closed. I smell her slick, even before Micah growls at its taste.

Fuck *me*, this is so hot.

But can my Hot Shot leave well enough alone?

Of course not.

Keeping one hand on Emma's head, he guides her forward to take us both deeper. We stretch her pretty mouth until it can't accommodate any more. When I shift, putting our dicks side-by-side instead, she hums her approval and sucks both harder.

Gunnar shifts to slip his other hand in front of me and grab hold of my knot. With firm, slow motions, he kneads the throbbing mass until it swells for him.

Fucking *fuuuuuck*.

I curse, palming his ass harder, kneading it the same way he's working my knot. Micah slurps more of Emma's cream, his hips bucking into the air as he does.

Emma's face is rapturous. With eyes half-lidded, she licks the underside of both of our dicks, then slicks the space between them. Gunnar moves his fingers with more purpose, trying to drive me toward a faster finish.

Always trying to win, my Hot Shot.

As if I'd ever let that happen.

I grasp the bottom half of his shaft, knowing Emma won't be able to take both of us that deep, and start jacking him off while she swallows around her mouthful. He groans, the sound mingling with the moan that vibrates over both of us as Emma comes on Micah's face.

FUCK.

My core clenches as release bursts out of me. Knot expanding into Hockey Boy's rhythmic squeezes, cock spraying down Emma's throat and all over Gunnar's dick. He chokes on a growl, his ass twitching as he follows me over the edge.

Right where Emma and I wanted him.

chapter
fifty-six

WATCHING Emma swallow two loads from my packmates while I stare between her naked breasts and feel her pussy gush all over my mouth?

Holy shit.

My Alpha lunges, and so do I.

We sense the pack leader stirring across the nest, but that isn't important right now. In this moment, all that matters is sinking *my* knot into *my* omega.

She wasn't cramping before—but having an orgasm without one of us wedged inside her must have triggered some. I feel them hit; her pussy fluttering in a way that feels similar to a climax but doesn't come with the delicious squirt of cinnamon cream she usually gives us.

When she squeaks a second later, I fly into action, clamping my hands around her thighs and lifting her onto my waiting erection. I shove into her right away, relief bursting across my field of vision like a shower of sparks.

God, she feels so *good.*

It doesn't matter how many times I have her—every thrust into her slick perfection is like coming home.

She needs it hard this time, so that's how I give it to her, jacking my hips up and letting her ride me fast. It doesn't take long for her inner walls to clamp and *pull*, popping my knot into place.

"That's right," I rough out. "Come all over my knot. Fuck, yes, sweet girl. Milk this cock until your insides are soaked in me. I want your pussy to be glazed with it."

I really do. Pumping my release into her and then locking it all in fills me with untold satisfaction. And knowing she already has Gunnar and Zane's warming her belly makes it even better.

"My well-bred baby," I grind. "So full with all your alphas' cum. We all want to mark you, keep you stuffed with as much of us as we can."

Her pussy snatches my knot as she comes again, the pleasure wracking her body in a hard shudder. My knot expands, sealing us together when I make good on my threats and paint her depths.

We both go down hard, me falling onto my back and Emma landing over my chest. Her back expands on short pants, but her eyes are already closed, her features slack.

Fuck. My sweet love.

She may be in good spirits, but her body is *exhausted.*

Worry takes root in my chest as I watch her melt into my embrace, her eyelids never so much as flinching. It's been five whole days, and she still isn't truly coming around. Tomorrow is Christmas—and I know she'll be so sad if we miss it.

"This never happened during any of my volunteer sessions at

the clinic," I murmur to the others, feeling Knox approach as Gunnar and Zane untangle themselves from their heap of sweat-misted muscle. "She's clearly wrung out. I wonder why her Omega isn't satisfied yet."

Our pack alpha starts purring when he gets to my side. I turn, letting Emma slip into the space between us so we can both soothe her if she wakes up again.

Gunnar and Zane start up, too. The four rumbles rolling together help me unwind a bit. My tired bones sink into the mattress. I soak in the silence and start to maybe even sleep a little before Gunnar asks, "Is it possible her Omega is *too* satisfied?"

My eyes crack open at the same moment Knox turns to frown over his shoulder. "What do you mean?"

"Like," Gunnar posits, "if the other alphas made her feel like shit for being in heat and needing them, maybe this is the *opposite* of that?"

I'm not sure I follow, but Zane does. He goes wide-eyed as Knox narrows his gaze and clarifies, "So, her Omega is getting what she's needed this whole time and doesn't want to give it up?"

Collective silence swells between us.

Until Zane curses, of course.

"Fuck," he laughs, "Are we doing *too good* a job?"

Gunnar shakes his head, peering over Knox to gaze lovingly at our omega. "Nothing could ever be *too good* for her. *Look* at her."

Knox smirks softly. "Agreed. Still, I think Micah has a point. Tomorrow is Christmas. She'll be devastated if she wakes up after it's passed. I think we need to give her a jolt. *Thoroughly* wear her Omega out."

Zane sighs, joking, "I mean, I have some ideas, gramps, but we're all going to have to stretch first—"

Gunnar scoffs, punching his arm. "You're such a dick. This is *serious*. I want to bond with her *now*."

Zane agrees, his second sigh sounding more genuine. "Okay, okay. Let's get real. Anyone have any thoughts?"

I mentally tick down her list, scratching out things we've already done—*DP, cockwarming, spitroasting*—

There's only one thing left.

And about a dozen ways to combine it with her favorites.

"I think I have a plan."

chapter
fifty-seven

THE NEXT TIME she wakes up, Emma is bundled into my side.

Her eyes are still hazed, and she doesn't say my name, but when I cup her cheek in my palm and scent-mark her forehead, I get a tiny smile that almost seems lucid.

I love that her Omega has felt so safe with us, but I also miss our girl. Her jokes and questions and eager curiosity. I know Emma's still in there—I can see her right now—but she shouldn't have to miss our first Christmas as a pack.

And Micah's plan is *insane*.

Part of me wants to try it purely to see if it will actually work.

Another part can't resist the unmatched pleasure of being in

Emma's sweet little cunt, no matter what lunacy I have to put up with to get there.

But mostly, I feel in my bones that I'm right about this. Her Omega is glorying in experiencing a heat with alphas who adore her—one big shock to her system might be enough for Emma to start feeling her way out of the haze.

"Hi, sunshine," I murmur into her hair. Through the pod's skylight, the last flecks of twilight fade into the clouds. "You let us all sleep for a bit, huh?"

She must have. After that last round, the four of us discussed our plans and then huddled around her for whatever rest we could scrape together. The sun was still shining when we all closed our eyes, so a few hours must have passed, at least.

I know that's a good sign, even before Micah burrows closer to Emma's back and skims his lips over her shoulder. When his hazel gaze snaps to mine, I can basically hear his thoughts.

She's cooler.

Which means now is a good time for us to do this.

A deep vein of anticipation carves its way into my abdomen. I look down at her drowsy face and love expands to block my throat, turning my voice into a hoarse rasp. "What first?"

"One more round," he says slowly, thinking while he examines her profile. "Then, I think she'll be ready for us."

Em hears that and lets out an excited squeak. The tiny whine rouses Knox, who lurches upright behind me. One glance between Micah and I has his stoic face splitting into a quick grin, though his tone is rough from the growl that echoes in his throat as he watches our omega stretch out her limbs. "There's my baby girl."

Zane pops up, too. "Holy shit," he mutters, rubbing his brow with the heel of his hand. "Is that what *sleep* feels like?"

He flashes his signature smile when he sees the way I'm clutching Emma to my chest, then turns to Micah. "We're good to go?"

Micah shrugs, sitting up. "As long as she is."

Zane purrs, crawling over Micah's lap to get between Emma's legs. He sets his face against her belly and nuzzles there, humming, "Mm, what do you think, *shona*? Are you ready for a special treat?"

Her gaze sparkles while she nods, whining for a third time. Knox kneels up, reaching over to pet her hair. "You were a good girl, resting for us. Now that you have your strength back, you get all four of your alphas at once."

The sticky, mouth-watering sweetness of cinnamon buns fills the nest. Thick and so warm—absolute perfection, especially when it blends with all of our scents.

Zane makes a pained sound, his brow pulling tight, and I realize she's doused his chest with slick. When he sees the sheen of wetness glazing his pecs, he drags his finger through it and brings it to his mouth.

My brain breaks a little, but I'm not alone. Emma's whole body quivers against me, her next whimper desperate.

"Alpha, *please*."

"Let's do it now. I don't want her hurting," Knox grunts.

His steely dominance lights a fire under all our asses. Micah shuffles to one end of the nest on his knees while our pack leader scoops Emma into his burly arms. Zane stares after her like a waiter's just snatched his favorite dessert away before he could even take a bite.

I snort and slap his back. "Come on, Pretty Boy."

As he snaps to his knees, all panther-like grace, I see he's already harder than I am. His long cock bobs against his abs as he goes to the spot opposite Micah and lies down.

Something about the way he moves—without a care in the world—undoes the sudden tension surrounding my lungs. I've never done what we have planned before, but Zane told me he'd handle it and I believe him. Especially when I see how relaxed and happy he is, smiling softly as he watches Knox coo to our omega.

"So proud of you, honey," he's saying. "You've done so good."

She purrs back at him, the small sound as bubbly and sweet as her moony smile. Knox can't seem to keep a straight face when he looks at her—another grin splits his features and he drops a kiss to her forehead.

"You want this?" he checks, inhaling her scent for any hint of distress. "All four alpha cocks at the same time?"

Her next whine is a bit growlier, like she's sick of all of us baiting her and wants her damn treat.

Fuck, she's adorable.

I chuckle, moving closer to the others. Lingering beside Zane until he rolls that dark, playful gaze up to mine. "Fancy meeting you here, Hot Shot."

Rolling my eyes, I nod at his erection. "How am I doing this?"

His lips twitch up at my impatient tone. "You're getting on top of me," he replies, all indolent charm.

"I'm bigger than you," I point out, unease swooping through my stomach... along with something that feels a lot like excitement.

His brow quirks. "I'm longer than you."

He means his dick. And that much is true—I'm wider, and my body likely weighs more, but he has the length for sure.

I glance down at myself and over at him again, contemplating. I hate to admit when I'm out of my depth—which is probably something I need to work on now that I'll be in a pack—but I actually have no fucking idea what I'm doing when it comes to stuff with Zane.

He's always kind about it, though. Sweet in a surprising way that reminds me why I decided he's good enough for my sunshine.

"It's okay," he says, softer. "Just sit at the bottom of my torso, facing out, and slide down until we line up."

I follow his directions. He props himself up on his elbows, biceps and traps bulging as he steadies us. With impressive core stability, he holds his body still while I awkwardly sling my leg over his hip.

His abs tighten under my ass as he lifts his pelvis slightly, waving his hard length between our spread thighs. "Good," he grits. "Lie back..."

I listen, reclining as he does the same, until he's underneath me with the back of my head on his left pectoral.

Chai spice rises off his throat, thick and hot. I feel my own scent swell in reply, balls tingling.

"Good," he praises again, much quieter. His right hand clasps my shoulder and pushes lightly. "Now lower."

That part makes perfect sense. I bend my knees a bit and slide against him until our dicks brush, both of us sucking sharp inhales through our teeth.

When the back of my knot presses into the front of his, he chokes on a growl. "Fuck, Gunnar."

Emma answers, gasping a moan. When I glance across the mattress, I see that Knox and Micah have her propped between them, stroking and rubbing at her without any penetration. Preparing her—because she's about to be as full as an omega can possibly get.

The thought alone makes my cock kick. It jerks into Zane's, the glistening tip smearing wetness against mine. Emma watches while he reaches his long arm down and starts jacking us slowly, rolling our wide, warm cockheads together in the way I've come to love.

My head falls back on a pant. *Fuck.*

Emma loves that shit, too. My dirty, beautiful girl watches with rapt attention every time we touch each other, and now is no exception.

Her pink tongue darts out to lick her upper lip as I buck into Zane's hand, pleasure zinging up my spine when he presses his spread fingertips along the veins pounding up my girth.

Fresh perfume fills the nest and Knox huffs it down, growling low in his chest as he brings our omega over to us. Moving with care, he lifts her over our laps.

"I want you to ride these alpha cocks, baby girl," he husks, eyes glowing down at her. "And if you can manage that, Micah will fill your tight little ass, too."

Zane holds our shafts together, aligning us both with Emma's pussy. I feel the heat of her before she even touches me—wet warmth that bathes the last sliver of air between our bodies.

Under mine, Zane's dick hardens even further. His extra length allows him to line us up just right. And the second Knox lets Emma go?

She *plunges* down.

Oh, holy fuck.

A shout tears out of me as her pussy glides around our swollen heads, pressing them tighter, smothering them in slick. Slippery muscles massage Zane and I against one another, every inch even more breath-taking than the one before it.

HOLY FUCK.

Micah's chest vibrates on a purr while he slides into Emma's back, holding most of her weight while still letting her ride us. Knox stands beside our tangle, reaching down and lightly gripping our girl's hair in his fist, muttering praises.

"So goddamn beautiful. Your cunt was built for this, omega."

Under me, Zane gnashes his teeth in a snarl. One of his hands comes up to grasp the hair at my crown while the other releases our cocks and moves to Emma's hip.

Micah holds her up and Pretty Boy directs her pace, yanking her as far as she can go on every thrust. Stuffing our cocks into her silken whirlpool of heat... until she's nearly taken us down to the root.

"Fuck, I want to come," I bite out, catching Zane's rhythm and matching the pump of my hips to his. "You're so fucking *perfect*, Em."

Over the slope of her shoulder, Micah nods his agreement. He scoops cinnamon slick off her thighs and gathers it in his palm. When he exhales hard, I assume he's covering himself in her essence.

"That's my good little miss," Knox rumbles, stroking her face.

"So good, we're all going to give you our cum at the same time. You ready for Micah to stretch that cute little asshole?"

She keens, squeezing the *absolute life* out of me and Zane.

Jeeeeesus.

Fucking her suddenly feels like fighting for my life. I *have to* pound my throbbing cock into her, feel the way she grips me, feel the way Zane's hardness glides against my own.

The harder I thrust, the more he slows, dragging in loud breaths and pulling at my hair while he curses. He lets me fuck her fast and furious, moving his hips in small circles under mine, rubbing the head of his cock against the underside of mine until I think I'll go crazy from the tingles sparking there.

Emma's body bucks as Micah starts to work his way into her ass. Zane and I both snarl—Micah's cock is huge, and having it pressed under Zane's makes our tight fit even snugger.

Way snugger.

Shit. Fuck. Damn it.

Emma's mouth hangs open while she squirms over the three of us. Micah bands his arm around her waist, lifting her into the rolls of his hips and mine.

Zane's hand drops from my hair to my thigh. He holds it against his in a demanding way that tells me he's back in control.

I'm shocked at how easy it is to let him take over, setting a new pace in time with Micah's. When the fireman alpha pulls back, Zane and I shove in deep. When we drop down, Micah surges forward.

Emma whines and moans, begging incoherently for bites and cum and more, more, *more.* Knox gentles her every time, waiting until we've all found a steady cadence before completing our circuit.

"Open up for Daddy, baby girl," he directs, sending a soothing beat of steadiness over all of us. "Let me finish filling you up."

Her bright eyes tear, happy sobs catching in her throat as he tilts his rigid cock between her lips.

"Shh," he soothes, gritting his teeth while she licks him, "You're okay, honey. You're doing so well. We all love you so much, Emma."

"So much," Micah pants, dropping his forehead to her shoulder with a groan. "God, guys, I can't—"

I know the fucking feeling. My balls are so tight, jiggling over the soaked heat of Zane's knot while his cock slides along mine. Emma's walls squeeze and glide around us, tugging on both shafts when they're not milking Micah. Her throat works as Knox steps closer, giving her the last few inches of his girth.

She's *glorious*.

A goddamn dream.

Ours

Mine.

Zane feels me slow as I watch her in awe. He thrusts for us both, rolling in those smooth undulations he's so skilled at. "Good boy," he murmurs, all silk and sin. "You knot her, okay? I'm about to go off all over your nice, thick cock. Get you all lubed up to shove deep and seal both our cum in."

Ungh.

Holy—

Fucking—

God.

His fingers dig into my thigh as he thrusts one final time and explodes. With a broken groan, I grind upward, barely giving him time to pull out before I lose control and knot Emma.

Feeling the new width stretching her through the thin wall between us, Micah curses and pushes deeper, a serrated sound ripping from his center while he comes, too.

Emma starts to twitch. Her slippery heat and Zane's release surround my throbbing girth, swirling in the most perfect sensation I've ever experienced. My mind blinks offline, instinct overtaking me as Emma bears down, her own orgasm drawing mine out.

Knox waits until we're all spent to fall over the edge. When

Zane catches me against his chest, hooking an arm over my shoulder and across my neck, our pack leader relaxes.

His watchful, protective gaze snaps back to Emma's face. All the tension leeches out of his body as he gives into her starved whines and shoots down her throat.

Micah is there to support her when she collapses. Knox shakes off his climax and follows, going to his knees at her side.

For a long moment, we all focus on remembering how to breathe.

Then, I hear a tiny oh-so-beloved giggle. And the words, "Oh holy *night*."

chapter
fifty-eight

MY BRAIN FEELS BLURRY, like an unfocused camera. Or maybe just a really smudged one.

Either way, the small bulbs dotting the rim of this round room give off hazy halos I can't quite hone in on. Instead, my eyes latch onto the small, distant pinpricks glowing above.

Oh.

Stars.

They're *beautiful*. A cosmic soup swirled into warmer shades of midnight, like thin clouds instead of clusters of light.

My vocal cords tingle as if I've just spoken for the first time in a while. Or maybe in a different voice than the one my Omega's been using.

I reach up to touch the place in my throat where the words echo—

And devastation sinks through me.

My fingers fumble on either side of my neck, searching, but...

It's blank.

I eke out a whimper, but a rough hand cups my cheek, interrupting. "Look at me, baby girl. I'm right here."

My head lolls for a moment, spinning. The command wasn't a bark, but I still feel compelled to obey. Which makes sense as soon as my gaze finally finds the burning blue orbs staring down at me.

Alpha, my Omega tells me.

Knox, I whisper back.

I'm so relieved to remember his name, I grin over my disappointed tears. "Kn-Knox?"

His purr roars louder, even as his face falls. "What's the matter, honey? Was that too much? Did we hurt you?"

Long, cool fingers wipe the sadness from my cheeks, another purr crowding into my side. I turn and find beautiful hazel eyes full of worry.

Micah.

"Sweet girl," his hoarse voice whispers. "Are you having another cramp?"

The roiling ache in my belly seems quiet, actually. I may not be totally out of my haze, but the heat has broken, and I should only need a few more rounds—if any.

But, right now, I don't want anything other than—

Them.

Their bites. Their *bonds.*

My fingers tremble against the unbroken skin of my throat, my bleary eyes swimming from Knox to Micah, wondering where my other alphas are. Why they didn't stay.

They must have changed their minds.

I probably made too much of a mess. Or got too needy with my whines and purr-seeking.

Disbelief still reverberates through my murky mind. Because...
no.

*No, they wouldn't leave me. They both promised. Gunnar
especially.*

I'm used to that hopeful, positive voice being wrong. But a
second after the thought finally forms, they both appear,
crowding behind Knox and Micah.

Of course they're here, my Omega says, self-assured. *They're
ours.*

The whine ringing through the air—*oh, that's me?*—cuts off.
My eyes roll up in a laggy blink, scanning their familiar features.

The gloriously gorgeous one with his furrowed glossy brows is
my Zane. And the shredded Adonis with pain written across his
expression is my hot shot, Gunnar.

He's here, looking at me like he'd give the world to erase whatever my face is doing.

He kept his promise.

It's not easy, but I force myself to *think*. They're all still here.
They all stayed, like they promised. And judging by how satisfied
my Omega seems, they took *very* good care of me.

Relief mingles with the tightness crowding my lungs. I try to
focus on that and not the empty crater at my center.

Telling myself it's okay.

It's *fine*.

It's—

"It's time," Micah murmurs, feeling my forehead. His eyes
drift up to one of the others, but his smile grows. "She's ready for
you, alpha."

Ready? For what? More?

I mean, my pussy feels a bit, um, overused. *But I suppose I
could...*

He must have meant more *cuddles* because the creamy nest
blurs as Knox gathers me off the mattress and into his wide chest.
The hair dusted there tickles my cheek, a sensation so innately
familiar I know he must have spent a good bit of my heat holding

me just like this. When his purr quiets into a more intimate sound, I understand why.

It's just for me.

The second I relax, his frown dissipates. Soft blue beams trace my features before flickering back to Micah. "Are you sure? She doesn't seem to understand what's happening."

Gunnar crouches at my eye level, his gray-gold gaze swirling. "Em? Can you hear us?"

With another buffering blink, I manage a nod. The lines of his face pull tauter. "You seem so sad, though, sunshine. What's going on?"

Zane shuffles over, pressing his warm palm to my cheek while he frowns tenderly. "It won't hurt, *shona*." He leans closer, a hint of his usual spark igniting in those bottomless brown eyes. "I'll make it feel good for you, I promise."

A tingly rush trickles into the space between my hips. Perfume swirls into the nest while a burst of slick slips onto Knox's lap.

The rugged alpha growls, low but gentle. He tempers it, but the sudden rush of his dominance batters me.

When I look up and see him strangling a bark, I remember how often he does that. For me.

For *all* of us.

Instead of demanding, he rests his forehead against mine, murmuring, "I want to bite you, omega."

He—*he does?!*

Elation bursts through my body, but he's still *talking*. "Make us all one bond. But only if you—*oomph*."

Deep, masculine laughter fills the nest as I land on top of the pack alpha, climbing up his torso to rub my scent all over his face. Along with a few dozen kisses.

"Bonds, bites, please."

My desperate whine drops into a whimper as he bands his thick arms around my back and chases my lips, capturing them with a groan. "Hell, baby girl," he hums. "Did you think we'd changed our minds?"

Now would possibly be a good time to lie.

But we all know I'm no good at that.

Instead, a shrill keen tears out of my lungs. Within a second, the alphas have me surrounded, all purring and reaching for me.

"Never, *shona*," Zane gasps out first, his beautiful eyes glossing. "Fuck, I'll *never* change my mind about you."

Micah nods his agreement, dragging his fingers over the bare expanse of my throat while he husks, "You'll see, sweet girl. When I bite you—you'll see how much I love you. How I could never stop, Emma."

Gunnar pulls my attention away with a tender squeeze of his palm against mine. He bends close, whispering to me in that special way he has—the one that tells me he isn't just talking to me, but my Omega too.

"I wanted to wait for *you*," he explains, the gold streaks in his gaze shining brighter. "Because I want you both here. I *need* it to be both of you."

Tears spill down my face, and I sniffle, turning to the last alpha—the one holding me.

Knox swallows hard, his brow folded down. "It's been *killing* me, wanting to bite you every time I sank into that sweet cunt," he rasps. "I'm barely holding back right now, omega."

And then I feel it—the way his arms tense and quiver; the wild beat beneath the wall of muscle pressed to my temple.

My eyes round with surprise and excitement. The second he sees them, that warm, adoring smile curves his lips all over again.

"God, I love you," he murmurs, almost to himself. "Come to me, baby girl. I can't wait another minute to make you mine. *Ours*."

He rearranges me so I'm upright, the others helping to situate my legs on either side of his hips. His hardness stretches up between us, smooshed between my belly and his rippled abdomen. He ignores it, gathering me back into his purr until the sensation vibrates against my nipples.

"Alpha," I choke out, squirming closer, bouncing on my

knees. My teeth sing, wanting to clamp down on some of this magnificent muscle. He grinds his own jaw, drawing my focus to the way he flashes his canines. "Please, Alpha?"

His attention snaps to the others, issuing a series of intense looks. When he turns back to me, his alpha power is almost unbearably strong.

"You want us all together?" he checks. "Right now?"

The question alone has me rising higher on my knees, whining frantically. I nod. Knox's lips hitch up again.

With a firm arm wrapped at my waist, he lifts me and very carefully pushes his cock into me. I moan, my hips automatically stuttering, and his purr gets louder.

"Just feel me, honey," he murmurs. "I'm here for you to clench down on when these bites set you off."

Another desperate sound tumbles out of me, my fingers digging into his shoulders as his girth swells against my trembling inner muscles. Micah comes around my back, stroking my sides softly while he buries his face into my hair.

"I'm excited, too, sweet girl," he chuckles. A finger trails down between my breasts and over to the place where his hand always lands when he hugs me just like this. "I know where I want my mark."

"Me, too," Zane smirks, pressing his body into my left arm. His hand trails down my neck to my straining nipple, thumbing it. One thick brow curves.

"I promised to make it feel good, right, gorgeous? And it will always remind me of our first time, um, *baking cookies*." He winks, and I swear my heart stumbles. The quick flash of his grin immediately softens, and he scent-marks my shoulder.

Before I can restart my brain, Gunnar nuzzles my other temple, bending my arm between our bodies to scrape his teeth over my palm. "Right here," he whispers. "Where I can always reach for you."

Knox rubs his nose against my neck. "I think you need me

right here," he whispers. "Don't you, baby girl? Everyone will see it and know you're mine."

More tears must have started splashing from my eyes at some point, and I can't stop them. I don't even try. Because I don't need to.

If anything, the fact that I'm so happy I can't contain it just makes them all more eager. Their bodies press in; their scents swell and blend. Their purrs soften along with their hands.

They all love me, I marvel. *Because I'm me. Not in spite of it.*

Knox is watching my face for this exact moment. He sees the second that fact finally sinks in. And his bark is low but effective.

"*Now.*"

The pack leader bites first—a surprisingly cautious press of his teeth right into the softest part of my neck. He growls, his cock jerking in my core while his—his *soul* sinks into my center.

It's solid and strong. Burrowing deep. Standing steady. Rough and tough and so very lovely in the most quiet, dignified way. As sturdy and stately as the trees his scent evokes. And every bit as towering.

He's a landmark. I could wander a thousand miles and still turn around and see him there, right in the middle of all my mess. Waiting for me.

Because he would. I feel that. He would be waiting for me no matter how far I wanted to roam.

My body flutters around his while he comes, filling me in every way an alpha possibly could. I fall against him, ready to bite back, ready to collapse—

But then there's another bite.

Sinking into my palm.

I rear and whine, clenching on top of Knox as Gunnar *groans.* The warmth of his own release splatters my side, covering me in his scent as he grinds into my hip and holds my hand to his face.

He crashes into me like a lightning strike. Chaotic flashes of light followed by deep velvet darkness. It's beautiful, tinged with melancholy and the fiercest *depth.*

Gunnar hits hard, tunneling as deep as Knox, but in a crackling, searing sense. He shifts and shines. Goes dark, lights back up. Quick and enigmatic—but the darkness holds no chill. No, he's always warm. Always *good*.

And so very *mine*.

All that bittersweet shade slips seamlessly into the places it belongs. Underlining the brightest pieces of me. The same way that shadows underscore light.

We fit. And his soul may be a mystery he hasn't quite solved— but I know, in this moment, that it was made just for mine.

I feel tears to match my own, wetting my fingers as he nuzzles and licks at his bite, rubbing his lips there until I start to crest into another climax. Knox grunts, and Gunnar follows, covering me in another layer of his scent.

It's too much for Zane, who suddenly snarls, pivoting me as best he can and bending to suck my nipple into his mouth.

Dark eyes swirl up at me, blazing so bright that I almost miss the pure, heartrending *entreaty* underneath all his sizzle.

See me, he begs. *Pick me. Love me.*

And I have. I do. So very much that I sob as I grip his thick, perfect hair and shove more of myself into his mouth. He groans, low and pained, his eyes squeezing shut for only a second before they reopen, showing me the vulnerability he never lets anyone else see.

When my fingers soften and I tenderly brush his hair back, he holds my gaze and strikes, sinking into the sensitive skin just around the edges of my tingling nipple.

Zane.

I expected my fun-loving alpha to come exploding in, but he doesn't. He comes like a sinuous swirl of silk. Color and softness and every texture of love I could imagine.

The rough and carnal. The comforting and warm. The joyful and sweet.

So many strands, woven into this incredible person who chose *me*. And just wants me to choose him back.

We're so alike, but he's worldly and wise in a way I know I'll never be. Never have to be, now, because I have him here, deep inside.

I keep threading my fingers into his hair as he laps at the tip between his teeth. Making this feel good, the way he promised. Because underneath all that smooth color? There's *him*. All his stories and humor and the deepest well of empathy I could envision one man carrying.

And I love him.

I choose him.

I *see* him.

He is *mine*.

Zane pops off to lave at his claim, shivering. Which is when I realize he's covered my other side in a chai-spiced glaze.

Which means I'm only missing—

Micah.

He's the gentlest, of course. Moving carefully, crouching to the side and finding the place where my ribs meet my middle, rubbing his scent-mark there until I bear down on Knox and flood his lap with even more slick.

"There's my girl," Micah breathes, tight but calm. His lips brushing, then parting, then—

Ah!

He bites me *hard*. Claiming with a finality that somehow has me on the edge of another high. Because he may be patient, but he's clearly been *dying* to have this.

Me.

Hot seed hits the small of my back and dribbles down my ass at the same moment his essence unfurls through the tether he's offered me.

And it's... *utter devotion*. Loyalty so *fierce*, I didn't know it could exist. Commitment—sure and deep and *true*.

And it isn't only for me.

He will bend and break and rebuild—for *all* of us.

He's the glue. The tape. Tough, but somehow flexing to fit

around us all, holding things together, offering to pull himself apart just to lend the rest of us any piece we may need.

There's a beautiful selflessness to him. And actual contentment at the bottom of it.

He doesn't give to receive. He gives to *build*. Bridges, tunnels, trampolines. It doesn't matter. He'll make it—to make all of *us* into a *unit*.

For me.

He does it because he loves me. And wants me to have the family he thinks I deserve.

Now I do. Because of him, helping to hold all of this together while we figured things out, there are four loose strands curled into my center, waiting for me to complete them.

Micah feels me shift and hums quietly, releasing his claim with a reluctant huff that nearly makes me smile.

He may act like he has the patience of a saint, but now I know better. And as he flashes me a soft smirk, I can tell he senses my amusement at his expense.

It only makes me more impatient to finish the circuits they've started. So I can *hear* them. All of them, all at once.

I blink up at Knox's waiting face. His fingers shake as they press into my thighs, slipping over my sweaty, slick-covered skin.

Without a word, he swallows and offers me his throat. A gesture I know, somehow, he's never performed for a single other person.

I hide my answering tears there, smearing them into his bristled skin before I find my spot, up high, near the muscle in his jaw that ticks when we're taking years off his life.

I'm surprised by how aware I feel, almost as if all the blurriness I've spent days buried in has evaporated. I even smile a little as I lick at his skin, inhaling his cedar and pine while I think about all the ways the four of us will turn his hair gray for years to come.

The only downside to being so aware is the way my inhibitions come creeping back. *Do I know how to do this?*

My Omega is deeply unconcerned and basically in a cum-and-claim coma. *You bite them. Duh.*

Knox is kinder. When he feels me hesitate, his purr deepens. "You can do it, omega. That's the perfect spot. Here."

He shifts his hips and tucks mine, working his knot into me slowly, so that I feel every blessed inch. When it finally locks into place, I lose all rational thought, my instincts lurching forward, teeth snapping right into him.

Oh. *Oh.*

We both roll into another orgasm, his brutal-sounding as he roars and bucks up into my core. I clamp and flutter, overwhelmed by so many sensations. They swarm in and around, then suddenly settle, leaving me to squint through the haze of euphoria to see—

Oh! Oh! *Oh!*

It's him!

Knox chuckles breathlessly when he hears my excitement. An answering wash of warmth froths over our bond. *Yes, baby girl*, he thinks. *I'm here. Daddy's here.*

He spends a long moment just gazing at me, letting me experience the deep-seated swell of affection and adoration that rolls through him as his eyes trace my face. So satisfied and *proud.*

When he senses how surprised I am, the pride solidifies into blazing determination. *Claim your other alphas, little miss. I want you to feel how proud all of us are to be yours. Right now.*

The strength of his will is enough to spur me on. Whirling toward Zane.

Because he *has* to go next. I'm not sure how I know that, but I do.

Turning to him, I instantly sense that I'm right. I can barely see the beatific smile on his face—because his dark eyes *burn.* Begging.

I know the feeling so well; an empathetic scrape of longing flares in my gullet. It hurts, waiting to be chosen. Worrying you won't be enough.

Never again.

I think the words for both of us, feeling Knox's bone-deep approval as I lunge forward with a small sob, sinking my teeth into the smooth, flawless skin stretched over his pectoral.

Zane grunts, his hands flying out to catch my weight and stroke my hair back as our bond stretches taut and sizzles to life.

Zing.

He bolts into me like a shot—a tumble of color and joy. Awe. And such buzzing, brilliant happiness.

I expected the fireworks from him, but not the silky whisper underneath. *Shona*, he murmurs, *look how perfect you are.*

He shows me how our connection has filled every single corner of his body with pure, true elation. And something solid, settling in his center. Something new, for him.

Purpose.

You, he corrects, nuzzling his face into my curls. *I wandered around for years, never knowing what I was looking for.* Images fly through his thoughts, dozens of places and people and adventures, all of them tinged with a wistful sort of hollowness.

And then, a frosted window. A girl in a white dress.

And a *spark.* A *click*—his universe snapping itself together in a way that finally made sense. Everything he had been waiting for.

It's you, baby, he tells me. *You are my purpose.*

I believe him. I suppose I always did. But *feeling* it, *seeing* it, reaching into him to *touch* it. Joy squeezes fresh tears from my eyes. Zane kisses them away, smiling against my cheeks.

A zap pings across our bond, right into Knox's. Zane cuts him a misty, genuine grin. *Hey. Thanks.*

Knox nods, brusque, but we can both feel how much that one word touches him. *Of course. I'm glad you're here.*

Zane's throat gets thick. He shares the sensation with both of us, reaching over to squeeze our pack leader's shoulder. *Me, too.*

Gruff embarrassment fills Knox's side of our tether. Zane's answering pang of amusement has the elder alpha huffing under his breath. With infinite care, he shifts me off his knot while bending to nip at his claim.

"Who's next, gorgeous?" Zane hums, helping our alpha turn me to Micah and—

Gunnar.

Zane thinks his name the same second I do, gazing over at our built, gray-eyed hockey boy. A thread of searing *want* glows along our bond, woven into the braided strand that now connects us.

The second he realizes that I've sensed it, a tilting gasp of guilt follows his beat of longing. He thinks I'll be jealous or feel like he wants me less because of the way our clumsy hot shot makes his stomach flip. Instead, it only illuminates my own yearning.

My tiny purr starts up automatically. I feel my lips curve at Zane as I glance over my shoulder at his fathomless eyes.

Come here, I think, repeating the words he often tosses to me and Gunnar. Always so casual, as if they aren't the exact lifeline we both need. *I want you with me.*

A hard exhale quivers out of my beautiful alpha, but he doesn't argue. Tender appreciation laps at my insides. His hands find my hips, heedless of the mess they've all left smeared over my skin.

Gunnar's throat works as he slowly kneels up toward me. The gold flecks in eyes glimmer while his gaze swims, locking onto mine.

"Em," he husks, his features pulling. Fear flashes over his face, and he pants, pressing his palm to his chest. "Baby... it's dark in here sometimes. And I can't—I can't always find my way through it. Are you sure you want to—"

He breaks off as I stretch to put my arms around his neck, purring into his pecs while Zane snuggles into my back, reaching one arm around us both.

Yes, I'm sure, I think, parting my lips over the exact spot I chose for Zane, making sure they'll match. I carefully break his pale skin before repeating the words, funneling them down our tunnel as it snaps into place between us. *We both are, Gunnar.*

It *is* dark here, but I'm not alone. Zane stands behind me, physically and metaphorically. Peering into all of Gunnar's pain with me. Hurting for him, too.

Gunnar's chest expands against my mouth, his breathing ragged. *I'm sorry,* he starts, shame and sadness thick in his thoughts. *I can close the curtain for you, sunshine. You don't need to worry about all of this. I'll figure it out.*

Internally, Zane and I turn to each other for a blink. His certainty clashes with mine, filling us both until it overflows into Gunnar.

Sharp relief rears back at us, his strong hands clutching at our bodies as Zane's hand finds his nape and drags him into a tighter embrace. I purr for them both. Wetness kisses my crown when Gunner rests his face there.

Come here, I say, to Gunnar this time. Pulling him out of his shadows and into the center of our pack bond. It's glowing with joy—Knox's, Zane's, my own.

We all enfold Gunnar into that happiness, covering him completely. The piece of him clinging to the dark trembles... and then recoils, springing away from his pain and letting him sink into the rest of us.

Amazement glitters through his veins. *Emma,* he murmurs, just to me. *It's so much brighter in here than I even thought it could be. It's so—God, baby, how are you even more beautiful __inside__?*

Adoration twirls between us. *I love you,* he whispers. *I should have told you the second I touched you. That night, when you looked into my eyes and turned me inside out... I should have—*

But, no.

Because, if he had, we wouldn't be here and we wouldn't have this pack.

I feel that realization hit him. Holding me closer, he turns his head. Peering at Zane.

My beautiful alpha stares right back. And there, in the middle of the bond I've made, I feel their souls brush for the first time.

Hi, Zane says, with a flicker of warm bemusement.

Hey. Gunnar gives the sense that he would be chuckling, repeating Zane's own words back to him, the same way I did. *Fancy meeting you here, Pretty Boy.*

A flare of heat burns from Zane to Gunnar, razing a path right through me. Cinnamon perfume explodes, filling the nest and drawing Knox and Micah into our tangle.

My hazel-eyed alpha growls low, brushing his hand between my thighs to gather my slick in a possessive gesture that undoes me. The guys feel my attention shift completely, and each of them sends me bursts of affectionate approval.

Good girl, my pack alpha gruffs as I leap at Micah, knocking him onto his back. He rolls into the momentum, toppling me and pausing to hover there, his face full of guileless joy.

"You ready for me, sweet girl?"

I whine, staring into his perfect gold-green eyes. He immediately sinks his cock into my slick center, pumping deep and steady.

"*Please*, love," he grits, panting the plea. "Anywhere you want. I'm *yours*."

The absolute truth of that—and the fact that I can already feel it, despite his loose bond curled into the others—makes me frantic. My instincts guide me, turning my face to the arm braced beside my head. I clamp my teeth around the straining tendons there, marking him right where he always holds me—tucking my body into his with his forearm banded across my torso.

His bond flickers to life, the string tangled through my middle and over to Zane, Gunnar, and Knox's, too. They all exhale as the force of it hits us—showing them what I learned just minutes ago:

Micah is *strong*.

So much more than he ever let on. He could have challenged Knox or started a bid for his own pack with the others. He could have barked to get his way any of the dozens of times he compromised.

Instead, he took that strength and bent it into *support*.

Gratitude floods our tether from both sides—his and mine.

Memories fly from my half, showing him all the times he's steadied me and brought the others closer. Thanking him for everything he's worked so hard to build with me.

It takes a moment for me to realize I'm not the only one. Zane and Gunner and even Knox—they soak his soul with their own waves of gratitude.

He takes it, shaking as my teeth press deeper, and he comes, filling me the way he loves so much. I feel that, too; the profound *satisfaction* spreading through his center every time he claims me in this primal way.

Micah roars, flipping us to situate me on top of his thick cock, using gravity and my squirt of slick to pop himself into place. His knot expands when he feels my body react to his pleasure, trembling around him in my own shivery climax.

My other alphas groan in unison, their senses flooded by ours. All four of their scents swarm the air, entwining with mine. Hot splatters of release hit my back, my thighs, the curve of my ass. Micah hauls me into a hug, turning his face into my neck.

The bonds tied into my middle light up, pulsing as the guys send each other internal messages. I close my eyes and hold Micah closer while he gives one last twitch inside my pussy and kisses my forehead.

I'm in you now, sweet girl, he whispers just to me. *In every way. You're <u>mine</u>.*

The others let us soak one another in for a long moment before Knox mutters, *I assume you mean <u>ours</u>.*

Yeah, Gunnar echoes, nudging me internally. *<u>Our</u> omega.*

Zane's bond beams pure elation, followed by a flirtatious tingle as he eyes the mess on my back. *Our glazed little cinnamon roll.*

"Oh holy night," I laugh out loud. "*That's* the first thing you say in our pack bond?"

They all laugh as Micah lowers us, lying back to let the others press in at his sides. Zane reaches over Gunnar to tuck my hair behind my ear. "No regrets, gorgeous."

Not a one, Gunnar agrees, quieter.

Never, Micah agrees.

Knox simply flexes his steady reassurance. He turns his face to the skylight, noticing how the moon has passed over the center of the sky. *It's after midnight...*

Happiness sings through the center of our bond, all of them pouring their love and relief into me.

But it's Gunnar who presses his face into my shoulder, kissing me. "Merry Christmas, Em."

chapter
fifty-nine

THE FIRST GLIMMERS of dawn find the five of us, freshly showered, making our way downstairs for the first time in nearly a week.

My heart leaps when I'm greeted by a happy bark. McKinley bolts up from his dog bed and comes right to Knox. He drops to his knees to pet him, and I follow suit, giggling when I get a big lick across the cheek.

Micah thumbs at his phone, smiling. "I texted Patrick to let him know that your heat was over just after you fell asleep. He must have been awake and brought the dog back for us."

Sheesh. I owe Micah's brother, like, a zillion favors. Or maybe a zillion and *five*, considering the small stack of beautifully wrapped parcels stacked on the coffee table.

With a happy bounce, I turn to guys and squeal, "Your presents made it!" Micah grins, wrapping his arms around my waist while Gunnar kisses my forehead and Zane drapes himself over the hockey star's back, grinning. I look down at Knox, giving him the same puppy-dog eyes as McKinley.

"Can we open presents?"

His smile is as fond as the thump of love he sends into the bond. "Of course, baby girl. Breakfast first, okay?"

With an enthusiastic nod, I start to gallop toward the kitchen, already thinking up the quickest breakfast I can—

"No!"

All four of them shout the word in unison. It's happened once before, but this time, when I whirl, I find their expressions match the chagrin squirming in our bond.

Oh. They don't *want* me to cook?

"It's not that," Micah rushes out, having heard my thoughts.

"Only..." Gunnar grimaces. "Um..."

Knox sighs, rubbing at his thicker beard. "Baby girl, maybe Zane could teach you some of his—"

My shoulders drop as I shake my head, giggling some more. "Thank the *Lord*," I burst. "I *hate* cooking!"

Zane comes to me first, his deep laugh chiming as he swings me into his arms. "Then consider me your personal chef. I made a breakfast casserole last week anyway. It's in the freezer."

"On it," Micah chips, slapping his shoulder as he passes. "Coffee?"

"Hot chocolate?" I reply.

Gunnar grins and nods his agreement. "I'm with the squirt."

Knox gives in easily, shrugging before stomping to the back door to let McKinley out. He lights the Christmas tree and the logs in the fireplace while Gunnar and Zane settle me into their laps, sitting close enough for me to hook one leg between each of theirs.

Zane eyes the gifts on the table and then shoots me some accusatory side-eye. "Which one of us got *two* gifts, gorgeous?"

I frown, noticing his point. The long, flat parcel is Knox's. Gunnar's is the small tube. Micah gets the medium-sized box, and Zane's is probably the red bag trimmed in gold ribbon.

So, what is the large silver box in the center?

"This one isn't mine," I tell them, dragging it closer.

Gunnar reads over my shoulder. His brows pull down. "It says it's from 'the worst friends ever.'"

Micah rejoins us, sitting in the space between my dangling feet and the coffee table. Knox shoves the rest of the presents to the side and settles on the edge of the low table, leaning over his knees to examine our mystery gift.

A lump rises in my throat when I recognize the handwriting: *Meg's.*

"I think that's for me," I mumble.

Zane steadies the box, a pretty silver one, tied together with a glittering red ribbon and a pair of jingle bells. Now that I'm really *looking*, I recognize Remi's handiwork—she's always been the most fantastic gift wrapper.

Hurt curls in my middle as I stare at it, remembering how terribly alone I felt just a few weeks ago. And how none of my friends were there for me.

Gunnar's gentle melancholy meets mine along our bridge. He's a little sad, too—missing his mom. Wishing he could call her and tell her about me.

Somehow, knowing I'm not the only one with mixed emotions helps me exhale. With a couple of tugs, I pull the bow apart and unseal the lid. The first thing I see makes no sense.

It's... a flannel pajama set? With Christmas trees all over it.

Except the tag tells me it's a men's extra-large. There's also a small wooden ornament pinned to the lapel with Knox's name on it.

Frowning, I dig deeper into the tissue, unearthing a second set of pajamas. This time, covered in... nutcrackers? With *Gunnar's* name—

Oh.

Oh. Em. Gee.

I laugh for real that time, tipping my head back. A flurry of joy answers my own, along with a lot of curiosity. Flashing a wicked smile, I start handing out pajamas, plopping a pair in each alpha's lap.

"Oh no," Gunnar groans, his wistfulness fading into horror.

"Oh yes!" I chime, handing Zane the ones covered in gingerbread men.

He sputters in outrage. "I can't *wear* this, *shona*! I have a reputation to uphold!"

I shrug. "Take it up with the girls. This is what they sent, and since we don't have any other Christmas pajamas..."

Micah accepts his set with a slight grimace. "Candy canes?"

I bend to kiss his forehead. "Well, you do smell like peppermint."

My set is the last one in the box, of course. The same fabric, cut a little curvier, and patterned with all four of theirs. Nutcrackers, cookies, candy canes, and Christmas trees, all swirled into colorful chaos.

As soon as they see me pull them out, I feel their annoyance fall away. With grumbles and sighs, they all start to change. I grin to myself, standing to let Gunnar and Zane shimmy their flannel bottoms over their underwear—

And there, at the bottom of the box, I see a pair of mint-green heart-shaped sunglasses. Along with one more note.

An apology. From Meg.

I scan her note and smile. I'll have time to delve into it later. I already feel better though, knowing she was trying so hard to earn my forgiveness for something she did by accident.

The others exchange quizzical looks when I set the plastic frames on top of my head. But I just shrug and offer them a goofy grin. "It's a long story."

ZANE'S CASSEROLE has put us into a food coma by the time the sun finally fills the horizon. We sit in a cluster on the leather couch, quietly content while we watch the dawn break.

Well, *they* watch the dawn break. *I'm* admiring our Christmas tree.

It's like you guys, I think, showing them my mental picture.

Knox is the trunk, sturdy and unyielding.

Micah as the branches, stretching in all directions, holding us up.

Zane would be the ornaments, of course. All colorful and glittering.

Which makes Gunnar the tinsel—strewn in clumps, filling in the dark, empty spaces. Completing the whole thing.

Knox's approval warms my belly. He takes in my analogy and sends back a simple picture of his own—that same imagined tree, made up of them all, flickering to life.

You'd be the lights.

All three of his packmates agree, scent-marking me sweetly and sending me waves of affection.

Knox watches over us, his pride ablaze. Which reminds me...

"Open your present, Alpha," I say, pulling the long, flat package over to him.

The tissue tears under his calloused fingers, revealing the rustic wood sign engraved with three words:

The Beckett Pack.

Shock echoes through him. Thick silence fills the room while he blinks at his name, throat visibly working while his mind stumbles over the logistics of his gift.

"Honey... when did you have time to get this made? We only asked you to be our omega and form a pack as your heat was starting. You didn't make any calls..."

Of course he noticed that. Knox notices *everything*. It's why he's such a good alpha—his attention, his insight. All the things that made me so certain, from the moment we met, that he would need this sign one day.

Feeling a little shy, I show him a memory of calling the local woodshop and commissioning his gift, a week before any of them asked me to be theirs. Days before he decorated the cabin and called it my home.

I watch understanding bloom across his features. They're still somber, but undeniably soft, too. "Baby girl, you had this made for me *two weeks ago?*"

Nodding, I crawl into his lap and tuck myself under his chin. His free hand wastes no time coming up to hold my face against his chest.

"Even if it hadn't been me," I whisper, "Or *us*... you deserved a pack of your own, Knox. I always believed that."

A rush of emotion flows between us, his gruff with embarrassment. I understand why when he swipes at his left eye a second later, forcing down his feelings before they spill out. I plant a kiss at the edge of his brow, scent-marking him there. "You like it, Daddy?"

"I love it," he replies, low. His free hand molds to my cheek as his blue gaze delves into mine. "Best gift I've ever gotten."

He's talking about me. All of us. Our pack and our new bond.

Speaking of—

Gunnar hears his name in my thoughts, and I point to his envelope. "That one's yours, Hot Shot."

It took some doing, getting ahold of Remi's alpha, Smith, and asking him for this special favor. But it's all worth it when Gunnar unfolds the paperwork and four season tickets for the Timberwolves fall into his nutcracker-covered lap.

Light gilds his gray eyes as he lifts his head. "You're coming to one of my games?"

I grin. "Not one of them—all of them! I got season tickets for every home game, and Smith said we could use one of their pack boxes. He's already put our name on it!"

Gunnar holds up the paper to show them the grainy picture I printed on Knox's ancient fax machine. One of the Timberwolves' boxes, with a paper taped to the open door.

Gunnar Sinclair—the Beckett Pack.

Nearly tripping over Micah, Gunnar lurches and snags me from Knox, placing me on his own thighs and crushing me close. Zane watches us, smiling.

When our eyes meet, his brow quirks. "My turn?"

I nod, and he grins wider, knocking Gunnar's shoulder before he picks up his gift bag.

After some fishing, he pulls out the leather-bound book I had embossed with his name and our pack's. "What's this, *shona*?"

I can tell from the sheen in his dark eyes that he already knows. I sit up and lean over his legs, excitedly flipping the leather cover open to reveal the title page. "It's our family cookbook! For you to fill in with all your recipes!"

But the book ends up on the sofa beside him as he *tackles* me onto Gunnar. Kissing and scent-marking my face while pure joy sparkles inside of us.

"God, I love you, gorgeous," he breathes, reaching back and grasping the recipe book. "I'll start adding to it tomorrow."

Micah's curiosity adds to the happy chaos blurring between us. With one final brush of his lips, Zane hands me to the alpha at his feet. I reach for the last box on the table, offering it to my handsome fireman with a shy smirk.

"Here."

A moment later, he has the custom snow globe in his hand,

tipping it to the side and watching the white sparkles float through the water inside. "It's beautiful," he murmurs, bemusement prodding at our bond.

I point to the bottom. "Wind it up."

His long fingers twist the silver bar at the base of the stand. I feel all his muscles tense when the song starts up. Everything in him goes still while he listens, his mother's favorite song tinkling into the hush that's fallen over us.

"I tried to have her jewelry box fixed," I explain. "But the winding mechanism was broken. They saved the box just in case you still wanted it, but the repairman was able to fix the sound mechanism and put it in something else. I thought a snow globe since..."

"We were snowed in," he finishes, swallowing hard as he stares at the little cabin in the glass dome. "Wait, is that—"

I nod. "Yeah! The cabin!"

"Emma." His feelings are a muddle, all so strong I can't even begin to parse them. But he buries his face into my neck, where I feel his tears as much as I sense them in our bond.

He only lets a couple loose as he breathes heavily against my shoulder. I sense his bewilderment as he murmurs, "This is the most beautiful thing anyone's ever given me." A second later, his heart catches, and his exhale shakes. "Well, the second-most beautiful."

Micah leans back, sinking his hazel eyes into mine, making his meaning clear without words. Even before he says them through our tether. *Nothing will ever be more beautiful or precious to me than you.*

Above us, Gunnar sniffles, groaning, "Fuck. How do I turn it *off*?"

Zane hugs him from the side, laughing. "You *don't*, babe. Just let it happen."

Micah smiles at them, then at me. A spark lights his face. "I know we told you we didn't have time to get a gift for you, but we thought of one while we were all in the nest. Zane managed to get it together during one of his trips to the kitchen for food. We hid it under the back of the—"

He doesn't even get to finish before I'm clamoring over to the tree. They all follow, leaving their gifts on the table and coming to surround me beside our tree while I pull the last package from the back and rip the paper right off, revealing a gold eight-by-ten frame...

And my list.

Or, as Zane's handwriting states from the top of the purple paper: *Emma's Knotty List.*

"We thought we should keep it," Gunnar mumbles.

"Or, you know," Zane winks. "Use it. Over and over and over—"

Knox rolls his eyes before meeting my gaze. "This is a placeholder, little miss. Your real gift won't be ready for a few weeks. Can you wait and be surprised?"

I note the way they all instant drop their internal curtains. Watching them scramble makes me giggle. Giddy, I bounce in place with a nod. "Of course, Daddy."

He kisses my forehead. "That's my good girl."

Micah hums his agreement, petting my hair back. "What do you want to do today, sweet girl? Do you need more food? Or maybe a nap?"

I shake my head, sending them a mental image of exactly what I want to spend the rest of the morning doing...

They all freeze, turning to Knox for approval. With an indulgent smirk, he sighs. "All right, all right. But everyone needs their boots. And coats."

We all obey happily; each of my alphas helping to bundle me into a coat, boots, a scarf, and a hat.

The backyard gleams under a beautiful layer of white, prime for the taking. I wait until they're all distracted to bolt, laughing as I run for the cover of a distant bush.

Knox curses and Micah immediately gives chase. Zane snickers, nearly drowning out Gunnar's groan.

A flurry touches my temple just as another tickles my nose. I pause and spin, gazing up at the falling snow with wonder in my heart.

Because I did it.

I found my mates and brought them together. I ignored all the ways this seemed impossible; and I bonded them.

But more than that?

I *believed*.

In them, yeah... but I'd also believed in *myself*.

And I got everything I ever wanted.

chapter
sixty

Six Months Later

THE SECOND MY stick hits the puck, I know it's going in.

The buzzer on top of the goal sounds, flaring red as the opposition's goalie crumbles to his kneepads.

A defender tackles me into the boards, but he's too late. I've scored. The goal is good. And the Jumbotron on the ceiling—

Four, three, two—

Our stadium erupts, the packed stands exploding into cheers as time expires and we win.

We. Win.

Damon Mathers tackles me next, his grin flashing white as half of the Timberwolves pile on top of me. Cameras flash, cannons blow, and teal confetti rains from the ceiling, swirling down to cover the ice.

My disbelief dissipates as our team captain fists my jersey, shaking me with raucous shouts.

"Gunnar! You did it, kid! Great fucking shot!"

Holy shit.

Did I just win the Stanley Cup?

I guess so. Because that's my face on the Jumbotron. Just over the score.

5-6. Final.

For a moment, the silence in my center is disorienting. Then I remember—I have my part of our bond closed, blocking the others out so I could focus.

Whipping my head toward the stands, I scan for the box Emma secured as my Christmas gift. There, she and Zane jump up and down, both of them shouting while she waves her home-made glitter-glue sign over her curly head.

Number 49 is mine! it shouts.

I grin every time I see it and now is no exception. Even with shock reverberating through my entire body, Em always knows how to make me smile.

The way Zane looks when he's laughing definitely doesn't hurt, either.

I feel them then, impatiently waiting on the other side of my interior curtain. The second I drop it, they both rush in, bursting with love and clamoring excitement.

HOT SHOT! YOU FUCKING DID IT! Zane shouts through our tether. Emma echoes his enthusiasm, so happy for me that she can't even form words around her joyful giggles and sobs.

Pride floods me as Micah and Knox join them, the former projecting an image of everyone in Knotty Hollow gathered at the town's only sports bar, cheering. Even Knox, who looks like he's clapping so hard, he might break his wrist.

They both wanted to be here—but they had too much to do

up at the house. Preparing the surprise we've been planning for Emma since the New Year.

The last month has been wild. My training and playoff schedule; closing up our Orlando house and opening the cabin for our summer up in the Blue Ridge. All the deliveries and planning sessions we had to keep under wraps.

Lucky for us, our girl is extraordinarily trusting. And generally unobservant.

She's also been by my side every single day and night, supporting me in any way she possibly could while my team fought our way here.

A year ago, I may have lied to myself. Claimed that I kept her close to make our surprise easier to manage. But she's helped me come to grips with just how much I need my pack. And now, looking up at her beaming face, there's no shame curled in my middle.

All the nights she's held me to her purring chest and helped me overcome my game anxiety so I could sleep. All her patience when I had to stay late at practice or couldn't be home for movie nights. All the times I just needed a distraction and she happily bounced into my lap.

Gratitude swells to block my throat while I point my stick up at her.

She dances in Zane's arms—and I catch the flash of his grin while he thinks, *You won't get any sleep at all tonight, Hot Shot. I hope you're good with that.*

Skating toward my team's boisterous huddle in the center of the ice, I toss him a parting glower. *Don't think I didn't notice you going down on our omega during the intermission. I had my curtain up but the two of you are loud.*

He grins wider, shoulders shrugging. *Had to remind you what you were fighting for, babe.*

That parting taunt is enough to keep the smile on my face as we're presented with our trophy. There are pictures, speeches, more pictures. By the time we get to the showers, I'm so impatient that all four of them snicker through the bond.

Micah and Knox blink off, not wanting Emma to see any of the surprises set up at the cabin as they arrive home from the bar. While I stumble into my post-game outfit, Zane sends me glimmers of the celebration brewing outside the locker room.

The Pierson Pack is gathered, along with Emma's brother and his pack. Our omega mingles happily, oblivious to the way I watch her from the threshold.

Zane stands off to the side, looking cooly gorgeous in a pale blue linen suit that matches our omega's dress. He notices me first, clipping through the small crowd to envelope me in a huge hug.

Emotion bursts through our bond as his hand grasps the back of my collar. Without a word, he turns my head, catching my mouth with his.

I can taste Emma—her cinnamon sweetness, layered onto his lips. My cock jumps as he takes over, sweeping his tongue along mine. As effortlessly commanding and sensual as ever.

My heart pounds and I let him feel it. He hums, breaking our kiss to hold me closer and murmur low against my ear, "I'm so fucking proud of you."

I feel how true that is. His pride *glows*, fierce and bright, along our tether. I turn my face into his neck for a moment, leaving my scent along his throat.

He loves that. Every time Emma and I both do it, I swear he tears up. I hear him sniff now as we both straighten.

He doesn't hide any of his emotions, but he does cock his head in a teasing gesture, nodding at the collar he just mussed. "Always such a mess, Hot Shot."

I raise a brow. "Yeah, well, my stylist had his face between our omega's thighs."

He grins and shoots me a wink while he rearranges my collar. "Only during the first intermission. She was getting suspicious, so I came up with a perfect distraction."

"Mm," I hum dryly. "That's what you said last night."

Zane's smile grows. "Shame you had to save all your energy for this and couldn't join in."

Uh huh. As if he doesn't live to bait me. "I'm going to get you back for that, Pretty Boy. Tonight."

He looks so handsome when he laughs. My pulse stammers while he loops his arm around my waist. "You're welcome to try, babe. But I think we both know who usually wins our competitions."

Yeah. Both of us.

But Emma most of all.

She reminds us of that very fact when a deluge of dirty images flood the bond. I turn and find her grinning while she barrels across the room.

You checking us out, squirt?

Happiness thumps through our connection, even as she narrowly avoids tripping over her feet. *Only always.*

Zane and I both laugh. He stops before I do, reverence rippling through him while he sends me a brief glimpse of what I look like in this moment—with my eyes crinkled and my lips spread in a grin.

Your best look, he thinks.

I bend close enough to nudge his cheek with mine. His dark eyes fall shut while pure love sings inside of him. I absorb it and send some right back.

Showing him my own mental image, I raise my brows in question. *Together?*

He nods with a smirk. *Always.*

We turn and open our arms for Emma to leap into them. The second she hooks her elbow around my neck and leans into my embrace, the whole world makes sense again.

We won, I realize, the thought finally sinking in as she scent-marks my cheek and gushes her praise.

Zane lets her go on, petting her hair with his free hand and meeting my gaze over her shoulder, winking once more.

Come on, he says internally, just to me. *Let's get our girl home.*

LAST SUMMER, I rented a house on Lake Como.

It was a big place, right on the water. Smack dab in the middle of what is, arguably, one of the most beautiful, tranquil places on Earth.

But as I lie in the gold light creeping into our omega's suite, I feel myself smirk.

Because that was *nothing* compared to *this.*

Sunrise slips over Emma's exposed back and Gunnar's bare chest, filling all the dips and curves I spent the night worshipping.

They're mine, I marvel, still unable to believe my luck.

Emma senses the emotions swelling inside my chest and stirs. Green eyes flutter open, her gaze soft as she smiles from her place on top of our hockey boy.

Good morning, shona, I think, giving my most dazzling grin to distract her while I send Knox and Micah a quick heads-up. They both duck behind their curtains, hiding their surroundings from her.

Our girl doesn't even notice, God bless her. She's too busy following my appreciative gaze, looking down at Gunnar's body —and all the bruising bite marks we both left on him during our little, uh, *celebration.*

Think he'll be able to walk? she teases, raising a brow.

I scoff. *If he can, we'll just have to try harder tonight.*

That's if Knox and I feel like sharing, Micah interrupts.

We don't, Knox gruffs, sending us the mental equivalent of a scowl. *Especially after everything you three put us through yesterday.*

Their fake grumpiness is a nice touch, honestly. *I* know we'll all spend tonight as a pack, but, under normal circumstances, whichever two alphas stay behind at the cabin typically get dibs on our omega the first night she gets home.

Well, our *other* home.

In a way, the cabin will always feel like our "home base"; but we have this nice house in Orlando now, too. Knox bought it within a month of our bonding, as Emma's Christmas gift.

At least, that's what he claimed—her *real* gift will come later this afternoon.

Still, having Emma travel for Gunnar's games while the rest of us took turns going with her was torturous. Having this house enabled us all to travel together, whenever possible.

We definitely prefer to be together as a pack at all times. Hopefully, this week will be the last exception for a while.

Today, Gunnar, Emma, and I will head back up to the mountains for our summer vacation. And when it's time for Emma to start her new (former) job as a pee-wee school counselor next fall, we'll all migrate back here as a pack.

Micah is all set up with the Orlando Fire Department and I've slowly transitioned my socials from travel content to home-making. That was nerve-wracking, at first, but it turns out my followers *love* Emma.

I mean... *who wouldn't?!*

My girl is gorgeous, and her bubbly personality totally shines on camera. The more content I shoot with her, the more people beg to see her.

I only narrowly catch my train of thought before it turns to all the videos and pictures I plan to take today. I want to document every single moment of this surprise for her. It's been a long time coming and it's nothing less than everything our omega deserves.

Underneath her, Gunnar shifts and groans, clearly feeling the effects of two hours on the ice and three hours between me and Emma.

She giggles—and, I swear to God, the sweet sound still sends butterflies to my stomach.

"How you doin' there, Hot Shot?"

He keeps his eyes shut, but tests out his lower half, lifting his hips with a grunt before pouting. "You two are mean."

"Me?!" Emma squeaks. "I'm an innocent bystander!"

Gunnar and I both bark out deep laughs at that. "Oh please," I chortle, sliding closer to them both, sliding my thigh over our hockey boy's. "We all know better by now, gorgeous."

Knox growls through our bond. *You're a very naughty omega*, he tells her, only half-kidding. *Teasing Daddy the way you did yesterday.*

Micah's interior laugh is warm. *He might need to teach you a lesson, sweet girl*, he thinks. *But I have other ideas.*

He sends a few images of our sexy girl, stuffed so full of his cum that she drips. She shivers and perfumes. I feel his thump of smug satisfaction when Gunnar moans in tormented pleasure.

You're all mean, he grouses. *Let me sleep.*

No can do, I reply, slipping him the thought directly so Emma won't overhear. *They're all waiting for us.*

His eyes finally drift open, falling first to Emma's content expression and then over to me. *Big day.*

I think back on the months I've spent with them. How my life has changed.

For years, I chased validation from strangers. Looking for the ultimate vacation, the greatest food, the prettiest people.

It all seems so empty, now that I've found the greatest adventure I ever could have imagined.

It's not a mountain or an ocean.

It's a family. *Our* family.

I smile as I press into Gunnar's side, scent-marking his shoulder before I drop a kiss to Emma's forehead and send him one final reply.

Best day.

THE WAY EMMA runs and jumps into our arms will never get old.

I've been waiting *days* for this exact moment—the way her eyes glimmer, the glow of her cheeks, her unfiltered exuberance.

I bundle her straight into my body, kissing her face while she squeezes my neck. "Sweet girl. I missed you so fucking much."

No matter how many times we do this, she always has tears in her eyes when we reunite. A very small part of me will miss that, now that the season is over and there won't be any reason for us to be apart, going forward.

But, mostly? I'm so goddamn *relieved*.

In a way, this new year has been a new beginning. For each of us, for our pack. Today feels like the culmination of all of that. The end of our beginning.

And the start of our *future*.

Zane and Gunnar both slap my back in greeting, each taking charge of one of Emma's bags while I carry our girl out of the small, executive airport, toward the landing pad.

"Where's Daddy?" she asks, burrowing her face against my throat.

I hug her harder. "Home waiting for his girl. He sent me in the helicopter."

The first time those words left my mouth, they felt ridiculous. But I've mostly gotten used to our alpha's wealth over the last six months. It helps that he never flashes it for any purpose other than making our lives easier or making Emma happy.

In this case, he couldn't leave our compound with everything going on, but he wanted her home as quickly as possible.

Can't say I blame the guy.

Emma senses the roiling impatience climbing my insides, even with my thoughts concealed by my inner curtains. When she frowns in befuddlement, I grin and kiss the puckered V between her brows.

"Come on, love. We have a surprise for you."

That perks her back up. She squirms in my arms, doing a happy dance as she launches into a series of guesses.

"Is it a puppy?"

"Nope."

"A pony?"

Zane laughs, "No, baby. Can you imagine Knox's *face*?"

She pouts at that. Then suddenly rears back, eyes wide as she gasps, "Am I having a baby?"

I suppress the carnal growl that scrapes my lungs at the thought. *Not yet*, I think. *Give me another heat or two...*

Gunnar smirks at me and then shakes his head at her. "I think *you'd* be the one surprising *us* if that were the case, squirt."

She deflates. "Oh. Right. Then, *what is it*?!"

"You'll see!" we all chorus, loading her into the chopper.

Our pilot has an easy day. It's perfect weather—warm and sunny, with minimal wind and lower humidity than we had any right to expect this time of year. Within twenty minutes, Emma squeals over the hum of the blades overhead, her voice shrieking, "*What* is *that*?!"

The guys and I smile at each other. *You tell her*, Zane thinks, nudging me.

Yeah man, Gunnar agrees, *you did all this work. You should get to tell her.*

Their gratitude is palpable. I'm still getting used to the way they all appreciate me so openly. Especially my omega.

I stare into her pretty green eyes, absorbing her excitement as I point to the enormous white tent erected in our backyard.

"That," I tell her, "is our wedding."

KNOX

MY BLOOD THRUMS as I watch Emma take in her surroundings.

Our bubbly omega is markedly quiet, turning a slow circle in the center of the dance floor laid out over the grass. Her head tilts back, rounded eyes absorbing the bower of wildflowers strung above her.

Those were my idea. Something I remembered from the night she admitted her previous wedding plans really didn't have much to do with her preferences.

One of dozens of details the four of us hoarded over the past six months, waiting until she fell asleep each night to discuss how we could bring them all to life.

The simplicity of most of the things on her list still sends a tender pang through my chest. My baby girl didn't want anything lavish or ostentatious. She wanted wildflowers. And a donut wall. And some sort of booth for photos?

I let Zane field that one.

We all played to our strengths, in a way. Gunnar took charge of wrangling friends and family, inviting Emma's relatives, their friends from Orlando, Micah's family, and our favorite acquaintances in town.

Micah was on point for setup and entertainment. Zane jumped at the chance to pick a caterer, design a cake, and choose our clothing. Which left budgeting and logistics to me.

But every spare second spent plotting is worth it the second Emma's mouth wobbles into a watery smile. "It's like a dream."

No, I think, knowing she hasn't noticed me yet. *You are.*

She spins, finding me on the opposite side of the checkerboard floor tiles. With a squeaked sob, she bolts right for me and I swing her up into my arms, turning with a laugh.

"Hi, honey," I hum, marking my scent along her cheek. "How's my baby girl?"

"I'm—I—" she cries. "Knox, how did you all *do* this?"

The guys fill in around us, each of them touching Emma as they all smile proudly. "A lot of late nights," I admit. "But we wouldn't have had it any other way."

"Yeah," Zane agrees, cupping her cheek. "We wanted to give you the wedding you deserved, gorgeous."

"Everyone is coming," Gunnar adds, smiling over Zane's shoulder. "The Ospreys and Timberwolves both leant us their company planes. They left an hour after we did this morning."

Micah pets her hair back. "Patrick is already inside. He has your dress, and he's going to start your hair and makeup, if you want those done."

Astonished joy fills Emma's entire body as she bobs her head in agreement. "What about McKinley?"

God. Every day I think I couldn't love her more.

Every day she proves me wrong.

I whistle and our dog comes bounding into the tent, showing

off the bow-tie collar Zane ordered him. Emma giggles, wiggling her toes when he licks her sandaled feet.

"Well, as long as McKinley's in, I guess I am, too," she quips, casting each of us bright grins. "When do we need to start getting ready?"

Micah checks his watch. "Right now, love."

Her shocked delight echoes through all four of us. I let it sink into my center, balancing her on one of my arms while I reach into my pocket and pull out the ring we spent weeks designing.

I set the case in her hand, displaying the large oval diamond at the center, with four smaller ones clustered around it.

"What do you think, omega? Will you marry us?"

"I STILL CAN'T BELIEVE they did this!" I blubber, swiping at my eyes. "Oh crap, my mascara!"

Meg's smile is calmly amused. "It's waterproof, babe. We all know you better than *that*."

Remi pats at my hair, her deft fingers re-curling a strand that frames my face. The curve of her lips is much kinder. "We figured you'd shed a couple of tears today."

"A *couple*?" Lucy snorts a smirk, then schools her face into a serious expression. "Sorry."

Bridget laughs, the sound brighter than I've heard in a long time. "It's her wedding! Leave her alone!"

"Not a chance," Serena chimes, expression severe. "I'm never leaving this girl unattended at her own wedding ever again. Remember what happened last time?!"

They all groan while I giggle. *Yeah, I guess that was sort of a disaster...*

Except I found my mates because of it.

And now I'm here, under a waterfall of wildflowers, holding the bouquet Micah picked himself. I look down and send him a mental picture of the gorgeous blooms, along with another beat of gratitude. The rush of pure love I receive in return sends me right back into tears.

You're so welcome, my sweet girl. A second later, Gunnar sends me a loud thump of amusement and an image of Zane fiddling with Knox's bowtie.

The murderous look on my pack alpha's face is enough to make me giddy with giggles again. Knox's grumbles about his tuxedo have kept me in stitches while Patrick and the girls helped me get ready, carefully maneuvering me into the most gorgeous gown I've ever seen.

The dress is all creamy, candlelit tulle, with floral appliqués covering the bust, waist, and hips. As soon as I saw the deep-V neckline and thigh-high slit, I knew exactly which alpha was responsible.

Just as I suspect Zane is also totally milking our pack leader's annoyance, making a hundred unnecessary adjustments to his tie just goad him.

Yep! Zane confirms.

Meg notices me bouncing on my toes, grinning like a loon, and raises her brows, bringing me out of my head. "You good, sis?"

"Yes!" I burst. "Is it time to *go* yet?! I want to *see* them!"

"You just saw them like four hours ago!" Bridget replies. "Besides I think Jonah is still getting mic'ed up."

Serena grimaces. "I know Jo will be a great officiant, but I hope he doesn't make the mattress-mony joke again. We all tried to talk him out of it on the plane this morning."

We all frown at her and she sighs, "Matri-mony? Mattress-mony? Like for sex? Honestly, I don't even know. He's been spending too much time with Theo and Damon."

"Oh *boy*," Bridget groans.

Meg titters behind her hand while Remi fiddles with the strap of her lilac bridesmaid dress. "Okay," the little omega with dark curls announces. "Everyone looks perfect. One last picture?"

Lucy spins to the living room coffee table and picks up the collection of heart-shaped sunglasses sprinkled there. They're a minty blue-green, to match my own special pair the girls' dresses. We all slide them on and crowd together, smiling for the photographer.

Impatience flurries into my bond. Usually, that means Gunnar is about to come looking for me. Sometimes Knox. Now, it's all four of them, filing out to the ceremony set-up facing our mountain's cliff.

It's time, baby girl, Knox tells me. *We're ready to start when you are.*

I step up to the back door, peering out at the lawn. All the chairs are filled and Jonah stands under the flowery arch at the end of the aisle. There, off to the right, dressed in coordinated white tuxes, are my four alphas.

Waiting for me.

A giddy thrill blooms beneath my lungs. So many feelings and thought swirl inside of me, but most of all, there's awe.

How did I get so lucky?

Who knew anything could ever be this incredible?

They all turn and stare back at me through the window. Gunnar's voice answers, quiet and sure, *You did, Em.*

A deep vein of adoration flows from Zane. *He's right, shona. You knew all along that we would end up here.*

You believed in us, sweet girl, Micah adds.

And Knox nods, so full of pride I could burst from it. *You made this into a home and turned us into a family.*

Months ago, I might have dismissed their praise. Written it off as platitudes or convinced myself it was all some stroke of good fortune.

But, now, I feel their words reverberate through me, and realize they're *right.*

I knew it.

They all grin in reply to my smug internal cheer. Off to the side, a string quartet starts up and the girls begin to file out. I step out into the sun and smile up at the sky before turning to my guys.

The wedding march swells to fill the summer air and it's all I can do to walk instead of *sprinting...*

Despite that restraint, I still wind up tripping on the last step.

But my mates are there. And they catch me.

Together.

a note from ari

So far, on this journey, there is without a doubt one thing I am most proud of:

My readers.

I'm not sure how it happened, but these books managed to attract the kindest, most beautiful souls. Your humor and heart have inspired me so much and I will never be able to thank you enough for being here with me!

Giving my amazing readers love stories they can get lost in has become my ultimate goal. So it is with great excitement (and some nervous butterflies!) that I announce a departure from the MVP Omegaverse and the start of a new series:

Ari Wright's Royalverse.

These books will be everything you've come to expect in my writing—modern, RH/why-choose Omegaverse romances with plenty of spice and swoon. These are fairytale re-tellings in the absolutely knottiest way imaginable—and full of charming princes (or villains...). Our happily ever afters will have multiple fated mates and absolutely no choosing! The first installment, **Once Upon A Pack** is coming your way in just a few months!

To all my sports romance lovers—I promise, the MVP Omegaverse is still unfolding. **Knot Her Catch** will be available next summer and I'm *thrilled* to feature my first plus-sized heroine of the series for book five!

In the meantime, it is my sincerest hope that you will take this leap with me into my next chapter. And, hopefully, what will be the second of many series to come 🖤

Sending you all my love and gratitude!

xx,

Ari Wright

from international bestselling author
ARI WRIGHT

Once
Upon
a Pack

final cover
to be
revealed!

Ari Wright's
Royalverse

Want more?

KNOT HER

Catch

A WHY-CHOOSE

BASEBALL

omegaverse romance

PRE-ORDER NOW!

acknowledgments

I am so thankful that this list continues to grow!

To Kelly, my best friend, who has been by my side through this whole crazy year—no one has a better friend than you. From helping me brainstorm, to cheering me on, and letting me vent, none of this would be possible without you! I am beyond excited for our next chapter and all the crazy it will bring. You're going to crush it and I'll be right there with you!

To Katie, who is *pivotal* in *every single step* of this process, truly these books would not exist without you! It would be easy to thank you for all of your time, attention, and expertise, but you bring so much more to my life than all of that. So thank you for being my friend and a constant source of support. I love you!! And I'm sorry if I butchered the punctuation in this acknowledgment.

To the rest of the Spice Me Up team, Kendra, Amanda, and JL—how you keep from wanting to strangle me every time I pop into your DMs, I will never know. All of your experience and opinions are so valuable to me; and knowing I have friends I can turn to means more than anything.

For McKinley, on the other side of the rainbow bridge. Thank you for inspiring the sweet pup in this story! And to the best dog mom, god mom, and aunt-mom in the world, MR—thank you for letting me borrow his name!

Never least, always last, and never anything but loving anyway—Matthew, my husband. You won't read this, so I'll take the opportunity to admit that your coffee is, in fact, better than mine. Shhh —nobody tell him!

about the author

Ari Wright was once entirely sane, but then she realized sanity is overrated and decided to write sporty Omegaverse smut.

Because life is short, you know?

When she isn't writing unhinged romances, she enjoys drinking coffee to the point of excess, kitchen experiments, raising her littles, and trying to keep her plants alive (just kidding, her husband does that).

She loves really embarrassing music, moody weather, and any story where the bad guy gets the girl.

Because what's Happily Ever After without a little (or a lot of) spice?

You can follow her works in progress, favorite reads, and very pink aesthetic on Instagram!

Printed in Great Britain
by Amazon

53344296R00261